DARK VECTOR

BOOKS BY WARD LARSEN

The Perfect Assassin
Assassin's Game★
Assassin's Silence★
Assassin's Code★
Assassin's Run★
Assassin's Revenge★
Cutting Edge★
Assassin's Strike★
Assassin's Dawn★
Assassin's Edge★
Deep Fake★
Assassin's Mark★
Dark Vector★

★Published by Forge Books

DARK VECTOR

A David Slaton and Tru Miller Novel

WARD LARSEN

TOR PUBLISHING GROUP
New York

DARK VECTOR

A Forge Book
Published by Tom Doherty Associates / Tor Publishing Group
120 Broadway
New York, NY 10271

www.torpublishinggroup.com

Forge® is a registered trademark of Macmillan Publishing Group, LLC.

The Library of Congress Cataloging-in-Publication Data is available upon request.

ISBN 978-1-250-34352-9 (hardcover)
ISBN 978-1-250-34351-2 (ebook)

Our books may be purchased in bulk for promotional, educational, or business use. Please contact your local bookseller or the Macmillan Corporate and Premium Sales Department at 1-800-221-7945, extension 5442, or by email at MacmillanSpecialMarkets@macmillan.com.

First Edition: 2025

Printed in the United States of America

0 9 8 7 6 5 4 3 2 1

For Chelsea and Cori.
Your smiles will take you far.

DARK VECTOR

ONE

Colonel Maksim Primakov walked across the ice-clad tarmac of Skovorna Air Base, his boots crunching over frozen sleet. The big hangar lay before him, its high western wall catching the last rays of dusk as another frigid night descended. A Test Pilot First Class in the Russian Air Force, Primakov cut an arresting figure in his flight suit and winter jacket. He was tall and square-jawed, and his pace was steady. His carriage bordered on arrogant. The close-cropped brown hair was more a habit than a concession to regulation, the sign of a man who had neither the time nor inclination to bother with more.

Primakov drew to a stop near the hangar, then turned and surveyed his surroundings. Not for the first time, it struck him that Skovorna looked more like a salvage yard than an air base. The other airfields where he'd been stationed in recent years invariably flew advanced jets. Most of the ones he saw here had not turned a wheel in years. The skeletons of two IL-76 transports lingered at the fence line, their frames rusting after having been cannibalized for spare parts. A once-sleek MiG-29 stood statue-like on two flat tires, access panels on its belly swinging limp in the glacial breeze. Legend had it that the jet had diverted here due to a rough-running engine. A fleet-wide lack of fuel pumps, combined with rampant organizational ineptitude, had eventually doomed the aircraft to rot.

A year ago, Skovorna Air Base had been all but abandoned, an outpost from another era fading to irrelevance. Two rescue helicopters had operated from the main hangar, and an army training detachment taught survival skills to recruits in the surrounding forest. Those complementary missions—teaching soldiers how to survive harsh conditions, and retrieving those who failed—were all one needed to know about the airfield's remoteness. The nearest city of note, Chita, was two hundred miles west. The closest depot for food and supplies, a logistical outpost of the 29th Army, was a two-day drive in the summer.

In winter Skovorna could only be reached by air. Weeds thrived amid the cracks in the ramp and windows in the outbuildings failed in storms. On that sad trajectory, the airfield had been a year, perhaps two, from complete abandonment.

Then, last summer, Skovorna had been thrown a lifeline.

With the opposite of fanfare, its two active units were reassigned elsewhere. Soon after, construction crews began arriving. To any casual observer, of whom there were few—only the most ambitious trappers and hunters from Olinsk—the alterations at the airfield would have appeared trivial. The big hangar was sealed and spackled, and the main runway and a single taxiway were refurbished. The living facilities were updated, although not enlarged—the unit preparing to take up residence was roughly the size of the old detachment. From a distance, and particularly from above—the only direction that mattered—Skovorna would appear little changed. It had been selected for rehabilitation for two reasons. First was its remoteness. The second, and far subtler, attribute was its proximity to the Chinese border.

There were now three airworthy helicopters on the tarmac, Hip J models brought in for logistical support. Near the Hips was a transiting AN-26 transport that had arrived yesterday with an extensive array of test equipment. The markings on the cargo jet attested that it was Russian Air Force, although the provenance of what it carried, Primakov suspected, was likely from farther south. And then, of course, there was the other aircraft—the one parked in the heated main hangar whose doors were shut tight. The one that was Skovorna Air Base's *raison d'être*.

Primakov turned back to the hangar, and his pale blue eyes canted downward to study the parking apron. The concrete was dusted lightly with snow, but thankfully there was no ice. Taxiing an airplane here in winter was sometimes closer to ice skating, but thankfully there had been little precipitation in recent days, even if the temperatures held fast to the standards of the Siberian Plateau. It was the second week of January, and the program was on schedule, the only setback having been one major storm during Christmas.

Headquarters was pleased.

The colonel scuffed a boot over the ramp, and beneath the snow he noted a few loose chips of concrete. He frowned. This was one of his ongoing crusades. The surface was beginning to disintegrate, damaged by too many brutal winters, yet further repairs would induce delays. To mitigate the risk, he had ordered the active taxiways be swept every morning, and a second time in the afternoon if a flight was scheduled.

He checked the nearby vehicle apron and saw the big sweeping machine sitting idle. Primakov walked over and found no one inside the cab, yet when he opened the door a bit of warmth drifted out. A vodka bottle lay on the floor, the last drop sucked out of it.

His anvil jaw clenched.

Like any Russian military officer, he was accustomed to such battles, yet Skovorna was supposed to be different. The mission here was an experimental cooperative, a model venture between two great nations. It was working, to a point. Not once had Primakov had a request for funding or personnel denied, and the men and women assigned to the project—fifty-six in all—were among the finest in the Russian Air Force. Unfortunately, these days "the finest" was an appallingly low bar.

It hadn't always been so. During his company grade days, unburdened by commanding anything beyond his own airplane, Primakov had viewed the service as mostly competent. In those years, when the oil had been flowing, and when Europe had been a beach vacation rather than enemy territory, the Russian Air Force had been functional. He remembered new aircraft arriving from the factory, and having enough fuel to fly them. The crew chiefs had been capable, and even the conscripts did their year of compulsory service with little complaint. The horrors of Afghanistan had been largely forgotten, yet there were still enough skirmishes in the Middle East and the Caucasus to keep everyone sharp. Altogether, Primakov had felt as though he was part of an effective fighting force.

Then the rot had begun. The looting by the oligarchs turned excessive, and the regime overreached in Syria and Crimea. The death knell, plainly, had been the invasion of Ukraine. Experienced mechanics had been issued rifles that belonged in a museum and hauled off to the front. Stockpiles of hypersonic missiles and precision munitions, many of which Primakov himself had been involved in testing, were exhausted within months, most of them wasted on civilian targets. Against a far weaker Ukrainian Air Force, Russian fighter jets largely remained grounded. Deep targets were struck not by Russian bombers, but by cheap drones purchased from Iran and North Korea. Within two years the service had been nothing short of gutted.

There was a time when all of that had bothered Primakov.

But no more.

He kicked the sweeper's door shut and set out across the ramp.

TWO

The nearby administration building was just beginning to glow at dusk, the feeble yellow light in the windows almost inviting. Primakov pushed through the main door and was hit by a fifty-degree temperature differential. Two enlisted men at the operations desk snapped to attention as he walked past. He strode down the hall like a bowling ball in search of a pin and turned into the main briefing room.

Everyone was waiting.

Front and center was Colonel Yevgeny Nemanchik. On a wall near the building's entrance a Christmas-tree organizational chart displayed a photo of every officer assigned to Skovorna. Nemanchik's picture was at the very apex of the pyramid, yet the strand of yarn angling down one level to Primakov's picture had somehow fallen loose. No one ever asked how this had happened, nor had anyone bothered to correct it, including Nemanchik himself. Yevgeny Nemanchik was, and had always been, a content careerist, and never had he been more in his element than at Skovorna. His unit's performance was meeting expectations, and the test program was running ahead of schedule. His overseers, a handful of select generals in the Ministry of Defense, beamed at the results, as did their Chinese counterparts. As base commander, most of Nemanchik's short workdays were spent dealing with logistics: coordinating supply deliveries, signing off reports, and, most importantly, keeping the perimeter secure. Yet when it came to the true mission of Skovorna, everyone knew who was in charge.

"Maintenance?" Primakov said without preamble as he took the seat at the head of a repurposed mess hall dining table.

"The aircraft is ready, Colonel," said a capable major that Primakov had plucked from Ramenskoye, Russia's main flight test center. "Only two items are outstanding. The aircraft's backup VHF radio is inoperative—we are waiting for a part to arrive. The integral boarding ladder is also out of service, a minor mechanical issue."

Primakov nodded. Neither item was relevant to today's flight. "Weather?"

A junior sergeant stood. "Current conditions at the airfield are eight-tenths overcast, between two and five thousand meters, unlimited visibility. The temperature is just above the freezing point with light winds from the north. This should remain stable during the mission window."

"And the working area?"

"Restricted Area 1512 shows no cloud cover above five thousand meters. Winds aloft are a modest jet stream from the northwest."

"Excellent." Primakov's gaze snapped right, a mortarman retargeting. His eyes settled on the only man in civilian clothes. "Systems preflight?"

Lin Cheng was, Primakov allowed, the smartest man in the room. He was the chief designer at China Aerospace Corporation, and headed a contingent of four engineers who'd been sent to Skovorna. They were backed up by an entire team at the home office in Chaoyang. The joint venture was a new tack for both countries, and, in Primakov's view, an admission of their respective failures. Russia had always been good with engines and airframes, but it lagged precipitously when it came to what was most important in modern air combat—the fusion of stealth, electronics, and software. With China facing the inverse problem, the leaders of the nations had committed to joining forces secretly, aiming to develop a fighter that could truly challenge the West.

Lin Cheng seemed to vibrate in his seat—the man was a perpetual fusion of caffeine and anxiety. Bespectacled and built like a child's stick figure, his lack of physical presence somehow magnified his intellectual aura. Lin had an uncanny knack for translating equations, silicon, and electricity into a fighting advantage. He had overseen his country's side of the joint venture since its inception and, to Primakov's occasional annoyance, never hesitated to put his imprint on the test flights.

"All systems are operational," Lin said in impeccable Russian. "We will be running software update 6.22. The adversary radar will mimic the AN/APG-81 found on the American F-35."

"Why not the F-22 radar?" Primakov inquired. "That is a more potent air-to-air challenger."

"More potent, yes. But a less likely opponent. The F-35 will be built in far greater numbers than the Raptor, and it has been exported freely."

Lin had a point, but, in Primakov's view, the Raptor remained the greater threat. It was a classic divide of perspective. For an engineer everything boiled down to numbers, defeating the most probable adversary. A pilot simply wanted to be the best in the sky.

On another day, Primakov might have argued the point. Instead, he asked, "How accurate are your simulations of this radar?"

"There are limitations, mostly due to the size of the SU-35's antenna and its processing power. Yet my country recently acquired technical data on the Americans' latest modifications, the Block 6 upgrade. Our newest replication should bring the accuracy to within twenty percent."

Primakov showed no reaction to the dual digs in this reply. If Lin could be believed, China had again succeeded in stealing fresh intelligence on the F-35. And the subtext was that the Russian-built SU-35 radar was vastly inferior. This, in a nutshell, was what had given rise to the development of Vektor—a fighter that could close the gap with the West. In Primakov's opinion, they were getting close. The prototype in the adjacent hangar was uniquely capable, even superior to Western jets in certain scenarios. By partnering in its design, China and Russia were doing what neither could manage alone.

Primakov launched into his mission briefing. As always, it was part operational outline, part inspirational speech.

"Our test objective tonight is to validate Vektor's radar cross section. Takeoff is scheduled for 1740, one hour after sunset." Primakov used Moscow Standard Time, the universal clock of the Russian military in a nation that spanned nine time zones—and a nation that refused to recognize Greenwich, England, as a reference for anything.

"This is the sixty-eighth program mission overall," Primakov continued, "and the sixth of this phase. It is as important as the first, and I know each of you will conduct your duties as the professionals you are. By establishing a baseline for performance against Western air-to-air radar systems, we will advance our greater goal—to build a fighter that can bring victory over any jet in the sky." He paused for a patriotic moment before continuing. "Flying adversary tonight will be Major Borovin in the support SU-35. He will launch from Domna Air Base for a rendezvous in the working area at 1800."

The term "adversary" was a bit of dramatic license. The SU-35 would not be maneuvering aggressively, as a true enemy would, but rather droning through a racetrack pattern in the sky. As the two jets flew opposing courses, the SU-35 would try to "paint" Vektor using its modified radar. Primakov had always found such missions excruciatingly dull—too little maneuvering, too many digital assumptions. As he invariably told anyone who would listen, the most important weapons system on any combat aircraft was the pilot.

Major Borovin linked into the briefing via a secure video connection from Domna Air Base, and for ten minutes Primakov ran down his test card. He coordinated the altitudes and airspeeds to be flown, and what radar modes would be used for each of the eleven planned passes. After a few questions from Borovin, the connection was cut. Primakov ended with a flourish, imparting inspirational words about the glory of Mother Russia.

He adjourned the briefing and set out toward the life support room. The colonel was halfway down the hall when someone called his name from behind. He turned and saw a gangly enlisted man approaching with a clipboard in his hand.

"Sir, a letter for you from Moscow." The private held out a thin envelope, and Primakov saw his name and rank hand-scripted on the front.

"When did this arrive?" he asked.

"It came on the Hip this afternoon, the regular supply run. It didn't reach you right away because it was inside the top secret courier bag."

Primakov nearly asked who it was from, but then checked himself. He frowned and shoved the unopened envelope into the leg pocket of his flight suit.

The enlisted kid hovered with his clipboard, which no doubt held routing paperwork that required a signature. The pause was brief before he turned away and retreated to his desk. Classified document procedures might be serious business, but glaring colonels were far more persuasive.

Primakov continued down the hall.

At Primakov's previous base, Ramenskoye, the life support room had been the size of a tennis court, nearly a hundred sets of flight gear organized in neat rows. Here the division didn't even warrant its own room—one metal gym locker had been wedged into an oversized closet.

The locker's door squeaked when he opened it. Primakov removed his G-suit from a peg and began zipping it over his legs and abdomen. He then pulled his helmet bag and gloves from the top shelf, and as he did so his eye snagged on the photo behind. Taped up at the back of his locker was a less than complimentary snapshot of his wife: Oksana preening for a selfie with her father, the Kremlin in the background behind them. He had put it there not out of longing, but as proof of the bleak state of their marriage. Of all the pictures he had ever seen of her, this was the worst. With her face scrunched against the sunlight, she looked older than her forty-four years, and her smile was a clear forgery.

He had not looked at the image in months.

The letter in his pocket weighed mightily. Surrendering to curiosity, Primakov pulled it out. He found a single page in the envelope. It was, as expected, from his father-in-law: Chief of the GRU's Third Directorate, Major General Viktor Strelkov.

> Maksim,
>
> I am told your work brings great success. You are a credit to our country. I have spoken to General Sholokhov, and he tells me your promotion is imminent. I realize this would mean giving up the flying, but a man of your background and talents is not to be wasted. I assure you the privileges at headquarters for a flag-grade officer will prove well worth the sacrifice.
>
> In duty and honor, Viktor.

Primakov felt the all too familiar burn in his gut.

Sacrifice? Honor? This from a man who kept mistresses half his age. From a man who took pride in his links to the Russian mafia. Even this news, the promise of a promotion for Primakov, was surely calculated for self-advancement. Strelkov held the rank of an army lieutenant general, and in heading up a directorate he was destined for the very top of Russia's military intelligence establishment. Having a son-in-law promoted to general could only help his standing.

Primakov resisted an urge to crumple the message, crosscurrents tumbling through his head. Instead, he took a grease pencil from his flight suit pocket and scrawled a three-word message on the paper. He folded the letter and stuffed it back in the envelope. Again using the grease pencil, he crossed out his own name on the envelope and wrote his father-in-law's. Primakov checked his watch and saw that it was "step time." He set the envelope on the shelf near the photograph, gathered his gear, and headed for the hangar.

THREE

Primakov pushed through the door to the hangar and then went still—as he often did. The relationship he had developed with this aircraft was not unlike what might be had with a woman. Its beauty gave pause, a sense of anticipation. Even a year after first seeing her, the jet stirred something deep within him. He could only think of Vektor in the feminine, despite its menacing aspect and hard angles. The main body was shaped like an arrowhead, the wings cranked back at precisely forty-one degrees. This angle was matched by virtually every other joint on the airplane. Stealth was not about curves, but rather constant geometry. Keeping reflections to the narrowest possible band.

Vektor was the color of charcoal, her radar-absorbent skin unflawed by extraneous rivets and latches. The wings and twin canted tails were large, and her fuselage lacked the usual appendages. There were no missile racks or antennae, and the bare minimum of service panels.

Sergeant Pavel Nicoliev, Vektor's crew chief, was waiting by the boarding ladder.

The two exchanged a salute, and Primakov said, "Good morning, Pavel. Any new issues?" He had received the maintenance officer's briefing, but line crew chiefs always had the most intimate knowledge of their jets.

"No, sir," Pavel replied. "The power is connected and your inertials are aligned."

"Excellent!"

Primakov began a walk-around inspection of the jet, beginning at the nose and working clockwise. On the underside of the aircraft's chin, just ahead of the nose gear, he ensured the reflector beacon was retracted. Controlled by a switch in the cockpit, it had been added for calibrations early in the test program. When extended, the angular arm increased the radar reflectivity of the aircraft a hundredfold. It was the aviation equivalent of putting a loudspeaker on a submarine, the intention to give a baseline reference for comparison.

Primakov found nothing amiss on his walk-around. As he climbed the ladder toward the cockpit a crew began pushing the hangar doors open. The jet was tall, the rail of the cockpit four meters above the ground. Nicoliev helped him strap in, guiding the parachute latches to his harness before climbing down and pulling the ladder clear.

Instruments spun to life, and soon Primakov had the two big engines spinning. In the confines of the hangar the noise was deafening, but with his helmet on and the canopy down, Primakov heard only a low-frequency hum.

Adrenaline began to stir.

He had flown nearly a hundred different types of aircraft, putting jets through their paces in various experimental test programs. Vektor had proved the most challenging of them all. It had nothing to do with the jet, which handled marvelously, nor the systems being integrated. The problem had been dealing with so many surrounding distractions. Chinese engineers, the distant meddling of his father-in-law, a once-proud Air Force falling apart before his eyes. Suspicion, mistrust, corrupt bureaucracies. It was a miracle Vektor had gotten this far.

Yet in that moment, seated in the cockpit and with the controls in his hands, he felt something old and familiar. Within minutes he would be up in the air, pushing a cutting-edge jet to its limits. A message bloomed on the datalink—a contribution of the Chinese. Borovin's SU-35 was airborne and headed for the working area.

Primakov gave Pavel a crisp salute and began taxiing. The temperature had dropped ten degrees since sundown, but the taxiway remained free of ice. Vektor's test flights were exclusively undertaken at night, robbing the American satellites of the visual spectrum of surveillance. The hangar, too, gave cover, and its roof had been covered with a special coating to counter penetrating surveillance.

Even so, Primakov knew the Americans were watching.

Skovorna had no control tower—hardly necessary for an airfield with only a few flights a day—and so Primakov announced his departure on the common airfield frequency. He lined up on the runway, stepped on the brakes, and began a partial runup of the engines. Once everything stabilized, he pushed the throttles forward to the first gate. The great turbofans spun up to military power. Primakov did not, however, engage the afterburners. The aircraft was overpowered as it was, and in such cold conditions the extra thrust wasn't necessary. More pertinently, the burners used a prodigious amount of fuel—something he didn't want to waste.

He released the brakes and Vektor leapt forward, its nose bobbing down like a racehorse leaving a gate. Even without afterburners, the acceleration was breathtaking as the fighter thundered down the broad four-thousand-meter runway.

After five hundred meters the controls began responding. He pushed forward on the stick ever so slightly, the speed building beyond what was necessary to get airborne. Then he pulled back aggressively for an eye-catching departure—a bit of showmanship was inbred in all fighter pilots. Within seconds Vektor was accelerating in a sixty-degree climb.

Although Primakov would never know it, ten meters before the main wheels lifted off the starboard tire kicked up a shard of debris. It was not, in fact, one of the concrete chips he'd been worried about. In a dreadful irony, the foreign object was a 12mm steel bolt that had fallen from the bottom of the sweeping machine the previous day as it brushed away a light snowfall. At two hundred miles an hour, the tire was spinning at an extreme rotational rate, and its rubber tread seized the bolt and flung it upward like a bullet.

The impact occurred on the bottom of the right wing, two feet behind the starboard landing gear well. The bolt penetrated the outer skin yet had no other apparent effect. Oblivious to this entire sequence of events, Colonel Maksim Primakov pointed Vektor skyward and sped toward the working area at just below the speed of sound.

FOUR

"Natis One beginning baseline pass," Primakov transmitted the instant he was established in the working area. The call sign Natis One had been stolen from Chita Air Base, one more part of the smokescreen regarding the Vektor program. Even deep in Siberia, the Americans managed to intercept radio traffic.

The mission would be monitored by Chita range control, although the sergeant behind the scope there knew nothing about its purpose. His Soviet-era radar equipment barely picked up the SU-35, and painting Vektor would be all but impossible unless the aircraft turned on its transponder. The range controllers had been told their only duty during the missions from Skovorna was to warn if other aircraft came near the test airspace.

On the west side of the range, Major Borovin banked his Sukhoi into a hard left turn, and announced, "Bandit One turning inbound."

"Natis One copies," Primakov replied.

The pattern was an eighty-mile-long oval, the two aircraft positioned at opposite ends. Unlike air combat training, there would be no maneuvering. The test objective was simply to acquire radar data. On the first pass, designed for calibration, the radar reflector would be deployed. After that, the stealth evaluation would begin. Altogether, it was a dull night's work for the pilots of two high performance fighters.

Established on opposing courses, the two jets merged with a combined closure of over a thousand miles an hour. In the cockpit of the SU-35, Borovin saw nothing on his scope. After thirty seconds of tinkering with his radar, he said, "Natis One, confirm your reflector is deployed."

"Natis One confirms, reflector deployed."

A short pause, then, "Bandit One has negative contact."

With his radar display still blank, and nearing the point of the expected merge, Borovin scanned the night sky for flashes of red and green. His own navigation lights were shining bright, but he saw no sign of Primakov's.

"Natis One, say position," Borovin said. "Bandit One never picked you up."

Primakov did not respond.

"Natis One, do you copy? I did not paint you on that pass." Borovin's voice was calm, yet as he repeated the call twice more the tautness in his voice rose.

Then Primakov's voice shattered the silence. *"Natis One, Mayday! Mayday! I . . ."*

Borovin waited for Primakov to finish his radio call. Five seconds. Ten. Impatience got the better of him, "Natis One, what is the nature of your problem?"

Primakov did not respond.

Borovin established an orbit in the center of the working area, both his radar and his sharp eyes sweeping the night sky. He saw nothing, and for two minutes his transmissions went unanswered. The range control officer, having heard the distress call, also tried to raise Primakov. There was no reply.

In the cockpit of an SU-35, and at a radar station in Chita, two concerned men turned up the volume on their secondary radios. These were tuned, as a matter of procedure, to the universal emergency frequency. They listened, fatalistically, for the warbling tone that would indicate Colonel Primakov had ejected.

The range controller adjusted his radar to its highest sensitivity, as did Borovin, but neither held much hope—Vektor was, by design, a virtually invisible airframe. After ten minutes Borovin's gaze canted down, no longer searching the sky for navigation lights, but the ground for plumes of flame.

He saw nothing but blackness.

The sergeant on the scope in Chita quickly alerted his supervisor, a major, to the situation in Restricted Area 1512. An experimental jet, on a test flight neither of them knew anything about, had gone missing. After a brief back-and-forth with Bandit One, the major realized there was only one recourse. He issued a sector-wide search for a possible downed aircraft and sent an alert up the chain of command.

Skovorna Air Base was among the first to get the word. Colonel Nemanchik had just fallen asleep in a lounge chair in his quarters, a standalone apartment at the center of the compound, when a resolute knock on the door caused him to bolt upright—the universal reaction to night-time intrusions in Russia. Nemanchik never made any effort to align his workday with flight operations, and had gone straight to his quarters after Primakov's mission briefing. He neither knew nor cared about the vagaries of testing aircraft, and the base's logistical duties were more efficiently performed during normal working hours.

He belted his bathrobe, went to the door, and found an agitated lieutenant from the command post. "This had better be good," he growled.

"Sir, the jet has crashed!"

Nemanchik went rigid. There was no need to clarify *which* jet since there was only one on base. "When?"

"Less than an hour ago."

"What of Primakov?"

"We don't know. A search has begun. There are messages from headquarters that must be answered."

"I'll be there as soon as I get dressed." Nemanchik slammed the door in the lieutenant's face and hurried to the bedroom, his thoughts swirling. Just like that, a posting that had been going well, his possible stepping stone to flag-grade rank, was on the verge of failure. Had something gone wrong that could be laid at his feet? Shoddy maintenance? A drunken crew chief?

No, he thought more positively. *This could be an opportunity.*

His response to the crisis would be critical. It might even work in his favor. "Poor Primakov," he whispered as an afterthought.

Nemanchik gathered his thoughts as he dressed and was tying his shoes when he was struck by a grave complication. One phone call was necessary before he left. He diverted to the back bedroom, which doubled as an office, and stood before the great floor safe. The safe was an ancient item, the size of a refrigerator and bolted to the floor, and only he, as commander, knew the combination. His hand shook a little as he spun the numbered wheel, and it took three tries to get the combination right.

He hauled open the door and pulled out a special phone he'd been given. He turned it on and placed a call, steeling himself with each ring. If he screwed up with headquarters tonight, he might lose his next promotion. But this phone call could prove far more consequential.

After five rings, a distracted voice grumbled, "What is it?" It was midafternoon in Moscow.

"Sir, this is Colonel Nemanchik at Skovorna Air Base. I regrettably have some very bad news about your son-in-law . . ."

Colonel Nemanchik, Major Borovin, and the range control staff in Chita were not the only ones trying to determine the fate of Natis One.

Six thousand miles away, an athletic man with gray eyes stood stock-still at the back of the CIA's Tactical Operations Center. David Slaton watched and listened in silence, much as he had all those years when he'd lived on the tip of the spear. Today, unfortunately, with a reluctant grip on the handle, the instincts that had served him so well in the field felt remarkably deficient. His only weapon was communication. There was no offensive option, no way to seize the initiative. The sensory inputs that guided him in the TOC, monitors that gave sight and signal intercepts that provided audio, were not under his direct control. He could steer channels, prioritize feeds, but all of that took time. It was, he supposed, a comeuppance of sorts—he finally knew how his own handlers, most of whom had been dedicated and well-meaning servants, had felt during those years when he'd ventured into harm's way to do their bidding.

"Still no sign of the jet?" he asked as he moved to his right—as if that might give a better perspective.

"No sir," confirmed the duty officer, a dusky-haired man in civilian clothes seated behind a central console. "AWACS has the best chance of getting early hits, but they're eight hundred miles from the action."

"But they *are* on station, right?"

"Darkstar 22 is established in an orbit over the Sea of Japan, been there for nearly an hour."

Slaton edged toward the front of the room, weaving between workstations. The new TOC, which had been designed for SAC/SOG missions like this one, was effectively a stage—rows of keyboards and monitors, subdued indirect lighting, all of it overlooking three screens at the front. A smaller version of the National Counterterrorism Center, it was a perfect backdrop for the world's greatest reality show. The theater where the clandestine service's greatest dramas played out. At six thirty in the morning the sun was just rising outside, and the smell of coffee permeated the air.

The scope of today's operation was unusual. Time constraints had not allowed a full-blown interagency effort, so the CIA had retained operational control while calling in "guest help." The assembled team included specialists from the Air Force, Navy, and many of the CIA's sister intelligence agencies. Everyone had been on duty since midnight. Slaton was not unfamiliar with command centers, but today's mission came with one glaring new twist—for the first time ever, he was the one running the show.

"SIGINT?" he inquired as he reached the front row.

"Nothing new," said a woman in civilian clothes. She was an employee of the National Reconnaissance Office whose mission today, as implausible as it seemed, was to monitor communications in a flight test area half a world away. In low earth orbit above that airspace a redirected satellite was skimming frequencies voraciously in search of transmissions. NRO had refined their eavesdropping on two previous Vektor test flights, spin-ups for today's big event. Those efforts had achieved mixed results. Today they'd gotten intermittent UHF audio on the working frequency and snagged a partial upload from an aircraft datalink. The latter would require serious processing and analysis, which meant it was useless in real time. The cold truth of it all: despite having a tremendous array of assets, the combined U.S. intelligence agencies still couldn't cover every corner of Russia.

The focal point became the main screen on the front wall, a map of today's area of operation. To Slaton's eye, the vastness of western Russia had never seemed so daunting. A tiny red aircraft symbol, now east of Restricted Area 1512, floated tenuously across the big map. Its position was only an estimate based on the comm hits they'd intercepted, combined with an expectation that Colonel Primakov would stick to his plan. In essence, they were basing their coordinates on hope, and until they acquired something more concrete, they were effectively working in the blind.

Slaton was still getting a feel for what assets were available to him. He had taken over SAC/SOG a mere three weeks ago, and most of that time had been wasted in an anesthetizing gauntlet of square-filling and administrative briefings. For one of the world's preeminent field operatives, it was a private hell. Success today, however, might make it all worthwhile.

Eight weeks ago, a walk-in agent, Russian Air Force Colonel Maksim Primakov, had approached the CIA and begun passing information about an aircraft called Vektor. He was initially controlled through the Moscow station, yet once the accuracy of his information was validated by analysts, headquarters quickly became involved. The details Primakov was conveying, insights into what both Russia and China were baking into the next generation of air combat, was a gold mine for the taking. The agency typically angled to run such sources for as long as possible, although in Primakov's case the usual incentives didn't apply: he hadn't asked for money, hadn't been compromised by sex or scandal. On appearances, he was of the rarest breed—an agent motivated by either idealism or, more likely, some manner of personal grievance.

The CIA was just beginning its deep dive to determine Primakov's motivation when he threw them another curve. The senior test pilot announced, with forty-eight hours' notice, that he was planning to flee Russia in Vektor. This steered the entire affair, virtually overnight, into Slaton's shadowed corner of the agency: clandestine operations.

His eyes remained padlocked on the big screen with the same intensity he had once given a sniper scope. He watched and waited, and wondered loosely if this was a typical day on his new job. He had not been home for two days, although that paled in comparison to the weeks, sometimes months, he had often spent abroad doing field work.

He lasered in on the airplane symbol on the map, imagining a jet hurtling through the ether on the other side of the world. What precious little they had gleaned so far seemed positive—Primakov appeared to be following through on his promise to defect. Whether he could pull it off was the big question. Analysts had been gaming the odds of success for the last two days, and the obstacles seemed overwhelming.

As Slaton wondered what had driven the man to take such extraordinary risks, his trigger finger tapped the top of a console.

Where the hell are you? he wondered.

FIVE

Maksim Primakov was, in fact, two hundred and six nautical miles east of Restricted Area 1512.

He had turned off every system on the jet with an electronic emission. Radios, radar, transponder, datalink, telemetry, an experimental laser system. He'd shut off every exterior light and had even toned down the cockpit lights to make the flight instruments barely visible. At the very least, it would keep his night vision sharp.

There was a saying among fighter pilots that "speed was life." Tonight, however, that equation had been turned on its head. Range was life, which meant that he had to fly at an uncomfortably slow speed. As soon as he'd established his eastbound heading, Primakov traded airspeed for altitude. Vektor was now flying at 62,000 feet at the jet's maximum range airspeed—far below the MACH-2 plus it might have managed—in the name of conserving fuel.

This had always been the challenge: How far could Vektor fly on a single tank of gas? Its designed combat range, with no external fuel tanks, was eight hundred nautical miles. This assumed a round trip, so Primakov could roughly double that number. Working against him was that he had burned fuel in the working area while creating his diversion. More worrying at the moment was that the weather officer had been wrong—the winds aloft were from the northeast, giving him a slight headwind component instead of the expected tailwind.

The bottom line was what it always had been. As he tried to defect with Russia's most advanced aircraft, the nearest landing airfield, Chitose Air Base on the island of Sapporo, Japan, was fourteen hundred nautical miles away. If he could reach it at all, he would be landing on fumes.

Primakov gazed out into the clear night sky. He rarely found time to reflect when airborne, but the profoundness of the moment caused his mind to drift. In the scant moonlight he saw a low cloud deck to the east, clinging like a blanket over the Siberian wilderness. Directly below he saw a distinct outline of white, yet it took a moment to realize what it was—the expansive Zeya Reservoir stretching into the distance. In midwinter the lake was frozen solid, and reflections of moonlight from the ice were a stark contrast to the dense forest all around. The visibility was exceptional, the night sky studded with stars. It seemed almost prophetic, a kind of celestial blessing.

Primakov's musings ended abruptly. In his rushed separation from the working area, he realized he hadn't gotten around to the most important task—inputting the precise lat/long pairing he had committed to memory.

He typed in the coordinates of Chitose Air Base in Japan. The flight management computer took a few beats to run the math, and when the results arrived, they were close to his estimate. Heading 139 degrees, 1089 nautical miles remaining. Then a new message came to the scratchpad. One that he hadn't been expecting: INSUFFICIENT FUEL.

Primakov was more piqued than worried. The computer showed him running out of gas well short of Japanese airspace. He double checked the coordinates, convinced he had entered them wrong. That wasn't the problem. He verified the cruise flight level and winds, yet saw nothing amiss.

He sat mystified as Vektor streaked ahead unbothered. The fuel calculations were so far off it had to be an input error. Then a voice in the back of his head pulled his eyes to the fuel gauge and he instantly saw the problem. Primakov drew a long breath through his oxygen mask. The left and right fuel tanks showed a large imbalance.

How did I not notice it sooner?

He immediately began to analyze the discrepancy. Primakov knew Vektor's systems better than anyone on earth and he could think of only two possible causes for the imbalance. The simplest was that the right-side fuel gauge had malfunctioned. He turned off the autopilot, which he had engaged to lighten the workload, and his test pilot's hands immediately felt the problem. This was reinforced by a seat-of-the pants sensation: the airplane was flying crookedly. It suggested there really was an imbalance, and implied a serious problem . . .

Primakov looked over his shoulder, toward the right wing, and his worst fears were realized. In the dim moonlight he saw a trail of vapor streaming behind the jet. He had a fuel leak. Which meant he was going to run out of gas before he was anywhere near Japanese airspace.

Of all the contingencies he had planned for, of all the possible complications, a fuel leak had not been among them. He kicked the rudder pedals in anger. *Why tonight, of all nights?* If he had seen the malfunction thirty minutes ago, before making the distress call and breaking away, he might have walked everything back. He could have declared an emergency, returned to Skovorna, and let maintenance fix the problem. He could have retrieved the envelope he'd left in his locker and done it all again next week.

But now? Now there was no turning back.

An amber warning light interrupted his miserable thoughts. Amber, in the world of human factors engineering, was the color of caution. Red lights were reserved for the most serious warnings, those that pre-saged imminent disaster. The light in question, however, might as well have been crimson. The right engine was overheating. With the temperature gauge edging higher, the evidence could not have been more damning—he had an engine overheat *and* a fuel leak. The two had to be related.

A diagram of the engine fuel system appeared in Primakov's head, and he deduced the likely problem. Fuel wasn't simply leaking *out* of the wing. It was also leaking *into* the aircraft. He envisioned fuel sloshing through the wing box, sucking back toward the engine bay where the hot sections of two massive turbojets lay. It would be like pouring gas onto the exhaust manifold of a car.

He began making decisions as test pilots do, immediately and instinctively. He stepped through the engine shut-down procedure by memory.

Starboard throttle—idle.

Starboard fire handle—pull.

The engine coughed once, starved of fuel, and began spooling down. The jet yawed right as the thrust became asymmetrical. Primakov pushed the nose down and advanced the left throttle. Even Vektor, overpowered as she was, couldn't maintain 62,000 feet on one engine.

The overheat light extinguished, meaning the sensor had decreased below the onset temperature. The engine was cooling, the situation stabilized. *But for how long?*

There was an expanded checklist for the engine overheat, one that Primakov would have referenced on any other flight in his life. But tonight was different. Tonight he ignored the best outcome for the Russian Air Force, and instead viewed the situation through the prism of his own interests. He could be flying a ticking bomb. He had no idea how much fuel had leaked into the engine bay, but if the vapor ignited the aircraft could explode. There was no option but to land immediately. The question was, where?

Airfields, both military and civilian, were hardly an option. After landing, he might talk his way out of trouble for an hour or two, but suspicions would be raised. Air Force headquarters, not to mention a wary Chinese contingent, would already be in a state of panic after their prized experimental jet had gone missing. Everyone would wonder why Primakov hadn't responded on the radio after his initial "mayday" call. And why had he flown so far in the wrong direction? It was very possible someone would check his locker, find the letter amid his flight gear with a message to his father-in-law. At that point, Primakov would not be answering to his Air Force commanders, but to the FSB. Interrogations in a dank basement, and soon after that, certainly, a bullet in the head.

He suddenly regretted the message he'd scrawled on the letter. It was a mistake, a parting bit of bravado that was coming back to haunt him. It wasn't the first time he had been punished by his impulsiveness, but the stakes tonight were far greater than an interservice rivalry or fraternal squadron antics. The letter, quite clearly, was proof of his treason.

There could be no turning back, which meant his only chance was escape. He had to somehow get on the ground and make his way to the West. The great prize he had meant to deliver, Vektor herself, would be lost. *But my knowledge of her capabilities . . . surely that is worth something. Worth the risk of getting me out.*

He peered into the darkness below. The most obvious solution was to eject over remote forest. The small communications device in the leg pocket of his flight suit, given to him by the Americans, could be his salvation. Looking down he saw the ground increasingly shrouded by clouds, and the idea of ejecting seemed fraught with hazard. It meant rocketing out of a warm cockpit into a frigid night sky, at hundreds of miles an hour, then praying for a full parachute and an injury-free landing. Like all pilots, Primakov viewed ejection as a last-ditch option, only to be contemplated in the face of certain death. Then another complication came to mind: ejection would automatically trigger the emergency beacon in his seat. There was nothing he could do about that, and it meant his position would immediately be seen.

And not only would he be bailing out over Siberia in the winter, but it was now enemy territory. Primakov craned his neck left and right, desperate for another option. If he could find a place to put the jet down where it would remain out of sight, he might have a chance. He remembered what he had seen minutes earlier, and a third option arose. A middle ground of sorts. He took a hard look at the starboard engine instruments. The shut-down had been successful, the engine temperature still decreasing. He had time, but there was no telling how much.

Primakov banked the jet sharply into a high-G turn, reversing course.

Minutes later the low clouds began to break, and he saw what he had spotted earlier. The outline of Zeya Reservoir below, dim fingers of white grasping into dense forest. The lake was massive and isolated, nearly three hundred miles of uninhabited shoreline. He had flown over it many times, and he remembered seeing a small village on the distant south shore. Below him now were the northern branches, remote and wild, virtually untouched by man. At this time of year, there probably wasn't a soul within twenty miles. Best of all, after a particularly hard winter, the ice on the lake had to be meters thick.

But would that be enough?

He circled the northern edge of the lake, coaxing the crippled jet lower. Even on one engine Vektor was responsive at low altitude, muscling through the cold night air. He leveled off at a thousand feet, let the jet slow, and in the scant light he strained to assess the lake's surface.

Was it possible to land here? No matter how gingerly he touched down, there was no escaping the truth—thirty tons of steel and titanium and fuel would be transferred from lift-producing wings to a frozen lakebed. Was the ice strong enough? And then there was the matter of stopping. The lake was miles wide, but would he be able to bring Vektor to a stop on pure ice before skidding into the far shoreline?

Only one way to find out . . .

Primakov chose the longest stretch of lake for his makeshift runway. The wind, according to his flight display, was nearly calm. He dropped the landing gear and lowered the flaps, slowing to approach airspeed. He descended on a three-degree angle and paid particular attention to the radar altimeter—it would give him an accurate altitude above the frozen surface. At one hundred meters he locked his shoulder straps into place. At fifty he focused completely outside.

The landing lights reflected brilliantly off the snow-dusted ice—so brilliantly that Primakov had trouble estimating his height above touchdown. The ground came at him in a blur, and he concentrated on the radar altitude readout in his heads-up display.

At ten meters he cut the sink rate, wanting as soft a touchdown as possible.

Five meters.

Three . . .

One . . .

Vektor's wheels kissed the ice.

There was the slightest of bounces, but Primakov kept flying and the big jet settled. The ice seemed to hold but lift from the wings was still supporting much of the jet's weight. Primakov worked the flight controls furiously, trying to hold the nose up and use aerodynamics to slow. Ever so delicately, he touched the top of the rudder pedals to test the wheel brakes. He felt a thump and an immediate release, the anti-skid system intervening. He tried again, and the brakes pulsed inter-mittently. The jet was slowing, but barely. The outside world flew past in a rush of white. Primakov felt like he was skiing down a mountain, barely in control. Soon the aerobraking waned, and at eighty knots the nose wheel settled gently.

With all three wheels grounded, the ice was bearing the jet's full weight. He felt a momentary sense of relief, but that vaporized when he saw a vague outline ahead. Looming in the moonlight, the jagged shadow of the forested shoreline. Primakov stepped harder on the brakes. Nothing changed.

Vektor began to skid, the nose skewing left. The jet was out of con-trol, the world outside a maelstrom of reflections in the glare of the landing lights. A wall of timber at the shoreline loomed, as imposing as the side of a canyon. The brakes were useless, and with no directional control Vektor was sliding sideways. With the trees looming, seeming close enough to touch, Primakov braced himself. Sensing a need to do something, *anything,* he reached down and shut off the still-running port engine.

The jet slammed to a stop like a car hitting a guardrail. Primakov's helmet struck the canopy.

And the world went to darkness.

SIX

The search launched from three different air bases in Russia's Far East Military District. A dozen helicopters and fixed-wing aircraft sortied into the night, headed for a search box beneath Restricted Area 1512. None of the crewmen knew exactly what they were looking for: the alert message had simply stated that an Air Force jet had gone missing with one pilot on board. The type of aircraft was left to question, as was the airfield and unit to which it was attached. This was unusual, but it didn't affect the mission—unit patches had little relevance in a pile of smoldering wreckage.

The first notable discovery was what was missing—there was no ELT signal, the emergency beacon that should have activated if either the aircraft had crashed or the pilot had ejected. An ELT would greatly ease the job of pinpointing the crash site, but the search teams had other means available. They could scan the cold forest with infrared sensors and monitor emergency frequencies for distress calls. Failing that, the sharp-eyed airmen had an excellent chance of spotting flames at night in the desolate terrain.

All of this, however, relied on one faulty assumption. As the search teams converged on the search box, no one could know that they were, by over two hundred miles, looking in the wrong place.

Primakov sat stunned. His eyes fluttered open and he tried to remember where he was. Slowly, agonizingly, the misery of his situation came cascading back.

A fuel leak.

An aborted defection.

Zeya Reservoir.

He sat for a moment in Vektor's cockpit, gathering his thoughts in an improbably silent world. The sensory chaos of the previous minutes had gone to stillness. He heard the hum of a gyro winding down, a faint ticking as metal cooled somewhere deep in the airframe. A handful of lights on the panel in front of him were illuminated, essential instruments that operated when the battery was the only source of power—with the engines shut down, the generators had gone offline.

He performed a self-assessment. His head hurt, having struck the canopy, and one shoulder was wrenched tight by a harness strap. Otherwise, he seemed fine. He snapped the harness release and felt immediate relief. Outside he saw nothing but black. He reached down, retrieved a penlight from his pocket, and shone it on the canopy. A layer of snow blanketed the Plexiglass, obscuring his view of the world.

His gamble had paid off, such as it was. The ice had been thick enough to support Vektor and he'd survived the crash landing.

"But now what?" he said to no one.

He disconnected his G-suit, unlatched his lap belt, and pulled off his helmet. He had no idea what shape the airplane was in, but there was one certainty—the jet had a fuel leak. Primakov decided it was far safer to be outside the cockpit. He activated a switch and the big canopy motored upward. Frigid winter air hit like a wall. Skovorna had been near the freezing point when he'd taken off, but here, in the mountains and with night having taken hold, it had to be twenty degrees colder.

He decided to turn off the aircraft battery—he wasn't sure what good that would do, but no resource could be wasted in a survival situation. He stood gingerly, feeling a bit woozy. Looking back, he took in the jet's dim outline. From this perspective the fuselage looked intact, and clumps of snow had slung up onto the wings and engine intakes. The right wing was buried in a snowbank.

He looked over the canopy rail to the ground. Standing on the seat, he was fifteen feet in the air. This introduced another minor complication. He'd been briefed by the maintenance officer that the integral boarding ladder was inoperative. The ladder he'd used to reach the cockpit was back at Skovorna. Without much hope, he activated the switch to deploy the telescoping ladder. Nothing happened. Primakov tinkered with the system for a full minute before giving up. Something was jammed and the crash hadn't straightened it out. He would have to find another way down.

It's such a damned simple problem.

His eyes settled on the right wing. It was the same height off the ground as the cockpit but embedded in that snowbank. If he could get out on the wing and lie down, he could easily drop into the snowbank. An inelegant solution, to be sure, but steeped in practicality.

Before he did anything else, Primakov had two important tasks. He first "safed" the ejection handles using the provided blocking pins. Next, he removed the seat cushion and lifted out the survival kit. He dropped the kit to the ground on the starboard side. He was about to start moving when his list of priorities shifted again. He removed the communication device the CIA had given him from a zippered pocket. He had considered not even bringing it—the idea of communicating with the Americans during flight seemed wholly impractical. Now his life might depend on the tiny handset.

Primakov powered the device up and, as always, assumed he had a good connection. His only instructions on its use had come the first time he'd turned it on, a tutorial of sorts that had played through once, then disappeared. The phone was, on simple appearances, the latest Xiaomi model—a Chinese brand that had supplanted Samsung as the bestselling variety in Russia after sanctions had taken hold. In truth, the device was a message-only satellite transceiver that, if the tutorial could be believed, would work anywhere in Russia.

Time to put that to the test, he thought uneasily.

He pecked out a message, keeping it brief. He was sure that the CIA, who were coordinating his defection, must be wondering where he was. Were they still expecting his arrival in Japan? Or did they already know that something had gone wrong? As he typed, Primakov felt like he was walking a deft line. He needed to explain what had happened without diminishing the CIA's enthusiasm.

He sent the message, and then waited for confirmation. The phone seemed to be trying, but there was no acknowledgment of delivery of the message.

What if it doesn't go through? he wondered.

The only truthful answer was depressing. He would be left standing next to a wrecked airplane at the edge of a Siberian lake at the height of winter. No one on earth knew where he was, and the most likely chance for rescue would be from people who would torture and kill him.

The little wheel on the screen kept spinning. His grip tightened on the case, and he weighed sending the message a second time.

Then, finally, confirmation: MESSAGE DELIVERED

Primakov heaved a sigh of relief.

He pocketed the phone and mapped out his next move. To reach the wing, he needed to maneuver to the spine of the jet. To get there, the main obstacle was the canopy itself, which was every bit as wide as the tapered fuselage. With the canopy tilted back at a forty-five-degree angle, he would have to tightrope along the rail and grip its metal frame to reach the wing area. Without hesitation, he gripped the raised canopy, swung his right leg out into space, and began searching for a foothold on the other side.

Maksim Primakov had already made one mistake that day—leaving the letter in his locker in the life support room had been a monumental blunder. His second mistake, however, would prove far more agonizing. As he tried to shift his weight around the canopy, his left boot slipped on a chunk of ice.

Primakov fell fifteen feet to the ground, his arms windmilling all the way. It was the equivalent of falling off the roof of a house. The ice he landed on, solid enough to support a thirty-ton airplane, did nothing to lessen the impact.

An awful sound filled the night air. A crack not unlike a frozen tree limb giving way.

Only it wasn't a tree limb.

SEVEN

When Primakov's message arrived at the TOC in Langley, the watch officer was the first person to see it.

The second was standing directly behind him.

"Not what we were planning on," Slaton said evenly. He flicked a finger at the comm officer who transferred the message to the main display, sharing the bad news with the rest of the room.

FUEL LEAK. CRASH LANDED VEKTOR ON NORTHERN END OF ZEYA RESERVOIR. NEED IMMEDIATE EXTRACTION.

Slaton turned to his on-loan Air Force expert, Colonel Michael Westbrook. "Can this be real? Could he have landed this jet on a lake?"

The aviator's blue eyes narrowed as he studied the big map.

Yesterday, in the chaotic hours after Primakov had declared his intention to defect, the CIA had snatched Westbrook from his Pentagon staff job in the way that pirates might plunder a good cook. He was a graduate of the U.S. Air Force Test Pilot School and had broad experience flying experimental aircraft at Edwards Air Force Base, as well as a joint assignment to its U.S. Navy counterpart, Naval Air Station Patuxent River. On arriving at Langley, a bewildered Westbrook had been ushered straight to Slaton's office and told that an operation had fallen into the CIA's lap which required his expertise: a Russian test pilot, who had for weeks been supplying tantalizing information about a top secret fighter, had abruptly declared his intention to deliver it to the West.

Westbrook had been at Slaton's side ever since as they plotted a once-in-a-generation intelligence coup. He had helped plan the surveillance of Russian airspace and coordinated with the Japanese to receive Vektor at Chitose Air Base on the island of Hokkaido. Now, with one message, the entire operation had collapsed before their eyes.

After considerable thought, Westbrook mused, "In the dead of winter, in that part of the world? The reservoir must be frozen solid, so yeah, it's conceivable he was able to land it."

"What about a fuel leak? Does that make sense?"

"Things like that happen, especially in flight test programs—that's why you do them. Reaching Japan from Skovorna was always at the limit of the jet's range, so if Vektor suffered *any* loss of fuel it would have doomed the mission."

"Plot it!" Slaton called out.

It was now looking like a stroke of genius that they'd been able to deliver a special comm device to Primakov—a dead drop performed during the colonel's recent visit to Moscow. Aside from providing burst messaging capability, via satellite, the unit also embedded its position with each transmission. Within seconds the main map before them recentered and a vast lake appeared, one lonely circle highlighted at the extreme northern tip.

"Is there any way we can get eyes on that point?" Slaton asked, addressing a young woman at a workstation labeled NRO. The National Reconnaissance Office had mission oversight on all space-based assets. In his days as an operator, Slaton had long benefitted from overhead imagery. Now he was on the other end of the supply chain, not an end-user but a content provider, and he was still trying to get a grip on what resources were available.

"Nothing in real-time," she responded. "There's an NRO COMINT bird passing overhead in thirty minutes, but that won't give us a visual. The next imaging pass will be a Space Force Albedo bird in . . . two and a half hours."

Slaton took this in stride. Russia was a vast country, and Zeya Reservoir was a corner that rarely bore watching.

"Looks like your buddies at Groom Lake won't have a new toy to evaluate," Slaton said.

Westbrook had briefed Slaton on a special unit, based deep within the Area 51 Complex in the Nevada Test and Training Range, that flew foreign aircraft to study their capabilities.

"Apparently not," the colonel said. "But I wouldn't say all is lost . . ."

"Our pilot still wants to defect," Slaton said, finishing the thought. "Only problem is, he's . . . what, a thousand miles from the nearest friendly border?"

"Nine hundred and eighty-two," said the NRO analyst, probably trying to be helpful.

"I suppose it's my job to ask," Slaton ventured, "so exactly how valuable would Primakov be?"

"His information would be priceless," said Westbrook. "He's been involved in this project from the start, and based on what he's given us so far, he knows the airplane inside and out. He also promised to bring out all the technical data he could get his hands on—I assume on some kind of memory device. But if you ask me, even without any of that we're obliged to get him out. The guy put his life on the line for our benefit."

Slaton desperately wanted to agree. He had seen far too many sources and agents get cast aside when the going got rough. Yet there was another side to it, the possibility of double agents or entrapment schemes. What if Primakov was blown and this was a lure? What if the entire plot had been orchestrated by the GRU? Were the potential benefits worth putting American lives at risk? "From an Air Force perspective, what would be the options for getting him out?"

"I've done my share of search and rescue missions, and the hard part is done."

"The hard part?"

"We don't have to search. We know exactly where Primakov is, and we've established good comm. The problem is how to retrieve him without drawing notice so deep in enemy territory. Right now, I see two questions that need to be answered."

"Which are?"

"First, the Russians know by now that Vektor has gone down—but do they know where? Second, do they know what Primakov's intentions were? If the answer to both is no . . . then we might have enough time to put a mission together. It wouldn't be easy, and we would have to work fast. But if we *could* get him out . . . that would be half a win."

Slaton considered it, not bothering to address the other half. "All right, Colonel. I am putting you in charge of devising an extraction plan. Get with DOD and find out what assets are available for something like this—I want every option."

Westbrook acknowledged the order and set off toward the hallway.

Slaton's eyes returned to the big map. In the periphery, he felt other sets of eyes on him. There was an underlying tension in the room, and he knew what was behind it: an outsider had been brought in to head up one of the agency's most sought-after posts. There were countless people in the building, lifelong CIA servants, who, on paper, were more qualified than he was to take over clandestine operations. Slaton had neither confirmed nor denied the specifics of his own background, but rumors were flying. The basics were essentially correct: he was a career operator who'd gotten his start in Mossad. More damning were the musings that he was President Cleveland's golden boy. Beyond that there was little beyond whispers—hints of missions and assassinations that defied belief. Slaton had never cared a whit about his professional reputation, but he also couldn't escape it. Like it or not, he was leading these people. The best way to earn their respect, he decided, was to focus on his job.

Westbrook's questions loomed large, yet Slaton found his thoughts snagged on the second. Did the Russians know about Primakov's intention to defect? If so, finding the colonel would become their highest national priority. The GRU would swarm over every corner of Siberia until they located either him or his remains. Conversely, if no alarm had been raised, the crash would be viewed very differently. A top secret jet had gone down and its pilot was missing. A misfortune, to be sure, but not an existential crisis. And if they did find Primakov, but didn't recognize his duplicity, it was possible he could evade suspicion for a time.

Time, he thought. Buy enough of that, and there might be a window for extraction.

It occurred to him that the best source on how much the Russians knew would be Primakov himself. He edged toward the comm desk, and said to the operator, "I want to transmit a message to Talon." This was Primakov's code name.

The technician poised his hands over his keyboard.

Slaton knew from Primakov's file that he spoke solid English. He was also not a trained intelligence operative. For these reasons, he decided to trust the security of the comm network and speak plainly. He dictated, "Do you believe your intentions to defect are known to your superiors?"

The technician typed out the message and sent it.

Almost immediately, Slaton began to have second thoughts. Could he believe any response? Probably not. He knew Primakov's phone was physically on the northern edge of Zeya Reservoir, but anything more was pure conjecture. There was no guarantee that he was the one holding the handset. And even if it was him, could he be trusted? He felt himself sinking into what Anton Bloch, his mentor in Mossad, had always referred to as "the realm of smoke and mirrors."

Lining up a target in crosshairs is so much easier.

Slaton did not expect an immediate reply. Primakov would be busy trying to survive, and right now was probably running as far and as fast as he could from the wreckage.

"His device isn't responding," said the comm tech in a detached voice.

Slaton stared at him. "What do you mean? Has he turned it off?"

"No sir. With this particular unit, even if he turns it off, we should get an integrity ping. The battery can't be removed, so getting no response at all means one of two things. Either the battery is completely dead, or the handset has been damaged. Either way, given his situation, it means we've lost our only line of communication."

Slaton stood stunned. Then he realized that all eyes in the room were on him. "All right, Talon has lost comm. All information will have to come from other sources. What have we got?"

"I could authorize a satellite to maneuver," the NRO woman offered tentatively.

"Do it." His index finger swept the room and settled on the second-ranking agency employee, a senior analyst from the Asia division. "Find out if we have any assets in the area."

"Assets? You mean—"

"I mean people!"

"Sir, our networks in Russia have been decimated since the start of the Ukraine War. What little we do have is in the west . . . Moscow, St. Petersburg, the Black Sea. This part of the country is a black hole."

"Just tell me what we have. Non-official cover, diplomatic staff . . . I'll take a sympathetic pig farmer. We need somebody trustworthy who can put eyes on this crash site. It's possible Talon is what he appears to be, a high-value defector. On the other hand, this whole thing could be a counterintelligence op. Before we even *think* about committing forces to retrieve him, we have to be sure there's a downed jet on this lake and not an FSB welcoming committee."

"You really think Primakov could be a double?" someone asked.

"We don't have strong evidence either way. He might be legit, or Vektor could have been a trap from day one. It's also possible that he *was* legit, but he's been blown, and the FSB is now running his handset."

"But we intercepted those radio calls from the test range," said the NRO analyst.

All Slaton had to do was look at her.

"Oh, right . . . those could have been manufactured as well."

For twenty minutes Slaton stalked the room issuing instructions. He sensed undertows of doubt, but he didn't care. They had to get clarity. By the time he circled back to the man from the Asia desk, he was hanging up after a lengthy call.

"Well?" Slaton prompted.

"I'm told there's only one agency asset anywhere near this area— he's working an op in China, just across the border. It's a NOC from your section, fresh out of The Farm and on his third mission." The Farm was Camp Peary, Virginia, the CIA's primary training venue.

"A new guy . . . under non-official cover," Slaton repeated, wanting to be clear.

A nod.

"Where exactly is he?"

The analyst hesitated. "Well, that's the thing . . . they're not exactly sure."

EIGHT

Truman Miller was, at that moment, in very deep shit.

And not just figuratively.

He looked down at a swamp of frigid muck that came halfway up his thigh. The stench was overpowering. According to the diagram of the wastewater plant, which he had memorized that afternoon, this pond was built to process "partially treated" effluent. He had figured that for something between a foul ditch and a dirty swimming pool.

Wrong again.

In the dim light he saw trash mixed into the putrid scene. Plastic bags, face masks, the odd water bottle. It was rancid and disease-ridden, the same stew of flushed jetsam that went into sewer systems across the world. Awful as all that was, the pond itself wasn't the shock. He had never, *ever* expected to be standing in it.

This wasn't what Tru had imagined when he'd joined the CIA.

He sloshed slowly to his right, closer to the concrete side. The pond was roughly the size and shape of a football field and contained by a twelve-foot wall. Above it was open to the night sky, and a metal walkway lined the entire rectangular perimeter. Aerators worked feverishly in the middle, producing burbling fountains of foam that appeared green in the light of the overhead floods. There were eleven other ponds like it across the facility, which was situated four miles outside Hegang, China.

The sound of the distant pumps and sloshing spray obscured the sound of his movement. Looking up through the metal-mesh catwalk, five feet above, he saw two sets of boots outlined clearly. Tru himself had been on the walkway minutes earlier, his mission nearly complete—six of the eight vials were filled and sealed.

The collections were part of a new CIA initiative—biological intelligence—on which Tru had received a detailed briefing. Effluent samples, he'd been told, could be analyzed for a great many things. Disease outbreaks, such as COVID-19, could be tracked and traced. Local dietary changes could be discerned, which were an indicator of economic health. The signatures of certain radioisotopes could indicate mining work or weapons manufacturing. Even the mood of the local populace could be extracted from effluent, evidenced by hormonal variations over time. To the head-shed at Langley, the analysis of wastewater was a new frontier in intelligence gathering. Tru's personal view, particularly from his current perspective, was considerably more jaded. Standing thigh-deep in activated sludge, he silently cursed whatever bean-counter had come up with the idea.

According to his intel package, the facility was supposed to be minimally staffed at night. For that reason, most of his pre-mission planning had concentrated on getting in without detection. It seemed simplicity itself: transit ten miles from the hotel, breach the plant's rudimentary perimeter security, dip a few test tubes into the muck, and then make the reverse trip. For transportation he'd stolen a scooter from a food delivery driver who lived across the street from his hotel. If all went smoothly, he would lock the scooter back up after two hours with slightly less gas in the tank but no one the wiser. The chain-link fence around the plant was laughably simple—because who broke *into* a sewage treatment facility?

Everything had been going swimmingly until ten minutes ago when two men appeared outside the control building. Tru spotted them immediately, and initially he hadn't been worried. He saw them pause for a cigarette and chat for a time. When they began walking toward Pond Seven his attention ratcheted up further. Only when they approached the catwalk did Tru realize the depth of his predicament. He was effectively trapped. To the left the metal lattice walkway dead-ended into a wall. The men were approaching from the right. There was no way out, no chance of concealment on the catwalk. Above him was nothing but ebony night sky.

Which left only one option.

And a putrid one at that.

A trapdoor in the floor of the catwalk gave access to a descending ladder.

He had made it through and closed the door just as the men began clattering up the far end of the walkway. He considered perching there, just beneath the catwalk, but feared he might be visible from above. Or even worse, that the men might open the trapdoor for some unfathomable reason. The best concealment, he'd decided, was to descend into the muck and barnacle in the shadows against the concrete wall.

And that was where he was now—with his back against a brown-stained wall.

Yeah, everything's going swimmingly.

He heard the men approach and then pause a few steps short of the trapdoor. Out of twelve ponds, they had not only chosen his, but also ended up less than twenty feet from where he was hidden. They talked casually and began tinkering with some kind of electronic control box. Tru was fluent in three languages, but Chinese wasn't one of them. He had, however, taken a crash course in it after being assigned this mission, a month of immersive training on top of his other spin-up work. Thanks to that, he at least caught a few words—*electric, cold, coffee.* His comprehension of the situation advanced ever so slightly. Something had broken, a blown fuse or a short-circuit, and these two were trying to deal with it. They were also looking forward to getting back to the warmth of the control room.

A clump of brown bubbles spun past in the wake of the aerators.

For the last week he had been guiding a tour group through China, a loose cover that had so far seemed to hold up. He'd steered his ten charges through architectural wonders and shameless tourist traps. He had been chatty and social by day, carrying a blue sign over his head to highlight himself. On a handful of dark nights, he did precisely the opposite.

This night was to have been Tru's third, and final, trip to collect effluent samples, targeting a dated wastewater facility outside Hegang. The first two excursions had gone off without a hitch, late night forays from hotels in Harbin and Changchun. Those samples were now in sealed syringes in his suitcase, disguised and labeled as insulin. Tru had paperwork certifying that one guest in his tour group was diabetic, which was perfectly true, and it would take a jaded customs inspector, even by Chinese standards, to destructively inspect one of the vials. He was almost to the finish line—this time tomorrow night, he would be on a flight to Singapore, and from there a connection would take him to Los Angeles.

The agency had thought of everything . . . *almost.*

After five minutes, his patience began to wear thin. Each second felt heavier than the last. His toes were going numb, and the two workers on the catwalk seemed in no hurry. They were laughing about another man's wife and, worse yet, seemed to disagree on how to repair the electrical problem.

Tru's initial approach had been one of caution. Not wanting to raise an alarm, he figured he could just wait the men out. He took a step to the right and felt something spongy under his new tactical shoe. An aerator popped on thirty feet away, green water blossoming into the air. The conversation above turned heated.

His own internal squabble peaked.

As a new guy in Ground Branch, he didn't want to screw up on his third mission. The first two had been even more insipid than this one, albeit less smelly. He'd begun his clandestine life posing as a college-age missionary to Nigeria, the true aim being to map out illegal taps on oil pipelines made by a rebel group. In the second he had played the part of a graduate student, doing research in Kazakhstan that had nothing to do with Timurid architecture and everything to do with the government's search for rare earth metals. In both cases Tru had done all that was asked of him, yet both produced little of intelligence value. This mission to China, at least, had so far been a success, and he was loath to spoil it for a lack of patience.

The more basal part of his brain, however, which usually predominated, argued for action. *This isn't a damned high security military facility. It's a freakin' wastewater plant.* The two men would not be armed, nor would they be trained to fight. And his own close quarters combat skills were first rate.

A dirty diaper bobbed past in a swirling eddy. The two men were arguing openly now.

I've had enough of this crap.

He pulled the last two empty sample containers from his pocket. Using a gloved hand, he filled and sealed them, then slid them into his small backpack. He edged toward the ladder and silently began climbing. He was wearing black tactical clothing, so the chance of being seen while on the ladder was low. The risk would come when he emerged. The men were ten feet to the left of the metal-mesh trapdoor, and at that moment were standing shoulder-on as they addressed their problem. As he closed in, Tru discerned a relay box full of conduits and breakers. He would be approaching the men from their four o'clock—just outside their peripheral view.

And if they did see him coming? The creature from the rank lagoon?

That was their bad luck.

He paused at the top of the ladder, removed his latex gloves, and touched his fingers to the hinged metal panel he'd gone through ten minutes earlier. He paused, trying to remember if the hinges had squeaked when he'd opened it earlier. A reprimand from Bob Stansell, his primary instructor from The Farm, rushed into his head. *"It's the little mistakes that'll get you killed, dumbass."*

No, Tru decided, *they hadn't squeaked.*

He focused completely on the two men.

Based on the bottoms of their shoes, their orientation hadn't changed. They were still facing the circuit box. For a moment Tru considered holding where he was, waiting until the men left. But how long would that take? Effluent dripped from his shoes into the pond—each tiny impact sounded like a bomb going off. What if they couldn't make the repair and had to call in help? Could they even *get* an electrician this time of night? The drips kept coming.

Tru ended his mental haggling. His decision, he realized, had already been made.

Only one course of action would control the situation.

He gently lifted the access panel a few inches. No squeak, no reaction. Peering out for a better look, he planned his approach precisely. He had to cover ten feet across the open catwalk. To one side was the concrete containment wall that bordered the entire pond. To the other was a hip-high metal rail that kept workers from falling into the muck.

The nearest man, who was short and potato-shaped, wore a hardhat. This, Tru knew, was company policy—his CIA briefing file had included a plant operating manual translated into English. The taller man, who wore glasses and was rail thin, wasn't wearing one—a rulebreaker or a supervisor, possibly both. Against two unsuspecting, and likely untrained adversaries, Tru's expertise in close quarters combat would be decisive. He reminded himself to operate by the book: apply the minimum force necessary to achieve the desired result.

He lifted the panel and climbed silently onto the catwalk. Tru kept low, poised to accelerate if necessary. With his first step he angled behind the pair. Neither noticed him, and the burbling from the distant aerators covered a slight squish in his step. When he was an arm's length away, the hard part was done.

His movement became a blur. Tru set his left leg behind the farther man, reached for an arm lock, and levered him up and over the rail.

Before he'd hit the muck ten feet below, Tru was mirroring the move on the hardhat-wearer. The man managed to raise his free arm, and there was a half-hearted shout, but it did nothing to alter the outcome. He belly-flopped into the pond right next to his partner, who was flailing in the foamy wastewater.

Tru took off like a shot, thumping along the catwalk with all the grace of a stampeding buffalo. He was certain neither man had gotten a look at him, and even if they had he was unidentifiable beneath a black ski mask. They were probably still rubbing putrid water from their stinging eyes. All the same, he felt a strong urge to put this place far behind him. He had reached Pond Seven in a roundabout way, keeping in cover and pausing in shadows, avoiding the few known cameras—assuming the plant diagram he had been given was accurate. With stealth now blown, egress was all about speed and straight lines.

He flew down a staircase toward the lowest level, taking the steps four at a time, half running and half falling. It would have been cata-strophic had he not mastered the technique during training. *Concentrate absolutely on the lip of the step you want.*

The most direct route to escape was through a building he'd by-passed earlier. Its purpose hadn't been noted on the diagrams, but he figured it for a pump house. He pushed through a steel door and found the interior nearly black. Tru paused to let his eyes adjust, and soon dis-cerned the outline of a door on the opposite wall. He ran through the darkness but immediately crashed into a hip-high table of some kind. He sprawled over a console thick with what felt like levers and buttons, and one or two moved. All at once, the room came to life.

Floodlights snapped on and Tru saw two massive machines of some kind along the far wall. A buzzer sounded, and after a series of clunks, a broad conveyor belt began moving. In the machine's recesses he heard mechanical grinding sounds. Tru didn't know or care what the con-traption did—he was just happy to have enough light to see the distant door.

He darted across the dusty concrete floor and burst outside. He paused long enough to get his bearings, and then sprinted across a hun-dred yards of open space, keeping clear of the lone floodlight on the plant's southern boundary. He rolled under the perimeter fence at the cut he'd made earlier. He pushed the chain-link bottom more or less back into place, and then gathered a bit of vegetation around the base.

He set out on a dead run toward his stolen scooter, which was hidden in a stand of brush slightly over a mile away. With the threat having ebbed for the moment, Tru found himself assessing the night's mission. To the positive, he was glad he'd worn the balaclava—had the men gotten a look at him, with his light brown hair and Western features, he would have appeared disastrously out of place. One major complication avoided. As far as shortcomings, he decided a can of spray paint would have been useful for disabling the lens of a camera he'd discovered, above the catwalk, that hadn't been on the diagram. His biggest mistake had been to not bring some kind of makeshift waders, maybe high-mil plastic trash bags. His trail shoes had been ideal until the moment he'd stepped off the bottom rung of the ladder into . . .

Okay, lessons learned.

When he reached the scooter, Tru took one look over his shoulder. He could still make out the southern edge of the plant, and he noticed nothing unusual. No sirens, no searching flashlights, no shouted alarms. He thought there was a chance the two men might not even call the police. As caretakers of a water treatment plant, they were not hardwired to be security conscious. Nothing of value had gone missing, and there was no real damage done. The only circumstance of note was that two members of the night shift had been tossed into the sea of sludge they managed by—who? A madman? A drunk? Either answer promised little more than embarrassment. Given the resultant haranguing they would take from the day shift, Tru guessed a shower and a change of clothes would be the least humiliating option.

He hiked a leg over the scooter, but before cranking its whiny two-stroke engine to life he checked his comm device. It was a CIA-issued handset that had so far worked flawlessly. On outward appearances it looked like a ubiquitous iPhone, right down to junk contacts and spam email. Unlike a standard iPhone, it was satellite-capable, although in certain circumstances an umbilicaled antenna/repeater was necessary. It also held three applications that would never be available in the App Store.

Tru saw one urgent message. He read through it once. Then he read it again. It was a time-critical amendment to his orders and contained both good news and bad.

The bad was that his level of risk was about to ramp up considerably.

The good was twofold. As of this moment, he was no longer assigned to the shit-show. Better yet, he was getting the posting he'd wanted since joining the agency.

He was going to Russia.

Under a surge of swirling thoughts, he pocketed the phone, cranked the scooter to life, and pivoted toward the main road in a spray of dirt and gravel.

As Tru sped back toward Hegang, keeping just under the speed limit, he was blessedly oblivious to what was taking place behind him.

In the great building he had stumbled through, the machinery he'd inadvertently activated was still running unattended. The system, whose purpose he'd never bothered to contemplate, was in fact an industrial-grade pellet press. The wastewater plant had years earlier been selected as a test site for an experimental project to convert nitrogen-rich wastewater solids into agricultural fertilizer. The concept had fallen victim to various design flaws, and as a result had gone dormant.

As with most such failed initiatives, funding for shutdown and disassembly was hardly a priority, and the abandoned system had simply been left to rot. When Tru had accidentally triggered it to life, however, certain parts began working as advertised. Empty conveyor belts sprang to life, and the grinding mill set to churning, although there was no source material—chunks of dried effluent—present in the feed system. What *was* on the feed belt, however, was telling: the building had become a repository for junked machinery. Pipes, pump housings, sprinkler heads, and two dated computer monitors began riding the belt toward the grinder. The journey took a matter of minutes, and when the debris came in contact with the grinding wheels, the pulverizing began. For ten minutes the great steel wheels chewed harmlessly, grinding bits of metal, plastic, and glass. Then they encountered a five-meter length of steel cable that became ensnared in a housing flange. Soon after, sparks began blanketing a floor where tons of nitrogen-laden dust had accumulated.

The resultant explosion literally blew the roof off the building.

To the man who had initiated the chain of events, however, it was little more than a flicker in the mirror of his stolen scooter.

NINE

Never had four meters seemed so far.

Primakov tried to crawl toward the survival kit, crabbing through the snow, but the pain was excruciating. He grimaced and leaned back into a snowbank, breathless from his exertions. The last thing he needed in this situation was to pass out. He had no doubt his right leg was broken, a fracture midway between the knee and ankle. Pins-and-needles pain coursed through his lower leg. The only positive—there was no blood on the fabric of his flight suit, which implied the fracture wasn't open. He was shivering uncontrollably, shock setting in to compound the cold.

He looked longingly at the survival kit and tried to remember what it contained. Ever since first getting his wings, Primakov had undergone an annual survival training, various monotone sergeants prattling on about how the contents of the kit "might save your life one day." He, like most pilots, had paid minimal attention, his mind typically drifting to that day's test card or, years earlier, the night's combat mission. Only now did he admit that the sergeants had a point.

He was sure there was a flashlight in the kit, and that would be a godsend. So too, the thermal survival blanket. He vaguely remembered that it included matches, but making a fire was out of the question due to the attention it would draw. The same went for the signal flares, sea dye marker, and survival radio, not to mention the satellite beacon that utilized GLONASS, Russia's copycat iteration of GPS. All of that would be invaluable if Primakov wanted to be found. But as things stood? He supposed some of it might prove useful when the Americans came.

And surely they would come.

He stared helplessly across the divide, knowing his life depended on reaching the kit. The survival gear was packaged in a heavy plastic pouch, square and sized to fit beneath the cushion of the ejection seat. During an ejection, if everything went to plan, the seat frame would separate, leaving the pilot hanging in his parachute and the survival kit dangling by a tether.

The tether, he thought.

Primakov looked more closely and found it—a nylon strap coiled on the ground near the kit. *If I could reach that . . .*

Vektor had slid to a stop against the shoreline, and he looked around and saw one branch within reach. It turned out to be old and rotted, and when he picked it up a section broke off in his hand. The second time he took hold more gingerly and eased the branch toward him. It was brittle on one end but might hold up—if he was very, very careful. Even better, on the far end was the stub of a smaller branch that might work as a hook.

For five minutes Primakov reached out, playing the stick and teasing the lanyard closer. At the end, the stick was half its original length, but he was able to lean out and grasp the tail of the lanyard. By the time he dragged the kit next to him, he was completely out of breath. It was pathetic how far he had fallen. An hour ago, he had been soaring overhead in one of the world's most advanced combat jets. Now he was euphoric at the prospect of a few sips of water.

He broke the seal on the survival kit and dug in like a kid opening the greatest birthday present ever. With forced discipline, he began a careful inventory. Item by item, he laid out everything within reach. When he was done the tiny collection of food and gear looked desperately inadequate.

But combined with ingenuity, with every bit of self-control he possessed, it might be enough to save him.

Tru reached his hotel shortly after midnight.

The streets of Hegang were deserted, and he expected the lobby would be the same. The establishment would have rated a solid two stars in the States, which aligned perfectly with his cover. He was operating under the guise of a tour guide for a small group of Americans. An economy-minded bunch who had come for exotic adventure, they'd shown little interest in being pampered.

After turning the final corner, he paused beneath the red awning at the entrance. The hotel was an architectural train wreck, poured modernist concrete with the trimmings of a gothic cathedral. He had referred to the style as "communist boorish," which had gotten chuckles from the group, but put a scowl on the face of their minder from the Ministry of State Security. Tru had never, in his college days, imagined leveraging his knowledge about the history of architecture as a cover, but it dovetailed surprisingly well with clandestine operations. There wasn't a city on earth that didn't have historically significant buildings. Nor was there a shortage of people who wanted to learn about them.

Through the glass main entry, he surveyed the lobby and front desk. The hotel didn't have a bellman—it wasn't that kind of place—and he saw no late-arriving guests. The only person in sight, a night clerk perched sleepily on a stool behind the desk, was halfheartedly swiping through images on her phone.

Tru wouldn't typically want to be seen arriving at such a late hour, which was bound to draw attention, but with an eye toward his new assignment he decided to set aside his caution. His concerns became moot when, just before he opened the door, the clerk disappeared into a back room with a Styrofoam cup in her hand.

He crossed the lobby quickly, making a beeline for the emergency stairwell on the far side. Tru was generally good at moving quietly, but tonight it was hopeless. His shoes squished with every step; looking back he saw a trail of brown footprints across the length of the room, including the ornate rose-petaled central runner.

So much for stealth, he thought.

He disappeared into the stairwell and climbed to the third floor uneventfully. He paused for a moment at the fire door, heard nothing on the other side, and pushed through to the hallway. The light in the corridor was weak, the walls a sickly yellow hue. The distinct smell of mildew hung on the air. He reached his room quickly, the third door on the right, and was about to swipe his key card when a door creaked open behind him.

Tru closed his eyes.

Tried not to grimace.

"What are you doing skulking around at all hours?" asked Ruth Feldman. She was a seventy-six-year-old widow and retired middle school teacher. Tru forced a smile and turned. Ruth's bosomy outline nearly filled the doorway; she was encased in something between a nightdress and a muumuu.

"Hello, Mrs. Feldman. I might ask you the same thing. Are you not sleeping well again?"

Her lips turned to an upside down U.

Tru had been schooled extensively in operational tradecraft—dead drops, surveillance detection, picking locks. Getting rid of muumuu-clad busybodies in the middle of the night had not been in the curriculum.

Ruth was one of his ten charges, seven women and three men who had signed on for the "China Through the Ages" experience. Ten days, eight cites, four buses, and one very long flight from Los Angeles to Beijing. They were here to see the Great Wall, Ming tombs, and a seemingly endless parade of pagodas. The tour company was perfectly legitimate, a going concern for over thirty years. What was new was an owner whose husband had once served in the CIA's Clandestine Service, and who discreetly permitted the agency to insert the occasional NOC as a guide on selected excursions.

For Tru it was a manifestly tedious assignment, but he had a pretty good idea why he'd drawn it. He was on the bottom of the totem pole in SAC/SOG, a new guy learning the ropes. In addition to his low standing, he'd endured a bumpy ride through training. He had sailed through all the courses that truly mattered. When it came to trade-craft, martial arts, and weapons and tactics, Tru had excelled. He'd been far less enthusiastic, however, when it came to safety briefings and mission reporting. He had been written up repeatedly for a bad at-titude, and nearly washed out because of it. Then the chief of training, Bob Stansell, had gone out on a limb for him. Why he'd done so, Tru never understood; he had given the old cuss nothing but trouble. Yet Stansell had offered him one last chance: Tru would be released on his own recognizance, given a chain of lousy assignments until someone, somewhere was convinced that he was worthy of more. Tru accepted the deal grudgingly.

He hadn't been thrilled about this mission, but admittedly the tour guide gimmick was a perfect cover. By education, he actually *was* some-thing of an expert on architectural history, and with minimal prep work he had no trouble giving informative lectures on the tour's stops. His group co-leader—a legitimate guide—performed backup and handled the logistics. Until tonight, the operation had been running smoothly. Now he needed an excuse to extricate himself.

Ruth lifted her cane and pointed to the carpet. "You're dripping, Eric. What did you get into?"

This was the name they knew him by—Eric Nordgren. "I really couldn't say, ma'am."

The grooves in her forehead deepened. "I smell a bad smell."

Tru could only nod—he had been trying to ignore the stench for over an hour. "Yeah. I really should go get cleaned up."

Ruth checked the cheap watch on her wrist. "Breakfast is in six hours. We don't want to be late to the Sanbao Temple."

"I'm sure we'll make it just fine," Tru said. Ruth hadn't missed a meal or a bus yet.

Without another word, he opened the door and retreated into his room. He leaned his shoulders against the door, as if expecting Ruth to barge in, and heaved out a long breath. He tried to focus on the upside. His orders had changed, and his next mission, whatever it turned out to be, would surely be more important than guiding cranky American tourists through pagodas by day and wading through crap at night.

With no intention of making it to breakfast, Tru got back on track.

The first thing he did was check his room. He had left telltales on the bathroom door and two drawers, and the wedged threads were still in place. His suitcase was laying open on a stand, and he compared the contents to the picture on his phone he'd taken before leaving. Every wrinkle and crease looked exactly as it had. Someone had gone through his things on the first day of the tour, a search so clumsy it could only have been a message. The MSS was watching him, and they wanted to be sure he knew it.

He diverted to the desk and set aside notes he had drawn up for his next talk: "A Classicist History of the Pagodas of Northern China." It was the most pretentious title he'd been able to come up with. He poised a hotel pen over hotel stationary and composed a note to Janet Simms, the co-leader of the tour. On most days she handled travel details and dealt with their Chinese minders while Tru took the group on outings. Janet had not the slightest inkling that Eric Nordgren was a clandestine operative of the CIA. Nor was she aware that the tour's itinerary had been built by the CIA's China section to cover the cities from which it wanted wastewater samples. Pagodas could be found anywhere.

In the letter Tru explained, almost truthfully, that an emergency had come up and he needed to leave. He didn't mention family or illness, but the implication was clear. He also told her that he would coordinate his departure with the Chinese. This assurance would fall apart quickly, but the note would keep Janet out of trouble and hopefully confuse the situation for half a day. By then Tru would be long gone.

He kept it to a single page and signed off by saying that he had enjoyed working with her, which he had. He gave the note one neat fold and set it by his backpack. He would slide it under her door on the way out. He went into the bathroom, turned on the shower, and stripped off his putrid clothes. He stuffed the pants and socks into the trash can, then set the shoes and shirt on top. He would dispose of it all on the way out. Thankfully, he had plenty of clean clothes, including a second pair of trail shoes.

He glanced into the mirror as he waited for hot water. The grimy face that looked back belonged on a ditch-digger, but it was nothing a little soap wouldn't fix. Tru was twenty-eight years old, and in the best physical condition of his life. The instructors at The Farm had seen to that, and he'd kept up a brutal training regimen in the months since. His light brown hair was cut short and neat, and his face was clean-shaven. This was in line with his cover—the tour company insisted that its guides maintain a clean-cut look.

For six months, Tru had muddled through assignments that bordered on pointless. In each case he had tried to keep a good attitude, tried to hone his tradecraft and learn from his mistakes. The powers that be were testing him, making sure he was a team player, and for months Tru had played along. Now he sensed a shift. He wanted to believe it was based on merit, that they had confidence in his abilities. More likely, he reckoned, the reassignment was more a function of geography and a short clock. Time was of the essence, and he was the only cop in the neighborhood. Tru pushed away his conjecture. Whatever the reason, he was getting the shot he wanted. He was about to get into the real game.

He stepped into the shower and rinsed away the night's stench. It took the entire bar of hotel soap. Had he been of a more methodical mindset, he might have considered getting an hour or two of sleep. That wasn't going to happen. The mind-numbing mission that had brought him here was firmly in the rearview mirror, and what lay ahead was the chance for payback he'd been seeking for years. By the time Tru stepped out of the shower, he was the opposite of weary.

He was amped up and ready to go.

TEN

The flashlight was a godsend, yet Primakov knew it was important to conserve the batteries. He performed a quick inventory of the kit and saw all the things he remembered. There were also a few tins of food, water purification tablets, two containers of water, a folding knife, a lensatic compass, a signal mirror, and a machete. His hopes rose on seeing a first aid kit, but aside from a few bandages, the only thing of use were two morphine syrettes. The most worthless discovery was sixteen rounds of ammunition. On a combat mission he would have carried a pistol in the holster of his vest, but flying armed on experimental test flights had always seemed pointless.

Until now, he thought miserably.

He turned off the flashlight and was encompassed by a profound blackness, only a few stars visible through breaks in the clouds above. He shifted to take the pressure off his injured leg.

Having completed his inventory, he realized that his most important survival aid was in the leg pocket of his flight suit—unfortunately, on the right side. Minimizing his movements to keep the pain at bay, he reached down and was able to gently unzip the pocket and pull the comm device clear. In the darkness he removed a glove to manipulate the screen, but when he touched it, his spirits sank. He turned on the flashlight and his fears were confirmed. The phone's screen was shattered, the case severely cracked. A complete lost cause.

Primakov turned off the flashlight again, put the glove back on, and closed his eyes. His frustration crested, and he pounded a fist on the ground.

What else could go wrong?

The comm unit was his sole means of coordinating an extraction. Without it, would the Americans even come? He eyed the survival radio skeptically. If he turned it on, the emergency beacon would automatically activate, and the Russian Air Force would home in quickly. Unfortunately, that wouldn't bring salvation—it was more like ringing the Grim Reaper's doorbell. Freezing to death in the mountains seemed preferable.

Scenarios began pinging through his mind.

How long could he survive alone in the wilderness? If it weren't for his injury, he was sure he could manage for weeks. He might even walk out and make his way to the West. But as it stood? His survival now depended completely on the Americans. He had to hope the value of his knowledge outweighed the risks of a rescue. And if they did commit to retrieving him, how long would it take? Days? Weeks? Could he last that long without freezing to death?

Primakov pushed it all away. He had to maintain focus. *Just like a test flight,* he thought. *Small steps in sequence.*

Having been schooled in basic first aid, he knew what his first step had to be: he needed to immobilize his lower leg, and that meant making a splint. It was actually an exercise he'd practiced in training. If he could find two relatively straight sticks, bind them together, it would keep his leg stable.

The lanyard strap from the survival kit would work perfectly as a binding, and he could cut it with the survival knife. The problem was finding the right sticks. The one he had already used was too rotted. He used the flashlight again to scan the immediate area, and for the first time he was struck by the depth of the snow. It was nearly up to Vektor's starboard wing, more than three meters high. He scanned the light beam into the distance and saw far thinner layers on the ice-clad lake and upper shoreline. The dry climate in these parts rarely produced large accumulations of snow, and he suspected the high bank here was an aberration caused by the natural windbreak. It had actually served him well—the snowbank had caught the jet, kept it from careening into the woods.

Fireball averted.

From where he sat now, unfortunately, the big drift was an impediment. His flashlight beam settled on a branch poking out from the wall of white—the wood looked fresh, and a few dead leaves were still attached. The branch was roughly half as thick as his wrist, which seemed ideal. The problem: it was ten feet away. The branch he had used earlier would be useless for extracting it from packed snow.

Then Primakov got an idea.

He tied the lanyard to make a loop at the end, then converted it to a slipknot. A makeshift lasso. Taking careful aim, he tossed it toward the branch, trying to capture the exposed end. He missed badly and cursed.

Reeling in the lanyard for a second try, he felt suddenly lightheaded. Shock, cold, dehydration. Every problem he solved seemed to lead to two more.

He sat still and breathed evenly. He knew that if he didn't keep his wits, the cold would kill him long before the FSB got its chance.

His head began to clear. Primakov coiled the lanyard, spun the looped end, and with a silent prayer he tossed it out again . . .

Tru had the throttle wide open, but the little scooter maxed out at the metric equivalent of forty-five miles an hour. What it lacked in speed, it made up for with anonymity. The secondary road he had chosen was thick with motorbikes, their deafening buzzes violating the early morning stillness. The scooter also gave him an excuse to wear a helmet, which concealed his Western features.

He felt bad about stealing it. But only a little. He simply couldn't think of any better way to reach the Russian border. Buses, trains, rental cars. Any of those were sure to trip alarms in the world's greatest surveillance state. He had made an honest effort to compensate the owner—a plastic shopping bag, containing more than enough renminbi to cover a new scooter and a helmet, was knotted to the chain and lock he had picked. Admittedly, his motive for doing so wasn't completely pure—it bettered the chance that the guy wouldn't report the crime. As a precaution, Tru had swapped out license plates with a similar scooter before leaving Hegang. His CIA briefing had been clear on this point: the Chinese were unrelenting when it came to tracking vehicle license plates.

The bike's tiny engine whined and its front tire shimmied. The curving road ran through agrarian countryside, wintering farm fields interspersed with stands of forest. Despite the rising sun, the air felt colder, and the forty-five-mile-an-hour breeze only made things worse. Tru was glad he had packed a heavy jacket and gloves—Siberia, surely, wouldn't be any warmer.

After two hours, he stopped, dismounted, and checked his phone. There were no new messages from Langley, but he expected follow-on instructions soon. His initial orders were to make his way to a coordinate set three hundred miles north, across the Russian border. What he would be tasked to do when he arrived remained a mystery, but it had to be important. Important enough to risk sending an illegal paramilitary asset into a hostile country with little planning and a burned cover.

His immediate challenge was to cross the border clandestinely. The most simplistic solution, riding the scooter through an established border crossing point, was a no-go for a host of reasons. To begin, the papers he was carrying would raise flags with both Chinese and Russian authorities. The fact that he was operating a stolen vehicle, with a stolen license plate, didn't help matters. On top of all that, Tru had no good reason to be in this part of China, nor any justification for entering Russia. It left only one recourse: he would ditch the scooter in a remote area and simply hike to the Amur River—in this region, the dividing line between the two countries.

Thankfully, Tru had paid attention during training to the briefings on Russian border controls. He knew that Russia actively monitored only small segments of its 37,000-mile border—one and a half times the circumference of the earth. In most areas they didn't even try. This was one of the minor recompenses of authoritarian rule. Unlike the West, which expended considerable time and effort keeping illegal immigration in check, few of the world's downtrodden viewed Russia as a destination filled with hope. The Russians kept a tight watch on border crossing points, and surveilled critical segments with belligerent neighbors, but even there the priority was to keep people *in,* and to a lesser extent, track foreign visitors. The bottom line for Tru: vast swathes of frontier were protected by little more than the occasional warning sign.

Walking into Russia, however, did present problems. Once he crossed the river, he would still have over two hundred miles to traverse. That meant finding a new means of transportation, and time was critical. But he *would* find a way. His mission to China had been mind-numbing, yet this one felt real, operationally urgent. The border he was about to cross was more than geographic. He was moving from gray to black. From legends and lies to a high-wire without a net. It would be a chance to prove himself, to put his resourcefulness on display. And, with any luck, an opportunity to do what he'd joined the agency to do.

He was stiff from the long ride and began walking to loosen up. As he did, he studied the map on his phone. The app was different from anything Google had ever designed, tailored for operational use. Terrain contours, border control points, and military installations were all clearly displayed. Thankfully, this region was sparsely populated on both sides of the frontier. He saw mining roads and village trails that led to the river, and much the same on the Russian side of the dashed black line. After a long study of the terrain, he picked out the path of least resistance.

Tru then remounted the scooter, fired it to life, and set out into a new day as sleet began to fall.

Word of the crash of Natis One swept through the squadron building at Skovorna like a storm-driven wind, and by the next morning rumors, some reasonable, others absurd, began swirling about what might have gone wrong.

In such a small, insular unit, everyone had had recent dealings with Colonel Primakov, who was universally held in high regard, and it was only human nature that each person thought back to their most recent interactions with him. Along the same lines, one nagging worry began to settle in minds throughout the building: *Was I in some way responsible for this tragedy?*

It was felt by mechanics and the weather officer, by the squadron IT specialist and the corporal who drove the aircraft tug. Even the cook wondered whether his borscht might have turned the wrong stomach at the wrong time. Yet no one in the squadron had more to think about than Corporal Stefan Ivanov.

Ivanov ran the life support shop, a section that on most days was little more than an afterthought, but whose equipment could have proved decisive last night. The conceivable points of failure seemed endless. Ivanov wondered if the colonel's G-suit might have malfunctioned. Had he ejected before the crash? If so, why hadn't his emergency locator beacon activated? Had his parachute been packed correctly? Were the inspections on his seat and survival gear up to date? No one in the unit had more on his mind.

Such second-guessing was natural, but it would soon be formalized—sometime in the next few days, an accident investigation team would swoop into Skovorna. They would go over every bit of equipment, every record in Ivanov's little shop.

Had he gotten lazy, missed something?

To get ahead of these questions, and perhaps with a slight morbid curiosity, the corporal closed the door to his work room and diverted to the colonel's locker.

The locker was a basic item that would have looked right at home in any gym. The door wasn't secured in any way, and when he opened it, Ivanov found the space mostly empty—Primakov had been wearing the bulk of his gear. There was a spare G-suit, which Ivanov noted was current on its inspection, and on the upper shelf he found two pairs of flight gloves, still in their plastic wrappers, along with an unused kneeboard and grease pencil. A photograph of the colonel's wife and father-in-law, taped to the rear wall, gazed back at him forlornly. Ivanov frequented the locker in the course of his duties, and he had the impression that something was missing. Finally, it dawned on him—the second photograph was gone, the one of the colonel's son in uniform. Then the corporal's eye snagged on something he had never seen before—a simple white envelope on the top shelf.

He pulled it out and weighed opening it. Then he read the two names on front. Crossed through was *Colonel Maksim Primakov.* Scrawled above that: *General Viktor Strelkov.*

Ivanov froze. This envelope had not been on the shelf yesterday. The idea of Primakov's name being struck through and replaced by that of his father-in-law was unsettling in its own right—Viktor Strelkov was one of the most powerful men in Russia. But the fact that the envelope had appeared on the night of Vektor's disappearance? That was something Ivanov didn't care to contemplate.

He stepped back from the locker and closed the door. With the envelope in hand, he thought long and hard about how best to handle the situation.

Ivanov tapped the envelope twice on his opposing palm, then hurried toward the hallway and Colonel Nemanchik's office.

ELEVEN

Thump. Thump. Thump.

The blue racquetball hit within inches of the same spot on the wall. Every single time. The rebound carried five feet away to the chair behind the desk where the thrower caught it effortlessly. The rhythm was metronomic.

"You did this to me," Slaton said accusatively, pausing his pitches long enough to shoot a hard look at the vice president of the United States.

Anna Sorensen grinned. "Yeah, I guess I did."

They were together in Slaton's new office. She was seated in one of the chairs in front of the desk, while he was in the soft executive recliner behind it, leaning back with his heels propped indifferently on the polished mahogany edge. It had been the opposite configuration six months ago: Slaton playing visitor, and Sorensen seated behind the blotter he tried to ignore.

Back then, Slaton had been her go-to man in the field, an off-the-books operator with a knack for pulling America's ass out of the fire. And never had there been more heat than when an attempted assassination had left President Elayne Cleveland in a coma. Sorensen had tasked Slaton to find those responsible, a hunt that unnervingly circled back to the highest levels of the U.S. government. Only his intervention had kept the nation from self-immolation. As a debatable reward, the president had selected Sorensen to fill the vacant vice presidency. She, in turn, had arm-twisted Slaton into taking her place as director of the CIA's Special Activities Center.

"I'm not cut out for a desk," he said.

"Christine thinks otherwise." Sorensen was referring to Slaton's wife, whom she knew well.

"Are you telling me this was her idea?"

She laughed. "Your wife doesn't have a conspiratorial bone in her body. But I will confess, when I talked to her last week, she seemed happy with how it all worked out. Are they settled in yet?"

Christine and their children—four-year-old Davy and a newborn girl, Chloe—had just arrived in Virginia, their move from rural Idaho having been delayed by a number of complications, not the least of which was the arrival of their second child.

"They moved into the house three days ago, or so I'm told. I've barely seen them."

"You'll adjust, David. I did." Sorensen, too, had an operational background at the agency before she'd begun shooting through the leadership ranks.

"What if I don't want to adjust?"

"You know, during your time in the field I saw you endure some pretty harsh conditions. In all that time, I never heard you complain."

"When I was in the field, nobody listened to my complaints."

Thump, Thump.

Sorensen looked at the wall and saw hundreds, if not thousands, of small blue marks. "Does Bill Moore still have the office next door?" She was referring to the Deputy Director for Science and Technology, or DDS&T.

"Yep."

"Has he complained?"

"Nope. He calls it my therapy—says he takes it as proof of life."

"Right." She took in the rest of the office. The walls were bare, a few nails where she'd removed pictures and mementos. The only thing she'd left behind, perhaps with a touch of mischief, was a hideous pendulum clock mounted high over the door. It hovered like a swinging scimitar.

He saw her looking at it, went still, and asked, "What the heck is that?"

"It was handed down from the last director. I'm told it was requisitioned from one of Saddam Hussein's palaces."

"I thought trophies were frowned upon."

"Officially . . . but exceptions are made. So tell me, how goes the defection?"

"You didn't come here just to annoy me?"

"The president is watching closely. She still wants that briefing tonight."

"Tonight?"

"It's been on the schedule, David. Primakov was supposed to be in Japan by now."

He had been so preoccupied with the crisis, he'd forgotten about a meeting with the president of the United States. The meeting had been arranged as a victory lap for the agency, a chance to revel in the biggest intelligence coup since the Cold War. Viktor Belenko and his MiG-25 for a new millennium. Now it loomed like a wake. "Seems my management career isn't getting off to a flying start. Maybe she'll fire me."

"Are there any new developments?"

"We're pulling out all the stops, but so far, the only hard evidence is the message that came through this morning. Primakov crash-landed Vektor and wants us to get him out. After that, his comm went dead. We've been working all day to get a look at the target area. I've also got one of my people heading that way—he should be crossing into Russia from northern China as we speak."

"Wait . . . *what?*"

"He was our only asset anywhere near Siberia."

"A NOC?" she asked.

"He is now."

"David, you can't just send—"

A knock on the open office door interrupted. They both looked up and saw Ed Cole, the shift watch officer from the TOC.

"Sir," Cole said, "those overheads of the crash site finally came in. There's something you should see."

Slaton waved him in, and Cole took over the local network computer on the L-extension of the desk. The watch officer didn't seem bothered that the vice president was in the room—hardly a surprise, since he had worked with Sorensen for years. Soon they were all looking at a series of photos with exceptional resolution.

"These are a multi-spectral product," Cole explained as he fine-tuned the presentation. "Electro-optical cross-hatched with radar. We've run the raw data through our best enhancement algorithms."

From a half dozen images, he brought the clearest to full screen. Slaton easily picked out the sleek shape of Vektor half-embedded in what looked like a snowbank.

"So there it is," he said. "He really did manage to land it."

Cole zoomed in further, the pixels muddying. At maximum enlargement the figure of a man could be seen sitting near the airplane, his legs outstretched on the ice.

"Hello, Maksim Primakov," Sorensen said.

"Yes, that's our pilot. But there's something else of note." Cole used the cursor to highlight Primakov's outstretched legs.

"What's that on his right leg?" Slaton asked.

"Our two best technicians have gone over it closely and done some image comparison. Everyone agrees—Primakov's right leg is lashed between a pair of branches."

"Tree branches?" Sorensen repeated. "Why would he . . ."

Slaton closed his eyes. "This just keeps getting better and better." A headache pressed in as he tried to work through the implications of this new twist. "All right. If he *is* incapacitated, then it's more important than ever that we get our operator on the scene. Are there any updates on his progress?"

"Miller is making his way to the reservoir. The last time he checked in he was nearing the Russian border."

"Maybe we should send him a message to suggest that speed is of the essence. Something like, 'Situation critical, get your ass in gear.'"

Cole looked at him questioningly.

Slaton cocked his head to one side. "Okay, be more diplomatic. But he needs to expedite."

"Understood."

As soon as Cole was gone, Sorensen checked her watch, and said, "I'll see you at the White House—two hours."

"Any pro tips?"

"Wear a tie."

"I don't own one." This was true. Slaton could tie a wide variety of knots that held tactical applications, but he had sternly refused to learn the double Windsor.

"Find out what you can, give it to them straight. And you need to have a plan for what comes next."

As soon as Sorensen was gone, Slaton put in a secure call to Westbrook, who had gone to the Pentagon to coordinate with JSOC commanders. "How's that extraction plan coming?"

"We're making progress," said Westbrook.

"Have you seen the latest footage?"

"We have. Vektor is right where we expected, and our pilot is injured—possibly a broken leg."

"That's a wrinkle we weren't expecting."

"True, but it reinforces one of the options we've been considering. I can brief you on it tonight."

"Give me the twenty-second pitch."

"I'd like to hold off until I know if the platform we need is available."

Slaton said, "Okay. But just so you know, I won't be the only one you'll be briefing tonight."

"Who else?" Westbrook asked.

"Be at the White House, seven o'clock. And don't be late."

Westbrook put the receiver in its cradle. He had been given a small office in which to work, an empty conference room in the D Ring with a table built for six. At the moment it felt claustrophobic, like the walls were closing in.

Slaton had told him at the outset that the president herself had greenlighted Primakov's defection. Or more accurately, America's response to it. By all accounts, the Russian colonel hadn't asked for permission—he had simply made his decision and given fair warning.

As test pilots are prone to do . . .

He scribbled notes for his briefing, then made a final call to Vandenberg Space Force Base. With a plan taking shape, divided into two parts, he ran a timeline to be sure everything fit. By the time he left for the parking garage, Westbrook was feeling whipsawed.

Alone in the elevator, he took a moment to reflect. He was two months into his first Pentagon tour, the kind of "career enhancement" staff job he had put off as long as possible to stay in the cockpit. Until a few days ago, the posting had met every miserable expectation: he'd been mired in a soul-crushing bog of interservice meetings and PowerPoint presentations. Westbrook had been assigned—or as he put it to his wife, sentenced—to the Office of the Assistant Secretary of the Air Force for Acquisition, Technology and Logistics. According to the performance reports of his predecessor, it was a position that oversaw "Air Force research, development, acquisition, and program sustainment activities, with an annual budget in excess of $60 billion for more than 550 programs." Impressive as all that sounded, it was veritable purgatory compared to his previous job: commandant of the United States Air Force Test Pilot School.

Then, forty-eight hours ago, he had been thrown a lifeline, a short-term loan to the CIA's Special Activities Center. He had been intrigued from the moment Slaton briefed him in, recognizing the value of acquiring Vektor, not to mention talking to the only man who had flown her. Now Primakov's aborted defection had morphed into something more perilous—a speculative Special Ops mission that was fraught with risk. He sensed crosscurrents at play, interagency squabbles, all of them far above his pay grade. Westbrook himself viewed the idea of rescuing Primakov from a far more elemental standpoint. One very brave Russian aviator had put his life on the line to help America.

And if a rescue mission was launched? Then some very brave Americans would get a chance to return the favor.

TWELVE

Dusk in Washington was dawn in China. Tru ditched the scooter on a rural road a mile from the border and simply started walking. According to his navigation app, the nearest official crossing point was thirty miles southeast. The forest was thick, but he had no trouble defining when he reached the border—the Amur River spread out before him, and at this juncture it was a quarter mile wide. In any other season Tru would have been forced to steal a boat to get across, but in January, at the height of a deep and brutal winter, that wasn't necessary. The river was encased in ice from bank to bank.

He saw no sign of civilization in either direction, and his map confirmed he was in deep wilderness. The ice-clad river looked almost inviting, and it struck him how irrelevant borders were to nature. Every inch of territory on earth—the forests, seas, and skies—were professed to be controlled by people and regimes. Ultimately, however, such claims were patently transient, as proved so ably by history. Then again, Tru had no interest in trying to explain that concept to a team of Russian border guards.

He stepped cautiously onto the frozen no-man's land, testing the footing. The ice seemed solid. He slowly picked up speed, and by the time he reached the midpoint Tru felt exposed. The evergreen cover of the far bank beckoned. He threw caution to the wind and entered Russia on a dead run.

He paused inside the tree line and drew in the frigid air, his breath going to vapor. The forest here was no different from any other, still and quiet in the morning. Even so, he couldn't deny a surge of adrenaline. China, in the present geopolitical standing, was as much an adversary of America as Russia had ever been. But Tru viewed things differently. He would take up America's fight here because he was duty-bound to do so. That was what he'd signed up for. But his secondary motivation was deeply personal.

Four years ago, his life had changed. He had given up a promising academic career. Forsaken club rugby to concentrate on martial arts. He had abandoned a dissertation on neoclassical churches in order to fire thousands of rounds on the range. It was the Russians who had done unspeakable things to the person he cared about most in the world. And now, finally, it was time to extract some payback.

He checked the map on his comm device and set out at a steady pace. Not a breath of wind invaded to interrupt the silence. Bypassing an open glade, he saw a herd of elk in the distance, a huddle of brown figures foraging for winter grass. Farther on, he encountered lines of deep paw prints that he reckoned had been made by wolves. He saw not a single person.

The sun cut a helpless figure above the eastern horizon, its orb dulled by heavy mist. Tru moved quickly, and soon was perspiring beneath his layered clothing. He felt strong and alert, primed for whatever came. After so much training, so much forced patience, he was on the mission he'd been after. He didn't know where it would take him or how long it would last. He had no idea what to expect when he reached his objective.

But one certainty he felt to his marrow.

He was as ready as he could be.

"So this is what it is like to freeze to death," Primakov whispered to the wind.

Like all Russians, he knew cold. As a boy he had fallen into a shallow pond in the dead of winter. On a camping trip with Oksana—back when they were newly married and carefree—he had suffered a minor case of frostbite.

But this, he thought miserably. *This is on another level.*

His feet and hands were numb, and he was shivering uncontrollably. He was thirsty but the water from his survival kit had frozen solid. He felt fortunate to have made it through the night. To the positive, he'd succeeded in devising a splint for his leg. The sun was up but it had not yet broken through the clouds to provide warmth. His mind began drifting, and when he closed his eyes, his thoughts strayed to a faraway place.

The winter looked the same, yet the backdrop was different. Not pristine forest and clear skies, but muddy trenches and the tang of smoke.

Not isolation and silence, but men shouting orders amid whistling incoming rounds.

And there was no protection from any of it.

God, I'm cold. But it is nothing to what you endured, Nik. I am sorry, my son. So, so sorry . . .

THIRTEEN

"I've never been here," Westbrook said as he and Slaton walked briskly down the West Wing corridor.

"I'll arrange a tour later. Let me do most of the talking—the thing I need you to cover is the extraction plan." His head canted right to gauge the colonel. "You do *have* an extraction plan?"

Westbrook hadn't had an opportunity to explain his proposal. "It's a two-part effort. I'm coordinating the Space Force end, and General Carter is working the DOD side. The president will have to sign off, of course."

Slaton wished they'd had time to go over it, but the entrance of the White House Situation Room loomed. "Okay, let's hope she likes whatever it is."

The Situation Room, known internally as "the whizzer," had recently undergone renovations. The outer hall was sided in gleaming marble, more a forewarning than a welcome. The interior was relatively small, constrained by low ceilings, and the room's modest size made the main conference table stand out like a teak runway. The president's seat was at the far end, and a half dozen executive chairs lined either side. Monitors dominated the side walls and an array of communications gear lay in wait, a sea of green lights ready to link to any component of America's global military and intelligence arsenal.

The group of decision-makers gathered was larger than Slaton had expected. When the president greenlighted the mission two days ago, only Anna Sorensen and the director of national intelligence had been read in on Primakov's defection—a reflection of the importance placed on secrecy. Both were here today, along with the president, yet there were six new faces, some of which Slaton didn't recognize. The national security advisor and secretary of defense were in place, and there was no mistaking the dreadnaught-like figure of Army General Holston Carter, chairman of the joint chiefs. The other three wore civilian clothes, but no doubt held high-level positions in the administration.

It wasn't the sort of company Slaton was accustomed to keeping, and he couldn't decide if it was an upgrade over the usual cast of killers, spies, and reprobates. The collective expression around the table was expectant, which told him word hadn't yet leaked across the Potomac about the loss of Vektor. Then he realized why: because the person overseeing Primakov's defection had not forwarded the bad news.

And that person was him.

The collective leadership of the nation was expecting a happy post-mission report: pictures of an experimental Sino-Russian jet secreted away in a hangar at Chitose Air Base, a smiling Maksim Primakov giving his best *Top Gun* thumbs-up. He wondered, with perhaps a trace of hope, whether the transgression might get him fired.

He and Westbrook sank into the last two available seats, side by side at midtable with their backs to the wall. At the head of the room, President Elayne Cleveland cut an imposing figure, yet Slaton suspected it was something of an act. She had spent months recovering from severe injuries after the assassination attempt. Her progress had amazed her doctors, and the fact that she was back on the job at all was a testament to her tenacity. Unfortunately, equally tenacious were the troubles at the southern border, inflation, and a lagging economy. Slaton didn't have a political bone in his body, but he knew President Cleveland badly needed a win. Something to rattle the increasingly grim news cycle on a seismic scale.

As soon as the doors were closed, the president called the meeting to order. She got straight to the point. "Well? Did we get this jet we were after?"

Slaton stood. "No, Madame President, we did not. Roughly twelve hours ago, Colonel Primakov took off in Vektor from his base in central Russia. Unfortunately, something went wrong. We believe he had every intention of defecting, but the aircraft suffered a technical problem. We're still trying to work out exactly what happened, but we've confirmed that the jet went down in a remote area."

"*Went down?*" the president repeated, her voice filling the room. "Are you saying it crashed?"

"Not exactly."

"Then what?"

Slaton's gaze swept the table and saw all eyes on him. Unlike his last job, there was no place to hide, no executive ghillie suit that would protect him. "Some of you weren't briefed on this op from the beginning, so I should fill everyone in."

The president circled her hand rapidly, agreeing but impatient. Slaton had had personal dealings with Elayne Cleveland, and he knew that she supported him. He also knew she called people out when they screwed up.

"Colonel Maksim Primakov made contact with the CIA eight weeks ago. He was a walk-in, not on the agency's radar as a target for recruitment, but we were quickly able to verify his identity. He's a senior test pilot in the Russian Air Force, and for the last year has been involved in the development of a stealth fighter codenamed Vektor." Slaton went over China's involvement in the project and explained how Primakov had established contact with the agency through a diplomat in Moscow. "We were able to supply him with a communications device, and he made two dead drops during visits to Moscow—he travels there regularly to keep the defense ministry apprised of the program's progress. The data sticks he gave us contained technical information on Vektor. It was only a small amount, but our analysts deemed it highly valuable."

DNI Karl Fuller, a career spook who had been involved from the beginning, injected, "We suspect Primakov provided the data sticks to establish his bona fides, but that his goal all along, which he announced only a few days ago, was to defect with the aircraft."

Slaton picked up, "We promised to support his defection, and coordinated with allies in the region to help. He said he wanted to land at an air base in Japan, and when we consulted the Japanese, without divulging specifics, they granted us use of Chitose Air Base on Hokkaido."

"So," the president said, clearly ready to move on, "what exactly went wrong?"

Slaton moved to the far wall where a map was projected on a monitor. The eastern half of Russia was displayed, Japan to the right. "Primakov took off yesterday evening from a remote base in Russia's Far Eastern District. The test flights in the program always operate at night—the Russians and Chinese have been going to great lengths to keep this jet under wraps. Honestly, before Primakov reached out to us, we knew almost nothing about it beyond a few loose rumors. We have evidence that Vektor departed on schedule—our satellites snagged a few bits of comm from the working area." He highlighted a red-lined box denoting the restricted test airspace.

"Everything was proceeding normally until Primakov declared an emergency on the radio. He never gave us specifics about his defection plan, but we believe this 'mayday' call was a ruse. We think he turned toward Japan at that point with the intention of defecting. The pilot of another fighter, which was in the area to support the mission, tried to contact Primakov on the radio, as did the range controllers monitoring the mission. There were no replies. Soon after, the Russians launched an intensive search and rescue operation."

"Wouldn't the Russians have been tracking Vektor on radar?"

"That was the beauty of Primakov's plan. Vektor is a stealth platform, and since this particular mission was meant to evaluate its stealth characteristics, the jet's electronic beacon was turned off. Since it was also nighttime, Vektor would have been virtually invisible. We suspect that's why Primakov chose this particular flight to make his move."

"But you said the jet actually *did* go down," the president prompted.

"We did our best to track what was going on. After Primakov's 'mayday' call, we operated on the assumption that he was heading east toward Japan. Less than an hour later, we received a message from his secure comm device. He said the aircraft had suffered a fuel leak and he'd been forced to land on the northern end of Zeya Reservoir—this time of year, the lake is frozen solid. Embedded in the message was position information, so we know exactly where he is." Slaton directed everyone's attention to a red X on the map along a northern finger of the reservoir. "He's asking for an extraction."

"*Extraction?*" the president repeated. "You're saying he crash-landed this jet, and now he wants us to come into Russia and retrieve him?"

"It would appear so."

"That must be hundreds of miles from the border with Japan," commented Fuller.

"Actually, closer to a thousand."

National security adviser James Holden said, "The risks involved in an extraction mission that deep are off the scale."

"They are significant," Slaton said, not trying to downplay the gamble they would be taking. "General Carter and Colonel Westbrook have been researching options all afternoon." He introduced Westbrook, deciding it was time to let him take over. Slaton was as curious as everyone to hear what he had to say.

Westbrook, who was wearing dress blues, began a briefing he'd had no time to rehearse. "Technical problems aren't uncommon in experimental test programs, and fuel leaks *can* be catastrophic. Whatever malfunction Vektor suffered, it was obviously serious. The good news is that Colonel Primakov survived the crash, and he still wants to defect. The northern tip of Zeya Reservoir is remote, and essentially uninhabited this time of year.

"It's true that going in after him would be a major undertaking. Conversely, *not* rescuing Primakov also entails risk. The Russians are going to find him at some point. They'll learn he was trying to defect, and also that he had been in touch with us. They could go public with the failed defection to embarrass us, and also to discourage that kind of thing in the future. We also shouldn't lose sight of the intelligence value that remains. We know very little about Vektor, and while we can't get the jet itself, no one has more detailed knowledge of the airplane than Primakov. He also promised to bring out a trove of technical data, which we assume is still in his possession. If we can get our hands on that, it would compromise years of research and development work by both China and Russia. Beyond all that, there is also a certain moral obligation. Primakov put his life on the line to further American interests.

"General Carter and I have been trying to determine if there is a realistic chance of getting Primakov out." He nodded toward the JCS chairman, who took over.

"A mission like this faces a unique set of obstacles. My initial thought was to put together a substantial force—dozens of aircraft, at least. But that fails on a number of counts. To begin, the logistics would take weeks to put in place. In that amount of time, the Russians are going to find Primakov.

"There are two other factors in play. First, Primakov's communications have gone down. Either the battery on his device is dead or the handset is damaged. Whatever the reason, our only means of communicating with him is lost and likely unrecoverable. There is also a more practical problem. Based on our analysis of the most recent surveillance footage, we believe Primakov may have suffered a broken leg in the crash."

Carter paused to let that sink in as spines straightened around the room.

The president leaned forward and set her arms on the big table. "I trust you have *some* good news?" she prompted.

"I have options, ma'am," Carter replied. "To go this deep into Russian territory without drawing notice will require a highly nuanced operation. If we put American lives on the line, we have to do so with our eyes open. If the Russians detect a rescue mission and respond militarily—which, legally speaking, they would have every right to do—it could turn into a political catastrophe.

"My first task was to determine how much time we realistically have. It's dead winter in Siberia, and the conditions are extreme. If Primakov does have a broken leg, it will severely limit his ability to utilize his survival training. I've asked the opinion of our medical staff, and, given his injury and the current temperature, they project he can survive for between twenty-four and forty-eight hours. That clock began running yesterday."

DNI Fuller said, "If that's accurate, then we shouldn't even be talking about a rescue mission. The only humane alternative, as I see it, is to tell the Russians where Primakov is and let them pick him up."

"If we do that," Carter said, "we're not only verifying his attempted defection, but also confessing our involvement in it. It's essentially a death sentence for Primakov and leaves us with a diplomatic disaster."

"I trust you have something better?" the president said.

Slaton intervened. "We need to buy time, and that's where my section comes in. It turns out we have one operator in the general area. He was on an assignment in northeast China, just across the border. Recognizing that we had to act quickly, I pulled him off his operation and ordered him to proceed to the crash site."

The room went silent, until the president said, "You have already sent someone in? Without my authorization?"

"I did. He's a paramilitary operator, trained to work in the black. As it turns out, he also speaks fluent Russian."

The gathering of Beltway warriors fell silent. The new director of the special activities center had put himself on thin ice.

DNI Fuller asked, "How long will it take for your man to reach the crash site?"

"We told him time is critical, but there's a lot of ground to cover. He has to cross undetected into Russia, but from there the crash site is still hundreds of miles away. It's also very remote, which will limit his options for travel. I'd say it will take him at least twenty-four hours to reach the site. Thirty-six is more realistic. If he can find Primakov in time, our man is trained in first aid and his survival skills are top-notch. Since he's carrying communications gear, he'll be able to give us a better understanding of the situation."

"Who is this guy?" the DNI asked skeptically.

"Truman Miller. He's a highly trained deep cover asset, a recent graduate of The Farm."

"*Recent* graduate?" remarked the president. "Are you telling me this guy is a rookie?"

Slaton tried not to wince—some tortured soul in SAC with a twisted sense of humor had actually cursed Miller with that very codename: Rookie. "Essentially, yes. But he proved himself unusually resourceful in training. I think there's an excellent chance he'll reach Primakov."

"I don't care how resourceful he is," said the president. "One guy hiking into Russia can give us better information, and he might keep Primakov alive, but it also magnifies the greater dilemma—it will give us *two* people to extract. How can we do that without starting a shooting war?"

"That," Slaton said, "is something Colonel Westbrook has been working on."

All eyes in the room went to Westbrook, who'd been reading a message on his phone.

Slaton still had no idea what the colonel was working on. He yielded the floor thinking, *This had better be good.*

FOURTEEN

"Primakov is nearly three hundred miles from the current search box for Vektor," Westbrook began, "but that net will inevitably widen. The airplane came to rest half-embedded in a snowbank, but once the Russians start looking in the right area its infrared signature won't be hard to find. I'd guess we have four days, possibly five, before the crash site is located. That's clearly not enough time to put a large-scale mission in place. I've been working with General Carter to come up with an alternative, and we agree that a very small two-phase mission would have the best odds of success. The chances of it being detected are minimal, but not zero."

He paused, until the president said, "Go on."

"Until recently, I was a commander at the Air Force Flight Test Center at Edwards. As such, I have a good grasp of our latest classified programs. The first stage of this operation would involve sending a bare minimum of personnel and equipment to the crash site. If we can do that quickly, we think we can conceal Vektor's position and extend our window for an extraction. It would also give us a chance to go over the aircraft and possibly recover a few vital parts."

"What kind of insertion are you proposing, Colonel?" the DNI asked.

"Traditional airborne systems take time to move into theater, but at Edwards my squadron worked with both air and space systems that are not yet fully operational. One of these, codename Star Chaser, is perfectly suited to this situation."

"Star Chaser?" remarked Vice President Sorensen. "I thought that was years away."

"Operationally, yes. But we've been testing prototypes for over a year."

"Could you please enlighten the rest of us?" the president prompted.

"The design criteria are straightforward. We have long needed a vehicle that can deliver a small cache of men and material very quickly over great distances. The answer was a relatively low-cost, one-time-use platform—essentially, a fire-and-forget spaceplane. It's already flown successfully, so the concept is proven. As things stand, the greater program is in a holding pattern while future funding is decided, but one unused test platform is available."

"This Star Chaser could reach the crash site more quickly than a conventional aircraft?" inquired the president.

Westbrook suppressed a smile. "The mission we're proposing is exactly what it was designed for. With a load of two to four people, and a limited amount of equipment, Star Chaser can reach any point on the globe in less than three hours."

The room went to a stunned silence. The president settled back in her chair, her hands steepled under her chin. Eventually, she said what everyone was thinking. "Tell us more, Colonel."

Twenty minutes later, Slaton and Westbrook walked out of the meeting with separate but parallel marching orders. Slaton would concentrate on getting Tru Miller to the crash scene as quickly as possible, and then coordinate with General Carter for a final extraction plan. Westbrook would coordinate the Star Chaser mission.

"Do you think it'll work?" Slaton asked. "Star Chaser?" He had never before considered using a spacecraft for a boots-on-the-ground op.

"In flight test it performed well. But we've never attempted this kind of range before."

"How many people would you send in?"

"I'm planning on two. A pilot, and one specialist to exploit Vektor. Since we're talking about removing electronics, maybe cutting out a few skin sections to bring back, I think an Air Force mechanic would be ideal."

"Makes sense, I guess."

"There is one thing you could help me with."

"What's that?"

"I need a jet."

Slaton looked at him curiously. "Given that you're a pilot, I'm not sure how to take that."

"I need a ride. If we're going to launch Star Chaser, I have to get out to Vandenburg ASAP."

"Can't you manage it from here? You've got the president's authority behind you."

"We need to do everything we can to keep this mission secret, and for that I need to be on site. The rocket has to be configured for the right stage length, and an orbital profile needs to be calculated and loaded. I'll also need to brief the pilot."

"Sounds like you have someone in mind."

"I do," Westbrook said, not mentioning that there was only one option.

It struck Slaton that he had made similar requests regularly during his operational days. Which meant there was only one possible answer. "I'll have an agency jet standing by at Andrews within the hour."

FIFTEEN

Tru walked six miles before encountering a man-made feature—the cleared easement for some kind of underground pipeline. He followed it for a hundred yards before seeing a junction riser. A sign warned people to stay away because the pipeline carried oil. He looked around carefully but saw no sign of surveillance cameras. If there were going to be any at all, he surmised, they would be in places like this, the nodes where the pipeline was exposed. For the first time in his life Tru wished he was carrying explosives. One well-placed charge could interrupt the flow of oil to China for months, and probably cost the Russian regime billions. It would also create an international incident and, he was sure, exasperate his CIA handlers.

In the end, it was little more than fantasy. He wasn't carrying explosives, and his training for using them was rudimentary. Even if it were possible, it wouldn't be his best play. Tru had no idea why he was being sent into Russia, but it had to be important. Something that would give the regime a bigger kick in the balls than a blown oil pipeline.

He set out north along the easement, which would be faster than trudging through forest. In all likelihood, the pipeline would lead him to a town where he could find a means of transportation. The sooner he got a ride north, the sooner he would reach his objective. And then he could find out what the hell was going on.

Six miles later Tru saw the first signs of civilization. A check of his navigation device showed a small village less than a mile away. He veered east and found a parallel road, which seemed a more natural approach than tracking a pipeline. The place he came upon was small, no more than a hundred houses and sheds nestled in the lee of a minor hill. If it had a name, he never saw it—there was no sign on the main road announcing, "Welcome to Wherever," nor any notation on his CIA-issued electronic map. The only thing he knew for sure was that he was somewhere in the Jewish Autonomous Oblast.

A remnant of another era, the JAO was one of two self-governing Jewish regions on earth, the other being Israel. Here, in the underbelly of Siberia, the concept had largely failed. The severe climate was one reason, Stalin another, but the end result was irrefutable. A century after its inception, virtually all of the Jews were gone—they now comprised less than two percent of the local population.

For Tru, however, the JAO had one endearing feature, and it had nothing to do with religion: the oblast was neatly bisected by the Trans-Siberian Railway. A railway that could take him very near his destination: Zeya Reservoir. Referencing his map again, he saw that the main road through the village continued to Birobidzhan, the nearest town with a stop on the railway.

Thirty minutes later he was swaying in the back of a delivery truck, concealed amid crates of potatoes. The mossy-haired old man driving, who was oblivious to his presence, seemed in no hurry as he navigated from pothole to pothole.

Tru tracked their progress, and by eleven that morning they were nearing Birobidzhan. Prior to reaching the outskirts of town, he jumped from the back of the truck and rolled onto the siding. He kept low until the truck was out of sight, then quickly covered the final mile on foot.

Birobidzhan was more of a hamlet than anything urban, one square mile of Bolshevik construction and managed decay. He had no trouble finding what he was after, although it looked more like a salvage yard than a rail station. A half dozen derelict cars lay shunted onto sidings, and the main platform and station were a shipwreck of warped siding and rusted metal. The next westbound train, according to an ancient chalk schedule board, was set to arrive in twenty minutes.

Tru ducked into a shadowed alley across the street and used the time to weigh his next steps. He was carrying a considerable amount of cash, but all of it was in either renminbi or U.S. dollars, either of which would attract unwanted attention if he tried to buy a ticket. To buy one electronically from a vending machine was also a nonstarter; using his only credit card or downloading a payment app would leave digital breadcrumbs that could be tracked. It left only one option: to board the train illegally. He tried to keep a positive outlook. The prospect of becoming a train hobo was hardly James Bond material, but it was a big step up from wading through effluent.

The train arrived five minutes late in a clatter of noise, its diesel smudge staining the cloudless sky. Tru began to move. His primary focus, as it would be until he was out of Russia, was to avoid unnecessary contact with locals. It wasn't that he had doubts about his language skills, but was more a sad treatise on the Russian psyche. The core rot of the nation was sourced in the halls of the Kremlin, yet the roots of corruption spread wide. Suspicion in Russia was pervasive, even here in the distant eastern oblasts, generations of people who had grown up informing on their neighbors and mistrusting outsiders. It was an unforgiving way of life, but the only one most Russians knew.

He easily identified the station's main security feature—a lone sixtyish man in uniform with a billy club belted to his hip. He was burly and bored, and strolled the platform like a cop on a beat. *Easy to see, easy to avoid.*

There were a handful of passenger cars at the front of the train, but the rest were freight and tanker cars. He made his approach from the non-station side, slipping behind a pair of derelict boxcars, rusted and graffiti-laden, that had been shunted to a secondary track. He studied the westbound train carefully. Ruling out the passenger and tanker cars, he concentrated on twenty or so boxcars. They each looked essentially the same until he noticed one with a side loading door that was cracked open slightly. It seemed the best option.

Tru was about to step into the ten-meter clear area between the tracks when it occurred to him to check for surveillance. He spotted two cameras, one mounted on a light pole to his right, the second on the distant station building. This gave pause. Would anyone be monitoring the feeds in real time? It seemed unlikely. Still, he felt the urge to improvise. He had seen a pair of maintenance workers when he'd arrived, and it wasn't lost on him that they had been dressed more or less as he was: dark pants, heavy jacket, black gloves.

He looked around and saw a wooden handle on the ground—three feet of tapered hardwood that had once been the grip of an axe or a hand tool. Tru picked it up, pulled the collar of his jacket higher, and strolled out into the open. He made his way to the front coupling on the car he'd selected, keeping his pace slow, his carriage weary. Anyone watching would see one perfectly unremarkable railway worker. He disappeared momentarily between the cars, as if inspecting the coupling, and then reappeared and began moving toward the big side door. His eyes swept all around: the tracks, the station, the platform. There were few people in sight, and none were paying attention to the fake inspector. He approached the open loading door and paused as if checking inside. He used the handle to pry the door open further, and after one last glance to either side, he climbed inside.

Tru quickly gauged the interior. He saw a haphazard scattering of boxes and crates. The car was two-thirds full, stacked to the ceiling in some areas, a maze of gaps in between. The shapes and sizes of the containers varied, and stencils on a few gave away the contents. Machine parts and lubricants. Racks of rolled aluminum were tied down next to a half dozen diesel engines. A stack of crates near the back caught his eye, or more precisely, what was stamped on each one. A red diamond symbol surrounded what looked like a fractured bowling ball. Beneath the warning label was lettering in Cyrillic: Взрывчатое вещество.

Explosives.

Tru was about to investigate further when he heard voices outside. He edged toward the door, peered left, and saw two workers in overalls approaching. They looked casual, unworried—something that would change instantly if they saw an intruder. He eased the door shut but didn't allow the latch to engage. The interior of the boxcar went to black, only a few shards of light filtering through gaps in the sidewalls.

He heard the men talking as they passed by, and he followed their conversation easily: they were arguing over strategies to cheat the railway's overtime pay rules. The voices soon receded.

Tru studied the door latch and was relieved to see that it could be opened from both the inside and outside. He should have known that before climbing in. Another lesson learned—and another lesson that would be worthless in any other vocation on earth, with the possible exception of thief.

He was reasonably sure he hadn't been seen climbing into the boxcar. Neither of the cameras he'd spotted were angled in a way to have recorded his entry, so as long as he exited uneventfully at his destination, there would be no reason for anyone to check the footage.

Only when the train started moving did Tru relax. Even though it was midday, the car's interior was pitch black and he could see almost nothing. He tried to remember the arrangement of the stacks around him, but the moment he turned around he barked his shin on a crate. He cursed under his breath, wishing he'd taken a better mental picture before losing the light. He considered cracking the door open but was wary it might draw attention. Using light from his sat phone would waste precious battery power. Resigned to the darkness, he put his hands in front of himself and eased cautiously ahead until he felt a stack of boxes.

He sat down, settling against a large wooden crate. The rocking of the car made it anything but comfortable, and an unknown metal protrusion jabbed him in the spine. He pushed away from the crate and laid down on the steel floor. It was filthy and cold, and every vibration seemed to transmit into his skull. Within minutes his thoughts turned hazy, and Tru realized how tired he was. He had barely slept in the last thirty hours. *Rest*, as they were so fond of saying at The Farm, *is a weapon in itself.*

The train's movement became rhythmic, and his thoughts turned foggy. How much distance did he need to cover? How fast did a Russian freight train travel across Siberian wilderness? Tru came up with a range and decided it would take between five and seven hours to reach Ulak Station, the stop where the railway came nearest Zeya Reservoir. He checked his phone and saw that it had no signal—hardly surprising inside the confines of the metal walls. He shut the handset down and shoved it into a pocket. In an hour, maybe two, he would crack the door open to give the antenna a better look at the sky. He would check for mission updates, and a GPS lock would give him accurate position and speed. It would also give him a solid estimate for his arrival at Ulak Station.

His weary body began to relax. All in all, Tru was pleased. He had crossed into Russia without being detected, and was more or less on schedule. His last thought before he drifted off to oblivion: *This new mission couldn't be going any better.*

"Drop it!" Slaton shouted.

It was a two-word command he had issued countless times in his life, usually with reference to a weapon. Never had he said it with more conviction.

Christine looked over her shoulder, then ignored her husband and lifted a big cardboard box from a high stack. "I gave birth to our daughter three months ago," she said. "I'm not an invalid."

He rushed over and took the box from her hands. It wasn't particularly heavy. "We talked about this—you can unpack, but no lifting or ladders."

"*You* talked about it."

He set the box down and they stared at one another.

She broke into a smile. "I never figured you for a nervous father."

"And I always figured you for a common-sense doctor. You had a C-section; you're supposed to take it easy." He put the box on the dining room table. "When did this stuff get here?"

"The moving truck pulled in around lunchtime. It took the guys most of the afternoon to unload."

He regarded the small mountain of boxes and furniture, and shook his head in wonderment. "For most of my life all my worldly possessions fit in a one-bedroom flat that I hardly ever saw. Never figured I'd have this much stuff."

"That's what happens when you settle down and have kids."

"Is that what we're doing?"

"The evidence is devastating."

She was right, of course. Regular paychecks, health care coverage, 401(k). He even had a life insurance policy for the first time—at least, the first of the kind that paid monetary benefits.

He leaned in and they kissed. Then they did it again.

There was no getting around it. With a wife, a four-year-old son, and a newborn daughter, Slaton was in a family way. Such commitments and responsibilities were severely at odds with his previous way of life. They were also the primary reasons he'd accepted the job overseeing the CIA's clandestine operations.

Their new house in a cozy Virginia suburb was the final step to normalization. Or maybe it was just a surrender to reality. They had started out raising their son, Davy, completely off-grid, cruising the world on a sailboat that took them wherever the wind blew. After that they'd hunkered down on a ranch in Idaho, trying for anonymity in a world that increasingly precluded it. This, surely, was the final plunge into domesticity.

"Davy asleep?" he asked.

"Crashed in his new big-boy bed. Chloe's down too. How was your day at work? Or maybe I should say, days . . . you didn't come home last night."

"Started at headquarters, ended at the White House."

Her soft eyes narrowed. "Seriously? *The* White House?"

"The one and only."

She waited for more, but when nothing came, she simply reached for another box, albeit a smaller one.

"Nope."

She stopped and stared false daggers. "I'm fine," she said.

He pulled her close and they held each other for a time.

"How long can you stay?" she whispered.

"I should try for a few hours' sleep, but I have to get back in soon."

She pushed away far enough to meet his gray eyes. "Well, whatever this crisis is, I'm glad you're watching from a distance. It's somebody else's turn to be on the front line."

"I guess. It's funny, though. I never realized how tough it is on this end. Ordering people into harm's way . . . it keeps you up at night."

"Well, whoever's taking your place on point . . . I hope they're as good as you were."

"*Were?*"

She smiled and smacked him on the ass. "Go to bed, Mr. Spymaster."

"Care to join me?"

"Maybe . . . but first I'm going to find that corkscrew."

Slaton went upstairs. The bedroom looked like a warehouse explosion, boxes and furniture strewn all around. The good news was that the bed was made, and his toothbrush was on the bathroom sink.

He looked through the labeled boxes, searching for one in particular—he had marked it carefully, two thick Sharpie lines beneath the words BEDROOM CLOSET. He found it, by no small miracle, in the half-empty closet. He used a pocketknife to cut the tape, opened it, and removed what was right on top.

The black backpack contained everything he needed.

SIXTEEN

General Viktor Strelkov stepped down the stairs of the Hawker 4000 business jet with all the elan of a dropped bowling ball. He had a top-heavy build, thick in all dimensions but immensely wide, and a bulky trench coat only added to his ponderous appearance. Beneath those layers, hair grew on every part of his body save for his massive head. As if to compensate, he stomped into the Arctic air wearing a thick fur hat, the traditional ushanka, complete with ear flaps that framed two great wrinkles at the base of his neck.

At the bottom of the stairs, Colonel Yevgeny Nemanchik, commander of Skovorna Air Base, stood at something near attention. He was wearing his winter uniform, as were the two enlisted men behind him who looked very cold. Strelkov had kept them all waiting for the best part of twenty minutes, having instructed his pilot to pause on the runway before taxiing to the parking apron in order to make a routine phone call. Far more comfortable were the four men on the perimeter—Strelkov's security detail had preceded him onto the tarmac and were facing outward alertly.

The general studied Nemanchik with eyes the color of Ural crude. The man was shivering, and the lapel of his overcoat snapped in the wind. Aside from a few added pounds, he looked much as Strelkov remembered. He was a small man in every measure with decidedly un-Slavic features. Bulging eyes, bent posture, the hint of a hooked nose. Strelkov thought he resembled a gargoyle who'd fallen from a bell tower—imagery that dovetailed well with his seemingly eternal angst. He conversed with Nemanchik regularly by phone, yet this was only the second time they had met in person. The first had been a dinner in Moscow during which a deep understanding had been reached.

"Welcome, General," Nemanchik said. His voice was brittle and jagged, glass going through a grinder.

Strelkov grunted what might have been a greeting, then got straight to business. "Have you found my son-in-law yet?"

"No sir, we have not. Every available aircraft is searching, but the wreckage has not yet been located."

Strelkov paused to look around the base. He had never been to Skovorna, although he was intimately familiar with the base's mission. The lack of aircraft, the absence of bustle seen at most air bases, seemed peculiar. Then again, he supposed it was fitting for the most secretive airfield in all of Russia.

A frigid gust of wind thrashed the tarmac, and Nemanchik was unable to quell a full-body shiver. "Perhaps we should go inside, sir."

"Why not?"

The colonel led the way to a drab administrative building. Once inside, they proceeded down the main hallway where enlisted men threw their backs against the wall. Strelkov knew this was not a display of respect for their colonel. For all the Air Force's quaint customs and courtesies, no officer in Russia commanded deference like a general of the GRU.

Nemanchik turned into his office. Strelkov followed, and once inside he none too discreetly closed the door behind them.

The colonel sat behind a wide desk that seemed to fill the room—a clumsy attempt at power projection from a man who knew nothing about it. "So," Nemanchik lied, "I am happy you have come to visit our little corner of the world. I only wish the circumstances were more auspicious."

Strelkov didn't reply, but instead surveyed the office. It was just as he'd envisioned. Small, utilitarian, a few personal effects hung on the wall in a pathetic attempt to self-glorify. There was a picture of Nemanchik standing at attention while a lower-tier Air Force general pinned colonel's rank on his shoulders. Next to that was a yellowing class graduation picture from the Military Logistics Academy, Nemanchik all but invisible in the middle row. The man was model minion, a smaller than life presence who had already gone one rung higher on the career ladder than his leadership skills warranted. He was precisely the type of sycophant Strelkov preyed upon: a perpetual underachiever who could be nudged a bit higher at the price of absolute loyalty. Russia was full of such men, and Strelkov made his living off them.

He had targeted Nemanchik last year, orchestrating his promotion and plotting his assignment to Skovorna. His reasons were twofold. First was to keep an eye on a very important government program. Second was to keep an eye on his son-in-law. Nemanchik reported to him weekly. Was Primakov drinking? Was he seeing women? Viewing foreign websites? The GRU kept track of all Russians, and when it came to alienating citizens from their inalienable rights, no concessions were made for military officers. And such oversight was all but obligatory for the son-in-law of a high-ranking member of the GRU.

For the most part there had been little to report. Primakov was a moody workaholic who rarely saw his wife. Oksana Primakov, née Strelkov, worked at GRU headquarters at Khodinka Airfield on the western outskirts of Moscow—commonly referred to as The Aquarium. Strelkov had inserted her there years ago, and he used her much as he did Nemanchik—a trusted set of eyes to keep watch on things. By all accounts, his daughter's career was going well, and she was rising through the ranks with unexpected speed. Like her husband, Oksana put work above marriage. By all the evidence Strelkov had amassed, which was considerable, the only thing that had ever truly bonded the couple had been lost two years ago. The death of their only child had brought a deep estrangement, yet both appeared to be soldiering on.

Now the gods of chance had intervened, putting Maksim's fate in the balance, and Strelkov had come to spin the situation as best he could. This probably meant casting his son-in-law as a hero, which, if Nemanchik's accounts could be believed, wouldn't be difficult.

Maksim's only questionable behavior had occurred last fall—there were rumors he had become involved with a local woman, a divorcée who tended bar down in Zeya. Strelkov shrugged it off as "boys being boys," and in truth he had been relieved. He was an expert in finding weakness, in exploiting it, yet Maksim had long vexed him. As far as he knew, he had never otherwise strayed in his marriage, and he carried out his military duties to the letter, albeit with a fighter pilot's swagger. More maddeningly, he displayed a fundamental willfulness that had long exasperated Strelkov. Despite his best efforts, Maksim Primakov could not be intimidated, manipulated, or shaken from his antiquated code of honor. And for these reasons, the man had long been a burr in his ass.

"Tell me what happened," he finally said, the lengthy silence having had its chance to play.

"We are not exactly sure, General. The flight began as a typical test mission, but soon after Vektor arrived in the restricted airspace something went wrong." Nemanchik covered the facts as he knew them, and then promised that the Air Force would get to the bottom of the catastrophe.

When he finished, Strelkov was silent for a time. His wrecking ball head tilted left, then slowly right. As if gathering momentum. "What are the chances my son-in-law is alive?"

Nemanchik's lips parted, destined for a banal and compassionate reply. Probably something about hope or God's will. Strelkov's brooding stare interceded, conveying that anything but the unvarnished truth would be a mistake.

"I am not an expert in air operations," said the Air Force colonel, "but from what I have been told . . . it is a coin toss, maybe less. One would expect the colonel to have ejected, but if he had done so an emergency beacon should have activated. The same is true if the airplane had simply crashed. So far, we have heard nothing, so there are only questions."

Strelkov ran a hand over his darkened, anvil-like chin. It made a sound like sandpaper. "What of this message I received during my flight? You say you have something to report."

Nemanchik shifted in his chair. "To begin, I should tell you that I have seen nothing out of the ordinary in the colonel's recent activities . . ."

A weighty hesitation ensued, and Strelkov's oil-black eyes locked on. *"However . . . ?"*

"Well . . . I did notice that the colonel seemed somewhat withdrawn lately. He customarily ate dinner with the enlisted men in the mess hall, yet this week I never saw him there."

Another pause. Strelkov let it build.

"There is one recent discovery I must bring to your attention—the reason for the message I sent. I received it only an hour ago." He unlocked a drawer on his desk and pulled out a simple white envelope. "This was found in Colonel Primakov's locker this morning."

The black eyes squinted and the caterpillar brows above them creased. Strelkov took the letter and recognized it straightaway. It was the one he had sent, only his son-in-law's name had been scrawled out and replaced with his own. The seal was no longer intact.

"Who has seen this?" he asked, his eyes drilling Nemanchik.

"It was discovered by a technician in the life support section, on a shelf in Colonel Primakov's locker. Seeing that it was addressed to you, he brought it to me immediately."

"Have you seen what is inside?"

"Absolutely not, General."

Strelkov seized Nemanchik in a dead stare.

The man broke almost immediately—he could not keep eye contact.

Strelkov moved closer to the desk, his great bulk hovering. "Colonel, that is the one and only lie I will *ever* grant you."

A bobble-headed nod. "I am deeply sorry, sir. Yes, I glanced at it, but only once. I thought it might be something time critical, something to explain what has happened."

Without responding, Strelkov opened the envelope and extracted the letter. What he saw sent a chill down his thick spine. He weighed what it might mean. Whether it could explain the disappearance of Vektor. Any answer was evasive, misted by insoluble questions. The central theme, however, could not have been more damning. He put the letter back inside the envelope, taking his time as he prioritized his next steps. The first had to be local damage control.

He said, "I saw helicopters on the flight line, did I not?"

"Yes, General. Hip J models assigned for logistical support."

"I want one ready to fly in twenty minutes."

"Of course. Do you wish to join the search?"

"I want the aircraft ready. When it is, you and one other person will join me on the flight line."

"Who?"

Strelkov told him. He then dismissed the colonel to issue the orders.

As soon as Nemanchik was gone, he took out the letter and looked at it again. There were but three words, handwritten in what looked like black crayon. For Strelkov, no other words could have infused more peril.

Fuck you, Viktor.

The helicopter crew had many questions. Where would they be going? How much fuel was required? Strelkov did not answer any of them.

The crew flew one of the Hips across the airfield and set down on the tarmac in front of the administration building. As per Strelkov's orders, the engines were left running.

The moment the chopper touched down, seven people spilled out of the building. Strelkov was in the lead, outriggered by his security detail of four men. In the middle of the nervous formation were Colonel Nemanchik and a bewildered Corporal Ivanov who had been dragged out of the life support room.

Strelkov stopped fifty feet short of the idling Hip, turned, and took a long look at the two Air Force men. Seeming to reach a decision, he pointed to the corporal. A pair of his beefiest security men closed in, seized Ivanov by the forearms, and frog-marched him toward the idling helicopter. A third bodyguard fell in behind, and once everyone was on board he leaned into the Hip's flight deck and began talking to the pilots.

Minutes later, Strelkov and a dumbfounded Nemanchik watched the chopper lift off in a swirl of noise and blown snow. The Hip rose high above the airfield, and roughly a thousand feet above the main runway it settled into a hover. There was a flurry of activity at the side entry door, which remained open, and a flailing shape was suddenly ejected.

Yevgeny Nemanchik looked on in horror as Corporal Ivanov, still clad in his camouflage fatigues and boots, dropped like a human anvil, his arms and legs swimming all the way to the ground. He hit squarely in the center of the runway, a bullseye of sorts, and his body bounced once before falling still in a boneless heap.

Strelkov turned to a horrified Nemanchik and issued an extended stare. The colonel seemed to be vibrating, on the verge of a breakdown. Without a word, Strelkov strode away to the warmth of the administration building.

SEVENTEEN

It was the sense of touch that filtered in first, a tactile bolt arcing through the haze.

Tru had been drifting, caught in the murky haze between sleep and consciousness, when he felt a tug on his right hip. He startled awake, his right hand instinctively swiping down.

It struck . . . something.

The first thing he noticed was the side door of the freight car—it was cracked open, as it had been when he'd first climbed aboard. This introduced noise, gusts of frigid air, and enough light for Tru to make a more disquieting discovery: two men were staring down at him.

They were dirty and rough-hewn, with days-old stubble on their faces. The smaller of the two was pudgy with a pugilist's face and stubby T-Rex arms. He was holding his wrist, rubbing it as if it hurt. The other man, tall and thin, was brandishing an axe handle—the very one Tru had acquired at the rail yard. He was tapping it rhythmically in his opposing palm like a street cop with a baton.

Right away Tru realized he'd made multiple mistakes. After boarding the car, he hadn't searched the darkened interior thoroughly. The fact that the door had been cracked open to begin with should have raised his suspicions. He had also lost control of his only weapon.

And things had been going so well.

"What do you have for us?" the man with the handle asked in Russian.

Tru pushed up casually, rising onto his elbows, and replied in Russian. "My best wishes for a very nice day."

The taller man's eyes narrowed, no humor registering. "You are not from here."

Tru's grasp of Russian was excellent—one of the reasons the CIA had brought him on board—but regional accents were maddeningly subtle. He had no chance of passing as a local and saw no reason to try. "No, I am from Yekaterinburg."

The scruffy men exchanged a glance.

"What brings you east?"

"I am passing through. I took work in Vladivostok for the winter, a shipyard. Then they stopped paying us, so I decided to go back home." It seemed a reasonable story.

Tru shifted a bit higher, nothing threatening in his manner. He set his back against a wooden crate and studied the two men. Neither looked like the type to have done military service, although it was hard to tell in Russia given the recent lowering of standards. Conscripts and criminals were more prevalent in some units than professional soldiers. "Did either of you ever serve in the military?" he asked. "Maybe in Ukraine?"

The nearest man spit. "Whores, all of them. We are businessmen." The axe handle went over his shoulder. It wasn't an overtly threatening move, but Tru recognized it for what it was. The man had a solid grip on the narrow end, palm up. The weapon was now poised, like a cop on a traffic stop holding a big flashlight on his shoulder. "I ask you again . . . what do you have for us?"

"Actually," Tru replied honestly, "I was wondering what you might have for me."

After another exchanged look, the men started chuckling.

Tru sensed their mirth was manufactured, and he was proved correct an instant later.

The taller man lunged forward and brought the axe handle arcing down toward his head. Tru rolled quickly to his right and lifted his left arm protectively. The wild swing missed, and the axe handle did what axe handles do when they slam into solid steel—it ricocheted upward. Tru caught it on the rebound and easily torqued it free of the taller man's grasp, which had been weakened by the impact.

Tru was up on one knee in a flash. His first strike with the handle wasn't a swing, but a punch—he rammed the blunt end into the taller man's solar plexus. He grunted in pain and dropped to his knees. Tru rotated a half turn, the handle spinning toward the pugilist in a two-handed grip. The man saw it coming and raised both arms defensively, much as Tru had done. Distracted, he never saw the kick coming to his groin. As he buckled, Tru reversed with the handle, a crushing blow to the jawline.

Before he hit the floor, Tru was turning back to his cohort. The taller man was trying to stand, gasping, when the axe handle slammed down on the back of his skull. He dropped face-first onto the steel floor.

Tru readdressed the man who was writhing on the floor and holding his face. He raised the handle for a knockout blow.

The Russian crabbed backwards, his face masked in blood, and rounded a corner into a nook Tru hadn't yet explored. He followed the man as he neared a pile of loose equipment. There were a new pair of military boots, a table lamp, a computer printer still in its box. Nearby, just out of the man's reach, was a crowbar. It didn't take a detective to figure out what the two had been up to. They'd been going through crates, hoping to find something of value, when Tru had interrupted.

The pugilist looked up plaintively, blood streaming from his mouth. He coughed and spat out a red blob that contained at least one tooth. The man held out an open palm in a way that could only indicate surrender.

Tru hesitated.

For the second time in a day, he faced a decision about how much violence to impart. The first occasion, involving the workers at the wastewater plant, had been relatively straightforward. The two technicians had posed no threat. This was different. These men had attacked him, and if he let them live it could put his mission at risk. They had seen him, talked to him, and knew the direction in which he was traveling.

Tru had been told there would be moments like this in missions, instances where training, rulebooks, and operational goals didn't mesh for a clear answer. A voice from The Farm came to his head. Stansell again. *You never know how you're going to handle it . . . until you do.*

Tru never doubted his abilities. But the question of *how* he would employ them loomed large. He had crossed into Russia with an agenda that was, admittedly, more private than professional. Yet the crimes he hoped to avenge had been committed by a few rogue actors. These men weren't responsible for what had happened to his sister. They were no more than petty thieves.

He glanced at the taller man. He was sprawled on the steel floor, rolling slightly with the motion of the train, thoroughly unconscious but breathing. He turned back to the pugilist.

"Nyet!" the man whispered, staring at the poised axe handle.

Tru lowered the weapon.

Which turned out to be a mistake.

With surprising speed, the man lunged, his hand reaching into the pile of equipment. Tru moved fast, but not fast enough. A big-barreled handgun of some kind swung toward him. He had no time to discern the type of weapon. He only saw a massive-bore barrel that belonged on an artillery piece. The instant the barrel settled on Tru's chest he dove to the right. He registered a muffled *pop* as he flew through the air, followed by a brilliant flash of light. Then a crash as the round struck the crate behind him.

Having lost his grip on the axe handle, Tru bounded back up and dove toward the man. The pugilist was fumbling with the gun when Tru slammed into him, leading with an elbow. The two tumbled against the car's sidewall, but Tru was quickest to stabilize. The time for debate and moderation was past. Tru was quicker, stronger, faster, and had been trained to fight by the best in the business. He pummeled the beefy man with a merciless series of fist and elbow strikes, followed by a devastating knee to the temple. The man stopped moving, either out cold or dead.

Tru never had a chance to determine which. He heard popping sounds behind him.

Looking over his shoulder, he saw the entire front half of the boxcar immersed in red phosphorous sparks. He looked down at the weapon the man had dropped and realized it was a flare gun. The flare had blown a gaping hole in a midlevel crate, and whatever was inside had lit off like a roman candle. The container above it was smoking ominously. Red sparks and shards of phosphorous flew in all directions, lighting the interior in a brilliant glow. In the sudden brightness, Tru saw labels on stacks of crates he hadn't seen before. His translations weren't perfect, but they didn't need to be. Air defense flares, hand grenades, 5.45x39mm cartridges. Five crates next to the flares were the worst of all. *Mortar rounds.*

He was riding in a goddamn ammunition car. And it was now on fire.

More flares lit off, flames spraying toward the ceiling. The situation was nearing critical mass.

"*Shit!*"

He had a fleeting thought that a fire extinguisher might be a good idea. It disappeared when something big exploded, peppering the sidewall with shards of wood and shrapnel.

More secondaries cooked off behind the main stack. The entire car was about to blow. His ears ringing, Tru lunged toward the cracked door and shouldered it open wide.

He took one look outside. The train was traveling at a middling speed. More than twenty miles an hour, less than thirty. The railbed was dirt covered with patchy layers of snow. Under normal circumstances he would never have considered jumping. But riding a fast-ticking bomb was anything but normal.

Tru looked over his shoulder at the two men who'd attacked him. Neither was moving. A rush of thoughts flew into his head, conflicting voices which, in the desperation of the moment, might have passed for conscience. None of those thoughts ever resolved, because in the next moment he was sent flying into space by a massive explosion.

EIGHTEEN

Tru blinked once. His eyes slowly focused and he tried to move.

Pain began searing in. Right shoulder mostly, a few secondary sites. Cymbals in his ears reached a crescendo, pounding into his skull. Then the ringing was overtaken by what sounded like thunder.

He shifted to take the weight off his shoulder and managed to sit up. He remembered falling, and in the next instant doing his best to dampen his landing. Muscle memory from parachute training coming back out of nowhere—bend at the knees, roll when you hit, absorb the energy with as much of your body as possible.

And absorb he had. He rolled his shoulder gingerly. Painful but functional. He rubbed the side of his head, and his hand came away bloody.

More thunder.

He looked up the track and saw the train a quarter mile away. Multiple cars had derailed—how many he had no idea, but logic suggested everything behind the one he had been riding in. Probably close to twenty. Smoke billowed into a bleak winter sky as secondary explosions rumbled, shards of shrapnel spinning upward like errant fireworks. One of the central cars looked particularly hot, a blowtorch of flames shooting from a breach.

He considered how many mistakes he had made this afternoon but was quickly overwhelmed. Maybe he should begin a mental file: *Things to never do again.*

Not a bad idea, but now wasn't the time.

He rose to his feet uneventfully, sore but steady. He reached into his jacket pocket and pulled out his sat phone. He had been told it was a hardened model, and on appearances it seemed undamaged.

Score one for the Directorate of Science and Technology.

He turned it on, and as it spun to life his thoughts sidetracked. The two men who had attacked him on the train couldn't have survived the blast. He tried to convince himself their deaths were not his fault.

Tried very hard.

Training was training. But this was the real world. The two thugs would have killed him, of that he had no doubt. And they wouldn't have lost any sleep over it. On the other hand, they had no relevance to his mission. They were mere bystanders, although not the innocent variety. Irrespective of the right or wrong of the situation, one thing was crystal clear: Tru was, on some level, responsible for their deaths. Later tonight, or whenever he next had a chance to sleep, that would probably weigh on his thoughts. He would deal with it then.

Right now he had to move.

He checked the phone and the first thing he saw was the time. It was three in the afternoon. For whatever reason, the two Russians had let him sleep for hours before rousting him. They themselves had looked rough, possibly hung over, so perhaps they'd been passed out when he had boarded. There was no point in dwelling on it. He had to be near his intended destination, and a check of the phone's map confirmed it—he was only six miles from Ulak Station.

He looked again at the wrecked train. There was no one in sight, but there had to be people on the other side of the conflagration—the engine and passenger cars would almost surely have escaped the catastrophe, momentum carrying them to safety. He envisioned rattled customers and dumbstruck rail employees gawking at the pyrotechnics a mile behind them. Not wanting to encounter anyone, Tru veered into the woods to circumnavigate the scene. The smoke was an easy reference and thick forest provided concealment. As he moved, his aches and pains subsided, although his shoulder remained sore.

He had been walking for ten minutes, his limbs regaining function, when a massive explosion reverberated through the hills. He looked through the trees and saw a vast cloud of smoke and flame clawing into the sky. *Glad I avoided that one,* he thought.

He set back out, and with all the mental bandwidth he could muster, Tru tried to think forward. How might the crash affect his mission? As far as he knew, the only two people who'd gotten a look at him were now dead. For the next few hours, the authorities would be single-minded, reacting to a disaster rather than investigating its cause. At some point they would discover two bodies at the center of the blaze and suspicions would be raised. They might go back and look at footage from the rail yard in Birobidzhan in order to identify the men. If there was a camera he'd missed, they might conceivably see Tru climbing into the car. Yet even if that happened, they would probably mistake him for one of the two dead men. He had never officially entered Russia, and any traces of his short time in the boxcar—DNA or fingerprints—were fast being obliterated.

All of that would take days, if not weeks. And it would support an easy solution that was very near the truth: two vagabonds had accidentally set off the immolation. Tru could think of only one downside—when he reached Ulak Station, the level of watchfulness would be higher than usual. And that might make it harder to reach his objective.

When he was clear of the crash site, Tru veered back to the track. His aches and pains persisted, but he pushed onward, knowing they were nothing compared to what he would endure if he were captured as a spy. Seeing no one along the railway, and with the sun skimming lower in the west, he broke into a steady jog.

NINETEEN

An ill-tempered Bob Stansell stood in an elevator at the George Bush Center for Intelligence. Two other headquarters employees were with him. One, a squat fortyish man he pegged as an analyst, was trying to ignore him. Bald and slope-shouldered, he looked like a friar in search of a medieval fair. The elevator's other occupant, a woman, seemed to be studying the floor. Stansell looked down. His boots were filthy, and he'd tracked mud inside. He had made a cursory effort to stomp the worst of it off in the parking lot, but it was hopeless.

Her eyes moved up, no doubt taking in his overall encrusted appearance. His clothes were wrinkled and stained. He was probably emanating earthy odors. The woman, a matronly sort with a stack of files under one arm, made a clucking noise without meeting Stansell's eyes.

"Sorry," he said. "I just flew in from Africa. Good news is, I got most of the blood off."

She recoiled, probably trying to decide if he was serious. The truth was that three hours ago he had been on a tactical range at The Farm watching three particularly hopeless recruits spray lead across rural Virginia. It had rained the previous day, and the ground was a mess—which, in his considered opinion, made for ideal conditions. Or as he succinctly put it to his charges, "An opportunity to shine in a real-world setting."

The elevator chimed, coming to a stop on the fifth floor. Stansell said, "Y'all have a nice day," making no effort to hide his Texas drawl.

"This is the leadership floor," the matron protested.

Stansell said over his shoulder, "Hardly."

The carpet in front of him looked clean and pristine, and he found himself wishing he hadn't knocked off any of the mud outside. It was seven in the morning and Stansell was cranky—more so than usual. He had spent all night on the range, and after reprimanding the worthless pricks that passed for recruits, he'd been headed for his truck, thinking about a breakfast beer, when his phone lit with a priority message. He was to report immediately to headquarters for a meeting with the director of SAC/SOG.

Nothing good ever came from being summoned here, particularly for men like Stansell. It generally meant one of two things. Either his advice was needed for an existential crisis, or he had messed up bigtime. When he'd entered the lobby downstairs, he had surveyed the mood of the place and sensed nothing to indicate an emergency. The few workers he saw were chatting and moving lethargically—in other words, a typical morning at Command Central.

On the other hand, he didn't remember screwing up lately.

That he was to report straight to the SAC director's office was doubly worrisome. Not only was it an unusually high-level request, but he had never met the new man in charge. Stansell's reputation at headquarters had long been rocky, and he didn't know how many of his transgressions remained in his record. Previous directors had twice tried to get him fired. The first instance had to do with the rendition of an ISIS commander—Stansell had put the man on a C-130 from Afghanistan to Poland without prior agency approval. That minor lapse was amplified when, somewhere over the Caspian Sea, the man had jumped out the side door, without a parachute, from roughly ten thousand feet. The second near-termination had come when Stansell washed a young recruit, who happened to be the son of a senior senator, out of training.

In both cases, Stansell, a former Recon Marine who had been working clandestine operations for nearly twenty years, justified his actions with an operator's typical ineloquence. In essence, a "shit happens" defense. He'd explained that his comm link had failed in Afghanistan, although the malfunction could never be identified, and claimed the jihadi had decided to enter Paradise on his own terms. As to a badly broken nose on the senator's kid, he maintained the contact had come from a telephone pole on the obstacle course, and not, as the kid had whined, from a punitive encounter with Stansell's bony elbow. In both cases, and with little evidence in his favor, Stansell's job had been saved by the director himself, a bit of gratitude for the operational wins he'd orchestrated over the years.

Unfortunately, his get out of jail free card was no longer playable. The new director, Charles Eraclides, was the former agency IG, and Stansell figured that having a lawyer at the helm would likely doom his career. Yet there was one ray of hope. The new chief of SAC/SOG was, by all accounts, a former Mossad operator named David Slaton. Code-name Corsair. If even half the rumors of his exploits could be believed, Stansell figured the man might have an operator's perspective.

He turned into the deputy director's anteroom. The desk where the executive assistant normally sat was empty—it was still early for the office crowd. The door to the office, however, was open and the lights were on. Stansell went through and found the deputy director waiting for him. Standing beside the desk, Slaton was on the tall side and looked fit. His off-blond hair was a bit unkempt, and his clothes were more suited to a hiking trail than an executive suite. Most distinctive of all was a pair of penetrating gray eyes.

"Are introductions necessary?" Slaton asked, extending a hand all the same.

Stansell took a solid handshake. "Probably not."

"Good, because I don't have time to waste. Truman Miller."

Stansell shifted mental gears, "Uh . . . say again?"

"Truman Miller. He went through The Farm last year and you were his primary. I want to know everything about him."

"Have you seen his file?"

Slaton opened a desk drawer, pulled out a standard personnel dossier, and sent it sliding toward Stansell. He reached out to keep it from falling but it ended up perfectly perched over the desk's gold-inlaid edge.

"What I need isn't in the file. To begin, this guy came to us straight out of college. I thought SAC/SOG recruited only Tier 1 operators—Seal Team and Delta guys."

"That was our preference for a long time. But your predecessor thought we needed to broaden the pipeline."

"With good reason?"

Stansell allowed a grudging nod. "I'd say so. For one thing, the Tier 1 pool is almost exclusively male. That limits our options in certain scenarios. And then there was the hack."

"Hack?"

"A few years back, someone—we think the Chinese, although it was never confirmed—breached a firewall and got into the DOD personnel database. They scraped files, including photographs, on a good percentage of our active-duty military members. With no way to know exactly how much damage was done, it seemed like a good precaution to broaden our hiring pool. We still hire experienced operators. But we also bring on a handful of fresh faces, people who have never been on active duty."

"Okay, good to know," said the new boss. "So back to Miller."

"I've put a lot of trainees through the program, and I don't remember them all . . . but he stood out. Raw, impulsive, a commendable lack of respect for authority. I expect he'd kick just about anybody's ass in a bar fight . . . present company excluded."

Stansell thought he might have seen a stifled smile.

"He was a shitty driver, though."

"Driver?"

"Defensive driving—every recruit takes the course. Miller was a failure. Guess you could say he was more of an offensive driver, always running things over and sideswiping the adversaries like they were playing bumper cars. Claimed it was anger management therapy."

"Charming."

Stansell was on a roll. "All in all, I'd say he had the makings of a fine operator. Maybe a tendency to get out over his skis a bit, metaphorically speaking, but he never got out of control. And for what it's worth, he wasn't a complete virgin. He did serve a few years in an Army Guard unit to put himself through college—state-run military records weren't compromised in the hack."

Slaton's eyes canted down to what looked like a very thin personnel folder.

"It says in his file he almost washed out."

"He was close, and more than once. Procedural crap . . . nothing that mattered."

Slaton opened the folder. "Speaks Russian?"

"Fluently."

"Intelligent?"

"Highly."

"Physical fitness?"

"Off the charts."

"What are his weaknesses?"

"From whose point of view?"

Slaton looked at him squarely, and said, "The only one that counts—mine."

"I think I recall a minor hiccup on his psych eval. The report came back as NAFOD."

"NAFOD? What's that?"

"A term our doctors use—no apparent fear of death."

"Are you telling me he's some kind of psycho?"

"No, he's rational. That diagnosis was never worth much in my book. Hell, teens, twenty-somethings—they all think they're bullet-proof. That's why old farts throughout history send them to fight their wars." The square jaw flexed. "He also might have had some authority issues."

"In what way?"

"Didn't always go by the book—not if he thought there was a better way. We generally like initiative, but Miller pressed to the edge of . . . let's say rebelliousness. He was also a bit of a loner, which isn't nec-essarily a negative. We like operators who can work solo. He filled all the technical squares for graduation, no problem. But the leadership at The Farm had some reservations, so it was agreed his first few assign-ments would be non-critical ops. Basically, an attitude check to see how he functions in the real world."

"And?"

"No surprises," Stansell said. "He's not a great rule follower. But in my opinion, initiative and aggression are a solo operator's best weapons."

"Tell me about his survival skills."

"Survival skills? Like mountain man shit?"

"Yeah, mountain man shit."

"He's not like a Cherokee tracker or anything, but as I recall he did some hunting when he was a kid, spent time in the woods. He went through the standard courses like all trainees. SERE, Arctic survival, jungle survival."

"Arctic survival. So he can handle cold weather."

Stansell flicked a bit of mud off his boot. "When it comes to cold, he's a goddamn prodigy—and that's in the file. He was a top-flight biathlon competitor a few years back. Good enough to make the cut for Olympic qualifying. He just missed making the team at an age when most guys haven't peaked."

Slaton nodded thoughtfully. Biathlon, he knew, combined cross country skiing and shooting, and was one of the most physically de-manding winter sports.

"What about his tradecraft?"

"He was picking it up."

"That doesn't instill confidence."

"I'm not trying to instill anything. I'm just telling you how it is."

Slaton crossed his arms and nodded. "As it turns out, we've put him in a very delicate situation."

Stansell chuckled. "Delicate? Now that might be a mistake."

"In what way?"

"In the way that you can't put a silencer on a hand grenade."

Slaton frowned.

"Look, if you tell me what this is all about, I might be more helpful. What exactly have you got Tru doing?"

"Tru?"

"That's what everybody took to calling him."

"Like a call sign?"

"I guess you could call it that. Somebody used the name, and it stuck."

Slaton went silent for a moment, then said. "What I'm going to tell you doesn't leave this room."

"Okay."

"We've sent him into Russia. He was on a mission in northern China, a low priority op, when something critical popped up. It's time sensitive, and he was our only asset in the neighborhood. A high-value defector needs to be extracted from a remote location in Siberia."

"*Siberia?* Are we talking about a detention camp?"

"No."

"Government minister?"

"No. I'm only going to tell you that this mission was authorized at the highest level . . . *outside* this building. I need to be sure Miller is someone I can count on."

Stansell considered it, then said, "In that case . . . you might have a problem."

"Such as?"

"I don't doubt Tru will go in and try to retrieve your defector. He'll probably tell himself he's only following orders. But for a long time he's been dying to take a swing at Russia."

"Russia?"

Stansell leaned back, crossed a filthy boot over one knee. "Let me tell you what you need to know about Tru Miller . . . the part that's not in your file."

TWENTY

The town near Ulak Station, Ovsyanka, was as quiet as church on Tuesday. More a frontier outpost than anything urban, half the roads were gravel, and the only fitting name for the architectural style was "tumbledown." The few restaurants and stores belonged on the set of a Hollywood western, advertising reindeer steaks and outerwear fashioned from locally trapped pelts. Paint was apparently in short supply, many of the buildings left as naked planking. Smoke curled up from chimneys in all quarters, infusing the air with the scent of burning wood. Tru figured this for a plus—his clothes still had a smoky tang, having been singed in the explosion on the railway.

He kept his head down as he walked up the main street. In a town so small, he would be immediately recognized as an outsider, and at this time of year, the only strangers would be nefarious drifters or tourists who'd badly lost their way. Thankfully, with daylight fading and the temperature dropping fast, he encountered no one.

He had checked his phone before entering town, then quickly turned it off when he realized the battery was down to twenty percent. It was a fact of life in modern clandestine ops—and a point drilled home by his instructors—that power management was among the highest priorities in the field. If you lost comm, you lost the ability to call in help or share time-critical intel. Trigger discipline and countersurveillance were fixations in Hollywood, but a dead battery was more likely to kill you.

He turned into a coffee shop, one of the more contemporary storefronts in a Kruschevian lineup. Tru immediately saw everything he needed: food, drink, and electrical outlets. The young girl behind the counter looked like a typical stateside barista: she'd dyed a blue streak in her black hair and a metal ring dangled from her nose. She seemed disinterested as he purchased a large coffee, a sweet roll, two bottles of water, and a handful of energy bars. One water and the energy bars he stuffed into his jacket pockets.

A few other patrons were scattered throughout the place, all either engrossed in quiet conversations or mesmerized by their phones. Tru took a seat at a corner high-top near the front window. While waiting for his coffee to cool, he used the time to survey the place. The broad front window gave overwatch on the street and would probably allow a usable satellite signal. He noted one back exit, and a narrow staircase that led up to the second floor—probably the owner's living quarters. The only staff besides the barista was an older man in the kitchen who was likely the proprietor. Tru settled onto a metal stool that felt solid: a blunt force weapon if needed, or equally useful for breaking the big window as an avenue of escape.

Satisfied with his setting, he turned to the wall and found a standard C-type plug. Thankfully, the CIA had thought ahead—the charger they'd provided adapted to various outlet types and voltages. He plugged in the phone, canted the screen for privacy, and powered it up. The signal strength was fair, and a new message downloaded immediately.

CONTINUE TO ASSIGNED GRID COORDINATES ASAP. ASSET TALON INJURED AND REQUIRES FIRST AID. EXPECT EXFIL INSTRUCTIONS SOON.

After reading the message, Tru tried to fill in the gaps.

He had been told time was critical, and now he understood why. Talon was injured. The fact that he hadn't been given specifics on his condition seemed telling. It suggested something immobilizing, but not necessarily life threatening. He then considered the term "asset." In such broad context, it could mean virtually anything: he might be rescuing a wayward American civilian, a stranded CIA officer, or a Russian agent.

Possibly something in between.

Conspicuously absent was any plan for getting out. Exfiltration from this deep in Russia would be a monumentally complex undertaking, particularly given that the asset was injured. Virtually all the CIA's manpower in Russia was concentrated in the U.S. embassy in Moscow, six time zones away. The nearest border from which a military operation could be launched was at least a thousand miles away. Still, something was in the works.

Something.

Tru shifted to the map on his phone.

He was making good time. The border was behind him, and he

was less than fifty miles from his objective. Yet those last miles might prove the most problematic. A single road bordered the eastern shore of Zeya Reservoir, and even that came up short of the grid coordinates he'd been given—he would still need to traverse miles of heavy forest. There was no civilization whatsoever near the rendezvous point, and he wondered how the asset had ended up so deep in the wilderness. He decided the answer would come soon enough.

He looked outside, and on the nearby hillside he saw the same conditions he'd encountered so far. Relatively gentle terrain, moderate snow cover. Still, with almost fifty miles to go, reaching his destination on foot was a nonstarter. He had to find a way to move faster, one that wouldn't raise suspicion.

A work van crawled past on the slush-laden street. He might beg, borrow, or steal a ride, but not without complications. A kid on a bicycle pedaled past, and Tru watched him skid over a patch of ice. Too cumbersome and perilous.

Then a figure in the distance caught his attention. On the edge of town, a man skirted the surrounding forest. He was moving quickly, easily, and slowed as he neared a rustic low-slung building. The place was cut from the same timbers as the rest of town, but it didn't appear residential. The building was long and wide, with a chimney on either end. A dull yellow glow shone from broad windows. Given the size of the place, and the half dozen parked cars outside, Tru took it for a community center of some kind. Maybe a lodge or a spa. He knew these were common in small towns, and he sensed opportunity.

He observed the man closely, saw him draw to a stop just short of the lodge's front steps. Tru watched him break down his equipment.

And just like that, he had the answer to his dilemma.

TWENTY-ONE

"Tru Miller applied to join the agency after an event that happened three years ago," Stansell said.

"Were we recruiting him at the time?" Slaton asked.

"Nope—not even on our radar. He was in college, working on a graduate degree. The reason he applied had to do with his sister. Kate Miller was five years older, a surgeon. High achiever and very idealistic. At the outset of the war in Ukraine, she volunteered to help treat wounded refugees."

"Doctors Without Borders?"

"Not that specific organization, but along the same lines."

"And let me guess—her volunteer work ended badly?"

Stansell nodded.

"How did you find this out?"

"Tru told me her story near the end of his time at The Farm. Kate started out at a hospital in Poland, but as often happens in these situations, she got dragged deeper. She volunteered to work at a field hospital in Ukraine. From there she began making trips to collect critically wounded civilians near combat zones. It's not unusual. Volunteers go one of two ways when they see war up close—they either back off and head home, or they go all-in. In her case, it was the latter. On one of these trips to the front she and two coworkers disappeared."

"Disappeared?"

"That's where the story gets hazy. An aid station called to say they had a severely wounded child. There was a consensus that if the trauma team waited for approval to go in, the child wasn't going to make it. Kate, along with a nurse and a driver, decided to set out for the station. The truck they were riding in wasn't marked with a red cross—just had the NGO's initials spray-painted on the sides. They never reached the aid station. The army was told that they were missing, but in the middle of a war searching for wayward volunteers isn't a priority. No trace of the truck was ever found. They might have gotten lost, could have crossed the lines and been detained. Or they might have driven off a bridge or taken a direct hit from a drone or an artillery round. Bottom line, all three just disappeared."

Slaton nodded somberly. "Things like that happen in war."

"All the time," Stansell agreed. "Our State Department made some back-channel inquiries, but if the Russians knew anything about what happened, they didn't admit it. When Tru got the news, he was devastated—his words. He was extremely close to his sister, and the vacuum of information only spun him up further. Truman Miller is not, I can attest, a patient individual. After two weeks of getting no-where on the phone, he decided to take matters into his own hands. He quit school, packed a bag, and flew to Ukraine to search for his sister."

"That's rash."

"Like I said . . ."

"Did he have any luck?"

"Wouldn't call it luck, but he did have some success—more than he should have, by all rights. He hit plenty of roadblocks. Just getting into Ukraine in those days wasn't easy, but nobody could turn him around. He made his way to the clinic where Kate had been working and talked to some of her coworkers. They didn't add much to what he already knew, and he spun his wheels for weeks. But he didn't give up. He made a side trip to a holding area where Russian POWs were being processed, and the Ukrainians were sympathetic enough to let him talk to a few of the prisoners. He ended up talking to a Russian conscript, one of the few who managed to surrender without being shot in the back. When Tru showed him a picture of his sister, the kid said he remembered her. He said she'd been captured by a unit named Kolovrat."

"I've heard of them. Right-wing Wagner offshoot."

"About as far right as you can go. Fanatic neo-Nazis, mostly former Spetsnaz. The name comes from the symbol on their patch, a modified swastika."

"Not good company for a female doctor. What happened then?"

"Tru's story ended there."

"You mean he never found out?"

"Actually . . . I think it was the opposite. I think he was told that some terrible things happened to his sister. The kind of things that don't leave room for hope. All I can tell you for sure—the next day he flew back to the States. The day after that he applied for a job with the agency."

Slaton took a moment to contemplate how this could affect the current mission. "And he told you all this?"

"He did, although it wasn't in any official capacity. Tru was written up four times for acts of insubordination during training. A disciplinary board was convened, and the evidence was overwhelming against him. He was gonna get kicked out. The night before the board made their recommendation, I ordered him to join me at the bar for a beer. I knew there was something under the surface, and I told him as much. I said it was the closest thing to a confessional he was ever going to get. So he told me what I just told you, and the next day I met with Anna Sorensen."

Slaton looked at him, then picked up the file folder on his desk and began flicking through pages. "His close-quarter combat skills were off the scale."

"A couple of my instructors learned that the hard way—apparently he's practiced various martial arts since he was a kid."

"Russian language tested out at the highest level."

"So they say . . . not really my wing of the university."

"His marks on the range were exceptional."

"He was an Olympic-level biathlon competitor."

The new director closed the file, tapped his fingers on the manila folder. It was as if Slaton was trying to convince himself. "And here we are six months later. Miller is out in the field, and the most critical mission this agency has seen years is dependent on him. I take it you intervened in his dismissal?"

"The operations we undertake in this section are demanding, and my job is to make sure the agency gets the best and most capable individuals. I agree that Miller had authority issues. But I'm also of the opinion that certain trainees are special. They have an intensity that sets them apart. Problem is, there's generally a reason for that kind of motivation, and it's not always positive. In his case, I thought he was worth the risk. If he can maintain his focus, channel his inner rage—and I think he can—he'll get results." After a pause, Stansell added, "Rumor is that you've got an operational background. Maybe you've seen somebody like him."

The two locked eyes for a long moment. Slaton was about to respond when a soft knock on the door interrupted.

A lead analyst Stansell knew, Janet Clark, peered in. "Sorry to interrupt, but I've got the information you requested on Rookie's China op."

Slaton waved her inside.

"It was as you suspected," she said. "We also discovered a second incident that could be related." She handed over two folders with hatching on the cover that denoted them as classified.

"Thanks for getting this so quickly, Janet."

"Anything else you need?"

"No, not at the moment."

She nodded to Stansell, and then bid a hasty retreat.

Slaton scanned the first file quickly. He then moved on to the second and began shaking his head.

"What is it?" Stansell asked.

Slaton set the files on his desk. "We received some fresh intelligence a couple of hours ago. It seems a wastewater plant in northern China had a major breach. There was an unexplained explosion, and a hundred thousand gallons of shit oozed down a hill."

"And how is this pertinent?"

"Rookie was paying this plant a visit last night, at roughly the time it happened. It was right before we diverted him to Russia. His instructions were to get a few effluent samples for biological analysis. A couple of test tubes—that was all we wanted."

Stansell nodded with a straight face, then eyed the second folder.

Slaton tapped it with two fingers. "And now we have this." He removed three satellite photos and spread them on his desk like a hopeful poker hand. Stansell saw high-res overheads of what looked like a major rail disaster. Two dozen cars lay strewn across a siding and smoke billowed from the flaming wreckage. In the center was a crater the size of a swimming pool.

"This happened twenty miles south of Zeya Reservoir. A munitions delivery, obviously. Half the train derailed, and twenty-five cars went up like the Fourth of July. We even got a report from Japan about seismic activity."

Stansell tried to cover his mouth, but his snickering wasn't to be stifled.

There had been a time when Slaton would have seen the humor. Being in the driver's seat, however, gave one a different perspective.

For the first time he understood what he had long been putting his own minders through.

Stansell shrugged, and said, "Like I told you . . . delicacy is not in his skill set."

TWENTY-TWO

Westbrook landed at Vandenberg Space Force Base at eleven that night. He was the only passenger on a sleek C-37B, the Air Force's version of the Gulfstream 550. It was hands-down the best ride he'd ever had as a passenger.

He peered through the oval side window and took in the modest airfield. Vandenburg, even in the days when it had been run by the Air Force, had always been geared to space flight, and the single runway and small air operations building emphasized that point. The jet taxied straight to the transient ramp in front of base operations and its engines began spooling down.

He thanked the crew for a smooth and expeditious ride, and then stepped down to the tarmac to find a car waiting. It was a generic "blue steely" staff car, and would hardly be secretive off base, but he had only one stop outside the main gate, and dealing with the base motor pool was simpler than acquiring a rental car.

A staff sergeant wearing OCP camo stood waiting at the passenger door.

"Welcome to Vandenberg, Colonel," she said as he approached, adding a sharp salute.

Westbrook returned it, and said, "Thanks for being here."

When she reached for the rear door handle, he said, "That won't be necessary. I'll drive myself."

"But sir, my orders were to—"

"I'm amending your orders," Westbrook said evenly.

The sergeant relented, and two minutes later he had the fob for the car, a key card for base VIP quarters, and a morning appointment with the commander of the 2nd Space Launch Squadron.

The sergeant walked away to base operations, and Westbrook settled into the driver's seat. He couldn't resist one glance into the distance. Standing tall under floodlights at Launch Complex 3 was a heavy-lift Vulcan Centaur rocket. Its stillness in the black night only seemed to heighten the craft's potential for speed and power. It was the next-to-last component for setting their rescue plan into motion.

To tie down the final variable, he fired up the map on his phone, typed in an address, and set out toward town.

The road to Major Kai Benetton's apartment was like the roads outside all military bases. There were fast food restaurants, dive bars, and tawdry pawn shops. At least three used car dealerships offered quality pre-owned vehicles and easy financing. Even at ten in the evening there was enough flashing neon to do Vegas proud.

Westbrook drove at an easy speed, wanting a few minutes to re-calibrate his thoughts. On the flight from D.C., he had used the jet's comm suite to manage a complex chain of technical events—it was, after all, rocket science. The next hour would require a far more nuanced approach. It was one thing to revise a flight profile, quite another to convert a mind.

For Westbrook it was a relatively new challenge. When it came to flying airplanes, his analytic nature had always served him well. That was all about task management and spatial orientation. In recent years, however, he had advanced to command positions—his only chance to stay anywhere near a cockpit—which meant dealing less with airplanes and more with the men and women who flew them. His acuity for reading people had always been less developed than his sense for appraising airframe vibrations or the aspect of an approaching fighter. But he *was* getting better at it.

Kai Benetton was a case in point.

She had been assigned to his squadron at Edwards three years earlier, a captain straight out of test pilot school. Prior to that she had flown F-16s operationally, including a number of deployments to hot spots. She had fit into the test squadron well and flown a number of experimental jets. Then Westbrook had given Kai her big break, selecting her as one of two project pilots for the top secret program known as Star Chaser.

And that was what brought him here today.

The car's navigation display showed his route coming to an end. Benetton had been rotating back and forth between Vandenberg and Edwards for a year, and here she kept an off-base apartment, the usual twenty-unit infill whose salespeople were fluent in terms like "permanent change of station" and "unaccompanied tour." The complex was populated by senior enlisted personnel and junior officers, a few civilian contractors thrown into the mix.

The place seemed quiet, and he parked the car in a spot marked "Guest." Westbrook was about to get out when he saw the front door of number 16 open. Kai emerged with a man, and the two paused in a spray of light from the parking lot floods. The man was fortyish, which made him ten years her senior. Slightly built, he had a haircut so tight he appeared bald. His jeans and collared shirt looked, even from across the parking lot, a bit worn. Most curious of all—and a question no doubt fueled by Westbrook's new association with the CIA—was that the man was Asian. The two embraced as they parted, a gesture that appeared warm but not quite intimate. Not wanting to be creepy, he got out of the car and shut the door loudly.

Kai looked over as her guest was walking away. She didn't recognize Westbrook right away—during the flight, he had switched from his uniform to civvies, including an Air Force ball cap. Then Kai did a double-take, and he caught something fleeting in her expression. Embarrassment? Surprise? He still had work to do when it came to reading people.

"Hello, Kai."

"Hey, Colonel. Wasn't expecting to see you out here. Did you get fired from the Pentagon already?"

He smiled. "If only."

The two shook hands, military courtesy giving way to familiarity with neither being in uniform. He glanced obviously toward the Asian man, who was getting into an old Honda, but didn't comment, letting his silence be an invitation to explain. She didn't. She simply stood there, radiating her usual confidence.

"Like to come in?" she asked.

"Yeah, there's something we need to talk about."

The townhouse was straight out of a rental brochure, featureless furniture and neutral décor. Kai, too, would have been a perfect advertisement. She was average in height and slim, with raven black hair, green eyes, and olive skin. Her mother, Westbrook knew, was Hawaiian, her father a mix of Swiss and Italian. She was undeniably attractive, but it was Westbrook's take on her as a former commander that brought him here—Kai Benetton was one of the best, most instinctive pilots he'd ever worked with.

"I just made some tea," she said. "Get you a cup?"

"That'd be great."

She veered into a tiny kitchen and began fishing through a cupboard.

"Everyone here getting fired up?" he asked idly.

"T-minus three days," she said. "I'm set to head back to Edwards after the flight, and then a week in Palmdale to go over the numbers with the engineers." She paused long enough to give him a suspicious look. "But you already know that."

He cocked his head, admitting that he did.

She poured the tea into a unit mug—the squadron he'd commanded at Edwards—and handed it to him along with a spoon and a container of honey. The girl had a memory like a steel trap.

"I only wish I was taking this one up," she said.

The fifth, and final, Star Chaser prototype was scheduled for an unmanned mission in three days. The previous three flights had been manned after an initial unmanned flight. This last mission would be unmanned and take the spaceplane to its design limits. After landing at Edwards, the airframe was set to be transported to a hangar at the Skunk Works in Palmdale, California, put on a massive test jig, and pressed and pulled and heated until various parts of the airframe failed. Inglorious as it was, destructive testing was a normal part of any test program.

"I'm gonna miss her," she said, taking a seat at a tiny table in the eat-in nook. "Stinks that the last one has to be crushed."

Westbrook sat down across from her. "You and I fall in love with these machines, but you know how the engineers look at it—it's all about the data." He stirred some honey into his tea and took a long sip. "Turns out, though, there's been a change to the schedule."

She regarded him curiously. "Don't tell me they're moving the timeline right again."

"Actually, this time it's moving left. And it gets better."

Her eyes lit up. "Another *manned* flight? I get to take her up again?"

"Yes . . . but there's one big catch."

Her excitement veered to caution. "I'm getting an odd vibe here."

"Let me start from the beginning. A few weeks ago, I was reassigned on a temporary basis from the Pentagon to another government agency. Before I say more, understand that everything I'm about to tell you is classified at the highest level."

"Right, secret squirrel."

"Kai, when I say 'highest level' . . . I'm talking commander in chief."

This got her attention. "Okay . . . noted."

"Star Chaser is going operational."

"Operational?"

"I've been working with the CIA. They were recently approached by a Russian military officer who wants to defect. I think you'd recognize his name."

"A Russian officer that I would know? I've never even been to—"

"Colonel Maksim Primakov."

Crinkles formed at the corners of her eyes. "He's a legend in their test community."

"He is."

"And wants to *defect*?"

"Actually, he already has—or at least he tried to. He was going for a blaze of glory, trying to reach Japan in an experimental jet called Vektor."

"Vektor? So it really does exist."

"The rumors are true."

"Hang on—you've gone all past tense here. Are you saying something went wrong?"

Westbrook filled in the blanks.

"Wow. He actually put Vektor down on a frozen lake?"

"Smack in the middle of Siberia."

"Too bad. I would have loved to have gotten a chance to fly her."

"Me too. As far as the malfunction goes, you and I have seen it before . . . little glitches that happen at the worst possible time."

"This is all very interesting, but what's the connection to me and Star Chaser?"

"We won't get our hands on Vektor, but the jet is mostly intact. Primakov is at the crash site, in the middle of nowhere, and he's injured. But he still wants to defect."

She was silent, trying to keep up.

"I was at the White House yesterday, Kai. The president wants to get Primakov out. The first order of business is to reach him before he freezes to death." He paused there.

She looked toward the front window, which faced the distant launch complex. Then she looked back at him. "Seriously?"

"Major, we have a lot to talk about . . ."

TWENTY-THREE

The lodge stood precipitously above a swale, as if contemplating a leap into the forest from which its timbers had come. By the time Tru reached it, night was taking hold. The hills were going to shadow, the cold settling like a great slab.

He paused a hundred meters away, hidden in the dense woods, and absorbed the big picture. This was definitely some kind of community gathering place. He had seen two cars depart minutes earlier, but a half dozen remained outside. He discerned movement behind various windows, vague silhouettes masked by sheer curtains; a steady trail of smoke clawed up from the eastern chimney. Tru would rather have waited until the place was unoccupied, but that might take hours. It was time he didn't have.

After ten minutes of watching, he began to move.

The wind funneled down through the hills, and he covered the final fifty meters through sheets of swirling snow. He circled clockwise to the backside of the lodge, wanting a complete picture of the place in his head before venturing inside. Whereas the front side was dominated by a parking area and a busy façade of doors and windows, the back was simpler. There were two doors, one of which connected to a brick path that led to a stacked-stone fire pit. In summer, there would probably be comfortable chairs circled around a roaring fire, but in mid-January the pit was encrusted in ice and snow.

Tru focused on the western door in back, outside of which was his reason for coming—a beaten ski rack standing crookedly next to the landing. There were presently no skis in the rack, but he expected to find a good selection inside.

The building was probably fifty years old, and in a village where everyone knew everyone, he doubted there would be much security. He made his way silently to the door and paused outside. There were no deadbolts, no cameras in the rafters. A brief test of the levered handle verified that it wasn't locked. There wasn't a window through which he could see the room beyond, so Tru paused to listen. He heard raucous conversation from the far side of the lodge, where the chimney was working hard. A party was going strong, and with night falling he doubted anyone would be gearing up to go skiing.

After a full two minutes he was satisfied.

He dropped the door handle, eased inside, and was instantly enveloped by warm air. His eyes adjusted to the light, and Tru immediately saw two things of note. The first was two rows of doorless storage closets racked with ski gear. The second was a lanky young man, in his late teens, working on a pair of ski boots.

The kid looked up, more surprise than concern in his expression, and before he could say anything Tru took the initiative. "Shitty weather," he said. One of the first things he had learned during a brush-up on his Russian at ILI, the Intelligence Language Institute, was that the best way to fit in like a native in most cultures was to start cussing.

A quintessential Slavic shrug. "The usual."

"I'm looking for Ivan." Tru figured any place like this in Russia would have at least one regular by that name.

The kid, who had pasty skin and disheveled hair, said, "Which Ivan?"

Tru cursed inwardly. He had thought far enough ahead to prepare a contingency opener, but hadn't taken it beyond one line. "You know, the old guy."

The kid, who likely knew everyone in town near his own age—a category that would include Tru—regarded him skeptically. Then teen apathy took hold.

"Petrovic isn't here."

"Figures. Which locker is his?"

The kid's eyes gave it away, somewhere near the far end of the row. "Who are you?" he asked.

"I'm his nephew."

"Didn't know he had one," said the kid, going back to the boot.

"I haven't been here since I was a kid." He meandered toward the end of the row of lockers, his brain churning over how to proceed. Then he got a massive break. Responding to a shout from down the hall, the kid disappeared.

Tru immediately went to work. The second locker from the end turned out to be Petrovic's, his initials scrawled on the lip of the high shelf. Unfortunately, I. P.'s boots were at least four sizes too small.

Not knowing when the kid would be back, or whether he might mention the arrival of Ivan Petrovic's nephew to others, he decided speed was his best ally. With a quick survey of the other lockers, he grabbed a set of boots, skis, and poles that looked like an approximate fit. He then rearranged other gear to cover the empty spots. It wouldn't hold up to a close inspection but might buy him a few extra minutes.

Moments later, Tru was out the door and into the night.

Strelkov spent the entire afternoon in the administration building. Reports from the field were still arriving, but now with less frequency. And, correspondingly, less hope. No trace had been found of either Vektor or his son-in-law. No brush fires had been seen, no emergency beacon heard, nor had any suspicious events been reported by locals. It was as if Vektor and its pilot had simply vanished from the face of the earth.

If only it could be so, Strelkov thought.

With the onset of evening, his mood declined precipitously. He walked outside into the bracing night air and ambled toward the big hangar. There was no one in sight, which made perfect sense—the airfield's reason for being had gone missing. To one side of the hangar, he noticed a tendril of smoke rising. He rounded a corner and saw that it was coming from a half-cut oil drum behind a shed. There was a small utility truck beneath the shed, its hood propped open. Engine parts were scattered on a nearby bench. The deductions were simple enough to make. The base mechanic worked outside, and he maintained a fire in the barrel to stay warm. He would be in the barracks now, finished for the night.

Strelkov went to the work bench, picked up a crowbar, and carried it to the barrel. He prodded the embers to life, and as they glowed brighter, he took the letter from his pocket. With its corners fluttering in the breeze, it seemed thin and inconsequential. Yet the weight of what it contained portended nothing short of doom. He dropped it into the fire, watched it burn with fleeting satisfaction.

The thoughts searing through his head were far more intense.

What had become of Maksim? Vektor had been missing for twenty-four hours now, yet no sign of a crash had been found. Strelkov saw contradictions everywhere, yet the letter raised a possibility he could no longer ignore.

Fuck you, Viktor.

He and Maksim rarely saw eye-to-eye on anything. They were both too ambitious, too ruthless in their pursuits. For years they had gone through the motions of civility, more to advance their respective careers than to hold a doomed marriage together. Oksana and Maksim had long ago diverged, yet the final wedge in their relationship was the most damning. They had rarely seen eye to eye when it came to raising their only child, Nikolas. They argued over which academies he should attend and how his career should progress. Then their discord went nuclear in the face of crisis. The war in Ukraine had shattered many families, but none more thoroughly than theirs.

Maksim and Oksana rarely spoke anymore, both having given up, but divorce was off the table in the name of professional advancement. Strelkov, for his part, maintained cursory contact with his son-in-law. The odd letter, an occasional text message. He went through the motions with care—even general officers of the GRU were subject to surveillance. He viewed this continued contact as a precautionary measure, keeping a distant eye on a man who could potentially bring embarrassment to the family.

But this? Could he really have gone to such an extreme?

The last corners of the letter curled to ash, becoming one with the embers.

Strelkov's phone trilled. He removed a glove, pulled the phone from his pocket, and saw a message from GRU headquarters—more specifically, from a trusted underling to whom he'd given an assignment hours earlier.

Strelkov winced as he read the reply: It appears you were correct, boss. See attached photos.

He opened a file and saw three grayscale photographs from various surveillance cameras. His son-in-law was in each of them. Maksim in the company of a middle-aged woman at a café, and then two shots of the pair walking together. A second message made the disaster complete: Woman identified as U.S. embassy employee, confirmed CIA ties.

Strelkov sighed mightily. He had ordered the search immediately after seeing the letter. As far as he knew, Maksim had not been the subject of any official watch order. Even so, the surveillance state that was modern Russia captured voluminous amounts of raw data. So dense was the pixelated forest, it often took serious digging to uncover relevant nuggets. The GRU were the best at such mining, and few in the agency were as adept at as Strelkov's own minions. His instructions had been to filter the data with respect to three parameters: a lookback period of six months, facial recognition for known American spies, and finally his son-in-law's profile. And how quickly the results had come. How easily. *I only knew where to look.*

He immediately sent a reply, ordering that the information be held in strictest secrecy. His order was acknowledged immediately, and Strelkov pocketed the phone.

For all the animosity in his relationship with Maksim, for all the pain and mistrust, the possibility of a defection had never crossed Strelkov's mind. But now, surely, there could be no doubt. His initial reaction of incredulity slowly gave way. His son-in-law had always been a patriot, committed to Mother Russia, yet that very notion—the idea of a pure and good homeland—had been bastardized by the regime. Being a creature of that political biome himself, Strelkov knew how such a traitorous act would affect his own career. He would become that morbid punchline he and his senior brethren at the GRU often joked about over Tennessee bourbon and Cuban cigars: a man in search of a balcony.

He pushed away his miserable musings and focused on damage control. Maksim's intentions seemed clear, but how did that square with the current situation? Standing next to the dying embers, Strelkov thought about it long and hard.

Three scenarios came to mind.

First was that Maksim had crashed while trying to defect, both he and the aircraft lost somewhere east of Skovorna—the direction of the nearest border. The second, and most damning, possibility was that Maksim had successfully defected. Yet Strelkov had heard nothing about this through GRU channels, and by now there would surely have been rumblings of a Russian pilot arriving at an air base in Japan or South Korea with a top secret fighter. In either of these cases, there was little to be done. If Maksim had died in a crash, Strelkov could likely guide things to an uneventful end. On the other hand, if Maksim was standing in a hangar in Japan, giving the Americans a tour of Vektor, Strelkov was done for. In that case, Maksim would go out of his way to implicate Strelkov. *Fuck you, Viktor.* And if that was how it played out, Strelkov would end up in the same GRU basement where he himself had sent so many prisoners, no way out beyond a single bullet.

The third possibility, however, a hybrid of the other outcomes, required more thought. Rather disconcertingly, it fit all the known facts. Perhaps Maksim *had* tried to defect, but something had gone wrong. Maybe the airplane had suffered a malfunction and crashed. If so, it would have happened somewhere between the working area and the Pacific coast.

And if Maksim *was* still alive but stranded in the wilderness?

Strelkov had a gift for prioritizing, for extracting what was relevant in complex situations, and every self-serving fiber of his being implored one response: if Maksim Primakov was alive, and still in Russia, Strelkov had to be the first to reach him.

He poked the ashes one last time with the crowbar. The information he possessed was known to no one else. But to leverage that advantage he was going to need help.

It was time to make some very important phone calls.

TWENTY-FOUR

"Zeya Reservoir?" Kai said, looking at a map on her tablet computer. "How far is that?"

"Five thousand two hundred miles as the crow flies," Westbrook replied. "But then, crows don't make orbital profiles."

"Star Chaser's longest mission to date was less than half that."

"It was designed to reach any point on earth. All we need is the right rocket and a suitable payload."

"And putting down there? You realize I've only flown Star Chaser once, and on that occasion, I had ten miles of dry lakebed at Edwards to work with."

"You only used two miles."

"But on ice?"

"Ice is smoother than a lakebed . . . firmer. Braking might be an issue, but your touchdown zone is fifteen miles long. And we already know the ice can support a jet that weighs four times as much as Star Chaser."

"What about—"

"Kai, listen . . . there's a lot to work out. As we speak, Star Chaser is on the pad and being prepped. The payload is you, one other person, and a small amount of equipment. This is what the system was built to do, and you can prove its operational usefulness. If you do, I'm betting the program will be continued. On the other hand, I won't downplay the risk. You are effectively going behind enemy lines, and if things go south, we could be facing the biggest crisis since Francis Gary Powers was shot down in his U-2. I know it's a lot to think about, and I hate putting you on the spot, but I have to have an answer . . . are you up for it?"

She paused to think about it. "If I say no, it goes to Jack?"

Westbrook straightened and rubbed the back of his neck. Jack Stewart, a civilian test pilot employed by Star Chaser's manufacturer, was the only other pilot to have flown the prototype—he'd taken up the second and fourth missions. "I'm afraid Jack is DNIF," he said, Air Force jargon for duty not to include flying. "He broke a collarbone a few days ago, mountain biking. On top of that, he's technically a civilian—although I suspect he would have jumped at the chance. Honestly, Kai, you would have been my first choice anyway."

"So if I don't go, this mission doesn't happen?"

"We don't have the time to get another pilot up to speed."

"And the rescue of Primakov would be off?"

"We'd need a Plan C, and right now there isn't one."

She stood and paced a tiny orbit in the kitchen. "It's not exactly my department, but couldn't aiming Star Chaser at Russia set off a nuclear war?"

"We've thought about that. Russian satellites will register the launch, no doubt about it—that's what they're tuned to do. But this is Vandenburg, not a missile silo in Montana. There's already a mission on the books we can sub into, a civilian launch the Russians know about. It won't look out of the ordinary."

"What about the other end, when Star Chaser reenters the atmosphere over Russia? Might they not mistake me for a thermonuclear warhead?"

"Your trajectory and reentry profile will be completely different, and they don't track incomings well at low altitude. Aside from that, your projected point of impact is in one of the most sparsely populated areas on earth."

"I don't like that word—impact." Westbrook didn't laugh, and she moved on. "Any thoughts on who would come with me?"

"I'm thinking a mechanic. We need to exploit what's left of Vektor, remove a few boxes and extract samples of its coatings. I was thinking maybe Sergeant Diaz."

Kai grinned. "Yeah, Q would be perfect." Qualario Diaz was a master sergeant at Edwards, and something of a legend on base.

She asked, "What happens to Star Chaser?"

"It's a one-time-use platform, Kai. The obvious solution is to sink it in the lake."

She winced.

"Look, our engineers were going to crush it anyway on the test rig. I've ordered it stripped down for the launch, all classified systems removed. The basic airframe won't give the Russians much they don't already have."

"Okay, let's say all this works and we manage to reach Primakov. How do we get back out?"

"We're working on that."

Her green eyes held him.

"We will get you out, you have my word."

She looked distractedly out the front window. As she contemplated what he was asking of her, Westbrook noticed a small booklet on the nearby counter. On the front was a picture of an Asian man—not the one he'd seen her with but cut from the same cloth. What the booklet was about he couldn't say since it was scripted in Chinese.

She turned around and saw him staring at it.

"Who was the guy I saw leaving?" he asked.

"A friend."

"Didn't look like your type."

"Oh, he very much is."

He tried to read her but saw nothing beyond squadron-level humor. Even so, he couldn't let it go. "Is it something we need to discuss?"

"No."

A freighted silence ensued.

She said, "Colonel, you're asking me to ride a rocket halfway around the world, penetrate Russian airspace in an experimental spaceplane, and then land it on a frozen lake in the dead of winter."

"Yeah, that about sums it up."

"If I agree to do all that, I'll be relying on you to come up with a way to get me out."

"That's right."

"Then I need you to trust me."

Westbrook grinned. "Fair enough." He stood and said, "So does that mean you're in, Major?"

After a humorless laugh, Kai said, "I guess you've got your girl."

TWENTY-FIVE

Tru was making excellent time along the northbound road, the snow conditions being ideal for speed.

Night had fallen, but the darkness wouldn't be absolute for another hour. A rising three-quarter moon helped with illumination, highlighting rocks and gravel runoff channels. As long as cloud cover didn't intervene, he would easily have enough light to keep going.

He hadn't encountered any vehicles for the last thirty minutes. The one set of headlights he'd seen had forced him into the woods. Concealed behind a patch of ice-covered brambles, he watched a delivery truck pass harmlessly in the direction of Zeya. As soon as the truck was out of sight, he'd set back out.

The gear he'd stolen fit reasonably well, although he had to stop to make adjustments soon after leaving the lodge. Tru was sure an alarm had been raised there. The kid would have noticed the missing equipment, not to mention a missing stranger who had come looking for Ivan Petrovic. He would report the situation to whoever was in charge, but it would likely stall there. As things stood, one set of missing ski gear was closer to a curiosity than a crime, and it was nothing that would prompt a manhunt on a cold winter night. Even so, he kept a keen eye on the road behind him. He had done his best to obfuscate his tracks out of the village, but there was no hiding the twins trails he was leaving along the road now. New snow and wind would eventually blot them out, although that might take days.

He worked into a rhythm, his heart rate rising over gently undulating terrain. During his run to make the Olympic team, when he had been in peak condition and used the best equipment, Tru could average over fifteen miles an hour. He hadn't skied competitively in years, but he was still in good shape, notwithstanding a few dings from his altercation on the freight car. And unlike a biathlon course, he didn't have to stop repeatedly to take aim at fifty-meter targets.

Tru "swung through the gears" as the terrain changed, varying his technique for different gradients. The skis he had stolen were decent, if a bit dated, and thankfully the owner had applied a fresh coat of wax. His form gradually became smoother, more familiar, and it seemed almost strange not to have a bolt-action .22 rifle slung over his shoulder. It was an odd dichotomy. Never in his competitive years would Tru have imagined being where he was now: skiing through the hills of Siberia without a gun. And wishing very much that he had one.

"What's the per diem rate for temporary duty in Siberia?" asked Master Sergeant Qualario Diaz.

"You gonna file for an advance?" Kai asked.

"Maybe finance keeps rubles on hand."

"Doubtful. Truth is, where we're going, I don't think we'll be spending a lot of cash."

They had met in a staging building near Launch Complex 3. Westbrook had told them to expect launch sometime in the next twelve hours, assuming the president gave the final green light. It was a first for everyone to have flight approval coming straight from the White House.

Diaz was sorting through a toolbox. He extracted an adjustable wrench and set it in a modest pile of tools. Weight had to be kept to a minimum, and he'd been allotted twenty pounds for equipment.

Kai was glad Diaz had been chosen for the mission. There were countless unknowns in what they were attempting, and to undertake it with a stranger would only have hiked the stress level. A slightly built Hispanic man, Diaz was a first-generation immigrant, his family having come from Colombia. He had served as crew chief on a number of the aircraft Kai had flown at Edwards, and she'd always liked working with him. Not only was he a first-rate mechanic, but he had a solid sense of humor—something they would need in the coming days.

"So," she said, "they offered this to you on a volunteer basis, right?"

"Yeah, but Colonel Westbrook was pretty slim on details. He asked if I wanted to go for a ride on Star Chaser—operational mission support, he called it. He waited until I said yes, then told me the part about crash-landing on a frozen lake in Russia."

"You could still change your mind."

"The way I see it, not many mechanics get a chance to earn their astronaut wings."

"I don't think we're going quite high enough for that—not unless our trajectory goes haywire and we sling out toward the sun."

Diaz gave her a severe look.

"Sorry, couldn't resist. Everything will be fine." A text message from Westbrook blinked to her phone. Kai saw a green traffic light emoji and a time.

She pocketed her phone. "Better pick up the pace, Sergeant, the countdown has commenced. We're at T-minus eight hours."

TWENTY-SIX

After ninety minutes, Tru stopped to rest. His heart rate settled as he took a long hit from his water bottle. He rolled his shoulder a few times; it was still sore. More water, then a check of his navigation screen. He had forty miles to go.

He was about to pocket the handset when he noticed a new message. He tapped it open and read: Asset to be rescued is injured survivor of air crash. Maksim Primakov, Russian Air Force colonel. Expect arrival of support team within ten hours. Extraction details to follow.

His first thought was that Langley was extremely confident in the security of their comm. His second, as was becoming a habit, was to decipher what was left unsaid in the message. Tru was closing in on Talon, and Langley knew it—his comm device regularly transmitted his position. So now they were giving him more. He supposed they hadn't wanted to provide details earlier in case he'd been apprehended en route, and subsequently interrogated. It made sense, in a cynical way. But then, he had signed up for a cynical business.

His next thought was even more jaded. *I'm putting my ass on the line to save a Russian officer?*

He looked out into the frigid wilds. There was no runway, no civilization anywhere near the coordinates he'd been given. How could anyone survive a crash out here? How on earth would they get out? He figured he would find out soon enough. He powered down the handset and secured it in an inside pocket—better for keeping the battery warm.

He set back out into the darkness, pushing hard and feeling strong. The old familiar burn gripped his legs. He paused at regular intervals, downing water and snacking on the energy bars from the coffee shop. He never stopped for long. The temperature was well below the freezing point, and he needed to keep his muscles from getting tight.

He checked his map periodically, and it was nearly midnight when he reached the closest tangential point to his target. Somewhere in the nearby woods was an injured Russian officer, codenamed Talon. And Tru was his first responder.

It sounded simple.

But what complications awaited?

He was carrying almost no gear. Did Talon have shelter, basic rations? In conditions like this, hypothermia could kill quickly. He wondered what the Russians knew about the situation. Were they also looking for this guy? Hopefully Colonel Primakov could fill him in, provide a better idea of what they were up against.

The snow in the woods looked no deeper than what was along the road. As long as the visibility held, he estimated he would reach Talon within the hour.

Tru stepped off the gravel siding and pushed into the timber.

Westbrook stood by a whiteboard in the small conference room near Launch Complex 3. PowerPoint had its place, but sometimes simpler was better. "The launch is set for 1500 Local. We've come up with an orbital profile that will put Star Chaser on Zeya Reservoir in two hours and nineteen minutes. That'll be late morning there, which gives you a daytime landing."

Kai and Sergeant Diaz sat looking at the board. The colonel's amateurish artwork looked like something a grade school science teacher might have scrawled in front of a class: a big blue dry-erase circle for earth, and a red line curving up and around to the far side.

"Destination weather?" Kai asked.

Westbrook shuffled through a pile of printouts on the central table. "Latest is for a solid overcast deck at ten thousand feet, clear below that."

"I'm not going to see the landing zone until ten thousand? You *do* realize how steep the approach angle is? That gives me less than a minute to pick my spot and put her down—and there are no go-arounds in a glider."

"I understand that. You and I plotted a solid reference point, and Star Chaser's nav-track error has been minimal on every previous mission."

She shook her head. "It was tight on the previous flights, but those were all here in the States with perfect GPS coverage. Where we're going the signals might not be as reliable."

"If it was up to me, I'd wait for better weather, but what we have is doable—and it's an operational necessity."

"Says who?"

"President Cleveland."

Kai had no response for that.

"We suspect Primakov has a broken leg, so we're sending in some first aid gear."

"Who's going to play doctor?" asked Diaz.

"I've been told the CIA asset sent to make contact is trained in combat medicine."

"Has he reached Primakov yet?"

"Not that I've heard."

Kai said, "If he gets there in time, I'd like a condition report on the lake surface. And maybe an amateur weather report. I'll only have one shot at this, and the last thing we need is to be surprised by ice fog on the reservoir."

"Ice fog?" Diaz repeated.

"Kai," Westbrook said, "the chances of that are remote."

"True, but Q has a right to know what he's getting into." She looked at Diaz, and said, "By the time we reach the base of this forecast cloud layer, we're committed. If I can't see the ground, we will have no way to land."

Diaz nodded pensively. "So, you're saying our lives depend on a weather forecast . . . for the weather halfway around the world."

"Pretty much."

His dark eyes jumped back and forth between the two officers. Then he smiled. "Sounds like a great plan!"

Kai could only smile back.

Diaz was cleared off to get fitted for the spacesuit he would have to wear.

As Kai concentrated on mission planning, Westbrook found himself staring at the whiteboard. He suddenly had a bad feeling about the mission. Kai, like every test pilot he'd ever known, was hardwired to mission success. But he had been the one to suggest using Star Chaser. On paper it seemed a logical, if untested, option. Now the risks were mounting, and two people were about to put their lives on the line. It was . . . sobering.

Kai got up. "I want to go fly the profile on the visual trainer."

As she approached the door, Westbrook said, "Kai . . . wait."

She paused. "What's up?"

He nodded toward the door that Diaz had just gone through. Understanding, she looked outside. "He's gone."

He sent the red marker rolling across the table. "You made some good points, and it got me thinking. The risks in this mission . . . maybe they're not acceptable."

Her green eyes remained level, but she said nothing.

"You and I are wired a certain way, Kai. We're operationally oriented. Every flight, every mission, is about pressing the envelope, giving new operational capabilities. When the powers that be in D.C. said they needed a way to get Primakov out, I saw a rare opportunity to take a program live. To put a cutting-edge platform to good use."

"And now you're having doubts."

"I feel like I've put you in a position where you can't say no. I shouldn't have done that."

"But if I don't go, we scrub. You'd take serious heat for that. *Presidential* heat."

"I can deal with it."

She leaned on the doorjamb, thinking about it. "I appreciate your concern, boss, but I'm good to go. I think Diaz is too. And for what it's worth . . . I'm only doing what you would if you were in my flight boots." She turned toward the hall and was gone.

TWENTY-SEVEN

Primakov thought he was hallucinating. He could have sworn he'd heard someone call his name. He attempted to sit up, but it was hopeless. His body seemed frozen in place.

He had made it through the day, forcing himself to sip water and eat his meager rations. But now, with the onset of nightfall, he was shivering uncontrollably. The temperature had dropped precipitously, and the cold was sapping his strength, fogging his brain.

It had not yet broken his resolve.

He pried his eyes open but, disconcertingly, darkness persisted. He looked up, hoping to see a few stars, some confirmation that he was still alive. He blinked and distinguished the vague outlines of the forest. And then . . . something. An ill-defined figure stalking through the trees. Its movement was slow and wary, and he thought it might be an animal of some kind. Then, all at once, a human shape materialized.

A spike of adrenaline shot up his spine, but he remained perfectly still. Like few men on earth, Maksim Primakov understood the importance of staying calm in the face of danger. Somewhere in his mental haze, he realized he needed a weapon. His left hand blindly groped the ground beside him. He felt the rotted stick he'd used earlier and he gripped it firmly. It was useless as a club, but if he could jab his adversary in the face, he might find an eye. It was feeble and desperate, but he wasn't going to give up without a fight.

He remained motionless, his eyes mere slits. The figure came nearer and paused in front of him. Something metallic clattered to the ground—ski poles?—and the figure bent down in front of him. A light shined in his eyes, blinding Primakov. He lashed out, aiming the stick where the man's face had been moments earlier.

The motion didn't go far.

His wrist was seized in a viselike grip. Primakov struggled to get free, but as he writhed something shifted and a bolt of pain shot through his broken leg.

"Aggh!" he grunted, dropping the stick reflexively.

The intruder did nothing to press his advantage. The man let go of his wrist, and said in Russian, "It's a pleasure to meet you, Colonel Primakov."

To army bean counters in Moscow, who could invariably recite organizational charts by memory, GRU Spetsgruppa V was a subsidiary of the Main Directorate of the General Staff of the Armed Forces of the Russian Federation. To the soldiers who were temporarily hosting the unit—a middling infantry battalion on the outskirts of Irkutsk, on the northern shores of Lake Baikal—the visiting detachment was a crack Spetznaz squad.

The truth was far more nuanced.

The rise, and disastrous fall, of Yevgeny Prigozhin had brought a deep reckoning among the nation's senior military officers. The idea that a private military company had gathered such influence that it could challenge the nation's command structure was viewed with alarm, if not outright fear. Scores of fifty-something generals, a mostly soft and satisfied bunch whose destinies had long been determined by one man in the Kremlin, for the first time faced threats from outside the old-boy network.

There could never be true fidelity in the federation, reflecting a president who governed with the ruthlessness of a mob boss. And while Prigozhin's uprising had ultimately been crushed, it was a wake-up call for those near the top.

After considerable handwringing, a handful of senior officers began quiet campaigns to carve out combat units that were, for lack of a better term, personally loyal. It was easier than many expected. To begin, the state was footing the bill. With a few strokes of a pen, an existing unit could be reallocated to a new command on the organizational chart. More ominously, the debacle in Ukraine had brought a distinct thinning in the army's junior officer ranks. Taking the place of professional soldiers was a cast of hardened mercenaries and opportunistic prisoners, men whose loyalty could be had for a price. In essence, all one needed to create a private army was a bit of off-the-books funding and the right connections, and no flag-grade officer worth his salt lacked for either.

And few were so richly endowed as General Viktor Strelkov.

Which was how, in those early morning hours, a detachment of his personal security force stood stamping their feet in the cold. The squad of sixteen men milled about loosely inside an empty hangar. Dirty and smelly, the place had all the ambiance of a grease pit. If there was a heater it wasn't working, and at that moment it hardly mattered—the doors of the hangar were wide open. Outside, three Mi-24 Hind F helicopters squatted on the tarmac primed for launch.

The unit was a reapportioned element of Vega Group, or more formally, GRU Spetsgruppa V. A few of the team, including their commander, a captain, had risen through the regular army, but most had more checkered pasts. The war in Ukraine had decimated even the most elite Special Forces groups, the price of a relentless operational tempo in a seemingly endless conflict. Once a destination for the finest operators in Russia, Vega Group had been forced to dig deeper for talent.

Many of the new men were castoffs from Wagner Group, refugees of the purge that followed the attempted mutiny. Thousands of hardened mercenaries, caught up in the reorganization, had found themselves looking for jobs. Vega Group, desperate for replacements after suffering heavy casualties in the "special military operation," was a natural landing spot.

Some GRU commanders argued that the ex-Wagner mercenaries lacked the necessary discipline for units like Vega. Others, however, warmed to the idea. Lawlessness in the military had become increasingly accepted, even encouraged on the front lines. Free from any code of conduct or legal oversight, civilians could be terrorized freely and conscripts shot in the back as a means of motivating others. This was the Russian way, and it wasn't anything new. The Russian Revolution, World War II, Afghanistan, Chechnya. Brutality was a mere tactical advantage to be leveraged, a force multiplier. And who better to bring it to units like Vega than a contingent of Wagner castoffs who'd spent most of their adult lives thieving, raping, and pillaging with impunity.

Captain 1st Rank Oleg Volkov took stock of his men. The mood was loose, everyone smiling and joking, and piles of gear were scattered haphazardly on the cement floor. For veterans of Ukraine, Syria, and Africa, the prospect of flying around Siberia for a few days to search for a downed pilot was something near a vacation.

The call from Strelkov this morning *had* been a surprise, and not only to Volkov. His men looked sleepy, and a few were marginally drunk. One had a crotchless woman's thong hanging from his ruck like a trophy. Volkov took issue with none of it—at least, not yet. This was a zero-notice call-up, and they'd gotten back from Africa only a few days ago. There, over the course of a month, they had delivered nine cases of rocket propelled grenades, trained a local militia how to use them, and then returned to Irkutsk with a significant cache of uncut diamonds.

Wagner might have gone into the shredder organizationally, but its business model was alive and well. With Strelkov's blessing, the unit had split the diamonds evenly—half for the general, half for the team. Such compensation packages were standard in Russia's private armies, and his men wouldn't have it any other way. They thrived on unfixed incomes, enduring privation for months and then enjoying the plunder afterward. On arriving in Irkutsk, the party had begun, and for three days his men had been doing what soldiers did after any trying deployment. Drinking, whoring, sleeping . . . rinse and repeat.

Volkov checked his watch. It was almost time. On a folding table he saw the coffee urn he'd ordered, and it looked to have been hit hard. By the time they landed at Skovorna Air Base, five hours from now, everyone would be ready.

He was about to give the command to board the helos when, through the open hangar door, he noticed a man out on the flight line. Having appeared out of nowhere, he stood completely still, a fearsome wind snapping the sleeves of his parka. Against another backdrop, he might have been waiting for a bus on a cold Moscow night. He was tall and powerfully built, with severely weathered features. His wild black hair and beard looked as though they'd never been groomed. Everything about the man exuded strength—not the kind built in a gym or grown with chemicals, but the kind sourced from a thousand generations of inbreeding.

Volkov recognized the man, having worked with him once before at the behest of the general. That mission had been a hunt through the wilds of Kamchatka for an army deserter—no run-of-the-mill teenager, but the son of a now-disgraced foreign minister. Volkov's men had eventually captured the young man, but it was Tarkhan, the Siberian Cossack, who had tracked him down.

The question of why he was here was perturbing, but there was little Volkov could do about it.

He walked out onto the tarmac and stopped directly in front of him. Tarkhan was just as he remembered. Brickhouse shoulders, hands like anvils. The only thing new was the ice clinging to his mustache. Neither made an attempt to shake hands.

"You are coming with us," the captain said, not inflecting it as a question.

"Those are my orders," the Cossack replied in the voice Volkov remembered—a voice that did to words what cement mixers did to rocks.

"I find myself wondering why. You are a tracker. This pilot we are looking for isn't running from anyone. If he is alive, he will want to be found."

The Cossack said nothing, and Volkov wondered if the man's orders were different from his own. The general had hinted this would be a special mission . . . a secretive mission. The fact that Tarkhan had been brought in as well emphasized the point.

"You will ride on the last helo," the captain said, pointing to the rightmost aircraft.

Without so much as a nod, Tarkhan turned and headed for the chopper. Watching him go, Volkov was struck by something he'd noticed before—the Cossack moved with a slight limp, some ancient misfortune never quite resolved. In spite of it, his stride was unerringly constant, the human equivalent of a crooked metronome. He had encountered countless dangerous men in his day, an inevitable consequence of fighting the shadow wars. The Cossack, however, was something else.

Not deadly. Not frightening.

He was . . . inevitable.

TWENTY-EIGHT

In survival situations, the most important factor is always the will to survive. Maksim Primakov, thankfully, was as stubborn as they came.

For the best part of an hour Tru prioritized his tasks. Primakov was clearly suffering from hypothermia, fading in and out of consciousness, which meant providing warmth was critical. He had found the Russian propped against a snowbank near the jet, a dangerously exposed position with no protection from the wind. A fire was mandatory, but again, building one in the open was a nonstarter since it would be easily spotted. The only option was to move his patient into the nearby forest.

Having carried in almost no gear, he was thankful for the survival kit from the ejection seat. He used the small machete and paracord to create a makeshift sled from tree branches, and was able to drag Primakov into the woods with minimal stress on his broken leg. When he began building a fire Primakov objected, fearful it would highlight their position. Tru argued that their position wouldn't matter if he died from hypothermia. He feathered up a pyramid of kindling and retrieved the matches from the survival kit. The match hissed and caught on the first strike, its tiny flame cutting the darkness like hope itself. Once the fire was burning steadily, Tru began melting snow for fresh water in a small tin cup from the survival kit.

He gave Primakov one of his last power bars, small pieces at intervals, and regretted not buying more. Soon the warmth and food took hold, and the colonel began to stabilize. He seemed more coherent, his gaze steadier and his voice clearer.

Tru's attention inevitably went to the big jet. Resting precariously at the edge of the ice-clad lake, it looked hopelessly out of place—like an eighteen-wheeler on a sandbar at sea. The agency had never told him how Talon had ended up in such a remote corner of Siberia. Of all the possibilities, this had never come to mind—a sleek fighter skidding to a landing in the frozen wilderness.

"Nice jet," he said in English. Tru had so far addressed Primakov exclusively in Russian. It was time to test his patient's language skills.

"She is called Vektor," he responded.

"How exactly did you end up here?"

The Russian eyed him. "You are CIA?" he asked. The accent was heavy, but his grasp of English was solid.

"Something like that."

"And they did not advise you of my situation?"

"My instructions were to reach an injured person and provide aid. Not much more."

The colonel filled him in on the rest of the story. He covered his background as a test pilot, his plan to defect, and how a fuel leak had forced a speculative landing on the reservoir.

When he seemed finished, Tru looked skyward. "In that case, I'd guess the Russians will be looking for you."

"They will search, yes. But for now, I think they are looking in the wrong place. When they last saw me, I was hundreds of miles west of here."

"So that's where the search will be centered?"

"Most likely. I can tell you I've heard no helicopter activity here since arriving."

"Could they know you were trying to defect?"

"No . . ."

Sensing hesitation, Tru gave Primakov a hard look.

"There is one person who might deduce my intentions," he said. "I left a letter for my father-in-law . . . an error on my part."

"What did this letter say?"

"Nothing specific about my plan. I simply told him to fuck off."

Tru suppressed a grin. "Will he share this letter with the authorities?"

Primakov chuckled reflexively, but it ended as a cough. When he recovered, he said, "He *is* the authority. General Viktor Strelkov is chief of the Third Directorate of the GRU."

Tru stiffened. "You're married to the daughter of a GRU general?"

The pilot shrugged. "My relationship with Oksana has mostly ended, but divorce was never an option."

"If the GRU learns the truth, that you were trying to defect—that might cause some serious complications."

"This was my thought at first. But it might not be so bad. If Strelkov realizes what I've done, he will have every reason to keep it to himself.

Such a scandal would end his career. And in this regime? Viktor would be guaranteed a very bad accident. His only chance would be to find me to gain control of the situation."

"You mean, find you before the Air Force does?"

A nod. "I know how Viktor thinks. He will likely give them misdirection."

"I guess that makes sense." Tru looked out over the reservoir. There wasn't a light in sight. "Would he have the assets at his disposal for a search out here?"

"He is a general officer of the GRU, and his directorate oversees Asia. He can have whatever he wants. His only concern will be to cover his actions so they do not raise suspicion. Those below him on the GRU ladder would happily stab him in the back to promote their own careers."

Tru had studied Russia widely on an academic level, its economy, politics, and history. For over a century the Russian people had been anesthetized into submission, first by the Soviets, and then, after a fleeting romance with democracy, by the man from St. Petersburg. What Primakov was telling him only reinforced his standing opinion: Russia was as corrupt a nation-state as existed on earth, in effect a crime syndicate that controlled the world's largest nuclear arsenal. Those in charge relied on the collective apathy of the populace: lies given and accepted was the perpetual expectation, a nation sleepwalking through a narcosis of mistrust.

He looked again at the jet, its sharp-edged outline clear in the dim light. It appeared undamaged, although one wing was buried deep in a snowbank. "Will the jet be easy to spot?"

"Not as easy as you might think. The greatest risk will be helicopters with . . . what is the English word . . . heat signature."

"Infrared."

Primakov nodded. "I have worked with many such targeting systems. Now, in the middle of the night, the airplane is roughly the same temperature as its surroundings. Having one wing buried in snow helps obscure its shape. At dawn and dusk, however . . . then we have a problem. The aircraft's metal skin heats and cools differently from the lake and forest. Each time the sun rises and sets, there will be an hour, maybe two, when the jet will stand out to such sensors."

"I could throw some snow on the wings."

"It might help, but still . . ."

"How long do we have until the search expands to this area?"

"If it were only the Air Force, I would say weeks. But Viktor, he is clever. If he realizes what I was attempting, it is not so hard to guess the route I would have taken. He will be the first to arrive. And there is something else to consider. If he can find us, he will have no interest in interrogating me or putting you on display for a show trial. His only hope for political survival is to hide any trace of my attempt to reach the West."

"Which means eliminating any trace of us."

"Da." The Russian regarded him at length. "It must have been difficult to reach this place. I should thank you for coming."

"You're welcome."

"Tell me your name."

"Most people call me Tru."

"Tru? As in truth?"

"I wouldn't go that far."

Primakov chuckled. "You are sounding like a Russian already."

TWENTY-NINE

Tru went into the forest to collect more firewood. He returned to their makeshift campsite to find Primakov fast asleep. He added two logs to the fire and watched them begin to burn. Fatigue was setting in. Aside from a brief rest on the train, he had been going nonstop for two days. He needed sleep.

He made one last account of their basic needs. He had built a crude shelter, a lean-to above Primakov constructed from evergreen boughs cut from nearby pines. Water, too, was under control: he could melt all the snow necessary to keep a steady supply. Food was more problematic—virtually none remained. He could acquire more by hunting, or seeking out civilization, but it wasn't critical. Humans could survive for days without nourishment, the body adapting.

He looked warily up at the sky. The fire was inside the tree line, but that would provide only marginal concealment from a good IR sensor. He checked the time. The assistance promised by Langley was due to arrive in six hours. Extraction, by the wording of the message, was going to take longer. He wondered what the hell a "support team" consisted of. The agency had virtually no assets in this part of Russia, which was why he'd gotten the call to begin with. Might there be Russian agents nearby, sympathetic locals? He decided that was unlikely, and given the importance of the operation he doubted foreign nationals would be deemed reliable. What about a quick-reaction military unit? He looked skyward again and imagined a SEAL Team hurtling earthward in a HALO jump through the great slabs of cloud. Having gotten that qual in training, he knew it would be all but impossible—a SpecOps unit could never be delivered this deep into Russian territory in so little time.

Speculation was pointless. All Tru could do was trust that Langley had a plan. He decided it was time for a sitrep. He settled near the fire, pulled out his phone, and typed out the pertinent details. As had been drilled into him in training, he kept the message short and concise.

Contact made with TALON. Situation stable. Awaiting support.

He then began a shopping list, requesting nearly a dozen items, including an IR camo tarp, food, pain meds, and blankets.

Then, almost as an afterthought, he added one last item: weapons. Tru hit the send button.

He had no idea if any of his requests would be honored. Given the time constraints, it was doubtful they *could* be honored—whatever help was coming, it was likely already en route. Still, it couldn't hurt to ask.

He glanced at Primakov, saw him sleeping soundly. With the thermal blanket from his survival kit wrapped around him, he looked like a polyethylene burrito. The forest was still and silent, the only noise an occasional crackle from the fire. Coherent thoughts gave way to sensory detachment, and when Tru finally drifted off the dominant thought in his mind was all too predictable.

What the hell have I gotten into?

The sitrep was routed directly to the TOC, and it reached Slaton as he was finishing a late working lunch. He put down his sub, wiped a bit of mayo from the corner of his mouth, and read the update.

For the most part, it was good news. His conversation with Bob Stansell had raised doubts about how Miller would perform, but so far the kid had come through. Primakov was alive, holding his own, and there was no immediate threat of them being discovered. That said, simply reaching Primakov in the wilderness had been the easy part. They were not, quite literally, out of the woods, and the risks were about to rise exponentially.

Slaton was mentally composing the update he would send to the White House—positive in tone, dutifully cautious—when the woman at the comm desk said, "Sir, do you want me to forward the supply list from the message to Colonel Westbrook at Vandenberg? We're four hours to launch."

"Yeah, good call."

The woman began typing on her keyboard.

Slaton immediately admonished himself. She was absolutely right—pushing the supply list forward was the top priority. How had his mind jumped elsewhere? *A few weeks in this place and I'm becoming one of them.*

He quickly righted his thoughts. The Star Chaser mission had sounded promising when Westbrook first laid it out. Now it seemed fraught with peril. Rocketing an experimental spaceplane into orbit and then penetrating Russian airspace? It was a damned moonshot. Or worse yet, the launch and reentry could conceivably be mistaken for an ICBM. *First week on the job, and I'm going to start a nuclear war.*

Even if the spaceplane worked as advertised, the plan for getting everyone out of Russia remained stuck on a drawing board in the Pentagon's basement. He wished the president had poleaxed the whole thing from the get-go. But now that she'd approved it, the mission was out of his hands. Maybe out of everyone's hands. How often had he seen this from the field? Grandiose schemes that took on unstoppable momentum.

He looked at his hand-scrawled schedule for the day, which had been mushrooming by the hour. DOD, NRO, Space Command. What had begun as a limited, low-risk venture—letting Primakov fly Vektor into their lap—was blowing up into a pending catastrophe. It occurred to Slaton that only one thing remained under his exclusive control: Tru Miller.

What can I do to help him?

The global map on the big monitor seemed vaster than ever, and he zeroed in on Vandenberg Space Force Base. In a triumph of aspiration, a thin red line arced up from the launch site, reached around the world, and terminated at Zeya Reservoir. The projected orbital path of Star Chaser, perfectly clean and uninterrupted, no allowances made for contingencies—of which there had to be dozens. Slaton had seen countless operational drawing boards over the years, but never had one looked so precarious. He sat deep in thought, ignoring the rest of his sandwich.

He picked up a phone and put in a call to Westbrook.

The colonel answered immediately. "What's up?"

"We just got word from our man on the ground. He requested some supplies."

"Yeah, the list just came through. It's pretty last-minute, but I'll do what I can."

"Most of it was stuff we were already planning on. But there is something that's bothering me. I'm concerned about how the Russians might react to this launch and reentry. I really don't want to start World War III."

"Yeah," Westbrook said, "DOD has a contingency for that. It's been in their back pocket ever since they conceptualized Star Chaser." He detailed the plan to mimic a planned civilian launch.

"Sounds like a good insurance policy. Try to make it sound as boring as possible."

"Will do."

They went over a few more issues, and when Slaton ended the call he felt slightly better. Then he went straight back to worrying.

What if the launch was scrubbed? From his admittedly terrestrial viewpoint, that seemed to happen more often than not in space flight. Bad weather, frozen fuel pumps, computer glitches. If Star Chaser didn't lift off on schedule, the entire plan might have to be abandoned. Was there an alternative, an option that carried less risk?

Slaton found himself drifting to a mindset that was old and familiar. Regardless of what happened with Star Chaser, successfully extracting Primakov from Russia would be dependent on one thing. The same thing that had been relied upon for millennia, before spaceplanes and jet fighters and satellite communications: it would all come down to boots on the ground.

In this case, a single pair.

And what bothered him more than anything: Today someone else was wearing them.

Kai was in the life support room, going over her flight gear with a tech sergeant, when Westbrook came through the door.

"We've got a slight load alteration," he announced.

"That's a little last-minute."

"The CIA's operator reached Primakov. He has a broken leg, but he's otherwise in decent shape. The agency forwarded a list of supplies their guy requested."

He gave her a printout and she looked it over. "We already have most of this."

"I'll take care of procurement for the rest. The only thing I'm not sure about is this IR camo tarp. I've heard of it, but it's not something they'd have on a Space Force base. Maybe we can rush something in from Pendleton or Lemoore. I'll let you know within the hour, and we'll finalize the launch weight."

"All right. I'll make sure payload support and launch control know changes are coming."

Weight and balance calculations for space launches were critically important and measured to the nearest ounce. They were typically set in stone months before a launch, but Star Chaser's core mission—rapid response to any hot spot on the globe—demanded a different approach. Software had been created to fine tune load schedules and orbital profiles until the final moments before launch.

Westbrook disappeared, and Kai looked across the room at Sergeant Diaz. He was sitting in a chair and looked ridiculous with a massive plastic shell on his head. Oozing out from gaps in the globe were blobs of hardening foam. These would be sculpted away by a technician, leaving a custom inner liner that could be inserted into his helmet.

He called across the divide, "More weight coming, huh? Does that mean I gotta lose this?" He showed her a silver four-leaf clover on a chain around his neck.

"Nah, better keep it. We're going to need all the luck we can get."

THIRTY

Kai and Diaz were strapped into their seats. Star Chaser, mirroring the Vulcan rocket it was mated to, was standing on its tail. This put them in an almost fully reclined position. The dual windscreens in front of them were pointless for the moment—they could see only the inside of a giant composite cylinder. The aerodynamic fairing was necessary for launch, and only after reaching the stratosphere would the clamshell separate and fall away, a prelude to the end of Star Chaser's boost phase. Until that happened, their picture of what was going on outside would be limited to feeds from two exterior cameras. One showed where they were going, the other where they'd been. The latter would soon show the planet Earth.

After an initial flurry of activity on the radios, there was now a lull. They'd reached one of the built-in holds in the launch sequence, and it gave Kai a last chance for reflection before hurtling into space.

As with her previous orbital flight, she found herself lost in deep thought. The idea of separating from earth, even a glancing excursion through the heavens, was profoundly liberating. It somehow reinforced how badly humans were behaving, the honesty of the universe contrasting with a world gone off-rail. The decline of democracy, the rise of autocrats. Rampant lawlessness and corruption, and a widening of gulf between haves and have-nots. Humans seemed unable to assimilate the technology they were creating, and soon that technology, in the guise of AI, would self-generate at an ever-increasing rate.

Her philosophic musings were cut off in the most terrestrial of ways.

"What if I need to pee?" Diaz asked.

Kai blinked and recalibrated, looked over at him. He looked distinctly uncomfortable, his wide-eyed face framed by the bulbous helmet.

"Do you have to go now?"

"No, but this space suit . . . it took an hour to put it on."

"It's a short flight, you'll be fine."

"But what if I can't hold it?"

"Then just go."

"In the suit?"

"Trust me, it's been done."

Their ridiculous conversational thread, which was being recorded for posterity by cockpit microphones, was mercifully severed by a radio transmission. *"Launch sequence picking up."*

The clock began ticking down again.

Kai turned to the next checklist.

From half a mile away, Westbrook took in the scene at Launch Complex 3. He was standing outside the launch control center, a bunker-like building that housed the team overseeing Star Chaser's mission. The spacecraft was poised atop the Vulcan Centaur rocket like an arrowhead on a shaft, yet at that moment it was invisible. The white payload fairing needed for aerodynamic protection provided another advantage today: no one without authorization could possibly know what was inside. Not the civilian employees at Vandenberg, not passersby on the nearby Cabrillo Highway, and, most importantly, not the operators of satellites passing overhead. This was hardly unusual, since many of the launches from Vandenberg carried classified payloads, but it was also a reflection of Star Chaser's history.

Having overseen the test program, Westbrook knew more than most about the vehicle. It was an offshoot of a spaceplane that delivered crew and supplies to the space station. Those few who had seen Star Chaser often made an association, on first glance, with the original space shuttle. It did draw from that design—high-Mach aerodynamics being what they were—with the primary difference being scale. The new craft was roughly one quarter of the original shuttle's size, a mere thirty feet long and twenty-five feet wide. The other dissimilarity involved its wings. Currently folded to fit within the payload fairing, the spacecraft's wings would deploy after launch with a notable upward cant—like a bird coming in for a landing.

It's avionics and systems were bare bones, saving weight and creating usable cargo volume. There were also no classified systems on board, a necessity for a craft that was, in effect, a disposable delivery system meant to be abandoned in enemy territory.

Reflecting its black-ops roots, the spacecraft's very name was steeped in misdirection. Despite launching toward the heavens, its true mission was solidly terrestrial. Indeed, those privileged few in the military and intelligence communities who knew of its existence had coined a different nickname.

They called it Crisis Chaser.

With his eyes alternating between the primed Centaur rocket and the countdown clock, Westbrook realized how accurate that name was proving to be.

THIRTY-ONE

The radios were alive as technicians ran protocols. Kai responded to a few, but mostly she stayed busy monitoring systems. She was happy for the distraction. Somewhere in the back bay of her brain she was uneasy about this mission, and in a way she hadn't expected. In her years of test flying, there had often been apprehensive moments—anyone who didn't admit to them was either a liar or psychotic. The idea that she was about to ride a rocket in an experimental spaceplane wasn't the problem. It had to do with their destination. And what she might face when she got there.

Sitting next to her, Diaz fidgeted with his gloves. He'd gone through a nonstop day of training and preparation. And while the thought of launching into space had initially struck him as a once-in-a-lifetime adventure, now it was getting real. For the next few hours, he was little more than a passenger on his first stratospheric flight. Only when they landed on a very cold lake in Russia would his work begin.

He checked the forward-looking camera and saw nothing but blue sky. "It's a long damn way from Cartagena," he whispered.

"What?" asked a distracted Kai.

"Oh . . . I was just saying, I really liked the training."

She gave him a questioning look. With the visor of his helmet raised, his unease was apparent.

"You've flown this thing, right, Major?"

"Once." She began flipping switches, and as she did a T-shaped knob fell off. She caught it before it tumbled back into the cargo bay.

He looked at her disbelievingly.

"It's only a landing light switch. Too bad I don't have a mechanic who could put it back on."

"I could go back and get a screwdriver from—"

"I'm kidding. It'll be a daytime landing."

He looked suspiciously at the control panels where hundreds of other switches were waiting to fall off.

"It's okay, Diaz. It's a solid machine, same as all the others we've worked with."

"*Ten minutes,*" said a voice over the radio. "*Autolaunch sequence initiated.*"

A clock with big red numbers began counting down on the central display. For the next nine and a half minutes a constant stream of chatter ran between Kai and the launch controllers. Everything was professional and systematic. By the twenty-second callout, Diaz was smiling. He was about to go on the ride of his life.

6 . . . 5 . . . 4 . . . main engine ignition . . .

Diaz's smile vaporized.

The noise inside the cockpit was moderate—nothing like the roar outside, which was rattling windows for miles—but Star Chaser began shaking violently. It felt as though they were at the epicenter of an earthquake.

Kai could barely focus on the instruments as clattering noises filled the air.

Diaz, worried that something had gone wrong, seized his armrests in a death grip.

The voices on the radio, however, remained calm.

"*Liftoff . . .*"

The acceleration was gradual, pressing them into their seats as the rocket lifted skyward. The altitude callouts from launch control became a progress report.

20,000 feet.

Ever so slowly, the pressure increased.

30,000 feet.

The vibrations began to dampen, and at the two-minute point it became easier to see the instruments. The accelerometer showed 2.9 Gs.

The engines throttled back slightly, and the two exchanged a look as they became lighter in their seats.

"*Max Q.*"

Diaz tried to control his breathing. It was sensory overload like nothing he'd ever experienced.

Things continued to stabilize, the push behind them lessening.

"*Main engine shutdown.*"

The vibrations virtually disappeared, and the cockpit went quiet.

"Okay," said Kai. "Now for the fun part."

She directed Diaz's attention to the windscreen. There was a muffled burst, and before his eyes the two great clamshell fairings flew away. More chatter on the radio, a nudge from behind, and the ride went silky smooth.

"There you go," she said. "We're flying."

His jaw literally dropped as he looked outside.

The earth lay before them through the window.

And they were flying upside down.

THIRTY-TWO

Viktor Strelkov woke before sunrise, and without even getting out of bed he checked his messages. With relief, he saw there had been no new developments overnight in the search for Vektor. Looking out the window he saw a leaden morning, the sun blotted away by low overcast clouds. He wondered how that would affect today's search.

Having slept poorly, he went to the bathroom and turned on the shower. As he waited for hot water, he looked in the mirror. The face that stared back was the same as ever—which was to say, thick-jowled and rough. His nose was a map of burst capillaries, and deep wrinkles grooved his forehead. It was one of the few compensations for growing older that after a bad night's sleep one generally looked no worse than the day before. He increasingly found himself relying on such rationalizations, which seemed far easier than exercise regimens or eating whatever made Greek fishermen live to be a hundred.

He showered, dressed, and twenty minutes later rolled into the administration building like a wrecking ball gone rogue. His first three words were directed to a corporal at the front desk. "Sausage, eggs, coffee."

The corporal rushed away, a man on a mission.

Spines straightened as Strelkov continued down the hall, yet he issued no more orders. At the last door on the left, he turned inside and sat heavily behind the commander's desk.

Last night he had informed Nemanchik that he was commandeering his office. The colonel, of course, gave no complaint, and from that toehold, in the few hours before he retired, Strelkov had seized Skovorna Air Base in its entirety. He would be the first to receive all communications relating to the crash of Vektor, and he assumed operational control of the base's small helicopter detachment. The colonel's adjutant would be at his beck and call. Nemanchik himself was relegated to running errands. Word of Corporal Ivanov's fate had spread through the building like wildfire, leaving no doubt as to who was in charge.

Strelkov gazed out the window and surveyed his new domain. He took no satisfaction in appropriating an air base; it was simply a necessity. The fate of his son-in-law remained an open question. They still had no crash site, no radar data, no locator beacon. Aside from one "mayday" call on a very dark night, Vektor had fallen off the face of the earth.

Except it most certainly hadn't.

His suspicions had deepened overnight—the primary reason he'd lost sleep—and he was glad to have this remote base from which to operate. Self-renditioning could prove an advantage on both offense and defense, and Strelkov was—*damn you, Maksim Primakov*—being forced to play both. Here he would be close to the action, and better able to manage the flow of information. Best of all, by taking up residence at Skovorna he would avoid the treacherous halls of headquarters. Regardless of one's station there, you never knew who was listening. Worse yet, allegiances in The Aquarium held the sureness of quicksand. Friends didn't become enemies before your eyes. They did it behind your back.

Nemanchik appeared in the doorway. He looked smaller than ever. "I spoke to the cook about tonight's dinner menu," he began. "Apparently there is no red wine. I could have some flown in on today's supply run—the quartermaster in Chita owes me a favor." The man wore his sycophancy like a straitjacket.

"You have vodka?"

"Of course, General."

"That will do. And forget about dinner. I want a roster of the personnel here who can—"

Strelkov stopped in midsentence. The sound of approaching helicopters began rattling the window. Both men looked outside as a flight of three Hinds arched in under the steel-gray sky. They circled the field once, the building shivering under the clatter, and then settled onto the apron, their rotor wash throwing clouds of snow and ice.

"I didn't know we were expecting arrivals," Nemanchik said hesitantly, his eyes flicking outside.

Strelkov realized he might have made his point too severely yesterday. He had learned the hard way—or actually, others had—that you could only terrorize people to a point, after which they became dysfunctional.

"I am bringing in a special unit to aid in our search." The word "our" was all it took. Nemanchik's visage went from caution to something near curiosity.

The rotors outside fell still, and under a pall of mist uniformed soldiers began streaming from all three helicopters. Hauling weapons and gear, they looked professional, confident. The last man who stepped down was different. He wore a heavy jacket the color of deer skin and large winter boots. Whereas the platoon in front of him was exclusively ethnic Russians, the civilian looked to be from the East. His broad face had rounded features, his black hair was wild, and an ungroomed mustache and beard concealed any expression on his face.

"Who are they?" Nemanchik asked.

"The soldiers are a very capable GRU team . . . they perform missions for me under special circumstances."

"And the civilian?"

"His presence does not concern you."

Nemanchik didn't query further, and Strelkov decided it was time to give him a chore—he wanted the office clear to meet the arriving contingent.

"How many Chinese are here at Skovorna?" he asked.

"There are four technicians."

"There is no need for them to remain. Use one of our Hips to send them away."

"Send them where?"

"The nearest border crossing point will do. Tell them all work on Vektor is temporarily suspended. We will keep them apprised of the accident investigation."

"I should consult General Kozlov at headquarters. He has been adamant that we keep a positive working relationship with the—"

Strelkov only had to glare.

"On the other hand, I could tell headquarters that the Chinese contingent chose to go back of their own accord . . ."

"An excellent idea."

"They will be gone within the hour." The colonel disappeared, leaving Strelkov alone.

He stared at the big map in silence. One of his first orders after seizing Nemanchik's office was to have a regional map tacked to the back wall. It depicted the eastern half of Russia in all its barren glory— terrain contours, winding rivers, thousands of miles of untouched shoreline. Outposts of civilization were few and far between, and military installations fewer yet. To those in Moscow, the Far East was an afterthought, a place to be plundered for resources, perhaps home for a few prisons. Otherwise, it was a land to be ignored.

Strelkov heard commotion down the hall as the commandos entered the building. Then two distinct sets of footsteps came up the hall and fell still outside the door. Two men waiting.

He spun around in his chair and saw Captain Volkov and the Cossack.

"Enter."

They came in, the captain taking the lead. He stood rigidly at attention. The civilian followed, casual but alert—an animal in the forest sensing its surroundings.

"As you both know," Strelkov began, "you have been brought here to search for a missing jet. The aircraft in question, codename Vektor, is an experimental fighter that we have been developing jointly with the Chinese. To this point, nothing has been found. It is *vital* that we locate the crash site." Strelkov paused for a moment and stood as if to emphasize what would come next. "You are probably wondering why I am here. An accident such as this would not normally concern my directorate, but in this case, I have a personal interest. The man piloting this jet was my son-in-law, and I very much want to learn his fate."

"If anyone can find him, it is my team," said the captain.

The Cossack said nothing.

Strelkov turned toward the map and pointed to an oblong box marked in red tape, the outline of Restricted Area 1512. "The search is currently focused here. While our military forces are generally competent, I believe in this case they have erred. They are looking in the wrong place."

"What makes you say this, sir?" asked the captain.

"They have so far found nothing, despite over a hundred sorties flown. It is a broad area, no doubt, but I feel we must expand the search box. I think we should look to the east."

The captain seemed to stifle another question, probably since his first had not been answered.

"You have three helicopters at your disposal, Captain. Divide your men accordingly." The general referenced the map, and with his finger he circled an area well to the east of the red box. "You will perform a grid search in this region, flying at low altitude."

"My boys have sharp eyes," Volkov said. "If Vektor is there we will find it."

"I want my own helicopter," said the Cossack, speaking for the first time. The words came from deep in his chest, closer to a growl than skillful diction.

The general looked at him questioningly.

"Searching from above is not enough," Tarkhan explained, "There are few people in this region, but they might provide valuable information. It's possible they have heard something, seen something. In remote areas like this, an airplane crash will stand out. Hunters, trappers . . . they would be the first to know about it."

Strelkov nodded his assent. He liked what he was hearing. Given the criticality of the situation, he had to pursue his search by every possible means. Tarkhan was offering a path he had not considered. "You may use one of the Hips, take it wherever you wish. But concentrate on the area I've identified."

The Cossack said nothing, his face expressionless. A slate wiped clean.

"I want to be very clear on one point. If the crash site is found, you must be the first to the scene. You will report any findings immediately, and *only* to me."

The two men nodded in turn.

For ten minutes Strelkov went over the search plan and communications protocols. He then dismissed the men. The captain performed a sharp about-face and disappeared down the hall. The Cossack didn't move.

Strelkov eyed him silently. The man had a distinct presence. Tall and big-boned, he exuded strength. His broad face and flattened features gave nothing away. Strelkov had spent a lifetime around unsmiling men, yet this one was different.

Just as he had been told.

"Why am I here?" Tarkhan asked.

"Because you are paid very well by my agency to do a job."

No response.

The creases deepened on Strelkov's broad forehead. "I was given your name by a colonel in my section—Andreyev. I needed someone who is familiar with this region, and he said he had worked with you before. I think it involved tracking down draft evaders who were hoping to become lost in these parts."

Still the Cossack remained silent.

Strelkov flicked a finger toward the door. Tarkhan turned and closed it.

"I am told you prefer to work alone," said the general.

A nod.

"Then that is what you will do. I will forward to you any intelligence I receive. You have free rein to pursue this search as you see fit. Volkov and his team will also be looking for Colonel Primakov. They are an experienced unit with many resources at their disposal. But I also want someone who knows the forest, who can find people."

"And who can kill?"

"I think 'hunt' was the word Andreyev used. I wasn't precisely sure of his meaning."

"I think you understood very well."

Strelkov's eyes narrowed. He wasn't used to being challenged.

The Cossack stepped toward the map, his huge head tilting in contemplation. After an extended look, he said, "East . . . why?"

"Certain intelligence I have received suggests that is where we should look."

The Cossack turned, his eyes a deadpool black. "I have intelligence too. I think I know why you look here." He raised his hand to the map, and from the original search area he spread his open palm eastward, eventually touching the Pacific Ocean.

Strelkov gave him a severe look. Hunter or not, this man needed to understand who was in charge. "Your job is not to speculate. You are to find Vektor, and more importantly, my son-in-law."

"And when I do?"

The general glared, but still the dark eyes did not yield. He did, however, after a time, give a single nod.

"We have an understanding, then?" Strelkov asked.

"We do."

THIRTY-THREE

The midcourse phase of flight would last less than an hour. Kai wished it was longer.

There was virtually no sound. A few fans hummed behind the instrument panel and the air system kept up its white noise. The thrum of rocket engines was gone, leaving only an occasional pulse from the OMS maneuvering motors. Hundreds of miles above the earth, there wasn't even a brush of slipstream noise to prove they were flying.

She quickly got her housekeeping chores out of the way, flipping a few switches and verifying their course. She made mental notes on the performance of various systems—Star Chaser was, after all, still an experimental aircraft, and she was a test pilot. Her most satisfying discovery was that the inertial systems, which had performed marginally on her first flight, appeared to be dead on.

She looked over at Diaz and saw him gazing pensively out the window.

Kai remembered doing the same on her first mission. The scene outside was a sight to behold. The stars appeared infinite against the velvet blackness beyond, and the curvature of the earth was readily apparent. You could see a thousand miles in every direction. Oceans, continents, vast weather systems swirling, the whole world set out in the texture of a dream. The God's-eye view was hard to describe to those who had not witnessed it. For Kai, it was a study in contrast. Vulnerability and dominance, strength and insignificance. Some might be convinced that there could only be a greater power. Others would see proof that science was the ultimate authority. Her own take was that if everyone could see what she was seeing, the earth backdropped by the blackness of the heavens, they might be more inclined to coexist.

"Why are we flying upside down?"

The question broke her musings. "In zero Gs orientation is meaningless. Flying this way gives us a better view of the earth."

Diaz looked awestruck.

She directed his attention upward—which would soon be down. "That's Madagascar, and we'll be coming up on India soon."

"There are billionaires who pay a lot to get this view."

"And look at you, getting government per diem for travel."

He was too starstruck to laugh.

"Sierra Charley Four, show you on course, reentry IP in five minutes. Expect comm blackout in three."

Kai acknowledged the call from mission control. The extreme heat of reentry would preclude normal communications, and after that the radios had to remain silent for security reasons. From this point on, Star Chaser was going black. Kai's only support would be the mesmerized jet mechanic beside her.

Colonel Westbrook's voice came on the radio. *"You're autonomous now, Kai. Good luck."*

"Copy all. OMS green, nav checks. Give our friends a heads-up. Kai out . . ."

Two checklists later, a message flashed to the main display: REEN-TRY SEQUENCE INITIATING.

Star Chaser nosed earthward, rolled right-side up, and began the final dive of its brief and glorious service life. One last time, Kai looked down at the earth in wonder. Then she tightened her shoulder harness and reached for the controls.

Tru was sleeping soundly when a vibration from his phone stirred his senses. He sat up abruptly, and the world came into focus. A snow-dusted forest and distant hills. It was early morning in Siberia, daylight trying to take hold. The air was glacial and unmoving. He stretched and instantly felt pain in his shoulder, a reminder of yesterday's low point—being blown out of a boxcar packed with ammunition.

Today will be better, he told himself. Which was followed by, *Is that what passes for optimism in clandestine operations?*

The fire had almost died out, and he ignored his phone long enough to get up, stir the embers, and drop fresh wood on top. He would soon have to go foraging for more—most survival skills were simple, but they did require time.

His movement apparently woke Primakov, who was stirring beneath his thermal blanket.

With the fire glowing brighter, Tru checked the message: SUPPLY INSERT IMMINENT. PREPARE TO ASSIST UNLOAD.

He stared at the screen, dumbstruck.

Primakov apparently noticed. "What is it?" he asked.

"They say we're about to get a supply drop." He looked skyward, then out across the reservoir. He didn't hear any engines, which ruled out a helicopter or snowmobile.

"How will this happen?" Primakov asked.

"I have no idea. I wish they'd be a little more—"

A resounding *boom* shook the air, then echoed across the valley. It sounded like a clap of thunder, but looking up Tru saw only the usual dank overcast.

"What was *that*?" he wondered aloud. "It couldn't be a thunderstorm this time of year. Are there mines around here where they might use explosives?"

When Primakov didn't answer, Tru looked and saw him smiling. "That," said the test pilot, "is a sound I know well."

Kai watched her airspeed closely. Star Chaser had just gone through a series of S-turns, a maneuver designed to decrease speed. As they decelerated through Mach 1, she kicked off the autopilot and went to manual control. She was effectively flying a glider—the flight controls responded perfectly to the joystick in her hand, but the spacecraft had no thrust whatsoever. It all came down to what pilots called "energy management." The descent profile had been programmed to give a ten-mile-long final approach, ending with a touchdown in the center of the reservoir near the arm where Vektor had landed.

Reentry had gone flawlessly, Star Chaser's tiles holding up to the three-thousand-degree heat. Yet now Kai faced a problem. Looking outside, she couldn't see the ground. The weather report, updated just before launch, had been for high broken clouds and good visibility. Looking out the window she saw only a solid blanket of white.

The situation wasn't critical yet. She was presently flying by the flight director on the heads-up display, which consisted of two circles. One represented the actual flight path, the other the desired path calculated by the computers. All Kai had to do was keep one circle inside the other, the world's simplest video game. That, however, would only work to a point—the flight director wasn't designed for landing. If she didn't see the ground before touchdown, Star Chaser would crash into the frozen lake.

The path straightened out seven miles from touchdown. Star Chaser was at thirteen thousand feet in a twenty-two-degree dive, hurtling toward the lake and dead on profile. The maneuver reminded Kai of dive bombing in an F-16.

Except I can't see my target.

Diaz muttered something from the right seat. She tuned him out, her concentration absolute.

At two miles the flight director cued upward, and she raised the nose. This cut the descent rate and Star Chaser began to slow. They were immersed in a cloud deck, the world enveloped in mist. She hoped the coordinates for the middle of the reservoir were accurate, as well as the measurement of its altitude above sea level—these were the baselines for the entire profile, and with no visual backup an error could be catastrophic.

When the radar altimeter hit two hundred feet Kai lowered the landing gear. Three green lights illuminated on the forward console, confirming the gear was down and locked. They were seconds from touchdown, still in the muck.

One hundred feet. Nothing but fog. She felt a slight buffet, Star Chaser whispering to her, complaining that she was getting slow.

At this point, had Kai been in a fighter, she would have gone around and tried again. Or barring that, simply ejected. Neither was an option today. She eased the stick back, trying to stay airborne just a little longer. The whisper became a shout, the airframe rattling as speed became critical.

"Airspeed low!" blared an automated warning from the overhead speaker.

"No shit!" she barked back at the robotic voice.

Suddenly the clouds turned to wisps, and Star Chaser burst into the clear. But it wasn't salvation. The frozen lakebed swept past in a visual rush, yet the dim light provided little contour for depth perception.

"Turn on the landing lights!" she shouted.

Thankfully, Diaz had reattached the switch, and he reached up and slapped it on.

It was like turning on a light in a dark room. Kai's crosschecks turned rapid-fire.

The picture outside.

Radar altimeter.

The ice.

Airspeed.

Her hand worked the joystick furiously, constant small corrections to settle Star Chaser back to the planet. The forward visibility was marginal, the horizon a mere suggestion.

Twenty feet. She lifted nose smoothly, breaking the descent rate further, playing the raging aerodynamic buffet.

Ten.

Five.

The main wheels touched down and nothing disastrous happened—the ice held.

She carefully lowered the nose. Very, very carefully.

This had been a major discussion point with Colonel Westbrook back at Vandenberg. Star Chaser's nose gear was not a wheel, but a skid. The designers had thought it simpler, saving weight and complexity, and perfectly suited to test flights on the expansive dry lake beds at Edwards Air Force Base. None of them had ever imagined setting down on a frozen Siberian lake.

Still, the skid was shaped like a blunt snow ski, in theory perfectly suited to ice.

In theory.

The skid kissed the frozen surface, and other than a slight grating sound everything seemed smooth. Which left only one problem.

Stopping.

Star Chaser had touched down at two hundred knots—well in excess of two hundred miles an hour. Kai tapped the foot pedals to engage the brakes. Nothing changed. She added pressure and felt a slight deceleration. Primakov, surely, would have encountered the same problem—stopping an aircraft hurtling across a sheet of ice.

The mist unexpectedly parted, and she could see into the distance. The shoreline, thankfully, was at least a mile away. Kai didn't want to go anywhere near it. This was also something she had discussed with Westbrook: the plan was to stop in the middle of the lake, if possible, where the water was deepest. With the brakes barely working, Kai had only one more option to slow.

She hauled back on the stick and the nose rose slightly, the spaceplane's aerodynamics still having a grip. Then she shoved the stick forward and Star Chaser slammed down on its nose skid. She did it repeatedly, working into a cycle, each iteration becoming more violent.

"What are you doing?" Diaz shouted.

Kai kept the oscillation going, no time to explain. On the fifth bounce she got what she wanted—Star Chaser's skid failed, and the spaceplane's nose thumped down onto the ice. The nose cone dug in heavily, and after one violent jolt the rotation began. Star Chaser spun clockwise and the world went to a blur. It was like the teacup ride at the county fair. The grating noise rose to a crescendo as if they were spinning over a gravel road.

Her shoulder straps locked against the tangential forces, and Star Chaser bounced into the air. It came down hard, then more spinning and grinding. Finally, the rotation slowed, the crunching noises lessened. Then, with one great jolt, everything went still.

Kai didn't move for a moment, waiting, assimilating. She turned and looked at Diaz. He was ashen.

"Well," she said speculatively, "that went well." She looked outside at their icy surroundings. "Hopefully this is the right lake."

He looked at her wide-eyed, and in a thin voice said, "Right lake?"

"I'm kidding. We did it. The hard part is over."

Ever so slowly, Diaz shook his head. He pointed to the angled forward windscreen. "Actually, maybe not. I think we're on fire."

Kai looked outside and saw nothing but smoke.

THIRTY-FOUR

The hotline had been established to prevent a nuclear war, but it wasn't the one most people knew about.

The original "red phone" connecting the Pentagon with the Kremlin, today a secure messaging link, was a safeguard that had been in place since 1963. Yet a second hotline between the two nations had become increasingly necessary.

Of the roughly ten thousand satellites in orbit, half were no longer operable, and with tens of thousands more on the drawing board, the sky was becoming a veritable junkyard of debris. The bits and pieces of satellites and rockets that rained down regularly had become a serious complication in an era of increasingly sensitive missile warning radars. The issue of false alarms had to be addressed.

The solution, initiated in 2010, was a direct line connecting U.S. Space Command's Combined Space Operations Center in California with Russian Space Force's Main Center for Missile Attack Warning outside Moscow. The system functioned well, but like any form of communication, was subject to misuse, and even deception.

As it was today.

The dispatch from California was brief and succinct, and had been transmitted, after careful consideration, seventeen minutes before Star Chaser began its reentry maneuver. This would give the Russians time to advise radar operators to watch for the contact, but not enough to research the source of the debris.

At 0128 GMT we expect a malfunctioning NOAA satellite to deorbit somewhere in the vicinity of the Russo-Chinese border.

Orbital generalities were included. The satellite was described as the remains of GEOSAT-7, an aging geological mapping platform. It had been chosen because the actual satellite was indeed malfunctioning and scheduled for deorbit. More pertinently, its visible and infrared imaging sensors were relics of another generation and would hold little intelligence value. Any scraps that survived the inferno of reentry would hardly be worth retrieving, and the fact that it would go down in a remote region of Siberia would further diminish interest.

Everything played out exactly as the Americans hoped.

A Voronezh-VP radar, located at the Mishelevka Radar Station outside Irkutsk, picked up an untagged target to the south on a steep reentry profile. Having been forewarned, the commander of the unit stood behind the operator and watched with detachment as the remains of a dying American satellite tumbled through the upper atmosphere. As was his duty, he recorded the contact in the daily log, but otherwise took no action. The debris was not a threat to any populated area, nor was it projected to fall near any strategically sensitive facility.

In time the Russians would uncover the ruse. They would go back over the data, run orbital calculations, and make an association between the launch of a Vulcan Centaur from Vandenberg, carrying an unknown payload, and the fiery reentry over the Central Siberian Plateau. All of that, however, would be months in the making.

In the critical moments that morning, the entry of Star Chaser into Russian airspace was dutifully ignored. Just as the director of the CIA's Special Activity Center hoped it would be.

Westbrook had watched Star Chaser's mission unfold from Vandenberg's launch control center, but that show ended with the beginning of reentry. The DOD might get a few raw data hits from its constellation of space-based platforms, but those would not be echoed here. Westbrook knew the launch had been textbook, and that the reentry maneuver had begun as planned. Other than that, he was in the dark.

As technicians around him eyed their scopes and assimilated data, the test pilot bowed his head ever so slightly, closed his eyes, and took a different path. He said a brief prayer for Kai and Diaz.

Two thousand miles east of Vandenberg, Slaton was in an operations center at the Pentagon. As the mission to extract Maksim Primakov advanced, the Defense Department was becoming increasingly involved. He supposed it was only natural, and the launch of Star Chaser had crossed a bureaucratic Rubicon—the CIA's TOC was no longer the hub, and he was forced to visit the Pentagon to watch things play out.

And play out they had. A burst of orbital data confirmed that Star

Chaser was somewhere near Zeya Reservoir. Where exactly, and in what condition, had not yet been verified. Whatever the outcome, there was no turning back.

Slaton was staring at an electronic map of the Earth when someone called his name from across the room. He turned and saw an E-3, who looked like he belonged in high school, holding up a hardwired phone. "Sir, secure call for you from the White House."

Slaton walked over and took the handset.

"Well?" asked a voice he instantly recognized.

"So far, so good, Madame Vice Present."

"That still sounds weird," Sorensen said.

"Tell me about it."

"The launch went okay?"

"All good until we lost tracking on reentry. The feed you have at the White House is the same one we're looking at. If everything went as planned, my guy on the ground should be sending a sitrep soon."

"Okay. How's the extraction plan coming?"

"General Carter is finalizing things as we speak. He told me he briefed you on the basic idea."

"He did, but the president and I want to see more details before we commit."

"Carter should be back at the White House in an hour or two."

"I'd like you to come as well."

"Actually . . . I have a better idea. DOD is running this show now, and the only asset I've got in play is our boy Rookie. I think the best way for me to be useful is to head to Japan and make sure this mission is squared away."

"David, JSOC is perfectly capable of running an op."

"This one's unique, and I've been on the leading edge myself a few times. It's a lot of time zones, but if I leave now, I can reach Hokkaido with a few hours to spare."

"I seriously don't think you need to—"

"As I recall," he said, cutting her off, "my predecessor had a habit of jetting off to forward operating locations to oversee *my* operations."

Silence on the White House end. Sorensen had done precisely that.

"I'll use a Company jet," he promised. "That way I'm in the loop the entire time."

A pause, then, "All right, I won't stop you. But understand one thing, David. You are now the director of the Special Activities Center. You will not under *any* circumstances take part in this operation. If you set one foot on Russian territory, so help me, I will have your ass! Are we clear?"

"Crystal."

The call ended.

Slaton couldn't suppress a veiled smile. He quickly placed a call to check on his ride to the airfield. The jet was already fueled and ready to go.

"A sonic boom?" Tru asked, repeating what Primakov had just said.

"That is precisely what it was."

"Russian Air Force?"

He considered it. "Possible, but unlikely. The Air Force flies many fighters which are capable of exceeding Mach 1, but there are no military training areas nearby."

"Could it be part of the search for Vektor?"

"No. Search patterns are slow and methodical. Speed is the last thing you want."

Tru looked down at his comm device. "Then maybe it was our delivery."

A thoughtful pause from the colonel. "Your military has many aircraft for secret missions . . . so yes, it is possible."

Tru walked closer to the shoreline, then stepped out onto the frozen lake. He scanned the sky and saw nothing but a low gray mist, a few breaks in the clouds to the east. Then he looked lower, across the ice, and something to the west caught his eye. Not an aircraft really, but a . . . disturbance. Against the misted horizon, perhaps two miles away, he saw a peculiar cloud. He couldn't discern the source, but it seemed to be growing, gray-white swirls boiling upward.

From where he sat, Primakov could have no hope of seeing it.

Tru called out, "I see something on the lake. I'm going out to have a look."

THIRTY-FIVE

"It's not smoke," Kai said.

She was standing next to Diaz on the thick ice, her helmet in her hand. Thinking that Star Chaser was on fire, she had blown the emergency escape hatch. Two explosive bolts threw the hatch twenty yards across the ice. They'd clambered outside quickly, and now had a better view of the situation.

Star Chaser was nose-down on the ice, her tail elevated. Scorch marks were evident along the lower hull where protective ceramic tiles bordered the aircraft's metal pressure hull. The remains of the skid were somewhere beneath the nose, which had plowed down into the ice. That was the source of the mist.

"Steam?" he ventured.

"Yep. Those tiles absorb thousands of degrees of heat on reentry. They'll cool quickly, but not fast enough to—" A sharp cracking noise cut her off and Star Chaser's nose sank further.

The reality of the situation struck Kai. Back at Vandenburg she and Westbrook had discussed the very scenario she'd encountered—the spaceplane might be hard to stop as it hurtled across the ice field. They had predicted the brakes would be marginally effective, and the colonel had come up with the idea of bouncing the nose until the skid failed. It was an inelegant solution, but seemed practical. There hadn't been time to run it by the engineers. It had just been two pilots spitballing, the way they'd done in the squadron bar back at Edwards. Now it had come back to haunt them.

Kai had stopped Star Chaser in the middle of the lake as intended. The plan all along had been to sink her, and the deeper the water, the better. A small explosive charge had been included in the cargo load, and the CIA's man on the ground was supposed to employ it to breach the ice after unloading. That whole concept was now going up in smoke—or actually, steam. By breaking the skid, she had put the superheated tiles in contact with the ice. *How could we have missed something so basic?*

"Come on! We need to unload the gear right away!" She scrambled toward the now-gaping entry door.

"Why?"

"Because I screwed up! Star Chaser is about to burn through the ice and sink. We can't let the supplies go down with her!"

They clambered back inside and began loosening the tie-downs on two hundred pounds of tools and gear. Kai grabbed a case of MREs and threw it out onto the ice. Diaz followed with a tool kit. She was freeing a second box when she heard another *crack,* far larger than the first. Star Chaser tilted to one side.

Kai moved to the hatch with another load but stopped dead in her tracks when she reached the opening. Ten feet away she saw a man in a dark ski parka. He was huffing like he'd been running, and there were flecks of ice in his light brown hair and stubble beard.

He looked back at a woman in a spacesuit.

"Hi," he said.

"Hi," she said back.

They stood there for an awkward moment, each trying to process the other. It was Kai who finally ended the standoff. "Well, don't just stand there. Give us a hand."

All that morning, the three Hinds carrying Captain Volkov's team flew cross-hatched patterns above the virgin forest of Amur Oblast. The helicopters refueled twice, which gave enough time for the men to get food and coffee, and for the captain to call Strelkov to provide updates. They were effectively performing the same search the Air Force was carrying out—flying over wilderness in the hope of spotting smoke or wreckage—but in a completely different area. They also stopped at the only two civilian airfields in the region and searched every hangar thoroughly. In the course of it all, they had virtually no contact with the local populace.

Two hundred miles south, another helicopter landed in the middle of the town of Ovsyanka, kicking up dust in the center circle of a dormant soccer field. The locals who were outside stopped to watch the arrival, and a few curious drivers pulled to the side of the road. The Hip was clearly a military machine, its brown and green camo paint the same as a thousand others in the Russian Army. The man who stepped out of it, however, was anything but a soldier. His clothing resembled what the local fur trappers wore, and his plodding bearing, accented with a slight hitch, would have looked grossly out of place on a parade ground.

Tarkhan forged ahead with purpose. He knew Captain Volkov was furiously scouring the wilderness for signs of the crash, just as Air Force crews were doing far to the west. He was convinced they would fail. He had been born and raised here, on the Southern Siberian steppe, and he knew the land's vastness. He knew this was a place that seized men and made them disappear. Simply taking flight and looking down, no matter how sharp one's eyes, no matter how many sets were used, was a senseless waste of time. It was like looking for one fish hidden in the sea.

Finding a man here would take time and patience, and the best resource was the people who knew the land. Having the Hip at his disposal was an advantage, but not because it could drill endless circles in the sky. It allowed him to cover more ground, visit more towns. Ovsyanka was his fourth stop this morning.

The town was a typical eastern outpost, small and quiet, imbued with an almost curated insignificance. In spite of his uneven gait, Tarkhan's pace was unremitting. He stopped only once to question an old woman. She was too old for fear, but young enough for contempt. All the same, she answered the big stranger's questions. Guided by her directions, five minutes later, Tarkhan climbed a set of chipped-concrete steps and entered the police station.

A sergeant behind a worn desk regarded him cautiously. In this era of mobile phones, even in a backwater constabulary like this, he had probably been forewarned: an outsider had arrived by military helicopter and was looking for the police.

"My name is Tarkhan. I am performing a search." He did not drop General Strelkov's name, nor his GRU rank. Having arrived as he did was authority enough.

"A search for what?" the sergeant replied. He wore his caution like a suit of chainmail.

"A fighter jet crashed two days ago. The wreckage has not yet been found."

A nod. "We heard there was a search west of here."

"The search is expanding."

"What do you want from us?"

Tarkhan told the sergeant what he had told other sergeants this morning. "I want to know if you have had reports of unusual occurrences lately. Loud noises, brush fires, strangers nearby."

The policeman chuckled. "We have had all of that."

The Cossack's dark gaze deepened. "Where?"

"There was a train derailment, east of here on the Trans-Siberian line. Twenty-five cars, half of them loaded with ammunition. Went up like a Victory Day fireworks show. They will be cleaning it up for a month."

Tarkhan frowned. "I am looking for something less dramatic. One pilot and a bit of wreckage. Maybe you know men who hunt and trap, spend time in the woods. If any of them come across something unusual, strangers or fresh campsites, I want to know about it."

The sergeant's forehead went to furrows. "Campsites?"

A lack of response from the stranger earned a shrug.

"There is a reward for useful information," Tarkhan added. He leaned down to a nearby desk, requisitioned a pen and notepad, and scrawled down a phone number—he didn't bother with his name. He pushed it toward the policeman.

The sergeant dragged it closer and promised to keep an eye out.

Tarkhan turned to leave, but then he paused. The general's words from the previous day came back to his head: *Certain intelligence I have received suggests that is where we should look.*

He stood for a long moment, thinking about that. He turned back to the sergeant. "This derailment. When exactly did it happen?"

"Yesterday."

"What time?"

"Maybe . . . three in the afternoon."

"Do they know what caused it?"

"I talked to one of the investigators. He said they found two bodies in the ammunition car that took the worst of it. Drifters, no doubt. They started a fire, probably to cook or stay warm, and . . ." He made an exploding motion with the fingers of both hands.

"Two men, you say?"

"That's what I was told—not that there was much left of them."

"Where is this investigator?"

"Mikhailov? He is where he has been since yesterday—at the scene. Marker 1421, nine kilometers east along the line."

Tarkhan turned toward the door without thanking the man. He also didn't remind him about calling with new information—the hint of a reward took care of that. He pulled out his mobile and placed a call.

Strelkov picked up immediately. "You have found something?"

"It is probably nothing. But your people can help decide." Tarkhan explained what he wanted.

"I will take care of it."

"Has Volkov had any luck?"

"No more than the Air Force."

Minutes later, Tarkhan was back on his helicopter flying eastbound along the gently curving rail line.

THIRTY-SIX

The man who met them said his name was Tru, but before the civilities could go any further, he insisted they get to work. In light of the situation, Kai didn't argue. Up to this point she had been in her realm: sitting in a cockpit with flight controls in her hands and tasks to perform. Now, standing on a sheet of ice in Russia next to a mortally damaged spaceplane, she was completely out of her element. And Tru Whoever was her and Diaz's best hope for getting out.

They heaved supplies and equipment onto the ice as fast as they could. Since the cargo bay was tight, they improvised a system. Diaz loosened the tie-downs and handed packages to Kai. She relayed them out the hatch to Tru, who then carried them a short distance away. It was a simple and reliable scheme.

Until it wasn't.

They had transferred almost half the load when a loud *crack* caused everyone to freeze. Star Chaser lurched suddenly, her nose dropping into what was now a gaping hole in the ice. Clear water enveloped the nose cone, and more steam than ever began boiling around them.

"She's going down!" Tru shouted.

Kai threw a big tarp through the hatch, then leaned out to take a look. Another jolt, and the spaceplane settled lower. The deck was canted steeply nose-down, and water began pouring inside. "Time to get out, Diaz!"

"I've only got a few more—"

"Now, Sergeant!"

Kai clambered toward the angled opening, and Tru hauled her out by the arms. She slipped as she got clear, and they both went tumbling onto the ice. She turned and saw Diaz at the hatch. He reared back and tossed a big toolbox outside. It flew a few feet and smacked down with a thud. Then the ice sheet between them collapsed.

Star Chaser lurched left, its right wing flinging skyward, and quickly began to sink. Diaz disappeared—the rolling motion had spun the escape hatch skyward.

"*Diaz!*"

The spaceplane daggered down by the nose and the hatch came back into view. Diaz was nowhere to be seen.

Kai rushed toward the edge of the ice, only to be jerked back by her upper arm. She landed on her ass. "We have to get him out!" she shouted.

Tru said, "I'll do it!"

Having already thrown off his jacket, he picked up a tie-down strap that had ended up on the ice and secured it to his waist. He handed her the other end, and said, "Anchor this as best you can."

With the hatch going under, he shuffled to the edge of the ice shelf and launched himself toward Star Chaser. He splashed into the icy water. Kai held the strap firmly. It was roughly twenty feet long, enough to reach the sinking spaceplane, but with nothing to secure it to, she simply wrapped the end around her shoulders and sat down on the ice.

Steam from the superheated tiles billowed into the air, enveloping everything in a cloud of white. The hatch disappeared beneath the surface with Diaz still nowhere in sight. Tru dove down toward it. Soon Star Chaser's tail was all Kai could see, air burbling to the surface all around.

She felt a tug on the strap as it reached its limit. She squirmed closer, as near the edge of the ice as she dared—if she fell in, they might all become stranded and freeze to death. Another tug, harder this time, and then the strap went slack. She saw no sign of either man as the tip of Star Chaser's tail disappeared amid chunks of floating ice. Pulling lightly on the strap she felt nothing but slack. She reeled it in with both hands until the empty S-hook clattered up onto the ice.

"No, no, no!"

The water fell calm for a few interminable moments, bubbles and ice-clad eddies all that remained. Then, finally, a writhing figure burst to the surface—splashing frantically. Moments later, Tru came up behind him. Both men were spitting water, gasping for air.

"Here!" Kai shouted.

As soon as their eyes were on her, she coiled the strap and heaved the S-hook toward them. Tru caught it on the fly, and quickly locked arms with Diaz. Kai sank lower on the ice and hauled the strap in, the heels of her boots digging in for purchase. When both men got their arms to the edge of the ice sheet, she did her best to act as an anchor, keeping the strap taut and pulling for all she was worth. In a maelstrom of splashing and kicking, Diaz flopped up onto the ice. He then turned and helped Tru claw his way out. Both crabbed away from the breach, limbs spread wide to disperse their weight.

When they were finally clear, both men rolled onto their backs, shivering and exhausted.

No one spoke for a time as three bodies and minds recalibrated.

The last bubbles from Star Chaser percolated to the surface. Kai said breathlessly, "Well, there goes a hundred and ten million dollars."

"What kind of aircraft was that?" Tru asked.

"I'll explain later. Right now . . ." She got to her feet and went to the pile of supplies they'd managed to salvage. She opened a container that was full of winter clothing. "We need to get you both into something dry."

Thanks to Colonel Westbrook's foresight, they had brought two changes of clothing for everyone. There were layers of thermal protection, shirts and pants, and also heavy ski jackets. None of it was military-issue, nor was it anything stylish. This was intentional—on the off-chance they encountered locals, they would at least appear to be civilians. It didn't take long for the two men to change, and in the bracing temperatures modesty gave way to survival.

Kai changed as well, having no need for a spacesuit without a spacecraft. She used zip ties to secure her and Diaz's suits to the blown escape hatch, then pushed it all across the ice and watched it disappear into the big hole. The last vestige of Star Chaser sank into the icy water.

Tru pointed to a spot on the distant shoreline. "Camp is over there. There's no way we can carry all this, so grab what's most important. We'll come back for the rest later."

Kai grabbed a bundle of olive-drab blankets and a container of survival gear. Diaz and Tru picked up containers of food and medical supplies.

"Did the comm gear make it off?" Tru asked. "I requested a couple of handsets and extra batteries."

"We brought it, but that box didn't make it off."

"What else did we lose?"

Diaz said, "Some food, a few tools, a camera. I'm sure there's more, but I'll have to check the manifest later."

Kai said, "There was also a case with some weapons and the explosives you were supposed to use to sink Star Chaser."

Tru reflected, "I guess that sort of worked out."

With all they could carry in hand, they cast a collective last look at the swimming-pool sized hole and the small mound of equipment next to it. It was half a victory. And half a defeat.

Sodden and spent, the three Americans set out across the ice as a lashing wind began to rise.

Tarkhan ordered the pilot of the Hip to make one orbit over the accident scene. The scale of the disaster was clear. Heavy cranes had been brought in, and the derailed cars were being dragged aside. The intensity of the fire was evident, at least two boxcars having been reduced to molten heaps. The steel carcasses of those cars that were simply battered and dented were being lined up at the edge of the forest, where they would likely remain for eternity. The track itself, the vital Trans-Siberian Railway, was severely damaged, a giant crater waiting to be filled in. The surviving cars, those at the front of the train that had escaped the catastrophe, sat unscathed a half mile away.

The chopper deposited Tarkhan in a clearing a few hundred meters from ground zero. By the time he reached the scene, everyone was watching him, and for much the same reason he had drawn attention in Ovsyanka: the arrival of a civilian, unannounced, in a Russian Army helicopter, was sure to draw notice.

He had no trouble identifying the man in charge—in the middle of a group of three, he was the only one not wearing a hardhat.

"Mikhailov?" the Cossack asked straightaway.

"Yes. And you are?"

"I need information," Tarkhan said, as if not hearing the question. "You found two bodies in the wreckage, is that right?"

Mikhailov's hesitation was brief. "Yes, there." He pointed to the mangled car at the bottom of the hole, little more than a heap of liquified metal atop a mostly intact wheel carriage.

"Is that where the trouble began?"

"We are certain of it. The idiots started a fire in a car full of explosives."

Tarkhan looked up and down the track. "Have you determined exactly where the problem began?"

The investigator pointed up the track to the west. "There is a green evidence flag nearly a kilometer up the track. That's where things started lighting off. The red flag halfway there is where the first explosion caused the derailment. The ammunition car sat here cooking for a good ten minutes before the big secondary did this." He gestured to the crater.

Tarkhan studied it, then referenced a few of the battered cars nearby. "Was this car like the others? One loading door on the right side?"

"Yes."

He asked a few more questions, then ordered Mikhailov to write down his mobile number.

Tarkhan walked up the track toward the two flags. He reached the red one and saw the breach in the track—a crew was beginning to make repairs, but it would be days, if not weeks, before the rail line could be used. He kept going, and on the way to the green flag he paid particular attention to the siding on his left. He saw gouges in the gravel bed, dozens of sets of footprints tracking in every direction. There was also trash, probably left behind by the repair crews—food wrappers, mostly, and a shattered vodka bottle. Farther on he found a few scraps of singed paper, fallout from the conflagration. He reached the green flag, then walked a hundred yards past it.

There Tarkhan stopped.

His theory was highly speculative and would be difficult to prove. Any supporting evidence here had been thoroughly trampled. It occurred to him that the general had the best chance of validating his idea, and Tarkhan hoped he'd taken his request seriously.

Satisfied there was nothing more to be seen, he turned back and headed for his helicopter.

THIRTY-SEVEN

The wind came out of nowhere, a sharp twenty-knot gust sweeping in from the north. Kai kept next to Diaz, who didn't look a hundred percent. He had no apparent injuries, but a few minutes in the frigid water had severely sapped his strength. Kai was feeling it as well, even though she was perfectly dry. She had done duty in plenty of cold weather stations, but for a girl from Hawaii this was an outlier.

Tru, conversely, seemed to have gotten a second wind. He forged ahead ceaselessly in spite of the cold.

"We're going to need a fire," she called ahead.

"Already have one going."

He paused to let them catch up, and she studied him more closely. He was roughly her age, maybe a couple of years younger. A solid six feet tall, he was in excellent physical condition, and had been keeping a steady pace across the ice. Even so, she sensed he was holding back for their sake. His light brown hair was trimmed neatly, but he hadn't shaved in a few days and a blond-shot beard was taking over his face.

"Thanks for what you did back there," she said once they came alongside.

"Yeah, I owe you one," Diaz added.

He looked at them guardedly, his whiskers spackled with ice. "That's why I'm here . . . I think."

"By the way, I'm Major Kai Benetton."

"Air Force?" he asked.

"Yeah. And as I'm sure you've gathered, this is Diaz. First name, Qualario, master sergeant, USAF." She waited a beat, then prompted, "And you're just . . . Tru?"

"Yep."

Another empty pause. She supposed it was a CIA thing—not a call sign, but a codename. Cryptic and evasive, as if his real name only came on a need-to-know basis.

"Well, nice to meet you, Tru." She looked out ahead. "Where exactly are we going?"

He pointed shoreward. "Reference the tallest tree, then go right a hundred feet or so."

Her sharp eyes swept the shoreline, and all at once it materialized out of the forest backdrop. Sleek lines, sharp edges, twin vertical tails canted outward. *Vektor.*

"My God. He really did pretty it. He landed her on a frozen lake."

"I was impressed. But you might have one-upped him with . . . whatever that was you brought in."

"Experimental spaceplane, Star Chaser. Takes off on top of a Vulcan rocket, separates for a suborbital trajectory, then glides in for a landing."

"Glides? As in no power?"

"There are a couple of thrusters, but those only work in space."

"Huh. So that wasn't our ticket for getting out."

"Nope. Star Chaser is a one-and-done platform."

He looked at her questioningly. "Which means there are now four of us stuck in Siberia. That's how they drew it up?"

"It seemed like a good idea at the time. With Colonel Primakov being injured and the geography what it is—there was no way to extract you quickly. It was decided a supply mission would buy time."

The man whose name might or might not have been Tru looked back at the distant hole in the ice. "Sounds expensive." He set out walking again.

"It was," piped in Diaz. "But this is exactly what Star Chaser was designed for. It can take a limited load anywhere in the world in matter of hours."

Tru shot a glance at the darkening sky. "Any idea what the eventual plan is to get us out of here?"

Kai said, "When we left, it was still a work in progress. I can tell you they're pulling out all the stops—they really want to get their hands on Primakov."

"And who exactly is 'they'?"

"The CIA is the lead agency, but the president is making the calls."

He looked over his shoulder as if to read her. Probably trying to decide if she was serious. "The president, huh? Guess I shouldn't be surprised, given the risks involved."

"How is Primakov holding up?"

"He's immobile, broken tibia. Aside from that . . . he's cold and hungry."

Diaz said, "So I guess we do a little camping until our ride home shows up."

When Kai chuckled, Tru whipped around, anger boiling over. "Do you two have any idea how much shit you're in? We are one thousand miles inside enemy territory! The Russians are searching for us, and if they find us, they will consider us spies. That means no protections under the laws of war." He looked directly at Kai. "And in case you've missed what's gone on in Ukraine in recent years, prisoners, especially women, are not treated well. The Russians are animals, and they . . ." His words tailed off.

After a short beat, Kai responded sharply, "You're right, Agent Tru, or whatever the hell your name is, we are in deep shit. But this was a volunteer assignment. Diaz and I knew when we signed up that Star Chaser was a one-way trip. We came anyway!"

The two stared at one another, neither relenting.

He finally said, "Truman."

"What?"

"My name . . . it's Truman. My friends call me Tru."

Her gaze never wavered. "Okay . . . Truman."

"Yeah, well . . . enough conviviality. We need to find some cover."

Even the most hopeless bureaucracies sometimes stumble their way to success.

With low expectations, General Strelkov had forwarded Tarkhan's request for assistance to the appropriate GRU headquarters division. The ask was a relatively minor one, and on appearances seemed unrelated to the search for Vektor.

He assumed that Tarkhan wanted the information as a means of barter, something to trade for more relevant knowledge. Mutual favors between agencies were an essential component of Russian governance—in truth, the country would likely collapse without them. Most were minor corruptions. A case of vodka might be exchanged for details on how a boss was skimming funds; intel on which foreclosed businesses might soon be available for reallocation could be swapped to help a teenager dodge a draft notice. Such arrangements existed in all societies, private ledgers of convenience, but in Russia they were a fundamental cog of day-to-day life.

GRU headquarters was generally held to reside at 76 Khoroshevskoe Highway, yet the truth was more sprawling. Its reach into the buildings surrounding that address had spread like administrative ragweed, rooting outward and consuming everything in its path. The section where Strelkov's request landed was known as Unit 45921. The GRU reveled in such number-play, both for the sake of anonymity and the suggestion of mass.

The unit's mission was, in its own colorless parlance, "the coordination and processing of distant internal watchfulness." Muddled as that sounded, 45921 actually served a vital function. The Russian Federation rambled, from east to west, for over five thousand miles, and many of the more remote territories had large non-Slavic populations. Keeping watch on such a disparate populace had always been a challenge, yet the digital age had opened up new possibilities. Unit 45921 was the GRU's tie-in for the surveillance of thousands of remote towns, villages, and outposts—places that fell within the federation's borders, yet whose local authorities were less than reliable. It was a monumental task, and given the constraints of its budget, the unit had no hope of actively monitoring over a million distant feeds. It functioned, in effect, as a digital first responder that could appropriate surveillance channels to help put out faraway fires.

The unit's office was buried in an acutely soulless building on the edge of the sprawling GRU campus. The furniture was a remnant of the Brezhnev years, and the heater rarely worked. As if mocking its purely digital mission, the walls were lined with a parade of standard file cabinets. Inside them were countless yellowed folders, stamped with various levels of classification and the old KGB emblem, that no one seemed to have the authority to destroy.

On a good day ten people showed up for work; this day, as it turned out, was something less. The message from Strelkov was shared across all seven occupied desks—the tasking had, after all, come from a general officer—and everyone set to work. The first order of business was to track down security footage, if any existed, from a rail yard in Birobidzhan. More specifically, a forty-minute period during which an ammunition train had stopped briefly the previous day.

To everyone's mild surprise, they learned that not only were three cameras installed at the rail yard, but they were functional, and the

footage was available for immediate transfer. After a few essential protocols, the security officer in Birobidzhan sent the data in a matter of
minutes.

From there, the team dove into the second part of the general's tasking.
And that was where the problems began.

THIRTY-EIGHT

"Welcome to Forward Operating Base Vektor," Tru said when they reached camp.

He introduced the newcomers to Colonel Maksim Primakov, and noticed that Kai and the Russian seemed to connect right away. Not wanting to waste time on test pilot shop talk, he interceded.

"We have a lot to get done here." He stoked the fire as he talked. "Our comm gear went down with the ship. That's going to complicate things. I've got one handset with forty percent on the battery, and in cold like this that won't last long. We need to compose a sitrep and tell Langley what's happened. After that, I need to hike out and retrieve the rest of our equipment."

"Do you want us to come?" Kai asked.

"I put together a gurney to move the colonel yesterday—with a few modifications, I can turn it into a sled and manage on my own. There's no hiding on the ice, and the less group exposure we have the better. Anyway, you and Diaz need to get to work on Vektor. Our orders are to exploit it to the maximum extent possible."

"They wanted pictures," Diaz said, "but we lost the camera."

"My phone is good for some pics, but like I said, battery power is at a premium and right now comm takes priority. Keep a log of what you want to photograph, and we'll try to get to it before we leave."

Tru issued tasking, and even Primakov was given chores—the fire had to be tended, and the colonel was ingloriously assigned to be chief stoker and commander of wet clothing to be dried. Diaz diverted to Vektor. Once Tru and Kai agreed on what needed to be in the sitrep, he turned on the handset, typed as quickly as he could, and hit the send button. He powered down immediately.

It was early afternoon, and he wondered if he should wait for darkness before setting out to recover the supplies. He would be exposed on the ice for close to two hours. That said, one man pulling a sled wasn't particularly suspicious. Aside from the sonic boom, they had heard nothing to suggest a search in the distance—in this kind of isolation, with the air so cold, the sound of an aircraft would register long before they could get a visual. There had also been no sign of civilians—there were a handful of villages along the reservoir, and while the nearest of them was ten miles away, a chance encounter with locals couldn't be discounted. Given his language skills, Tru reckoned an accidental meeting would be manageable as long as Vektor wasn't in sight.

He decided the sooner he retrieved the equipment, the better. He bulked up his makeshift gurney with extra branches and paracord, and then tested it on the ice. It worked as expected—nothing durable, but solid enough to carry what they'd salvaged from Star Chaser. The outbound trip would be easy, but he guessed hauling the supplies back would be a workout.

He set out alone toward the big hole in the ice. Not for the first time, he was struck by how this mission was morphing. Two days ago, he had been driving toward an effluent pond on a stolen motorbike in Hegang. Now he was humping over a frozen lake in Siberia. He had initially been fired up about being sent into Russia, imagining a chance to exact the vengeance he'd long sought. Instead, he was stuck playing defense, responsible for the safety of three people, one of whom was Russian. And while they were all technically soldiers, if their position was uncovered, he didn't expect much combat support from two test pilots and a mechanic. It also didn't help that the weapons he'd requested were at the bottom of the reservoir. It all added up to one thing—avoiding contact with the enemy was paramount.

He picked up speed, feeling vulnerable in the open. The sled was running smoothly behind him, but the thoughts in his head were more jarring. Tru felt as if the op was slipping out of his control. He regretted his earlier outburst to Kai and Diaz, but frustration had gotten the better of him. He had entered Russia expecting to play offense, yet with each new development it felt more like a retreat.

Every decision, every step, seemed a retrograde move. He wasn't acting but reacting.

And he didn't like it one damned bit.

Sorensen spent most of the night at the Pentagon fine tuning the extraction plan with General Carter. Vice presidents didn't typically immerse themselves in JSOC mission planning—but then, most vice presidents didn't have backgrounds in clandestine operations. At the edge of midnight, the two set out to the White House to give the president an update.

The limo carried them over the 14th Street Bridge, and from there the driver weaved his way to East Executive Avenue. From that vantage point Sorensen had a good view of the southern portico of the White House. Lights were burning bright all around, and she wondered if it was like that every night.

"Who else will be joining us?" Carter asked.

"Not sure. At this hour, it might be just the president."

"I wish our plan didn't have so many variables."

"There are a lot of moving parts, but nothing that can't be overpowered by unlimited resources."

He looked up from his briefing sheet and eyed her. "You're as worried about this as I am."

"Yeah, pretty much."

The wheels of the limo squealed as the driver turned into the parking garage, and moments later two Secret Service agents were ushering them upstairs. They were taken, not surprisingly, straight to the Oval Office.

Sorensen was the first through the door and she diverted to one side. Carter came in behind her with all the enthusiasm of a gladiator entering a lion pit. As it turned out, aside from the president, two others were waiting: national security advisor James Holden and DNI Karl Fuller occupied the far side of the world's most famous office.

President Cleveland wasted no time. "I thought our new SAC director was coming."

Sorensen replied, "David took a flight west—he wanted to oversee the mission from up front."

The president's gaze narrowed. "Up front?"

"He's headed to the mission launch point. When it comes to operational detail there's nobody better and we're only going to have one shot at this."

Apparently mollified, she moved on. "I'm told Star Chaser landed successfully on the reservoir."

"They set down right on schedule and Rookie made contact with the crew. We just received an update. The team are starting to go over Vektor. There are, however, some minor complications."

The presidential head canted warily.

"I don't have the specifics," Sorensen continued, "but apparently Star Chaser sank into the lake."

"I'm confused," said Fuller. "Wasn't that the plan all along?"

"Yes, but it didn't happen as expected. Along with her other cargo, Star Chaser was carrying a small shaped explosive charge. The intention was for our operator to employ it to fracture the ice beneath the spaceplane, sinking it in the deepest part of the reservoir. We figured if we could put the vehicle out of sight, we might keep the Russians from knowing it was ever there—or at the very least, make it hard to salvage. For reasons that aren't clear, Star Chaser began sinking soon after landing. The crew were able to unload some of the gear, but much of the load was lost."

"Anything critical?" asked the president.

"The biggest loss was all three comm units. We still have one usable sat phone, thankfully, the one Rookie is carrying."

"Will that be enough going forward?"

"Marginally, yes. There's no way to recharge it where they are, so Rookie will have to conserve battery power. We also lost two discreet navigation beacons—those would have helped during the rescue if the weather takes a turn for the worse."

"Okay, so we've delivered partial supplies, and we're exploiting Vektor. Let's hear the plan for getting everyone out."

This put General Carter on the hot seat. The mission to extract was firmly on the DOD's shoulders.

He said, "The mission is taking shape and we've begun moving elements into place. There is only one aircraft that can reach that far into Russia and bring out three passengers and equipment—the CV-22 Osprey."

Everyone in the room had a basic familiarity with the Osprey. It was a tilt-rotor vertical takeoff and landing aircraft, flown by both the Air Force and Marine Corps. When it came to penetrating Russian airspace, however, it had one giant flaw.

It was James Holden, a retired admiral, who played devil's advocate. "The Osprey isn't stealthy. It's one thing to have Star Chaser fall out of the sky like a blob of space junk—with a little misdirection, we got away with that. But there's no way an Osprey is going to penetrate Russian air defense networks without being seen."

"You make a valid point," Carter allowed. "But I think we've found a way around that . . ."

THIRTY-NINE

USS *Boxer* scythed a choppy path through the southern Sea of Japan. The seas were heavy; a low-pressure area had descended from the north and a bitter twenty-knot wind cut across the deck.

Boxer was a *Wasp*-class amphibious assault ship, and while it didn't pack the punch of the Navy's big nuclear carriers, it was a capable strike platform with its complement of AV-8B Harriers, F-35 Lightnings, and various helicopters and support aircraft.

Boxer had been west of Fukuoka, Japan, steaming toward the East China Sea for an exercise with the South Korean Navy, when her tasking had suddenly changed. She was ordered to turn northeast at best speed and remain in Japanese territorial waters. Instructions regarding a special new mission would soon follow.

"Still nothing?" asked Captain Dave Longmire, *Boxer*'s skipper, when his exec appeared.

Standing on the catwalk outside the bridge, the wind buffeted both men's jackets in light drizzle. Captain Carl Emerson had gone down to check on things in the combat information center.

"One new comm. Sometime in the next ten hours we can expect a couple of arrivals." Emerson zipped up his jacket against the wind. It was mid-afternoon, and once the sun set the temperature was forecast to plummet.

"Let me guess . . . Ospreys?"

"Didn't say, but the fact that the original message mentioned V-22 maintenance support . . . it stands to reason."

"CINCPAC is playing this tight."

"I was thinking the same thing."

"What do you make of this random point in the ocean we're headed to?" the skipper asked. Their amended orders had given them a new destination: a grid pairing west of La Pérouse Strait, the narrow body of water that separated Sakhalin Island from Hokkaido.

"Probably the same as you. It's as close as we can get to Russian territory without poking the bear."

"A jumping off point?"

"If that's what it is, it'd be risky. An aircraft as unstealthly as an Osprey—you can't hide from radar in that airspace."

"Well, whatever they're up to, I'd say it's sourced pretty high."

"Agreed. Smells like a total black op."

Longmire, who had spent most of his career flying Hornets, looked up at the scudding gray clouds. "Tell you one thing, I'm glad it's not me landing in this shit tonight."

"Like I've been telling you since the academy—surface warfare is the way to go."

Kai looked out across the lake. Their CIA minder was a mere dot in the distance, but he was moving smoothly, keeping a good pace. She guessed it would be different on the way back, when he would be sled-dogging a hundred pounds of equipment behind him. She wondered if she should have insisted on going with him. There was no clear chain of command between them. She could even imagine Primakov trying to assert his authority—they were, after all, on the colonel's turf, and he outranked everyone. Kai tried to keep a positive outlook. With any luck, rescue would come soon, and no contentious decisions would have to be made.

For now, their greatest enemy was the cold. It seemed to go straight to her bones, even though she had put on an extra pair of thermal pants and a second heavy shirt, and switched out to a pair of waterproof trail boots. It had been a mistake to not prioritize retrieval of the comm gear, but at least they'd salvaged the heavy clothing before Star Chaser had gone down.

Diaz had also layered up, and he was going over Vektor feverishly. He might have been a worthless copilot, but there wasn't a mechanic in the Air Force she would rather have on that job. Primakov was presently digging into an MRE—beef stroganoff in a pouch. It wasn't her personal favorite, especially since she was trending vegetarian, but he seemed to be enjoying it.

"Our snake-eater seems wound pretty tight," she remarked to the Russian, gesturing toward the lake.

He shoveled in another mouthful of beef, not put off by the fact that his meal was cold. The MRE heating pouch had proved inadequate, and the simple cooking gear they'd brought was at the bottom of the lake.

"Tru?" he said, pausing his heavy-duty plastic spoon. "He is very focused, and that is what we need. He reached me quickly and warmed me before I froze to death. Is he one of your Navy SEALs?"

"I don't know what his background is. But given that he's here, doing what he's doing . . . probably something like that."

He looked at her questioningly, then scooped another spoonful of beef. "I heard the sonic boom announcing your arrival. I have to ask, one pilot to another, what kind of aircraft brought you here?"

"That would be classified."

Primakov smiled. "I have risked my life to help America, and still you do not trust me?"

"I barely know you. But I'll tell you about it when we get somewhere safe. We're not quite out of the woods, so to speak, and it's probably in everyone's best interest that I don't share too much."

The Russian was undeterred. "Given how quickly you arrived, and the distance from the nearest border . . . Star Chaser, I think."

It was her turn to smile. "I guess you get intelligence briefings too."

"Of course . . . but I learn far more from reading *Aviation Week*." He was referring to the trade publication that gave detailed insight into the latest developments in air and space technology. "The openness of your society is both a strength and a weakness."

"Tell me about it." She looked at Vektor. Diaz was crawling across the jet's spine between the wings. "So, fill me in on how you ended up here."

He grunted painfully. "Everything was going to plan. I separated from the working area and was on my way to Japan when I noticed a low reading in the number two fuel tank. I looked back and saw fuel streaming from the wing. The calculations were simple enough—there was no way I could reach the border. Then the situation got worse. The right engine overheated."

"Fuel leaking into the hot section of the engine?"

"That was my conclusion. I saw two choices—put down immediately or eject."

"Couldn't you have diverted to an airport?"

"That, unfortunately, was not an option." He told her about the letter he had left his father-in-law . . . and also *who* his father-in-law was.

"Yeah, I can see that would have put you in a tough spot."

He pointed to the jet. "I explained the fuel problem to your sergeant, and he said he would try to locate the cause."

"If anyone can do it, it's Diaz."

He looked up at the sky, the clouds having cleared. "I remember as a child how vast the world seemed. The sky and the stars, the lakes and forest. The older I get, the smaller it all seems."

"I know what you mean. Maybe it has to do with our profession. The perspective from above is different, seeing from horizon to horizon every time you go up."

"And you have been in space—that must make it even more so."

"It does. The curvature of the earth, the black void all around. We're all floating on that big blue marble." She turned toward Vektor. "I should go see if Diaz is making progress." Kai then paused and gave him a circumspect look. "I was told you were bringing out some data."

He reached into the zippered breast pocket of his flight suit and extracted three thumb drives. He then put them back and zipped the pocket closed.

"I think you and I are going to have a lot to talk about," Kai said.

"Yes, we will . . . but all in good time."

Kai found Diaz beavering away in the engine bay. He had two panels dropped and his head was inside, the beam of a headlamp dancing deep in the jet's bowels. Not wanting to interrupt, she looked elsewhere and noticed a makeshift rope ladder hanging from the canopy rail. Primakov had told her that Vektor's integral ladder was inoperative—the indirect cause of his fall—and Diaz had clearly improvised a replacement. Seeing the canopy open, she couldn't resist.

She climbed up, double-checked that the ejection seat was safe, and settled into the cockpit.

It was designed for someone Primakov's size, giving Kai plenty of room. She couldn't determine the functions of most of the switches since they were labeled in Cyrillic, but it looked like a standard array of systems and armament controls.

There was one thing that struck her as different from other Russian fighters she'd seen: a set of four multi-function displays dominated the instrument panel. She had previously flown two Russian jets, expropriated by various means to the West, and both were generations behind in terms of software and weapons integration. The displays in front of her weren't powered up, so there was no way to tell what was under the digital hood, but she reckoned the electronics had come from the Chinese side of the house—according to Primakov, Vektor was a joint project between the nations.

She heard a rattle at the canopy rail, and Diaz's smiling face appeared.

"So, what do you think, Major? Any match for a Raptor?"

Kai smiled. "Hard to say without knowing the beeps and squeaks. These days, lethality is all about radar and missiles. But in the hands of the right pilot, yeah, this might be trouble. What about you—find anything interesting?"

"I'm pretty sure I've isolated the fuel leak. There's a puncture on the bottom of the right wing, behind the wheel well. Probably ran over debris on takeoff and kicked something up that penetrated the skin. The fuel tank is right above the hole. It's only the size of a quarter, but it definitely would have vented. Most of what leaked probably went overboard, but a bit drained back toward the starboard engine. I can see a hot spot outside the compressor section. There's no real damage done, but if it had burned another ten minutes it would have gotten ugly."

"Sounds like the colonel made the right call. I'll let him know."

Diaz looked suddenly contemplative. "I know it's out of your hands, Major . . . but any idea how long we're going to be here?"

"Our salvation remains a mystery. I'd say hope for a day, plan for a week." She looked back along the big jet's spine. "As soon as our CIA friend gets back with the equipment, our first job will be to be string up those tarps—we need to get Vektor under cover."

"Too conspicuous?"

"To a good infrared sensor? This thing would stand out like Times Square in the Sahara."

FORTY

Tru was stunned by the shades of white in a Siberian winter. As a former biathlon competitor, he had spent countless hours in cold-weather environments. Yet something here felt different. The opaqueness of the ice, the purity of the snow, the softness of the high clouds. Color, texture, brightness. The more he looked, the more disarming it became, a spectral vision that never stopped evolving.

Now, as the sun neared the western hills, the translucent surface of the reservoir was falling to gray. Despite having unzipped his jacket, he was sweating as he humped the sled over the ice toward camp. He'd reached the hole where Star Chaser had disappeared thirty minutes earlier, and found the breach already covered by a thin sheet of ice. By morning there would be little beyond a rough patch in the lake's surface, nothing to mark the final resting place of a top secret American spaceplane.

He'd been taught how to make a makeshift sled in Arctic survival training. Clearly, he hadn't paid enough attention. He'd lashed a half dozen extra branches to his jury-rigged gurney, and on the outbound haul it had worked well. Then he'd loaded it down with the supplies. Tru did his best to spread the weight along the length of the sled, but when he tried to move it the resistance was excessive, the ends of the outside runners digging into the ice. He saw only two options: tough it out for an hour, or split the load and make a second run. With night fast approaching, he'd chosen the former. Next time, he decided, he would use more branches, bind them more tightly, and shave the bottom surfaces smooth.

Yeah, next time.

The sledding was tough, but he was halfway back to camp. He couldn't help but reflect on the circular track of his life. Eight years ago, he had been immersed in biathlon, punishing his body even more severely than he was now for the sake of sport. Then college intervened, and he'd prioritized mind over body. Tru had always been fascinated by architecture and history: the practical, religious, and scandalous motivations that gave rise to buildings, neighborhoods, even entire cities. Studying the lines and logic of an ancient structure was like delving into the minds of its creators and benefactors. Then, just when it seemed like he'd set the trajectory of his life, tragedy intervened.

And here I am, right back where I started. Cold and hurting.

He moved cautiously, but the awkward load caused him to slip on the ice time and again. Keeping a constant speed was a struggle, and his progress became increasingly choppy.

Tru paused for a breather, the strain getting the better of him. He was reconsidering whether to abandon half the load and come back for it later when his thoughts were instantly severed.

He heard the unmistakable thrum of a helicopter.

He scanned the sky and spotted it to the north. A blunt shadow sweeping low over the hills. It was a Hind, although the exact model escaped him. D, F, J. There was no end to the damned variants. Then he discerned a second, and a third in trail.

The direness of his situation hit hard. He was at least a mile from the shoreline. Even if he left the sled where it was, there was no chance he could conceal himself in time.

And running would only draw attention.

The Hinds were heading west—not toward him, but on a parallel course. There was a chance they wouldn't see him in the gathering dusk. That hopeful notion was shot down when the lead Hind banked sharply and began flying directly toward him.

Tru didn't panic.

Oddly, it was quite the reverse. His thoughts seemed to slow down, acquiring an astonishing clarity. He put himself in the place of the lead helicopter crew, tried to assess the picture as they would—whoever *they* were. Since these were clearly military birds, he assumed they were part of the search for Vektor, although three aircraft flying in formation seemed counterintuitive. Vektor wasn't visible from where he stood—it sat shrouded behind a small peninsula of timber. Yet the Hinds were higher, with a better angle, and if they looked in precisely the right direction . . .

This set Tru's first decision. He didn't want the crewmen looking at the shoreline—he wanted their eyes on him. He began walking again, but on a different track than he'd been holding—a small bit of misdirection away from Vektor. He hadn't been leaving noticeable tracks on the ice, so it might be convincing. He was sure Kai and the others would hear the helicopters, and he envisioned them dousing the campfire and taking cover.

He plodded across the ice, doing his best to present a stark, relatable image. This was something that had been drilled into him during tradecraft training. Blending in was straightforward on a city street teeming with people or in a crowded train station. But when you were isolated, without crowds and confusion, the best move was to present a plausible image. Look like someone who *should* be there. In present circumstances: he was a lone man in a desolate place, battling the elements to scrape out a living. He had thankfully covered the loaded sled with a blanket, so what was beneath would be a mystery from a distance. He could be a hunter hauling a deer or elk carcass. Or a local recluse stocking his cabin with cans of food and bags of grain.

The reverberations of the rotors built as all three Hinds approached. He wondered how they would handle the situation. He was alone and would not be mistaken for Colonel Primakov. He doubted they could imagine his involvement in the loss of Vektor. The crew would almost certainly envision him as a local, a hunter or a trapper. Yet that brought its own kind of trouble—they might think he was good for a few questions. But would the pilots risk setting the big choppers down on the ice? Primakov had proved it could be done, but only in the face of a dire situation.

The helos vectored slightly to one side, and when one came abeam Tru got his first close look. The Hind was the aesthetic opposite of Vektor, not sleek lines and stealth, but blunt protuberances and ungainly armament pylons. The overall impression was distinctly buglike, the chin-mounted gun probing out like a stinger. A side door was open amidship on the lead aircraft and he saw four men in winter tactical gear. They were studying him, conversing. Two held rifles but they weren't pointed in his direction. Not yet. The lead Hind swept into a wide turn and the others followed, circling like a school of sharks.

The noise became thunderous, rotor wash sending swirls of snow across the ice. The lead helo came to a hover, and Tru saw the pilots gesturing, conferring with someone in back. They were debating whether it was safe to put down.

This was the moment of truth. Tru did the only thing that seemed natural in the situation. He waved. This brought more talking, gesturing, and finally the man who was central in the open side door replied to his greeting—a rude hand gesture.

Never in his life had Tru been so happy to get flipped off.

There was a distinct pitch change, the engines throttling up, and the lead helicopter flew directly over Tru, dusting him with snow in its whirling vortices. Soon all three Hinds were thrashing off toward the far side of the reservoir.

Tru took a long, deep breath, let it out slowly.

He couldn't avoid imagining how it would have played out if the pilots had been more adventurous and landed. There would have been no hope of talking his way out of the situation. Language skills or not, the soldiers would have checked the sled. Among his supplies they would have found military-grade infrared tarps, tools proudly made in America, and U.S. Army–issue Meals Ready-to-Eat.

At that point, his options would have ranged from abysmal to suicidal. If he could have stolen a weapon, he might have put up a good fight. Yet his odds in a firefight would have been grim. With nowhere to hide, he would have been battling a dozen armed men, not to mention three helicopter gunships. The only question: not whether he would have been killed, but how many of the bastards he could have taken with him. Because for Truman Miller, in Russia, being taken prisoner was not on the menu.

As the Hinds receded into the western dusk, the cold truth sank in: he had narrowly avoided his private Waterloo.

Tru stood there for a time, thinking.

Remembering.

Finally, he set back out toward camp.

When he reached it, the first order of business would be to conceal their position as best they could. The Hinds would not have departed if they'd deemed him a threat, yet someone's curiosity might be piqued. The helicopters could return, or a foot patrol might follow up. If he didn't have a wounded man in his care, the obvious choice would be to pull up stakes and move. Primakov's injury, however, precluded that option.

As he trekked shoreward, Tru used the time to self-critique. Had he put himself in a bad position? Yes, but not without good reason—retrieving the supplies was vital. The appearance of the helicopters was not unexpected; it had simply come at a bad time, when he'd been exposed.

He remembered Kai's offer of help earlier. What if he had taken her up on it? On the one hand, her presence might have helped sell the picture: a man and a woman striving to survive in a remote frontier. Then the alternate scenario ran in his head, and anger set in. What if they had landed and Kai was with him? How would a band of Russian soldiers, deep in the wilderness, have reacted? He rode that idea farther than he should have before remembering another line from training: *In most jobs you can learn from your mistakes. This isn't one of them.*

Tru distilled the encounter to two conclusions.

He had been damned lucky.

And in his second life-or-death confrontation in a matter of days, he hadn't flinched. He had made the right calls.

Non semper ea sunt quae videntur. "Not always what they seem."

This was the motto of the 486th Flight Test Squadron at Eglin Air Force Base in Florida. The Latin phrase, coyly scripted on the squadron patch, laid bare the truth of the unit's faux designation: no "test" work was performed by its pilots. The Squadron flew the C-32B Gatekeeper, a highly modified version of the Boeing-757 airliner. The interiors of the jets were very different from the sister ships flown by Delta Airlines: there was a high-end communication suite, a cabin that could be configured for various combinations of cargo and personnel, and a rest area for additional crewmembers on extended flights. The exterior was quite the opposite, as if someone had ordered the aircraft wrapped in a plain white envelope. The only markings were those mandated by international law—a registration number and an American flag to denote the country of registry.

The 486th's real mission was as vague as it was secretive: the unit provided quick-reaction transport, in support of time-critical missions, for the State Department and the CIA's Special Activities Center.

And quick they had been.

A C-32B was waiting at Andrews Air Force Base when the generic government sedan approached. The steward standing at the bottom of the boarding stairs, a master sergeant wearing a flight suit, didn't really know what to expect. His crew, who had been on alert at Eglin, had gotten the call four hours ago. One passenger was to be delivered ASAP from Andrews to a military base in Japan.

A man emerged from the car and walked quickly to the stairs. He carried a standard backpack and was wearing a winter jacket. Given another backdrop, he could have been heading out for a trail hike.

"Good morning, sir," the sergeant said. Since the man appeared to be civilian, he didn't salute.

"Good morning," their guest replied.

"Any luggage?"

"You're looking at it," the passenger said, gesturing to what was on his back.

The man ascended the stairs two at a time, which wasn't lost on the sergeant. Whoever this guy was, he was in a hurry. Five minutes later, the stairs were pulled back, the chocks removed, and the big jet was taxiing on a single engine. In order to save precious seconds, the second engine would be started on the way out to the runway.

FORTY-ONE

There were three multi-spectral tarps, and Tru worked with Diaz to drape them over Vektor. Tie-downs were included, high-strength line similar to paracord, and they used all of them as insurance against the unpredictable wind. The tarp's green-camo scheme wasn't ideal for winter terrain, but it worked well to muddle Vektor's distinctive visual silhouette, and also gave protection against sensors of certain wavelengths. To distort the picture further, Tru and Diaz piled snow and tree branches randomly on the tarp.

When they were done, Diaz went back to working on the airplane. Tru saw Kai engaged with Primakov. Their conversation appeared casual, and from a distance he caught a bit of the exchange—Kai was relating her flying experiences. It gave every impression of two pilots passing time. Had she been CIA, Tru might have thought differently. He would have assumed manipulation, and that everything she was telling him was fabricated. That was how an agency interrogator would handle a source, but with Kai it didn't fit. There was something genuine about the major. She was smart and capable, but deception simply wasn't in her locker.

He looked around and weighed what to do next. For Tru, waiting for extraction was like waiting for a storm. He didn't know exactly when it was coming or how challenging it would be, but like a Boy Scout gone nuclear he was determined to be ready.

He regretted that they hadn't retrieved the weapons from Star Chaser, but of far greater consequence was the loss of the comm gear. He had checked for messages once each hour, but with less than a twenty percent charge remaining on his sat phone, he had no choice but to increase the interval. The last time he had powered it up, he quickly referenced the map application. The nearest civilization was a tiny village called Khvoyny on the opposite side of the reservoir. He researched it quickly on the agency database: the town's two hundred and twenty-six residents lived on twelve streets. It was marginally seasonal, with an economy that was a two-legged stool—gold mining and forestry. Altogether, a inconsequential outpost in a vast wilderness. Yet for Tru, the town held one great attraction—electrical outlets.

He was running a risk-benefit analysis of a visit to town when Kai walked over and sat down next to him.

"How's the colonel holding up?" he asked.

"As well as can be. We mostly talked about flying. He can tell us a lot about Vektor, not to mention a few other airplanes he's flown."

"I'm wondering what he can tell us about himself."

"What do you mean?"

"I'm curious what drove him to defect."

She shot a glance at Primakov—he'd taken some pain meds and looked half asleep. Kai lowered her voice. "I brought that up, in an oblique way. It was strange, but he actually sounded pretty patriotic. He grew up in the Soviet era, went to the top military academies. He said he doesn't like what Russia has become—the corruption, the cronyism. Eventually the war in Ukraine came up, and when it did, he clammed right up."

Tru's gaze went dark. "Do you think he flew missions there?"

"I didn't ask, but it's doubtful. He's been doing test work for ten years, which generally keeps a pilot off the front lines. But there was definitely something there."

The spark Tru had felt died down and he found himself distracted. Kai had pulled her black hair into a short ponytail. Absent the trappings of rank and profession, she was very attractive. She was also on task. She'd been getting information out of Primakov, even if it was in a good-cop way. Best of all, he didn't see signs of stress. The cold, being stranded in enemy territory—none of it seemed to bother her. She was composure personified. But then, he supposed that went with the territory of being a test pilot.

He got up and went to the pile of blankets, plucked two off the top, and handed them to her.

"No fire tonight?" she asked. They had doused it earlier when the helicopters had come near.

"Better not. Maybe in the morning."

"Sounds like you had a close call with those Hinds."

Tru had told everyone about his encounter. "I got lucky," he said, which was true. Then he lied. "I'm not sure what would have happened if it had landed." He looked out across the ice. "We need to set a watch tonight."

"A watch?"

"I was definitely seen. I don't think any alarms were raised, but it's possible somebody will come looking for us."

"So you want us on guard duty."

"I don't think we have a choice." They locked eyes for a moment, and he tried to read her. She seemed to be weighing an argument. Kai was a major in the Air Force, and if Tru had a rank in the CIA, it would be considerably lower. Right now, however, none of that mattered. It was all about whose expertise was most relevant.

Like a good officer, she recognized it, and said, "I'm in."

"I'll take the first three hours," he said. "You can do the next shift, then Diaz and the colonel can take their turns."

"You're really going to put Primakov to work?"

"Like it or not, he's part of the team."

A look of amusement spread across her face. "This whole thing sounds like some weird scenario from leadership school."

"Does it? I wouldn't know—must have missed that training block."

After locating and acquiring the footage from the train station in Birobidzhan, Unit 45921 moved on to their secondary task, which, on its surface, was straightforward: they were to search for suspicious persons on the recordings, and if at all possible identify them.

The first pass was promising. Near the end of the video, minutes before the train departed, a man appeared on the non-station side. At a casual glance he might have been a railway employee—he was dressed in workman's clothes and carried a tool of some kind over one shoulder. This impression held as he meandered between a few of the rail cars, seemingly performing inspections. Then, near the end of the recording, he inexplicably climbed aboard a boxcar and didn't reemerge before the train departed.

This was highly suspicious, and while no one in the room knew the reasons behind Strelkov's interest, they realized the general was onto something. The footage had reasonably good resolution, and after running it through their best enhancement algorithms—which was, after all, the unit's specialty—they got a solid capture of the intruder's face.

And that was where their run of luck ended.

For the best part of a day, and into that night, the face was seined through the GRU's vast databases, which included facial profiles on virtually every Russian citizen. When this gave no match, the unit began the time-consuming process of running the photo through two secondary digital libraries. The first was a compilation of all foreigners whose images had been logged by immigration control as having entered the country in the last twelve years—when the surveillance program had begun. The second, and far more extensive, library involved images that had been vacuumed up through various GRU cyberattacks: driver's license and passport files pilfered from scores of countries, profiles vacuumed from social media, and the digital bounty of raids on various government and corporate computers across the world. By the internal estimate of the GRU, which was likely inflated—bureaucrats were the same everywhere—the agency had the faces of over half the world's population on file.

This last comparison was the most time-consuming, but eventually a handful of possibilities were flagged for closer study. All, unfortunately, failed more precise matching algorithms, not to mention the experienced eyes of the unit's top analysts. By one a.m. the next morning, the process reached an end point. The face from the rail yard in Birobidzhan could not be identified.

It was disappointing, but not unusual—and in certain ways, the lack of identification was an answer in itself. With a ninety-six percent certainty, the man was not Russian, had not visited Russia in recent years, and his picture had not been acquired in the course of cyber operations. Who this ghost was, and what he was doing in a backwater train yard on the edge of Siberia, was of little concern to the sappers of Unit 45921. The supervisor was confident his people had done their best, done it quickly, and he packaged their findings in a succinct report.

At two that morning he sent an email summing their work, along with the acquired raw footage, to Viktor Strelkov. The e-soldiers of Unit 45921 then went home for a much-needed rest.

FORTY-TWO

Captain Volkov walked into the enlisted mess hall at Chita Air Base and saw his men occupying two tables. After a short night they had taken the place over, which wouldn't win any love from the local contingent. The captain had rousted his men early, but even after breakfast and coffee they were a tired and surly bunch. He knew they were frustrated, and he felt it as well. Vega Group was an action-oriented unit, and for two days now they had been flying endless grid patterns in a search that seemed hopeless. It didn't help that their recent Africa trip had put money in everyone's pocket, while success here held no such promise. By every measure, this mission the general had saddled them with was a tough sell. Volkov was tired of telling his men to stay focused, and they were tired of hearing it.

The highlight of their previous day had been dusting some local idiot who'd been lugging a sled across the reservoir. They had spotted only a handful of people in the last two days, most of them near the few villages they'd come across. Volkov had come up with one idea for streamlining the operation. They were wasting too much time going to and from the search box, returning to Chita every few hours for refueling. For this reason, he had sent a request to the general last night, and to his mild surprise it had been immediately approved.

He went to the head of the room to address his men.

"I understand your frustration with this mission, but we must carry out our orders as the professionals we are. I do have good news this morning. A temporary fuel depot is being established in a small mining town inside our area of operations. I have also arranged accommodations for us there. This will allow more time on station to successfully complete our mission. Do you have questions?"

"How long will we stay there?" a jug-eared corporal asked.

"The missing aircraft must be found, but I cannot imagine it will take more than a few days."

"Does this town have women?" asked the senior sergeant, a hairy fireplug of a man. Laughter and heckling broke out.

"Every place has women. But in a town like this, they probably shave more often than you, Drugov."

More laughter, and the mood lightened noticeably. His men needed to let loose, and tonight they would. Volkov, too, was relieved. With more time available to search, perhaps they would find the crash site soon. And then, surely, they could move on to something more lucrative.

Strelkov was on the phone in Nemanchik's office, getting the latest on the Air Force search, when he turned and saw Tarkhan in the open doorway. He startled only slightly. The Cossack had a way of appearing soundlessly. It was off-putting—and, he was sure, intentional.

He ended the call, and said, "That was the Air Force. There have been no new developments overnight. They are expanding their search marginally in all directions."

"What of my request?" Tarkhan asked, as if Strelkov had not spoken.

"Headquarters spent the night working on it. It was as you suspected. They uncovered footage of a man getting on the doomed train at the rail yard in Birobidzhan."

"Only one man?"

"That's what I was told. Were you expecting more?"

The Cossack considered it, then said without elaborating, "One man makes sense. Show me."

Strelkov went to the computer on the desk and called up the images.

Tarkhan remained silent as he studied them. There were five in all, various captures of the man walking through the rail yard. The collar of his jacket was raised, and he averted his face from the cameras in a way that was purely professional. One frame, however, from a camera he likely hadn't spotted, provided a decent look at his face. It wasn't Colonel Primakov—not that Tarkhan ever imagined it would be. The features were vaguely European, although not conclusively. He could conceivably be an ethnic Russian, but more likely was something else. In the last image the man could be seen climbing into a boxcar—almost surely the one that was now a melted heap in a crater outside Ovsyanka.

Tarkhan's suspicions deepened. He noted the time stamps on the photos and compared them to the well documented time of the derailment. He turned away from the computer and regarded the wall map. With the general's eyes on him, his blunt finger traced the railway, from Birobidzhan to the point where the derailment had occurred. Then it kept going and settled on one of the places he had been yesterday: Ulak Station, and the nearby town of Ovsyanka. His eyes returned to Birobidzhan, and then continued in the other direction—not along the rail line, but into the wilds south and west.

"You have not been able to identify this man," Tarkhan said. It was near an accusation.

"No," Strelkov admitted. "The image was run through all our databases, but there was no match. Now, I have done as you asked. Tell me what this has to do with my son-in-law's crash."

Tarkhan turned to face him, his weathered features giving nothing away.

When he didn't reply, Strelkov's frustration peaked. He would have berated any other man in his command for such willfulness, yet something told him that wouldn't work here. The Cossack had a reputation as an excellent hunter, and he was beginning to understand why. It wasn't merely that he knew the forest. He understood his quarry. He had a gift for putting himself in the heads of those he was tracking—and also those he worked for. He had found a thread and seized it; the photos from the rail yard were proof of his instincts. Strelkov needed this man on his side, but that would require taking a risk.

"You and I must reach an understanding," he began, pausing for emphasis. Even for Tarkhan, such words from an overseer of the GRU would carry menacing weight. "There is something else in play, but I must have your word that it will remain between us."

"You have it."

That his response was immediate Strelkov took as a positive. There were no complex thoughts, no measuring of angles. This was a man on a mission, nothing more and nothing less.

"It is possible my son-in-law was flying to the West on an . . . an unauthorized mission. In the course of it, I believe the airplane went down."

"And you are not sure if he has survived."

"Precisely."

Tarkhan nodded. "This is what I suspected."

Strelkov was mildly surprised. "How did you reach this conclusion?"

"You have taken a personal interest that seems unusual, even if it does involve your son-in-law. And just now, when you were on the phone with the Air Force—they told you there was no new information, and you were not surprised. More relieved, I think. Also, you have turned the search to the east, but only using people who are under your direct control."

"You read people well."

"That is the best way to find them."

"What else? Tell me about the man who got on the train."

"Simple. He is American."

"American?"

"Your son was an officer, a test pilot. Such men are not impulsive. He would have told the Americans of his intentions, and so they too were watching that night. If the colonel had successfully defected, the GRU would know it by now. So he has crashed. The Americans will know this as well. They will search for him using their spy satellites. If Primakov is alive, there is a good chance he remains in contact with them. He would be valuable, and they might risk an attempt to get him out. And if he did not survive—the Americans might still want to see the wreckage of this secret airplane."

Strelkov stood stunned. For days he had been focusing on the logistics of the search, distracted by setting up shop in Skovorna and keeping the Air Force at arm's length. He had loosely considered all the things Tarkhan was suggesting, yet he hadn't carried them forward to logical conclusions. Hadn't used them to guide his greater plan.

"You think the Americans have sent someone . . . either to retrieve parts of this aircraft or bring Primakov out?"

"Wouldn't you?"

"What else?"

Tarkhan again addressed the map. "Begin at the rail yard," he said, pointing to Birobidzhan and then arcing left. "The train carrying this man had an accident some hours later."

"Do you think the man in the video, this supposed American agent, *caused* the crash?"

Tarkhan shrugged. "I do not see how destroying a train would advance his mission. But by connecting the two we can see a path. He was moving west and north, toward the area where Volkov and his men are searching."

"But that is still a great deal of ground to cover."

The Cossack said nothing.

"Is there a chance you can pick up his trail?" Strelkov asked. "Track him from where the train derailed?"

"I began working on it yesterday."

"Did you make any progress?"

"I learned that there were two victims in the train crash. They could not be identified because the fire was too intense."

"Two, you say?"

The Cossack nodded.

"Might the Americans have sent two agents?"

"No. Only one man is necessary. Two would double the risk."

"Could one of the bodies recovered have been our man?"

"It is possible . . . but I suspect not." He tapped a tiny dot on the rail line. "If he did survive, his natural instinct would have been to continue to the next station, here."

"Ovsyanka."

"I went there yesterday, but there was little time. Now I know more. I will return today. It is a small place where a stranger, an American, would surely stand out. He would seek transportation in a place with few options. I will seek them out precisely as he would have."

"Yes, look into it."

"It would help to have a picture of his face."

"I'll send it to your phone."

Tarkhan shook his head, pointed to the nearby printer.

Strelkov turned it on. "What else?" he asked as the machine ran through its warmup.

Tarkhan surveyed the map. "You and your people should look back, in the other direction."

"Where? The coast? Kamchatka?"

A shake of the head. "He boarded the train in Birobidzhan, which means he wasn't on it coming in. Look south."

Strelkov looked at the wall map. "China?"

"That is the closest border, and easy to cross—I have done it myself many times. This man's face does not exist in our records, but the Chinese watch even more closely than we do. It is possible they can help identify him."

"Yes. The Chinese have an interest in Vektor, so it's not much to ask."

"I am not sure you should mention Vektor in your request . . . but I leave that to you. You have far more at stake than I do."

The two locked eyes for a long moment. Then, without another word, the Cossack turned and walked away.

FORTY-THREE

Tru knew the situation was getting critical; the cold was killing the battery on his phone. He had checked it briefly after waking and found a single message—one of the compensations of having a top-flight CIA comm device was that you didn't get spam. He read it, sent a reply, and turned the handset off immediately. He would get one more power-up, two at the most, before it turned into a rock.

He woke the others, and when everyone seemed coherent, he said, "The extraction plan is shaping up. As it stands, we're looking at to-morrow night."

"How will it be done?" Primakov asked.

"They want us to identify a landing zone on solid ground—no fro-zen lakes. I'm guessing a V-22 Osprey. That's the only aircraft with enough range and a vertical landing ability. At least the only one I'm familiar with." He settled his eyes on Kai. "Any secret programs we should know about?"

"A vertical landing aircraft that could reach this deep? Not on any drawing boards I've seen. I agree—it's going to be an Osprey."

"Langley didn't say how many to expect—any ideas? I'll need to know when I scope out LZs."

Kai considered it. "We could all fit in one, even if we take a few pieces of Vektor with us. But it'll be loaded down with fuel. It's possible they'd send a second for redundancy's sake—aircraft do break. I'd say two at the most."

"Okay. I'll scout out an LZ this morning. We need to be ready to roll when the time comes, which means having the colonel and anything we want to salvage from Vektor at the extraction point. In the near term, we've got a bigger problem. My sat phone is almost dead, and we can't afford to go dark. I'll have to go to the nearest town for a top-off."

"Is that safe?" Diaz asked.

"It's necessary. I'll wait for nightfall, and one full charge should be all we need." He paused for questions but got none. It wasn't lost on

Tru that all three of his charges were wrapped in thermal blankets. "I think we could all use a fire, but we have to be careful. If anyone hears a helo, no matter how distant, we douse it fast. If we can keep our position hidden a little longer, two days from now we'll all be having a hot meal in a warm place."

Tru had been trying for an uplifting image, but the somberness of the faces looking back told him it had fallen flat.

"Yeah, I know," he said. "We won't talk about the alternatives."

Strelkov kept the minions at The Aquarium busy. His usual mode of running operations, honed through years of ruthless experience, was to divide elements of a mission among different units. By drawing manpower from different divisions, and ensuring there was no communication between them, he alone would have access to the combined product. This kept midlevel supervisors mostly in the dark, and also introduced a degree of competition. His method did introduce risk—giving more individuals knowledge of portions of a given op—but it invariably raised his level of control. And in the GRU, control was everything.

It was by this scheme that he assigned Tarkhan's follow-on request to a small department in the China Division, which was conveniently lodged in his own Third Directorate. The GRU's relationship with China's Ministry of State Security was no different from what existed between intelligences agencies around the world: transactional mutual assistance, veiled by self-interest and mistrust.

He had given the China Division its marching orders that morning, a simple request that was to be forwarded to its mirror division in Beijing: kindly ask if they could, with due haste, put a name to a face that had been seen in a rail yard in Birobidzhan.

Irrespective of whether the Chinese succeeded, they would surely be suspicious. The request to expedite would be honored, although not out of any altruistic desire to help their neighbor to the north. If any match was made, the MSS would study the results carefully, reckoning that an advantage might be had.

As it turned out, the face from the rail yard got an immediate hit using the MSS's facial recognition software, and for the simplest of reasons. Three days earlier, an American guide had gone missing from a tour group in Hegang. A second guide from the group claimed that the suspect, Eric Nordgren, had been forced to return to the States to attend to a family emergency, yet no record could be found of his leaving the country.

No nation on earth monitored its transportation hubs more closely than China, particularly when it came to foreigners. Even so, losing track of one American had seemed, at least initially, no more than a clerical error. Immigration authorities had put out a watch order for Nordgren, and his profile was sent to checkpoints nationwide. After that simple response, however, the matter had largely been forgotten.

The photo from the GRU shook things up, although not in a major way. Even for an organization as conspiratorially minded as the MSS, the match of the photo from Russia did not seem particularly alarming. The man supposedly named Nordgren had not been seen in days, and since the Russians were asking about him, the natural assumption was that he had gotten into trouble north of the border.

The MSS was happy to wash its hands of the entire affair. A midlevel analyst built a file containing a photo of Nordgren, captured during his arrival in Beijing, along with his passport information and a single paragraph explaining the circumstances of his disappearance. He sent this information to a midlevel counterpart at GRU, along with a suggestion that a future favor was now owed. A reply expressed thanks and a promise that the favor would of course be returned. Within minutes of the email reaching The Aquarium, it was bounced onward via a secure network to Skovorna Air Base.

Seated at his desk in the commander's office, Strelkov studied the photo thoughtfully, comparing it to the image from the rail yard. He saw a young man with square features, a clean-shaven face, and neatly combed hair. Having spent thirty years matching faces in government registries to candid photographs, he didn't need facial recognition software—this was the same man. He rose from the desk and went to the wall map. Hegang was not far from the Russian border, and when he connected the dots of that city, the rail yard in Birobidzhan, and the subsequent fiery train crash near Ovsyanka, Strelkov saw a nearly straight line. If that wasn't convincing enough, based on the passport and legend, the man was most assuredly an American intelligence operative.

Altogether, it was the best news he had gotten in days, and he knew who to credit.

Tarkhan, clearly, had picked up the scent of his prey.

FORTY-FOUR

Tarkhan reconstituted his search precisely where he'd left off. His helicopter delivered him to Ovsyanka where he called upon the same constabulary and, as it turned out, the same policeman he had seen the day before. This time he presented a picture of the man he was after—the rough image from the rail yard. The slothful sergeant claimed to have not seen him. Tarkhan wasn't the least bit surprised.

"The train that crashed," he asked, "was it scheduled to stop here?"

"It was."

"This man was on that train. I think after the wreck, he came here to seek transportation. Have you had any reports of missing vehicles?"

"No."

"Do any buses pass through town?"

"This time of year, only one—the bus to Irkutsk every Sunday. If he came after this train wreck, as you say, that would not have helped him since it happened on Wednesday."

"What about traffic? Do many vehicles pass through town?"

"Almost none in the winter. There are two roads, one running east and west, the other heading north. This time of year, all are treacherous due to the conditions."

Without so much as a word of thanks, Tarkhan got up and walked outside.

The sun was peaking on midday, but in the frigid air it gave more light than warmth. He was making little progress today. There had been delays leaving Skovorna—the helicopter had suffered a mechanical problem, and it had taken over an hour to fix it. Still, his patience never wavered. The same could not be said for his pilots, who had gone up the street to find something for lunch.

Tarkhan didn't want to eat. He wanted to think.

Outside the station a single police car sat parked on the curb. Old and weather-beaten, it probably saw little use; virtually any place in town could be reached on foot in a matter of minutes. He went to the sedan, removed a map one of the pilots had given him, and spread it across the metal hood.

The map, which was of sufficient scale to cover thousands of square miles of taiga, was daunting at first glance. The general had told him the Air Force units searching for Vektor were expanding their search box, yet in all likelihood, they were still over a hundred miles to the west. Volkov and his men were flying circles in the correct oblast, but they too had come up empty.

So much ground to cover.

Tarkhan's instinct had been to backtrack, banking on the idea that the Americans might have sent someone to the crash site. He had second-guessed himself for a time, concerned that the notion was distracting him from more direct leads. Now, however, he had proof—a face to go with his theory. *Yes*, he thought, *if anyone knows where Primakov and Vektor are, it is the Americans. Find this man, and he will lead me there.*

He looked down to the bottom of the street. If this American had come to town after the derailment, seeking a means of transportation, he would have walked in from that direction.

Tarkhan folded the map, slid it into his pocket, and began walking.

He would do the very same thing.

The aircraft was buffeting heavily, jolting Slaton's shoulders repeatedly against the nearby bulkhead. The two pilots in front of him were all business as the vague silhouette of USS *Boxer* materialized out of the gloom.

Slaton's previous experience with carrier operations had come from the back seat of an FA-18 Super Hornet. That had been a wild ride in terms of acceleration, and for that matter, adrenaline. This was altogether different. The Osprey was getting rocked by gusty winds, and from his vantage point on the cockpit jump seat, situated centrally behind the main crew stations, he could barely see *Boxer* a mile ahead. Rain showers had been raking the Sea of Japan for the last day, but the pilots seemed confident of getting aboard.

Reaching this point on the globe had been an odyssey worthy of Homer. The C-32B he'd boarded at Andrews had delivered him, with one stop for fuel in Fairbanks, Alaska, to Osan Air Base in South Korea. There he had transferred to a CV-22, the Air Force version of the Osprey, flown by a deployed detachment from the 8th Special Operations Squadron from Hurlburt Air Force Base in Florida. Not for the first time, Slaton was struck by the global reach of America's military, the depth of assets at his disposal. And not for the first time, he was happy to have them.

At half a mile he could see *Boxer* more clearly. Two other CV-22s were already on deck, along with a few helicopters and a pair of F-35 fighters. The waves below were churning, their whitewater crests sweeping airborne on the wind. They were flying directly into that wind, *Boxer* having maneuvered to give Chaos 44, their call sign, a headwind to lessen its groundspeed.

The deck that initially looked like a postage stamp grew larger in the forward windscreen. The aircraft commander, who was flying from the left seat, worked the controls furiously. Slaton heard the Osprey's big propellers change pitch, tilting as they slowed, and soon the aircraft was practically hovering above the deck. Touchdown was surprisingly smooth, either the talents of the a/c or a fortuitous gust of wind. He didn't ask which.

They were immediately marshalled to a clear area, and as soon as the engines shut down the aircraft was surrounded by a virtual rainbow: a swarm of men and women in colored vests. An officer arrived right behind them and made his way to the starboard-side entry door. Slaton thanked the crew for the ride, unstrapped, and encountered a Navy captain when the door opened.

"Mr. Slaton?" the captain asked, shouting to be heard over the noise of the auxiliary power unit.

"That's right." He stepped down onto the flight deck.

"Welcome aboard USS *Boxer*!"

They heard helicopters twice that morning—once just after sunrise and again at noon. No one ever got eyes on them. The sound was distant and seemed to come from the far side of the reservoir, although it was hard to tell given the muddled acoustics of the bowl formed by the surrounding hills. Just to be sure, they doused the fire each time and the relentless cold took its grip.

Tru found himself thinking ahead. Unlike yesterday, his trek across the ice tonight would be all about speed. With no sled and virtually no gear, his goal would be to minimize his exposure as he crossed the divide to Khvoyny.

Diaz had spent the day going over Vektor. A primary objective had been to get as many pictures of Vektor as possible, but the only camera that wasn't at the bottom of the reservoir was critically low on power, so his only recourse was to identify points worth photographing once Tru's phone was back in action. Diaz was presently engaged in a conversation with Primakov.

Tru looked for Kai but didn't see her by the rekindled fire. After a brief search, he found her in the nearby forest. She was sitting cross-legged, her upturned wrists on her knees and her eyes closed. The pose seemed familiar, and all at once it hit him. He came to a sudden stop, ice crunching under his boots.

Her eyes blinked open, something near a startle.

"Sorry," he said, "did I interrupt?"

"No, it's all good. I was just getting a little quiet time."

"Well . . . plenty of that out here."

"When are you leaving?"

"As soon as the sun goes down."

"I should take the first watch tonight."

"That'd be great." He nodded over his shoulder where Diaz and the Russian were still engaged. "What's going on there?"

"Not sure, but it probably has to do with Vektor."

Her eyes shifted down and settled on his hip—the only weapon in their possession, the machete, was hanging there in its sheath. "You think that's necessary?"

"If I did, I wouldn't go. Just a bit of insurance. If all goes to plan, nobody in town will ever know I was there."

She nodded, then picked up a generic blue ballcap from the ground next to her. She put it on, threading her ponytail through the back. "So, Tru Miller, tell me your story. How did you end up working for the CIA?"

He sat down casually, resting his forearms on his knees, and explained how he'd walked away from a life in academia.

"And this was Plan B?"

He started to smile, but it faded. "This wasn't ever on my radar. It just . . . happened."

"Well, for what it's worth, you seem pretty good at it."

He began lacing one of his boots tighter. "I appreciate your confidence, but all I've done so far is keep us hidden. If those choppers get a bead on us, there won't be much I can do."

"But they haven't . . . so you're doing a good job."

"You did your part with that spaceplane."

"The one that sank before we could unload it? I screwed up by breaking the nose skid—it was a bonehead move."

This time he really grinned. "Yeah, well . . . somebody once told me no op is perfect. I made a few mistakes myself on the way here."

"Such as?"

"I ran into some trouble at a wastewater plant in Hegang, China. Then I caused a freight train to crash—the Trans-Siberian Railway is probably still shut down."

"A freight train," she repeated.

"Long story. The point is, it's not the mistakes you make but how you react to them."

"Sounds like you're getting to be something of an expert."

Another smile.

"How long will you be gone tonight?"

"I figure three hours, maybe a little more." A long pause ensued, the silence of the forest taking hold. He said, "You were meditating just now."

Almost imperceptibly, her features tightened. Not embarrassment, but . . . something.

"Yeah. Ever try it?"

"No, but I knew someone who was into it."

"Old girlfriend?"

"No."

"Was she Buddhist?" Kai asked.

"No, she just liked the calming effect . . . it seemed to work. What about you? Buddhist?"

She stood and brushed a bit of forest debris from her hips, her figure backlit by broken shadows. "I guess you could say I'm searching."

"For what?" All at once, Tru realized he had no idea where this was going. Or why he was pursuing it. The rational answer would be that he wanted to know as much as possible about a member of his team. Or perhaps, after so many stressful days, he simply wanted a conversation that wasn't about Russians or landing zones. Deep down, however, he suspected it was none of that.

He got up and they stood face-to-face in the frigid air, far enough apart that the mist of their breath never mingled. To this point their interactions had been strictly professional, occassionally testy. This felt different. Felt easier.

She said, "When this Star Chaser mission came up, I knew I had to take it. I guess that's how I'm wired—I can't seem to back away from a challenge. I knew there would be risks, but I focused on the usual ones—aborted launches, system failures. This," she said, pointing out across the ice, "wasn't at the forefront."

"Sorry you came?"

"Not at all. I want to get Primakov out, especially now that I know him. But with Russians bearing down on us, and you all weaponed up. I guess that's a part of my career I thought I'd left behind."

He looked at her curiously. "Care to expand on that?"

"After pilot training, I spent my first five years in the Air Force flying F-16s. I went on two deployments to the Middle East and saw a fair amount of action. Mind you, we weren't in a full-scale war, nothing like Desert Storm or Iraq. We were facing an endless series of hit-and-run attacks. ISIS, Iranian-backed militias. They'd lob a few rockets at one of our forward operating bases, and we would get called in to respond."

"How did you figure out where the bad guys were?"

"That was the problem. Commanders had a lot of information to sift through, satellite and signals intelligence. But from my perspective, up high, the target tasking didn't always mesh with what I was seeing on the ground. Technology doesn't always clarify the fog of war— sometimes it makes it worse. We have surveillance platforms, smart bombs, drones, all of it controlled by guys drinking coffee in command bunkers thousands of miles away. Your trigger-pullers these days rarely get close to the enemy. At least, not close enough to see the proverbial whites of their eyes. From where I sat, twenty thousand feet up, you're just looking at a white dot on a screen or a set of coordinates. You might be bombing a building or a truck, but you never quite knew who was inside. Until one day . . . I did."

FORTY-FIVE

"I was flying over Syria," Kai went on. "Operation Inherent Resolve. One night, right before sunset, somebody launched rockets at our base at al Shaddadi. I found out the next day they didn't even hit anything, but in that moment, nobody knew it. Everyone was on high alert. A surveillance drone started tracking a car that was speeding away from the area the rockets had launched from. My wingman and I hustled over and got eyes on the possible target. We went through every protocol, and after a few minutes my wingman and I were cleared in hot."

"What were you carrying?"

"JDAMs, very accurate. Still, something about the whole scenario didn't feel right. We were task saturated, getting information from a lot of sources. But we had good clearance, so I rolled in hot. I sent a five-hundred-pounder chasing after a Toyota sedan."

"That's some overkill."

"Should have been, but something went wrong. Maybe a bad guidance package, a bent fin—who knows? The bomb hit a hundred meters left of target."

"Was that close enough?"

"It sure as hell would have rattled some windows. But that far away, there was no real damage to the vehicle. My wingman was about to roll in for a follow-up when the car stopped, the doors flew open, and six people went running across the desert. There were two adults and four children."

She paused, letting Tru imagine the picture. "Doesn't sound like a human shield scenario," he said.

"Nope. It was just a mistake somewhere in our operational chain. Maybe there was a different vehicle and we lost track of it, or maybe these people were running away from the bad guys. I nearly killed an entire family."

"And that made it personal . . . made it more real."

She nodded.

"Did it change you?"

"Maybe. My wingman and I talked about it. The next day I filed a report, explained how close we'd come to a disaster. Nothing ever came of it. From the brass's point of view, it was no harm, no foul. As it turned out, I rotated back stateside a few weeks later. I had applied for Test Pilot School, and right after I got back, I was accepted. I like what I do now, but it's a very different mission. And pilots with my specialty code are generally exempt from combat . . . or so I thought."

She left it there, and Tru said, "Kai, I don't think there's going to be any shooting around here. All the same, I have to ask . . . if it came to that, could I count on you?"

Her silence lasted longer than it should have. "Honestly . . . I don't know."

Tru should have been disappointed. Part of him wanted to launch into a speech, remind her that she'd taken an oath to defend her country. Another part appreciated her honesty. Or maybe her humanity.

In the end, he simply said, "I'll take the watch after yours." Then he turned and walked away.

Tarkhan moved slowly through the woods outside Ovsyanka, looking for any trace of human presence. He was quickly overwhelmed. Countless minor trails were pocked with boot prints. He saw discarded cigarette butts, empty vodka bottles, a decrepit sleeping bag, sodden cardboard boxes. He wasn't really surprised. It was the kind of scat found around all human settlements, the flotsam of what passed for civilization. He imagined teenagers coming here to escape their parents, drunk husbands to avoid their wives. Finding traces of the American here would be all but impossible. He paused and looked deeper into the forest, weighing the chance of picking up his trail farther out. A kilometer, perhaps two. He would have to go at least that far before the pollution abated. He decided there was a better way.

He turned back toward town and put himself strictly in the mind of his quarry. *I need a way to keep moving. I need food and water.* As he emerged from the forest, the town spread out before him, and his eyes went naturally to the main street: the place with the most vehicles, the most shops that would be open.

The most opportunity.

He walked up the street, and one of the first businesses he encountered was a coffee shop. Tarkhan paused, then turned toward the door. He found a handful of patrons inside, all sipping warm drinks and ignoring one another as they swiped at their phones. A girl with a blue streak in her hair and a ring in her nose stood near the cash register. She, too, was pecking at her phone.

Tarkhan approached the counter, and when she looked up the girl had no particular reaction. This was unusual. His size and menacing gaze intimidated most people, particularly women. This gypsy barista seemed immune.

"Were you working here two days ago?" he asked.

The girl nodded.

He pulled out the photograph. "Did you see this man?"

She looked at the picture and shrugged. Classic Russian indifference. "Men all look alike to me. I pay more attention to women."

Tarkhan's thoughts stuttered. Was she trying to tell him she was a lesbian?

He did not understand the youth of today. He had grown up on the Siberian steppe, the only issue of an alcoholic fur trapper and a battered woman. His mother died when he was seven, a beating that had gone too far. A beating he had witnessed. His father disappeared the next day and was never seen again. With no surviving family, young Tarkhan bounced between the homes of various neighbors until he was old enough to look after himself. He learned to hunt because he was hungry. He went to school because they served warm meals and had heat. He had not learned much in the classes, and he took regular beatings on the playground from the older boys. They didn't like him because he was different—there were few Cossacks in his village. This was an education in its own right. Tarkhan learned that only the strong survived, and so he taught himself to fight.

Things were different now. Young people were pampered and soft. Put them in the woods for two weeks, and most would die. Their worlds revolved around social media and tattoos, the influences of the West having taken their corrosive grip. For all their military might, the Americans wielded no more debilitating weapon than the woman named Taylor Swift.

He stared at the young woman and considered ripping the ring from her nose. Satisfying as the thought was, he knew it would accomplish little. He also suspected she was telling the truth.

"Do you want to order something?" she mumbled. Three silver studs on her ear caught the light.

"No."

Tarkhan went back outside and paused to check his phone. His fat thumbs fumbled over the screen, trying to make it work. He was not clever when it came to technology, yet he could not deny its utility. As if to affirm the point, a message from Strelkov appeared. He read it through and was encouraged. He had been right about China. The man he was seeking had been in Hegang three days ago. The message was accompanied by what looked like a passport photo. It was the same man, but a higher-quality picture than the one they'd gotten from the rail yard.

His initial sense of satisfaction ebbed. The photograph was an improvement, but how would it help him *find* this American? Tarkhan was convinced the man would have come here after the train crash. The next point of civilization was seventy kilometers distant—too far to travel on foot in winter.

He regarded his phone, wondering what else he might ask of the general. The GRU had vast resources, all of them at Strelkov's fingertips. Strangely, nothing came to mind. Surveillance in Russia might be pervasive, but it was concentrated in cities and towns. Places like this were different. In many respects, the wilds here were as mysterious, as unknowable as they had been a thousand years ago.

He pocketed the phone. He would simply have to rely on traditional methods, which had always been his strength. Tarkhan could track through the steppe like few men on earth.

But first one must find the trail.

He looked up and down the street. *Someone here must have seen him,* he thought. *I simply have to find that person.*

"I have a lot of concerns," said Major Vince Gianakos, who would serve as aircraft commander on the extraction mission. His sturdy build and dark features reflected his Greek ancestry. "The biggest is fuel."

Slaton was in a ready room on board *Boxer*, seated in a chair labeled CO. In this muddled joint operation, the question of who was running the show might have been up for debate had it not been for a definitive message from COMPACFLT that had arrived hours earlier: David

Slaton, Director of the CIA's Special Activities Center, would have the ultimate say on all operational decisions.

With the aim of keeping the mission, quite literally, off Russia's radar, the extraction of the team at Zeya Reservoir would be carried out by a lone CV-22 Osprey. Gianakos would be in the left seat, and his crew would be rounded out by a copilot, Captain Gus Bryan, and crew chief, Tech Sergeant Dane Jackson. Ospreys sometimes flew with larger crews, and the addition of a medical corpsman had been discussed, but with weight being critical it was decided to fly with a skeleton crew.

"How tight are you going to be on gas?" asked Captain Longmire, who was also seated in the front row.

"There are a lot of variables," Gianakos admitted. "We configured the aircraft with three auxiliary tanks, the max we can carry. If everything goes perfectly, we should get back aboard with a twenty-two-minute margin. For a six-hour flight, that's really tight. It's also highly dependent on our ingress scheme, which should keep us at high altitude for half the profile. Do you have any updates on that, sir?"

"We're still working out the details," Slaton said, "but so far everything is a go. We'll have a narrow window for launch—no more than ten minutes' notice."

"We'll be ready." Gianakos turned to address *Boxer*'s captain. "Just as a precaution, it would be nice to have search and rescue on airborne standby for recovery." It was all but an admission that the slightest miscalculation would put him, his crew, and his passengers into a very cold Sea of Japan.

Captain Longmire said, "We'll have helos in the air."

The briefing ran for another twenty minutes, much of it covering the route to Zeya Reservoir. Gianakos went over abort protocols, communications, and various contingencies. Slaton took mental notes throughout, logging a number of requests—no, he corrected, demands—that he would forward to JSOC and Langley.

When the briefing ended, Slaton pulled Gianakos aside. "I'll do everything in my power to make this work, Major. That said, I'd like to get your take on two possible modifications to the plan."

Gianakos listened closely. The first change he liked.

"Where are you going to find jet fuel in the middle of nowhere?"

"From a jet," Slaton responded. Gianakos had been told he was going in to rescue four people, one of whom was injured. He hadn't had a need-to-know about Vektor. Until now. Slaton explained his plan, and then asked, "Would that work? Is there any issue with an Osprey using Russian-manufactured jet fuel?"

"None that I know of, but I should run it by our tech staff. Jet engines will burn pretty much anything combustible. Over time you might have trouble with the fuel system gumming up, but for one mission it shouldn't be a problem. And an extra few hundred gallons *would* be very helpful. The question is how to transfer it. We'd have to figure out a way to drain it from the jet and haul it to the LZ. Any way you figure it, that would take time. I'm all for more gas, but I don't want to spend an extra hour on the ground to get it."

"Understood—I'll do some research. Seems it would at least be a good option to have in our back pocket."

Gianakos regarded him cautiously, and said, "And the second change?"

Slaton told him about it.

The Greek viewed this revision as far more problematic.

FORTY-SIX

Kai watched Tru set out across the ice. He moved quickly under the moonlight and soon vaporized into the dark. He was good at that, the coming and going. Disappearing when it suited him, appearing out of nowhere. It seemed a useful life skill, and she considered asking him for pointers.

No sooner was he gone than Diaz appeared.

"Can I show you something, Major?" he said, beckoning her with a nod.

She followed him to Vektor, and they ducked underneath the multi-spectral tarps. He turned on a portable worklight—thankfully they'd rescued that from Star Chaser, along with plenty of D-cell batteries. The aura beneath the tarps was something from Halloween, all jumping shadows and sharp-edged reflections. They ended up behind the aircraft's right main wheel.

"I thought you'd want to see the leak." He directed the light beam up through an open access panel in the wing box.

She looked up and saw the fuel tank clearly. "I don't see a hole."

"There isn't one anymore—I plugged it with some sealant I carry in one of my kits. The way the jet came to rest, it's not quite level, so not much drained after the landing. Still, with a campfire fifty feet away, I figured we didn't need to be dumping kerosene on the ground."

She moved to get a different angle and saw the repair. "It looks like a wad of chewing gum."

"That's what it feels like when you use it. Of course, it's actually a high-tech compound the Air Force probably pays a thousand bucks a tube for."

"So, no more leak?"

"Nope. The goop isn't a permanent fix—just meant to keep a jet in the air for a few more combat missions."

"What about the fuel in the engine bay?"

"I couldn't find any. Must have either burned off or evaporated after landing. I turned on the battery long enough to check the fuel gauges—the Russkies use funny units, but I figure there's about 21,000 pounds left."

"Maybe we can use it to light a signal fire for the extraction team."

"What?"

"I'm kidding. Too bad we couldn't have used the airplane battery to charge Tru's phone."

"No way to connect the two—fighters don't have outlets like airliners, and the volts and freqs are all wrong. You'd just fry the phone."

She backed away from the panel. "What were you and Primakov talking about earlier?"

"He was telling me where the boxes for various systems are mounted. I haven't started pulling them yet, but that'll save me a lot of time and trouble. I know we're going to want the radar and mission computers. Maybe the engine controls, and for sure the datalink."

"If Tru gets enough juice for his phone, we'll send some pictures home. They might have some requests."

Diaz began closing the panel.

Kai backed away to get a more complete view of the jet. In the muddled shadows Vektor looked ominous, an angry raptor caught in a cage. Still, aside from a few open panels and having one wing planted in a snowbank, the jet looked surprisingly intact. It had been an extraordinary feat of airmanship by Primakov to put her down unscathed.

Kai went back outside and saw the Russian in his usual spot, propped against a tree with his leg immobilized. He appeared to be dozing off. Not wanting to bother him, she grabbed a blanket and diverted to the edge of the ice. She picked out what looked like the least uncomfortable boulder and settled down to begin her watch.

She unzipped her jacket, hoping the cold air would help keep her awake. Then she fixated on the ice-clad reservoir. Tru was out there somewhere, prowling through a pitch-black night. Doing what he did best. Her eyes shifted to the great shadow that was Vektor. The thoughts that began brewing in her head were anything but meditative.

Zeya Reservoir covered nearly a thousand square miles, yet only a few corners of its jagged shoreline held pockets of civilization. Among the least prominent was the village of Khvoyny, a quiet township cradled in a secluded northern arm. Exposed and alone, it was the frontier equivalent of a lighthouse—a sight that was both welcoming and cautionary. The burden of winter only amplified its aura of contradiction.

Without the map on his phone for guidance, Tru was forced to use other means to navigate to the far side. He had already determined the course, and during daylight hours he used the small compass from Primakov's survival kit to pick out distant ground references. Once the sun set, stars filled the matte-black sky, and he easily transitioned to the overhead celestial grid.

The cold was remorseless, but the wind had thankfully lessened. There had been no new snow since he'd arrived, and it occurred to him that he should request a weather forecast in his next message to Langley. A storm would be in their favor for the near term, hampering the Russian search. Conversely, severe weather could delay their extraction.

He had no trouble finding Khvoyny. His star-chasing took him halfway across the reservoir, and from there the lights of the town flickered out of the gloom. As expected, it was a tiny place, yet as he closed in the lights took on a Vegas-like cast against the backdrop of wilderness.

Not wanting to approach the town directly from open ice, he veered right and intersected the shoreline a few hundred yards from the nearest structures. Tru had moved quickly across the reservoir, but he slowed as he neared the town. A stunted wooden dock, its pilings encased in ice, sat centrally on the shoreline. There was a gravel boat ramp, and nearby a few small dinghies and sailboats had been hauled up the bank and overturned. He saw two buildings directly on the lake. The nearest looked like a rustic restaurant that was boarded up for the season, while the other appeared to be a modest residence. The home looked occupied, lights glowing from two windows and a trail of smoke rising from the stone chimney.

Tru paused behind a stand of brush, double-checking that there was no one in sight, then ran low and fast toward the shuttered restaurant. He aimed for the awning-covered patio where hibernating tables and chairs rested upside down. On any summer day it would be a gathering place, lunch with a nice view. On a cold January night it was abandoned. It was the perfect place to hide—and possibly more.

He threaded through the upturned furniture and quickly found what he was after—an electrical plug. Hoping the power had not been cut for the season, he took out his phone and charging cable, and plugged in. To his relief, a lightning bolt symbol verified the phone was charging.

After putting the screen to sleep, he looked out across the village. It would take roughly twenty minutes for the phone to charge fully, and not wanting to waste time, he decided a bit of reconnaissance was in order; there was no telling what other needs might arise.

He ran back toward the forest, avoiding a shaft of yellow light from a lone sodium flood. Soon he was weaving amid trees to survey the town. The basic layout was simple: three parallel streets carried up from the shoreline to a flat glade, and from there wooded hills took over. The streets on the left and right were lined with modest residences, while the road in the middle, wider and in better shape, held an array of small businesses. There was a tiny clinic, a grocer, a café, and Russian Post. All were closed. The only public building that appeared inhabited was at the top of the main street, a bar called Czarina. The lights inside were ablaze, and even from a hundred yards away Tru could hear raucous shouting and thumping music.

He moved quietly from shadow to shadow. The forest's evergreen scent held fast in the rising mist. Within minutes he reached the top of the village. He watched two figures leave the bar and head down one of the side streets—a man stumbling badly and a woman fighting to keep him upright. Tru turned around, deciding he'd seen all there was to see. He was about to head back to the shoreline when a dank silhouette in the distance caught his eye. It sat in the open glade to his right, and when he realized what it was his heart rate jacked upward.

A military truck—some version of the standard ZIL-131 chassis.

Thankfully, it didn't look like a troop carrier, yet the olive paint scheme and stenciled lettering on the door were unmistakable: Russian Army. From where Tru stood, he could only see the front half of the truck, so he edged forward to get a better look. The forest thinned and a deep meadow spread out before him, illuminated in the spill of light from town. Tru got a better look at the truck, and he saw another like it.

Then he saw what was behind them, and everything crystallized. He was weighing what it all meant, how it might affect his mission, when the slightest errant sound caused him to freeze.

The snap of a dead branch.

FORTY-SEVEN

The trucks were fuel trucks.

Behind them in the meadow were three Hind helicopters—almost certainly the ones Tru had encountered earlier.

All of that was troubling enough.

The snapped branch, however, was a far more immediate threat.

Sound traveled well in cold, dense air, but thankfully the forest was dark. Tru turned slowly, minimizing noise and motion. He instantly saw the source of the sound.

Twenty feet away a soldier stood next to a tree. He was wearing a camo uniform and, based on his hips-forward stance and a faint splashing sound, he was taking a piss. A half-spent cigarette dangled from his lips, and as he relieved himself his free hand held a phone in front of his face. The light from the screen cast his features in a ghostly amber hue as his thumb worked the screen. The man had an assault rifle slung across his chest, muzzle down, in the patrol carry position—if Tru wasn't mistaken, an AK-12.

He tried to make sense of it.

Khvoyny was nowhere near hostile territory, and as far as he knew there were no military bases nearby where training might be taking place. Which left only one solution: the helos were here to search for Vektor. Yet if that was the case, why was this man in the forest? And why was he carrying a weapon in a no-threat environment? He reckoned it was possible his commander was a stickler, posting a guard on valuable army assets.

Whatever the reason, Tru couldn't dwell on it. He simply had to remain still. Remain invisible.

He had been caught in an exposed position—no more than a few leafless saplings stood between him and the guard. Tru's disadvantage in firepower was decisive—an assault rifle versus a machete. The blade on his hip was useless from where he stood, and reaching for the handle would require movement. His best ally was the darkness, particularly since the guard's night vision would be degraded from staring at his phone.

With all that settled, Tru chose the most difficult course of action. He did nothing at all.

He stood stock still, barely breathing. The man lowered his phone to zip up his pants. When he turned back toward the glade Tru lost a fifty-fifty proposition—the guard turned in his direction.

As he did, the man looked up, a fleeting glance that ended in a double take. Then he, too, went still.

Tru's presence had caught the Russian's eye, although he appeared more curious than alarmed. It would take precious seconds for his eyes to adjust, for his mind to distinguish the nearby shadow as human. Even then, the natural assumption would be that he was looking at one of his buddies, or possibly a stray local. If he'd had more time, Tru might have considered talking his way out of the situation. But if he waited even a few seconds, the window for action would be lost.

Tru launched himself toward the Russian.

Twenty feet wasn't a great distance. No more than the length of an average pickup truck. One-third of a bowling alley. To Tru it looked like a mile. Yet he did have one crucial advantage. In those vital seconds before being seen, he had been proactive. He'd mapped the clearest route through the saplings, checked the ground for logs and large rocks. Given the way the guard was carrying the AK, Tru knew he was a right-handed shooter. That right hand was presently holding a phone, and the barrel of the weapon was pointed 180 degrees away.

Tru had always had a decent sprint, but never in his life had he covered eight steps with such lightning speed. The soldier made the mistake Tru hoped he would make—he tried to rotate his weapon, thinking there was time to bring it to bear. Theoretically it could have worked. If the guard had fallen back as he spun, used a close-in grip, he might have gotten off a contact shot. At the very least, the situation would have gone loud to alert others. Instead, he tried to extend the AK into a standard firing position. The one he was comfortable with and had performed a thousand times on the range. That was the insidious downside of muscle memory.

Tru didn't allow it.

Machetes are a unique style of blade. More a tool than a weapon, they are optimized for cutting vines and clearing brush. Yet the item in his hand was new, its edge dulled by nothing more than a few days of chopping kindling, which meant the blade was well suited to his twin objectives. The first was to incapacitate the man's right arm and preclude his finger reaching the AK's trigger. The second was shock and awe.

Tru unsheathed the machete as he ran, performing a cross-draw with his left hand and raising it high. He scythed the blade down violently on the guard's upper right arm, felt it sink into flesh. The man grunted in pain.

The key to close combat is adaptation, adjusting sensory inputs. When you were too close to see what your opponent was doing, you had to feel his movement, counter as necessary. The guard was stunned and off-balance, flying toward the ground, his plan of getting off a quick shot shattered. Tru released the machete—in close, with no room to swing, the blade would be less lethal than other means. He focused completely on wrapping the man up, and when they hit the spongy forest floor intertwined, he twisted behind the Russian.

It helped that he was slightly bigger than his adversary, but his real advantage had been earned through countless days spent on training mats. Before the guard could react, Tru interlocked his arms in a deep rear chokehold. One forearm vised across the man's throat, while the other interlaced behind his head. The guard recognized his dilemma, but too slowly. His training kicked in and he wedged a flattened left hand beneath his attacker's forearm, a desperate attempt to relieve the crushing pressure on his larynx. Tru's hold, however, was devastatingly solid, making escape all but impossible.

Both men knew it was only a matter of time.

A chokehold can be applied in two basic variants. One cuts off the carotid, shutting down blood flow to the brain. This induces unconsciousness in roughly ten seconds but allows an equally quick recovery. With revival not in his game plan, Tru employed the second option—bone-crushing pressure on the trachea.

After repeated failed attempts to free himself, the guard began to panic, the brain's response to air starvation. He thrashed his legs, trying to throw Tru off balance, but nothing changed. The AK strapped across his chest was useless against an attacker who was behind him.

After thirty seconds the guard stopped moving. Tru didn't let up the pressure for nearly another minute. By then the muscles in his arms were trembling from exertion. He rolled away from the dead Russian, rose to one knee, and paused. He neither saw nor heard anything to suggest another guard nearby. The distant party at the bar continued unabated. Tru eased higher and scanned across the meadow. There was no one else in sight.

He rolled the dead Russian onto his back but could see little—there was almost no light at ground level. He removed his flashlight and very carefully turned it on, shielding the spill of light as best he could with his free hand.

The man's features were classically Slavic. He had short-clipped hair with a distinct widow's peak, large ears, and tobacco-stained teeth. He'd died with a look of surprise on his face, no doubt stunned by how quickly and decisively Tru had gained the upper hand. The guard's uniform displayed a sergeant's stripes and there was a patch on one shoulder—a gold-handled dagger over a silver shield. Tru was no expert on Russian military units, but this one he knew.

Vega Group.

Intrigued, he rolled up the man's sleeves, and on the right forearm saw more evidence. A Nazi eagle tattoo, common among right-wing mercenaries.

The world around him went on pause.

The mission to rescue Primakov faded to a backdrop, supplanted by something more personal. Replaced by the mission tasking sourced from his nightmares. For two years he had trained and compartmentalized, never knowing if he would get an opportunity to extract vengeance for what had happened to his sister. The chance that this man was directly involved in her disappearance was virtually nil. But the odds that he had served in Ukraine, or some other anarchic theater of operations, and terrorized someone else's sister? Those were very high. A virtual guarantee. The collapse of Wagner Group had spun countless offshoots, but there was one commonality among all its sickly progeny: they were populated by lawless paramilitaries for whom atrocity was a way of life.

Tru looked into the astonished, lifeless eyes, and felt no trace of remorse. Was that wrong? He thought back to his encounter on the train. The two thugs who'd attacked him there had paid the same price, yet afterward Tru wished it could have been avoided. This was different. One verifiable shitweasel was off the map of life . . . and Tru Miller was glad for it.

A drunken cheer from Czarina interrupted, and he purged the distracting thoughts as best he could. He spotted the man's phone nearby on the damp forest floor and retrieved it. A search for pocket litter turned up a wallet with ID, cigarettes, and a butane lighter. The fact that the guard was carrying identity documents, and also wearing a proper uniform, told Tru that unit security was at a low level. That made sense, he supposed. Operators working overseas strove for anonymity, but if these men were in fact searching for Vektor, they wouldn't view Khvoyny as a high threat environment. Yet it also raised a larger question: why would such a specialized unit be called out to search for a downed Air Force jet? Vektor was important, but it seemed a waste of valuable resources.

Tru considered how to proceed.

If he kept the phone and wallet, their absence would be noticed when the body was discovered. That would happen soon, and since the obvious cause of death was trauma, it would be like setting off a fire alarm. He contemplated hauling the body away, hiding it in the forest or sinking it beneath the ice, but that seemed equally problematic. He looked around, and his eyes settled on the meadow.

A plan began to form. More shouting from the distant bar caused it to accelerate.

Tru woke the guard's mobile phone and held it to the man's face, unlocking the device. He again shielded his flashlight, trained the beam on the guard's face, and took three post-mortem selfies. He did this precisely as he had been trained to do—one face-on shot, followed by a forty-five-degree angle from either side. The CIA's latest software would blend the varied aspects for a comprehensive facial profile that would, with any luck, turn up somewhere in the agency's databases. He removed the guard's military ID and took a photo for the record: Junior Sergeant Sergei Golubev, along with vital statistics that would soon turn to dust. More fodder for research. He kept the powered-down phone for eventual exploitation, but returned the wallet and ID to the guard's pocket.

He moved to the edge of the tree line. Before him the three big Hinds squatted ominously in the field, their rotors drooping in the dim light. He paused long enough to be certain there was no one else on guard detail, then ran flat-out toward the nearest helicopter. The midship entry door was open, a common method of keeping fuel and hydraulic fumes from building—in training he had paid close attention to the lessons on Russian military hardware.

Tru clambered inside, cleared the cabin, and then took stock of what was inside. It surprised him at first. But the more he thought about it, the more it made sense.

His plan began to build.

Then it came in a rush.

He vaulted back outside and disappeared into the forest.

FORTY-EIGHT

Captain Volkov took in the scene before him approvingly. He was sitting on a crooked stool, fondling a sweaty bottle of beer. His men had overrun the pub, and for the last two hours they'd been slamming down vodka and pawing at waitresses. A corporal was dry firing his Glock at the house mutt. At least two fights had broken out with the locals, most of whom had gone home fuming and bloody. The few that remained were now tipping back shots with his men, a camaraderie born of bruises and broken glass.

Volkov sanctioned all of it. For two days his men had been boring holes in the sky, scouring endless kilometers of wilderness for the remains of an air crash that might never be found. His men needed to blow off steam, to do what soldiers did when they weren't killing and marauding.

With the doors and windows shut against the cold, the place smelled like a moldering bar towel. Music thumped from a boombox, a playlist of vague Europop songs no one could name. The sound recoiled howitzerlike in the room's unforgiving acoustics. Volkov noticed the bar's corpulent owner sulking behind the counter—he was looking on hopelessly with a broom in his hand. He went over to the man, reached into his pocket, and pulled out a wad of cash. The GRU gave him a healthy stack before every mission, for use as he saw fit. On particularly dangerous assignments he disbursed it to the men as incentive pay. Occasionally, he used it to make amends in places like this. More often than not, he simply kept it.

Volkov peeled away what seemed like a reasonable number of bills and slapped them on the scarred bar top. "For your troubles."

The proprietor, a dyspeptic sort with salt-and pepper hair and a gray-stubble beard, looked at the cash, and then the room around them. The mirror behind the bar was shattered and overturned tables littered the floor. A light fixture shaped like a beer stein hung crookedly from its electrical cord, occasional sparks the only sign of life. The few barstools that hadn't gone to splinters had been righted and were occupied by shoulder-slapping men.

"That might cover the furniture, but not the bar bill."

A few more bills hit the counter.

The owner opened his mouth to say something else, and Volkov cut him off. "Don't get greedy. This will be the worst of it. My men may be back tomorrow or the next day. I'll tell them they've had their fun and that they must pay their tabs."

"And if the dog needs therapy?"

Volkov grinned. A hirsute hand swept up the cash.

The captain checked his phone for messages. Seeing nothing new from General Strelkov, he pocketed the handset. As he did, his fingers brushed the second phone in his pocket. The new burner he had used only twice, both times in the last week. He resisted an urge to check it. *Not until I have something to report.*

He settled back on his stool, and was about to inquire about food when a massive blast shattered the night. The entire building shook and waterfalls of dust clouded down from the rafters. Volkov's head whipped around, and through the ice-encrusted front window he saw glimmers of orange flame. His men had similar reactions, and at least two drew handguns. He ran for the door and burst into the frigid night. A chain of lesser blasts lit the sky, oranges and reds flickering against the surrounding forest. Behind him, his men poured out of the bar like the place had been teargassed.

In the center of the meadow one of their helicopters was going up in flames. His first instinct was to go back inside and ask the owner if there was a fire brigade in town. That notion was torpedoed by yet another explosion, this one followed by a string of crackling sounds—small caliber ammunition lighting off. His men were standing behind him, and when something pinged into a nearby wall, he shouted, "Everyone back inside!"

His men complied, all except Sergeant Drugov, who came and stood next to him. They were in partial cover behind a heavy wooden beam.

"Sergei was on watch, wasn't he?" Volkov asked.

"He wasn't happy about it, but yes. We left our weapons on board, so someone had to keep an eye on things."

Volkov scanned the meadow and the nearby buildings. "I wonder where he is. And what the hell caused this?"

The sergeant shrugged. "A problem with the helo, most likely."

"Let's hope the other two birds and the fuel trucks aren't damaged. Strelkov understands the cost of doing business, but to lose all our equipment while everyone is at the bar . . . that could be viewed as careless."

The two men swapped a glance, then watched helplessly as the big chopper was engulfed, orange flames boiling beneath plumes of black smoke.

Volkov wasn't particularly worried about Sergei's fate. But the question of what could have caused the inferno hammered in his head.

FORTY-NINE

The sound of the explosions in Khvoyny thundered across the reservoir. For the next hour, at the tiny encampment twelve miles away, theories about what might have caused them ran rampant. Diaz thought it might have been an industrial accident, Kai a military exercise. Primakov theorized it could have been dynamite being used in distant mines. Behind the curtain of all that speculation: the unspoken worry that Tru might have run into trouble.

Consequently, his arrival back at camp was met with palpable relief—a respite that ended immediately when they saw what he was carrying. Two rifles, multiple magazines, and a rocket propelled grenade launcher. He was also wearing a plate carrier vest.

He told them about his discovery of the Hinds and his encounter with the guard. The questions came in a torrent.

"Have you told Langley about this?" Kai asked.

"Haven't had the chance," he said, still breathing heavily from hauling the weapons across the reservoir. "But I've got a good charge on my phone now, so that's next on my list."

"And you took these weapons from the helicopter you set on fire?"

"Yeah. I checked all three birds, and each of them was weaponed up—basically what a small unit would carry into combat. I hadn't planned on engaging anyone, but after it happened, I had a body to deal with. A little arson seemed like the simplest solution. While I was working on that, it occurred to me that a few guns probably wouldn't be missed from the wreckage."

Kai said to Primakov, "How closely will an incident like this be investigated?"

The colonel considered it. "A helicopter catching fire is one thing . . . it happens. But if they find this guard's body with a gunshot or trauma? That would bring trouble."

Tru hadn't been specific about how he'd killed the man. "I took him out with a chokehold. It turns out he was a smoker, so I left a couple of spent cigarette butts on the ground near the Hind that went up. With any luck they'll bite on that as the cause, consider it a stupid accident."

Kai said, "It might work. I investigated a ground accident once involving a jet full of ammo and fuel—when you combine those, things really cook off. We heard the explosions from here, so I'd guess the chopper isn't much more than a pile of melted metal."

Primakov shook his head. "You are thinking only of facts and evidence. Never forget that Russians are suspicious by nature."

"Either way," Tru said, "the fire will buy us time. There were also some serious secondary blasts, so it's possible that one or both of the other Hinds are damaged."

"We should hope that is not the case," the colonel argued. "That would bring reinforcements. It would be better if none of this had happened."

"Look, I did what I had to do to keep our comm up and running. One man got in the way, so I neutralized the threat."

"Neutralized?" Kai said. "That's a nice word for it."

He shot her a hard look, and she relented.

"Sorry. You did your best in a bad situation. At the very least, we need to get word to Langley. They're planning an extract, and they need to know what's going on. Maybe they can put a satellite on this town to give us an idea of the fallout."

"A fair point," Tru allowed, dialing down his irritation. "I'll send a message soon. But there's something else we need to consider. This guy I ran into, he wasn't a run-of-the-mill grunt. He was Vega Group."

"What's Vega Group?" Diaz asked.

Tru looked at Primakov.

The colonel frowned, and said, "Spetsgruppa V of the FSB Special Purpose Center. Commonly referred to by its old KGB name—Vega Group."

"Special Forces?" Kai said. "Why would a unit like that be out looking for a missing Air Force jet?"

"A good question," Tru said. "It didn't make sense to me either . . . at least, not at first. But while I was hauling ass back across the ice, I had time to think." He looked at Primakov knowingly. "Perhaps you should tell everyone what you told me when I first arrived, Colonel."

All eyes settled on the Russian. He was propped against a tree, flames from the fire highlighting his strained features.

The Russian looked up at Kai and Diaz. "Your CIA did not

unearth as much information on my past as they should have. Or perhaps they did but neglected to tell you about it. My father-in-law is Major General Viktor Strelkov, chief of the GRU's Third Directorate. Vega Group is almost certainly operating under his command."

"Your father-in-law is pulling strings to find you?" Diaz surmised.

Kai intervened. "No. Only one unit is looking here, and that's not by chance. He suspects something."

Primakov nodded. "Well done, Major. As I mentioned to your CIA friend here, I committed an error before my departure. My father-in-law and I do not get along, and when I took off that night, intending to defect, I left a letter for him."

"A letter? Are you saying you confessed what you were doing with Vektor?"

"Nothing so direct, but enough to put the idea in his head that I was taking drastic action. Once Vektor disappeared, he probably deduced my intentions. Strelkov has vast resources at his command, so he knows by now that I never reached the West."

Tru said, "It wouldn't be hard to guess the direction of your planned escape."

"You are right. But that is all he knows. He will suspect Vektor has crashed somewhere in this area, yet he can't know the outcome. Did I perish with the jet? Survive an ejection? The truth, that I landed on this reservoir . . . that is something no one would imagine."

"So they won't look here?" Diaz ventured.

"Strelkov will look everywhere. If it ever came to light that his son-in-law was a traitor, he would meet the same fate all siloviki meet when they fall from grace. A high window, a radioactive doorknob, a doomed flight. His only chance of survival is to find Vektor, and more importantly, to find me before anyone else does."

"And if he succeeds?" Kai asked.

"The answer is clear." He pointed to the pile of weapons Tru had requisitioned. "This unit is heavily armed—not what one would need for a search in a friendly corner of Russia. If Vega Group finds us . . . finds Vektor . . . their orders will be clear. Eliminate every trace. This is Strelkov's only chance of survival."

"It looks like your boy is at it again," said Anna Sorensen across the secure video link.

Slaton was in a briefing room on one of *Boxer*'s lower decks. With him were Major Gianakos and Captain Longmire. On the other end of the link, in a White House room he didn't recognize, were Sorensen, President Cleveland, DNI Fuller, and General Carter.

"What's he done now?" he asked cautiously. Given that the call hadn't been scheduled, and who was involved, it had to be serious.

"We repositioned a couple of NRO birds to monitor the area around Zeya. This is some of the first footage we got."

The monitor went to a split screen and loops of surveillance footage began running. In the God's-eye view Slaton saw a small town on the shore of the reservoir. Just beyond that, three military helicopters sat parked in a field. As the footage ran, the view zoomed in on the helicopters. Slaton saw a lone figure running from one of the choppers toward the forest.

"Is that who I think it is?" he asked.

"It is."

Tru Miller disappeared into the woods. He then reappeared moments later hauling what looked like another man in a fireman's carry.

"It gets better," Sorensen promised, having obviously seen the footage multiple times. "I'll give you a little foreshadowing—the guy he's carrying is dead. Or at least, I hope he was."

Slaton sat transfixed as the scene ran. Miller carried the body into the center helicopter, then emerged minutes later hauling a load of gear and darted back into the forest. Soon after, a massive explosion filled the screen. The processing software couldn't keep up as repeated blooms of infrared turmoil washed the screen in shades of white. As the big chopper cooked off, the field of view widened back out. People began flooding out of a building on the edge of the main street. A few began moving toward the burning helo, but then quickly backtracked as secondary explosions lit off, white-hot incendiary trails streaking randomly from the blaze.

"The helicopters are Hind Fs," General Carter said. "One was obviously totaled, and it's possible another was damaged. Apparently, these birds brought in a detachment from Spetsgruppa V."

"Vega Group?" Slaton asked, trying to make sense of it. "How do you know that?"

"It came straight from the source. We just got a sitrep from Rookie. His comm device was nearly dead, so he took the initiative to sneak into town to charge it. In doing so, he inadvertently ran into one of these Russians."

Carter read Miller's message, a broad-brush sketch of the disaster playing out on the monitor. Rookie had encountered a man guarding the helicopters, killed him in an altercation, and then staged a fire to conceal the crime. From an operator's point of view, Slaton saw multiple mistakes—none of it should ever have happened. That said, he allowed that Miller's cleanup scheme was probably the best he could have done in a complex situation.

"He also sent a couple of pictures," Carter said. "Photos of the dead man and his ID. We've just begun running them through the system. Vega Group stays busy all over the world, so there's a fair chance he'll show up in our databases. If so, it might give us a better idea of who we're up against, and more importantly, why they showed up here."

The theater of devastation ran unabated on the monitor. Brilliant and insistent.

"How will this affect exfiltration?" Slaton muttered to himself.

The microphone clearly picked it up.

"We've been asking that same question," Sorensen said.

"So far we see no sign of a threat reaction from the Vegans," Carter said dryly, pronouncing it as if the Russians didn't eat meat. "It's almost midnight there, and the fire has burned out. In the near term, I think the Russians will assume this is an accident. But eventually they'll get a look at the wreckage, and it's possible Rookie left something incriminating behind. If suspicions get raised, it could create serious complications for our exfil op."

Slaton said, "I'm wondering why Vega Group is there at all. How far is this town from our people?"

Carter replied, "They're on the other side of the reservoir, roughly twelve miles away."

After a prolonged silence, the president chimed in for the first time. "I want to know how this affects the rescue mission. Do we still have a green light?"

The DNI said, "Rookie messed up. The last thing we needed to do was draw attention to the area."

"No," Slaton argued, "the *last* thing we needed was to lose comm with our people on the ground. He fixed that problem. I agree, he shouldn't have put himself in a position where he was forced to engage, but now we know we've got a potent fighting force not far from the LZ."

"But are we still a go?" the president asked again.

"I say yes," Sorensen responded. "But we need to send a message to

Rookie, tell him to hunker down. If nothing changes, we'll have them out in roughly twenty-four hours.

"I agree," the DNI seconded. "Waiting doesn't better our odds. But Miller needs to stay put. The guy is an unnatural disaster."

Slaton didn't argue otherwise, realizing there was nothing to gain from it. Miller *was* taking big risks. But the perspective from the front line was always different than the one from headquarters, and so far, the kid was getting the job done. In all honesty, he saw vague resemblances to the first missions of another elite operator.

Was I ever that reckless? he wondered.

The psych eval Stansell had mentioned earlier came to mind.

NAFOD. No apparent fear of death.

Maybe the shrink had a point after all.

FIFTY

Tarkhan spent the night in Ovsyanka, taking a room in an empty boarding house above a pub. His helicopter crew had insisted on returning to Skovorna Air Base, but he had seen no point in doing so. The trail he wanted to pick up was here, and time spent traveling back and forth was time wasted.

He had covered much of the town yesterday, hitting every bar and restaurant, the only outfitter, and then every business with an open door. No one recognized the face in the picture he carried. Today Tarkhan would pursue closed doors. Knock them down if necessary. He started at the edge of town, pounding on doors all along the street. A few were answered, but he learned little from residents who were clearly wary. He was accustomed to people being put off by his bluntness, and also his appearance, but it seemed a particular detriment today.

On the sidewalks in between his intrusions, he tried to think.

He could not discount the possibility that his quarry had somehow transited Ovsyanka unseen. If so, he would simply pursue the next most likely course. He would study the roads leading out of town and focus on those spurring north and west. He would make inquiries with anyone he encountered. It never occurred to him that he would not find the next lead. His only concern was time. The American was on his way to find Colonel Primakov and, assuming he was still alive, to spirit him away. This meant he would linger no longer than necessary in the course of his travels. Tarkhan considered what else the general might do for him. The camera footage from the rail yard had been a useful bit of intelligence. The GRU, plodding as it might be, did have its utility.

He turned up a stone path that led to a shambolic house, one of the oldest he'd seen. The stone walls looked to be mortared with mold, and the roof was pocked with rotted shingles. But one light shone brightly behind the curtained front window. He went to the door and beat on it with his fist. When no one answered, he did it again, the old wood rattling in its frame as if on the verge of collapse. He heard a shuffle of footsteps, light and slow. The door swung open to reveal an old woman in a housedress. She was a classic baba, thick-jowled and hunched by age. His daunting presence seemed lost on her as she regarded him with a scowl.

"What do you want?"

"I am searching for a man, a stranger who might have passed through town a few days ago." He showed her the picture.

Without even looking at it, she said, "You are the first stranger I've seen in months."

She tried to shut the door, but he blocked it with a boot.

"You are not a silovik," she said. "You are a Cossack."

Tarkhan looked at her more closely, and perhaps saw a trace of his own bloodline. The woman didn't know what to make of him. But she wasn't pushing on the door any longer. Without comment, he asked a few more questions, mostly about things that might have gone missing around her property. Cars, bicycles, food. Her annoyance seemed to grow with each answer. Pensioners, in his considerable experience, and especially women, were always the most difficult. The old ones had had their doors knocked on in the Soviet era, in the days of an iron-fisted Party and flourishing gulags. The bunch in Moscow who ran things today were every bit as ruthless, but distracted by self-interest— there was no profit in terrorizing old women on the Siberian steppe.

"You live alone?" he asked.

"My husband is dead. Go away."

Sensing another dead end, he backed his foot from the door and set out toward the road. He resisted an urge to look over his shoulder. Tarkhan had been shot in the hip ten years ago on a very similar side-walk. He had been hired to track down Yakut boys who were dodging conscription, and he'd figured out early on that you didn't have to chase them down—simply watch their homes long enough, and they always returned to their mothers. What he hadn't taken into account that day was a mother with a shotgun. Tarkhan had killed the woman with his bare hands as she tried to reload. He had never much under-stood women, yet on that day he learned what they were capable of. His hip would never be quite right, but the limp worked in his favor. People tended to underestimate him. The only real limitation was that he could no longer run fast, and this was of no consequence. Tarkhan never ran.

He was halfway to the street when he realized the old woman hadn't shut the door. He stopped and turned. She was staring at him.

"What about skis?" she asked.

"Skis?"

"I know someone who works at the lodge. He told me a stranger came there that night. He didn't stay long, but a set of skis went missing."

Tarkhan cocked his head sharply. "Who told you this?"

There was a long hesitation, and he let it play out.

Finally, the woman said, "My grandson. He works there a few days a week."

"Did the police investigate this theft?"

"No one made a formal complaint. I only know because Artyom mentioned it during dinner last night."

"Where is Artyom now?"

"He is working at the lodge as usual."

Before Tarkhan could ask, the old baba was giving him directions.

"Tell me he is dead," said Oksana.

Strelkov briefly pulled the phone away from his ear, regretting having picked up the call from his daughter. He hadn't realized how bad it was between her and Maksim. He *should* have known. "I have nothing new to tell you."

"But how can such a priceless jet disappear?"

When he had first told Oksana about the crash, he'd weighed giving her the truth: that her husband had been attempting to defect to the West. Now, as then, he could see no advantage in doing so. Only increased risk. Mortal risk. "We will find the jet."

"The Chinese must be furious."

Strelkov held steady. Chinese involvement in the Vektor project was supposed to be secret. Indeed, the entire project was highly classified. Still, he was not surprised Oksana had found out—she was, after all, his daughter, and by all accounts she had made the most of the cushy job he had arranged for her at GRU headquarters. He had been too busy in recent months to discuss it with her, but, when he'd last checked, her stock was rising swiftly. His hope was to steer her rise toward the General Staff, a section where he was lacking a trusted agent.

"This is not the time nor the place to discuss such rumors," he said sternly, pivoting away from the China question. Strelkov knew full well this call was being monitored—he himself had ordered surveillance on his daughter's phone.

"Why can they not just declare Maksim dead?"

"In time, that will happen. Just as it did with . . ." He couldn't bring himself to say the name.

There was a brief and blessed silence. Then she asked, "How long will you stay at this wretched place?"

"I won't return to Moscow until we've located him. Until then, let me know what you are hearing at headquarters. People there are ruthless, and they will spread any kind of ghastly rumor if they think an advantage can be had."

"All right, but . . . do you think there is any chance that Maksim is still alive?"

For the first time in days, since he had first advised his daughter of the tragedy, he sensed something deeper in her tone. Something old and honest. There had been a time, very briefly, when Oksana and Maksim had cared for one another. "There is always a chance . . . but it is very slim. I can tell you that—"

His phone pinged with another call. When he saw who it was, he said with relief, "Darling, I have to take an important call. I will ring you right away if there are any developments."

He switched to the incoming call with great anticipation.

Tarkhan never called without good reason.

Oksana stared blankly at her handset, but only for a moment. She was used to being cut off by her father.

She was sitting in her new office in the east wing of headquarters. It was the first office she had ever had with a window, and she looked out across the sprawling campus. The January of Moscow glared back with its endless palette of gray. Bundled workers hurried from building to building, innumerable tiny cogs in the vast machine. A machine with so many hidden missions, so many cross-purposes, it was a wonder anything ever got done.

Her eyes came back inside and settled on her desk. Or, more precisely, the picture on its far corner. The most prominent corner. The one that people saw when they walked in. The photo was the one constant in her career, displayed at every workstation, in every department that she, the general's daughter, had fluttered through: a candid shot of her, Maksim, and Nik on a beach in Crimea. *Twelve years ago? No, closer to fifteen.* She was actually smiling—perhaps the last time?—forty pounds lighter and wearing a daring swimsuit. Maksim was Maksim, striking and confident in his aviator shades. And then there was Nik. He was barely school-age, small for his age, all knobby knees and elbows. Limbs that never quite filled out.

Never.

Oksana tapped a finger on the hardwood. She would need a new picture soon. Did she have one of only her and Nik? Probably, somewhere. If not, she would order Unit 43125 to create one. Or was it 42125 that did the deep fake photography? The more she learned about this place, the more labyrinthine it seemed.

Someone would take care of it. Of that, she was sure. Because she was a mother who had paid the ultimate price.

And I will never let them forget it . . .

FIFTY-ONE

Captain Volkov regarded the molten heap that had hours ago been an assault helicopter. Little that was recognizable remained of the Hind. The heavy engines, which had been mounted high above the cabin, had crushed the fuselage. Four of its five rotor blades rested on the ground, while the fifth pointed skyward like some kind of warped aeronautical headstone. The fire had died out hours ago, but a few tendrils of smoke still writhed up into the bitter morning air. The good news was that no unspent fuel or ammunition could remain given the intensity of last night's inferno.

The main discovery this morning, as they sifted through the wreckage, was the body of Corporal Golubev in the main cabin. This surprised no one. They had not been able to find him last night during the blaze, and it was assumed he had somehow been a victim of the conflagration.

Sergeant Drugov, who had been rooting through the smoldering mess, approached with something in his hand. It turned out to be a set of dog tags.

"It's Golubev," he said, handing over two discolored steel ovals.

Volkov took them, and after a brief look shoved them in his pocket. He would have to write another letter. There had been little left of the corpse beyond ashes, but that wasn't anything his mother needed to know.

"There is something else you should see," added Drugov.

He led the way to a forward section of the wreckage, where the entry door would have been. He pointed to the ground and Volkov saw two spent cigarette butts.

"You are suggesting this was the cause?"

The sergeant, who despite his heavy frame was something of a fitness nut, shrugged. "A nasty habit. But there is a reason for our rules about smoking near fuel and explosives."

Volkov wasn't convinced. "I see many possibilities. In time someone

will come to investigate, although these days, so far from Moscow . . .
I doubt it will be a priority."

"Have you told the general about it?"

"Yes. He was annoyed, but these things happen. He is already looking for a replacement bird, but that will take a few days. In the mean-
time, we are to continue our search."

The sergeant took in the scene. The team was busy cleaning up,
removing debris from the operating area and prepping the two remaining Hinds. "One of the other birds took a hit in the cabin—looks like a
30mm round from the chin gun. The crew chief says it's through and
through, no serious damage."

"Good."

"Both fuel trucks also escaped—one broken window, nothing more."

"Then we launch soon. Go find the pilots—we should go over the
search plan for today."

"Which sector?"

"Right where we left off, to the north and west."

The sergeant stomped away, a cloud of ash rising under his boots
with each step.

Volkov regarded the charred Hind, then looked out across the reservoir. This mission had seemed a soft one at first, but it was growing
more complicated. The fire appeared to be an accident, yet something
about it bothered him. Something about this whole mission bothered
him. Wherever the hell Colonel Primakov was, Volkov hoped they found
him soon. More than ever, he was ready to move on.

Kai hadn't slept well. The cold was part of it, but her tumbling thoughts
made things worse. Musings that had begun during her watch shift had
avalanched into something bigger. As things stood, they were going to
be rescued tonight. Unless the soldiers across the reservoir found them
first. Either way, her time on the lake was rushing to a conclusion. This
would be her last morning on Zeya, her last hours with these people.
How it would all end, however, was very much in question.

She looked at the shapeless blob fifty meters away, Vektor lurking
beneath its cloak. Again, her thoughts spun like a centrifuge.

She heard muted voices from beneath the tarp. Tru and Diaz were
discussing the jet's imminent postmortem, the dissection about to begin. She got up and walked over, shouldered under the cover, and found

them huddled near Vektor's right wing. Diaz was pulling the airplane's data recorder from an access port.

"This is the one they wanted first," he said.

"That's the black box?" Tru asked.

"Yep. Our new jets link up in flight test, everything downloaded in real time. The Russians are more old school. They pull the recorders after every flight. It's cheap and simple, but it does create a delay." He set the unit, which was the size of a cinder block and nearly as heavy, down on snow-encrusted ice. "Next come the avionics."

Kai moved closer and looked pensively at the belly of the jet. "How's that fix to the fuel tank holding up?" she asked.

"No leaks as far as I can see," Diaz replied as he taped over the data ports of the FDR.

"Good. And the battery?"

"Battery?"

"Yeah, is it keeping a charge in the cold?"

"I turned it on a couple of times to check some systems—it seemed fine."

"What about the APU?"

Diaz stopped what he was doing. He stared at her for a long moment. Tru did the same.

"Major," Diaz said, "what are you getting at?"

"I think you know." She shifted to look at Tru. "I think you both know. There's no reason I can't fly Vektor out of here."

Diaz laughed nervously. "You cannot be serious."

"I mentioned it to Primakov last night . . . hypothetically, of course. He agrees there aren't any showstoppers. With the fuel leak fixed, the jet is basically airworthy. Fuel would be extremely tight, but I can probably reach Japan."

Diaz looked at her incredulously, his crew chief's mind clearly logging how many "showstoppers" to bring up.

Kai studied Tru. Surprisingly, she didn't see the same level of shock. "Well . . . what do you think?" she asked.

He held her eyes for a long moment, then glanced up at the sleek jet. "It *would* be a real poke in the eye to the Russians." Then, like a slow dawn, his blond-stubbled face broke into a grin. "I think it's a terrific idea."

FIFTY-TWO

Tarkhan walked in the front door of the lodge and immediately encountered a hallway. To the left he heard a conversation, casual and animated, coming from double doors that led to a warmly lit room. He turned the other way and saw three doors along the interior wall. He examined the floor and saw heavy scuff marks leading toward the center door. He followed them and turned inside.

It was indeed the equipment room, and it was exactly as he'd imagined. Half the lockers were full of ski gear, the others jammed with heavy jackets and mud boots. Through an open closet door, he saw a massive gun safe.

A kid was standing behind a workbench adjusting a ski boot with a screwdriver. He was skinny and swivel-eyed, and while not particularly tall, his thinness made his torso appear long and his limbs short. Altogether, the human equivalent of a weasel.

"You are Artyom?" he asked.

The kid's eyes were already on him. Already wary. Tarkhan wondered if his baba had forewarned him that a stranger was coming.

"I am. Who are you?"

Tarkhan walked to the bench and stopped on the opposite side. He pulled out the photograph of his quarry. "You saw this man three days ago." It wasn't a question.

Artyom nodded. "Yes, he was here. He said he was the nephew of one of our members."

"He stole skiing gear?"

"Maybe. A set went missing. You are police?"

"I am looking for this man," he said, for the second time ignoring the kid's question. "I need to know where he went after this place."

"How should I know?"

"Did he say anything about where he might be going?"

"No."

"Did he take any other gear? Supplies for camping, food?"

"Not that I know about."

"Did you see him leave?"

"He left while I was out of the room."

"What about—"

"I cannot help you! Stop asking so many questions!"

Tarkhan's gaze fell to a dead stare. He walked calmly around the counter.

"Hey, you can't be back here!" Artyom protested.

The Cossack perused the work bench. He saw a hammer, a power drill, a hacksaw. Then he spotted the best thing of all.

"You should leave," the kid said weakly.

Tarkhan reached into a scrap bucket and pulled out a two-foot section of galvanized pipe. He turned toward the kid.

"Wait . . . you can't—"

Two massive hands seized the scrawny kid by the collar and lifted him into the air. He spun the boy around, slammed him across the oak worktable, and extended his right arm. He slammed the pipe down viciously on his five bony fingers.

Artyom screamed.

"Which way did he go when he left?"

"How could I know? I came back here, and he was gone."

"You must have seen tracks in the snow later, when you left to go home."

"I . . . I don't remember."

The pipe came down on his forearm this time, shattering bone. When the screaming stopped, Tarkhan said, "Remember now."

"Aahhh! Yes, yes . . . I was afraid he had stolen the gear. I looked and there were some tracks! But I am not sure they were his."

Tarkhan asked a few more questions, each of which was met by a shake of the head. By then Artyom was curled in a ball on the floor and sobbing. He looked up at the Cossack as if he were the grim reaper. The boy thought—no he *knew*—that death was upon him. He gave Tarkhan no more useful information about the American. Which meant he had nothing more to give.

"Tell me the combination to the gun safe."

The kid did so without hesitation, his ruined arm cradled to his chest.

Tarkhan went to the safe, opened it on the first try. Inside he found a dozen weapons of various types. Most were relics, and some looked as if they hadn't been fired in years. He removed a Makarov that looked like it was in decent shape. He unloaded it, checked the action, and deemed it serviceable. He surveyed a shelf full of ammunition, picked out a full box, and stuffed the gun and the bullets into the pockets of his great coat.

"You have a car here?" he asked.

"Yes."

He reached down and patted the pockets of the kid's jeans, found the keys in the front left. He pointed the pipe at him. "Forget me. Forget this." He dropped the pipe. "If you call the police, it will be bad for them. Worse for you."

He turned away and headed for the door. Halfway there, he paused. A locker with a partially open door caught his eye. The members of this lodge did not only ski. They were outdoorsmen, and some hunted. He reached into the locker, requisitioned what he wanted, and was gone.

Boldness was one thing. But Kai Benetton was never cavalier. The four of them settled around the campfire to settle the question of the moment: Was there really a chance they could get Vektor airborne again?

Primakov, the only pilot who had flown her, was central to the discussion. He was also very much in favor of Kai finishing what he'd started. "The biggest problem will be maneuvering on the ice. The jet ended up close to shore, but I think the ice is still thick there. The right main wheel has sunk down slightly, but the other two look solid. The greatest risk will be when you start your turn toward the open lake. When the jet first moves the ice could fracture. If that happens, and any wheel sinks even a quarter of a meter, the gear assembly could fail. You would have no chance of getting airborne."

"There's no way to know ahead of time," Kai said, "we just have to give it a try. I say we launch right before the Osprey lands. Lessens the chance of being discovered for everyone. I should fly out at night anyway. Stealth is great when it comes to radar, but I don't want any MiGs getting a visual."

"Russian fighters have infrared," Primakov warned, "yet the range of such systems is limited. Without knowing roughly where to look, they will be searching the sky through a soda straw."

Diaz, who had spent thirty minutes checking various systems, gave his report. "I started the auxiliary power unit, and it fired up no problem." The APU was a small jet engine designed to power the jet on the ground. It also provided air to start the engines. "All the electrical buses came on line and the nav platforms aligned. I used the air to engage the starters. Both engines shed some ice but they're spinning freely."

Primakov said, "I recommend we start the APU twenty minutes before takeoff. Many systems can be affected by the extreme cold."

"That would burn more gas," Kai said, "and I'm already set to land on fumes."

"Maybe we can fix that," Tru said.

She looked at him skeptically.

"I think I might know where to find a truck with some jet fuel."

She looked at him incredulously. "Go back to town? After what happened last night?"

"Nobody would be expecting it. My biggest worry isn't that I'd get caught stealing a truck—it's sinking through the ice on the way back."

Primakov said, "The ice held up to Vektor, but I only used a small stretch of it. You would be spanning the lake from shore to shore. The weight of the truck is easy to estimate. The question is how thick is the ice on the far side of the reservoir."

"Is there any way to find out?"

"There is actually a good bit of science about such things. And we Russians are proud of our ice roads. Tell your people in Langley to research it."

"On what pretense? They don't know anything about this, and if we tell them—I suspect they'd shoot it down hard."

Kai said, "So modify the request. They've told us fuel will be critical for the Osprey. Tell them you're going to steal the truck in case it needs a top-off."

A brief silence ran as their plot thickened. The notion of flying Vektor out had been completely off-the-cuff. Tru suddenly felt like the head of a gang of thieves plotting an ill-advised bank heist. It led to an unavoidable question.

"Before we go any farther, there's something we should agree on," he said. "If we try to fly Vektor out, it'll be without command approval. That means we're putting our careers on the line. That doesn't bother me, but I want to hear from each of you."

He looked at Kai.

"It was my idea," she said. "I'm in."

Diaz was next to her. "What are they going to do, send me back to Bogota?"

Primakov broke out laughing. "Career? What career?"

FIFTY-THREE

The second call Slaton received from the White House was much like the first—it came out of the blue, leading him to think a problem had arisen. This time he took the video feed alone in the briefing room. As it turned out, only Sorensen was on the White House end.

"I'm having déjà vu," he said. "Correct me if I'm wrong, but last I checked you're vice president of the United States and I've taken your old job. How is it that I'm downrange and you're managing things on the command post end?"

"Because you're on probation."

"Thanks for the vote of support. What's up?"

"He wants to steal a fuel truck."

"I guess I don't have to ask to whom you're referring."

"Rookie just sent a message. He wants to go back to town tonight, steal one of those fuel trucks, and drive it across to the LZ. He asked us to research how thick the ice is on the reservoir."

"Is it possible to find out something like that?"

"CIA has a team working on it."

"Well, from this end I can tell you that more fuel *would* be useful. It would give the Osprey crew more options on their egress route."

"All I see is how much could go wrong. What if Rookie is seen or gets captured? It could blow the whole extraction."

"Believe me, nobody understands operational complications better than me."

"I should tell him not to do it."

"Is that a question?"

"I guess I'm looking for your opinion on the matter."

Slaton leaned back in his chair. For the first time in days, he was enjoying his job. "Have you learned nothing at all from working with me? It doesn't matter what you tell him. He's going to steal that truck."

Silence as Sorensen weighed it. Then, "So maybe I should just approve it."

His sigh carried across nine time zones. "No, Anna. You should leave this one to me . . ." He recited the message he would send to Rookie.

When he was done, she said, "Seriously?"

"Trust me on this."

The look on her face fell to something between pain and resignation. "Why do I feel like I've put a lunatic in charge of the asylum?"

He smiled but said nothing.

"What really scares me is that I see your logic. I wish I'd thought of it when I was dealing with my more recalcitrant operators."

"This job is actually easy. You just have to think like the enemy."

Strelkov slammed down the handset, his frustration building. Neman-chik's office had never seemed so constraining. He pushed away from the desk and diverted to the window. The bleakness outside seemed eternal.

He had not been able to reach Tarkhan all morning. He knew the Cossack had spent last night in Ovsyanka—as a senior officer of the GRU, he could track any phone in Russia. He had, in fact, spent the entire day there, which suggested he was onto something. Still, he had not bothered to check in. This morning Tarkhan's phone had begun drifting north, sinking into the wilderness until its signal flickered and was lost. Like so many technological marvels, the party trick of triangulating phones was worthless outside the range of mobile networks. Strelkov tried to take it as a positive sign. The Cossack had gone into the woods, and that was his element.

It was also where Primakov had to be.

If I only knew what he was doing . . .

The overnight news from the Air Force was as expected—they had still found nothing and continued to expand their search box. The president himself had actually sent Strelkov a brief message: he offered condolences on the tragedy that had befallen his son-in-law, and encouragement to use any and all resources to resolve the disappearance of Vektor. Far from a salve, it only heightened the urgency to put an end to the entire affair.

More worrying, however, was that the rumblings of suspicion he'd sensed at headquarters, steady in recent days, had gone abruptly quiet. If someone there knew Primakov had attempted to defect, they could ruin him in any number of ways. He considered calling Oksana to ask for her help. She was as much at risk as he was, perhaps more, and while she didn't have his connections at The Aquarium, she displayed a streak of cunning that could only be inherited. He decided against it for now.

His eyes settled on a Hip helicopter sitting dormant on the tarmac. The airfield was deathly quiet, as it had been for days. A concrete ghost in the midwinter gloom.

"What to do?" he growled.

The only surprise in the last twenty-four hours had come from Captain Volkov. One of the Hinds that had been hauling his Vega Group unit had caught fire last night and been destroyed. According to Volkov, the fire had been an accident. True to his nature, Strelkov harbored doubts. He sensed he was closing in, yet still Primakov eluded them. Tarkhan remained convinced that the Americans had sent a paramilitary to reach him. Strelkov saw no clear nexus between that theory and a helicopter catching fire.

Still, it gnawed.

He moved to the big map and located the tiny town of Khvoyny. He then traced a finger down to Ovsyanka. From there, Tarkhan had headed north. A twinge of encouragement set in when he connected the two. Tenuous to be sure, but encouragement all the same. There was still much ground to cover, but the activity around Zeya was central to the search he had envisioned—the most direct path to freedom Maksim could have taken.

The map was shrinking. The noose tightening.

So maybe, just maybe . . .

Zeya.

FIFTY-FOUR

Tru kept checking for messages, but on the matter of ice thickness his phone remained silent. The last update from Langley had come hours ago, confirming that exfiltration would take place shortly after midnight. It also reiterated that they needed coordinates for a landing zone. The LZ had been on his list of things to do, but he hadn't gotten around to it. To either help him, or perhaps emphasize their impatience, headquarters had included the coordinates of a few potential sites selected by analysts from satellite overheads.

He set out into the woods and checked the three nearest spots. The one he liked best was two hundred meters west, an open field on the edge of the reservoir. The ground appeared solid, there were no obstructions, and snow cover was minimal. This last feature, he had been told, was critical. They were going to be hauled out by a CV-22 Osprey, and vertical landings on heavy snow could lead to dangerous whiteout conditions. The only downside of the location was that it was visible from across the lake. Tru reasoned that the risk would be minimal; they would have the cover of darkness, and the Osprey was set to be on the ground for only a few minutes.

His recce took nearly an hour, and when Tru got back, he saw Kai and Diaz in the shadows beneath Vektor. They were engaged in what looked like a heated exchange. It ended quickly, and the mechanic set off deeper into the shadows shaking his head.

Tru walked over. "Problem?"

She paused a beat, then said, "It's not a big deal. Diaz has doubts about the ejection system."

"What kind of doubts?"

"To begin, Primakov pulled out the survival kit, which is functionally part of the seat. Diaz had trouble reinstalling it and he doesn't think it would separate properly. We've also been wrestling with Primakov's harness—it's too big for me, even after we adjusted it."

"So you wouldn't be able to eject?"

"Let's just say I hope it doesn't come to that."

"Then let's can the whole idea. You can fly out with us on the Osprey."

"No, it'll be fine."

He looked at her for a long moment. The steel in her gaze was evident. "And if I ordered you to come with us?"

"I'd say you're not in my chain of command."

A slow nod. "Yeah. About what I figured." He looked at the jet contemplatively.

"Don't," she said.

"Don't what?"

"You're thinking about disabling Vektor."

He tipped his head to one side. "Shoot out the tires?"

"Those engines put out a helluva lot of thrust. I could probably ice skate long enough on flats to get her airborne."

"Put another hole in the fuel tank?"

"Diaz has more goop."

"I could launch that rocket-propelled grenade I stole into the engine."

Her smile was spontaneous. Effervescent. "Yeah, that would do it."

The sun made an appearance, and her black hair began shimmering. Her green eyes were translucent, although more from what they held than from the reflected light. Tru felt strangely immobilized. It struck him that for two years now, since first immersing himself in this clandestine existence, he had left something behind. His commitment had been so deep, so absolute, that the rest of his life had gone gray and bland. Now the colors came rushing back.

He said, "What makes you want to do this with such a high level of risk?"

"I'm no adrenaline junkie, if that's what you're suggesting." She nodded toward Vektor. "This is what test pilots do. We learn about unfamiliar aircraft and take them up for trials."

"But this isn't the high desert over California. We're talking about a thousand miles of hostile airspace to reach friendly skies. Even if a Russian fighter doesn't shoot you down, you'll be critical on gas."

"I'll be flying at night, and if Vektor's stealth characteristics are anywhere near as effective as Primakov says they are, I'll be on my second beer at the O-club in Japan before your Osprey even lands."

He forged a smile. "I give you full points for confidence, Kai."

"Believe me when I say, test pilots are not daredevils. It's actually the opposite. Primakov agrees with everything I'm telling you. He says he would make the flight himself if he wasn't laid up."

"Okay, you win. I guess my part is to steal a fuel truck from right under the noses of a Special Forces unit."

"Now who's the adrenaline junkie?" She began walking back to Vektor.

"Kai . . ."

She stopped and turned.

"Yesterday you asked about my story, what brought me here. There is something . . . someone."

He told her about his sister, how she had gone to Ukraine and been captured by Russians. He told her about the incapacitating grief that sank into his soul, and how it had driven him to go search for her. "I eventually crossed paths with a small group of investigators—Ukrainians mostly, and a couple from the Baltic countries. They were operating under U.N. auspices to collect evidence for eventual war crimes prosecutions. Nobody knows whether that will ever happen, but the first step is to collect and safeguard evidence. They'd been traveling around the front lines interviewing people: former prisoners, locals, soldiers. They had no trouble documenting widespread torture, sexual abuse, and the execution of civilians by Russian soldiers. I explained that my sister had gone missing near a certain village, and the leader of the team told me they couldn't help. Yet one woman took pity on me. She pulled me aside and allowed me to see what they'd collected from the town in question."

"Any idea why she helped you?"

"She was Lithuanian, said she lost a brother in similar circumstances. She gave me three hours with the file from Sjeverne. They hadn't gotten around to digitizing everything, so a lot of it was on paper: documents, interviews, photographs. It was the worst three hours of my life—seeing what humans are capable of doing to one another."

"And your sister . . . did you find out what happened to her?"

Tru nodded, his voice going to a whisper. "One witness described a young American woman who'd been taken prisoner. His description fit my sister perfectly. He even said her name was Kate. They had beaten and assaulted her . . . at the end she was barely alive. Then the Russians pulled out of town suddenly one night. They locked almost thirty prisoners in the basement of a church, and roughly an hour after they left there was a massive explosion. Some of the locals figured they'd rigged it with explosives, others thought it was a missile. The locals dug through the wreckage and found only a few dazed survivors."

"But not your sister."

He shook his head. "No. Most of the bodies were shredded, un-recognizable. The townspeople buried them in a collective grave."

"I'm so sorry, Tru."

He stared off into the distance. "I was closer to Kate than anyone. Still am, in a way."

"I'm sure you were a good brother—you did what you could."

"No, a good brother would never have let her go in the first place."

"She was an adult. You can't blame yourself for her choices."

He didn't reply. Because clearly he did blame himself.

"What would she think about this?" she asked, gesturing to their camp. "About what you're doing now."

"She wouldn't like it. She'd say I was reacting to events, lashing out."

"And are you?"

"Probably."

"I disagree," she said. "What happened to your sister might have driven you at the beginning—but what I'm seeing isn't a vendetta. You're going after that fuel tonight—there's no revenge in that. All I see is a guy who's focused on a mission, on doing what's best for the team."

They locked eyes for a silent moment, then Tru headed off.

He walked to the edge of the reservoir, saw the sun high above the distant hills. The naked expanse of ice seemed wider than ever. He thought about what Kai had said, and realized she had a point. For the first time in years, he was making choices that weren't governed by retribution. He was focused on a mission, the immediate goal of which was to steal a fuel truck. He wasn't weighing how many Vega Group men he might encounter, or where they had served. He just needed to get the gas without blowing his own op. Without endangering Kai and the others.

How he was going to do that, Tru had no idea.

FIFTY-FIVE

Obscure units in The Aquarium were not the only ones getting unusual tasking.

One particular research cell deep in the Langley headquarters building was accustomed to bizarre requests. Truth be known, and as a point of pride, it was their stock in trade. That said, the determination of ice thickness on a remote reservoir in Russia was, even by their standards, a notable oddity.

Making the job even more intriguing was a specific request to calculate whether a 25,000-pound ZIL-131 fuel truck, either fully or partially loaded, could be driven across the lake with the ice at the current thickness. Allusions in the tasking order suggested the request had come from the *very* highest levels. Piecing it all together, and before their first keystroke, the team of researchers came to their first conclusion: someone at the White House wanted to know whether a Russian fuel truck could cross Zeya Reservoir, most likely in the next few hours.

Without bothering to consider the who or why of the crisis, five men and women went to work. Their quest began well. With mild surprise, they found volumes of open-source data on the ice thickness of Zeya Reservoir. Naturally suspicious of all information sourced from the Russian government, they crosschecked similar ice fields on lakes in other nations and found no reason to doubt the Russian numbers. They also learned that NOAA, in conjunction with a handful of universities in a global warming study, had been using a satellite to estimate ice thickness on lakes across the globe for years, Zeya among them.

Information on the capabilities of ZIL-frame fuel trucks was easily drawn from internal sources. The ZIL transport had been a staple across all Russian military branches for decades, and virtual treatises on its performance and capabilities existed. With those investigative ducks in a row, the team quickly collated, condensed, and crafted a report.

The answer was channeled back to the White House less than two hours after the question had arrived. It comprised three pages of text, as well as supporting graphs and equations, but could effectively be condensed to a single word: Yes.

Crossing Zeya Reservoir in a twelve-ton truck, under current conditions, posed no problems whatsoever.

Tarkhan left the lodge with measured optimism and the keys to poor Artyom's car. The good news was that he was closing in: his quarry had passed through this place three days ago. His new challenge was to pick up the trail.

There were dozens of paired ski tracks in the snow outside the lodge. Most were fresh, and he tried to discount as many as possible by logic: he ignored sets that led into the forest in groups of two or more, as well as others he discerned as being inbound. Only two sets departed in a way that made sense.

Thankfully, there had been no new snow in the days since the American had passed through. On this point, Tarkhan no longer had doubts—that was who he was chasing. An American agent, most likely from their CIA. He harbored no particular animosity for Americans. He felt equal compassion for all those he hunted, which was to say, very little.

Moving on foot, he began with the set of tracks that appeared older, less in expectation than as a matter of elimination. The twin lines ran along the siding of a road that took him west, away from town. They skipped over patches of icy runoff, and after less than a mile made a ninety-degree turn toward a decrepit house. The place was held together with a smattering of planks and patches, and leaning on a rail in front of the house were the skis that had presumably made the tracks. Having come this far, Tarkhan decided that a conclusive answer would be simple. He walked up to the residence and, without knocking, went right through the front door. A surprised couple, both in their sixties, looked up at him from twin bowls of hot cereal.

"Those are your skis?" he said, addressing the stunned man.

A deep pause ensnared the man as he gauged the intruder. The waddle-necked woman wore a head scarf and a scowl. Through some combination of good sense and Tarkhan's formidable presence, the man took the easy route. "Yes, they are mine."

"You were at the lodge recently?"

"A few days ago."

Tarkhan sensed nothing suspicious, either inside the house or in the man's simple responses. That being the case, he turned back outside and, in a rare display of good will, closed the door behind him. He backtracked straight to the lodge.

The second pair of tracks led north alongside the main road. Feeling confident, Tarkhan decided driving would be preferable. The kid's car turned out to be a decrepit old Lada. Tarkhan was not an experienced driver—he had never owned a vehicle himself—but he was generally proficient, especially in winter conditions. The Lada lacked the power and weight he preferred on icy roads, but its tires were decent, and the gas tank was full.

There was no traffic at all on the road and he drove slowly—on the left side and with the window rolled down—to watch the tracks as closely as possible. He had already checked the weather, and thankfully no new snow was expected—a circumstance that would have forced a more rushed approach. As it was, Tarkhan took his time. Even in the little Lada, he was making good progress, going faster than what any cross-country skier could manage.

He was gaining ground.

Unlike the previous trail, these tracks did not end quickly. His conviction continued to grow for two reasons. The first was that the tracks led north, which seemed the logical direction given the general's premise of Primakov's escape plan. The second, and more nuanced, reason involved the tracks themselves. The twin lines alternated between the road and the siding, keeping to where the snow cover was best. He also noted a tight symmetry in the skier's stride over flat terrain and climbs, and the downhill sections looked to have built considerable speed. Whoever had made these tracks was an expert skier, and he reasoned that the American would never have attempted such a conveyance unless he was confident in his abilities. It was all no more than conjecture, to be sure. But to Tarkhan it felt right.

After two miles the last residences gave way to virgin forest. His suspicions avalanched to certainty eight miles from town. He came upon a spot where the tracks suddenly stopped. He could see where the skis had been taken off—the footprints of large ski boots took their place and led into the forest. Another set nearby led back, and the tracks then continued. He could think of only one explanation for this: the American had seen a car coming. He had quickly removed his gear, gone to hide in the woods, and then returned after the car had passed.

He was twenty miles from town, the tracks continuing with fault-less ease, when the Lada began to bog down. The road deteriorated severely, and soon the car's rear axle sank into a hidden pit of slush. Tarkhan got out and deemed the situation hopeless. The wheels were deep in muck, the engine was smoking, and the road conditions ahead looked even worse.

He opened the trunk, removed the gear he had taken from the locker at the lodge, and hefted it on his back. He set out walking at a constant pace, the twin lines in the snow his compass.

The sun was getting low, darkness imminent as Tarkhan looked up the road. "I am coming, my friend," he whispered. "Coming very soon."

The Osprey looked cold as it sat hunched in the wash of *Boxer*'s deck lights. The weather continued to be poor, high winds and rain lashing the churning sea. The good news was that the forecast was for im-provement. By the time Chaos 21—the call sign of tonight's mission—returned to *Boxer,* conditions were expected to be better. And weather was always more relevant when it came to getting back aboard the ship.

And there was further good news. An Air Force F-35 had launched an hour earlier from Chitose Air Base to serve as a "weather ship," and the report from its pilot was favorable. In the critical airspace over the northern Sea of Japan, the skies above ten thousand feet were clear. Had that not been the case, Chaos 21 would have been forced to devise an entirely new ingress plan.

Having flown halfway around the world, Slaton was busy overseeing the final preparations. The cold rain stung his face, yet the wind at least softened the flight deck's usual industrial vapors—no exhaust fumes, no stench of hydraulic fluid. He cornered the Osprey's loadmaster as he was motoring the aft boarding ramp closed. "Is the package I gave you on board?"

"It is," said a lanky sergeant, whose name was Jackson. "You really think your guy downrange is gonna need it?"

"A little insurance never hurts." Slaton rounded the port side of the Osprey and joined a huddle of officers near the island. Major Gianakos was talking to Captain Longmire and his XO. The fact that he didn't have to shout was an aberration; flight decks were typically a deafening environment, but tonight's only mission had not yet started engines.

"All good?" Slaton asked as he approached.

"So far," Longmire replied. "Weather is good, fuel is on board, and the airplane is code one." He was referring to the jet's Air Force maintenance code. "One" meant that the aircraft had no discrepancies.

"Any updates on our ticket into Russian airspace?" Gianakos asked.

Slaton had spent much of the last hour coordinating with Langley. "They've got an eye in the sky locked on. As far as we can tell, the flight is on time."

"Let's hope, because without that we're an abort."

The next twenty minutes were a rush of activity. Colored vests took over and the flight deck was readied. After a final update from headquarters, Slaton gave the green light. Aircraft directors, plane captains, and fuelies scurried in every direction. Amid the beehive of activity, the ship's senior officers retreated to the combat information center. The crew boarded the Osprey, its entry door closed, and soon both engines were turning. The great twin rotors began whirling, and the signal to launch was given.

The Osprey didn't take off like a conventional jet from a carrier. Instead of a catapult shot, the aircraft simply tilted its rotors to the horizontal and rose straight up, much as a helicopter would. Chaos 21 did precisely that, albeit laboring slightly at its maximum allowable weight. The aircraft accelerated and immediately banked northwest. Once airborne, the rotors canted forward, and speed began to build. In a matter of minutes, Chaos 21 was chasing the vague glow of a deep winter sunset.

FIFTY-SIX

One hundred and ten miles northeast of *Boxer,* on the great spit of land known as Sakhalin Island, Boris Kafelnikov kicked the tire of his AN-2 Colt. The rubber sidewall felt hard, which told him it was either properly inflated or frozen solid. Probably both.

He hurriedly went through the motions of the rest of his preflight inspection, his collar pulled high—the temperature was −13 degrees Celsius. The beefy Russian removed the red covers that protected the pitot tubes from ice, pulled out the wheel chocks, and checked the lubricant level on the big radial engine—in recent weeks it seemed to be burning more oil than gas. Without delay, he climbed into the cockpit and began flipping switches. His first move after getting the engine started was to crank up the heat.

Kafelnikov looked over his shoulder and saw the usual westbound load in the cabin behind him—a few bags of mail and two crates of vodka. The reverse trip would be different, the cargo bay brimming as always with machine parts and electronics. Most of the containers would be plumaged with false bills of lading and fraudulent end user certificates. There was no telling where it all came from. Dubai, Romania, Morocco, Cyprus. The waypoints of Russia's high-tech smuggling schemes were, by design, a shapeshifting labyrinth. He and his old Colt delivered the illicit imports the last few hundred miles, one of the few constants in Russia's globe-spanning network of lies.

He taxied carefully over the ice-encrusted ramp, the Colt's tires thumping along as they warmed and gradually regained their roundness. The winds were strong tonight, yet another pilot had told him the ride above the cloud layers was smooth.

Because Kafelnikov never carried passengers, his little company was certified for single-pilot operations. In his view, he had stumbled onto the perfect job. The money was good, and six nights a week he made one simple round trip—two and a half hours west to Khabarovsk, an hour on the ground to load and refuel, followed by the reverse trip. If the weather was crap, he canceled. When the airplane broke, he waited. As jobs on Sakhalin Island went, it was easy money.

He soon had the old biplane clawing noisily into the sky, the dashboard rattling from the engine's heavy vibrations. The Colt was a relic of another era, an ungainly biplane, but it was stout and reliable—much like Kafelnikov himself. After a sweeping turn to the west, he talked briefly to an air traffic controller—Dmitri, as ever, working the sector's night shift.

Fifteen minutes later, the Colt was plodding along at twelve thousand feet, skimming above a heavy cloud deck. With everything stable, he engaged the rudimentary autopilot, pulled out his thermos, and poured a cup of coffee. Reaching into the back, he liberated a bottle of vodka from the nearest case, cracked it open, and poured a generous shot into his cup. The first sip was always the best. His eyes kept up an easy scan on the antiquated instruments. Last night a fuel pump had given him trouble, but tonight everything seemed to be behaving.

Content, he looked up and studied what seemed like a million stars.

Although Boris Kafelnikov would never know it, on this particular night the sky was looking back. The God's-eye vision was routed to the JSOC command center, and from there mirrored to the TOC in Langley, the White House, and the combat information center on *Boxer*. Dozens of leaders across the globe watched two radar returns float across the sky in a slow-motion ballet. The blips were separated by a prominent hatched line, the official boundary separating Japanese and Russian airspace. The blue dot, labeled Chaos 21, flew a course ten miles south of the demarcation line, a bird of prey stalking from a distance. The red dot, representing the AN-2 Colt, chugged unsuspectingly westward.

To everyone's relief, Boris was right on schedule.

President Cleveland, watching from the Situation Room, was accompanied by her national security staff and Vice President Sorensen. Also in attendance was Colonel Westbrook, who had just returned from Vandenberg.

"He's sticking to his usual route," Westbrook remarked. "That helps—it's only about twenty miles from Japanese airspace. The tricky part will be for Chaos 21 to jump the divide."

The president's gaze fell on General Carter, who was actively coordinating with three separate agencies.

"We're about to go live," he said. He then added in a rhetorical whisper what everyone was thinking. "I hope to hell this works."

From the outset, the exfiltration mission had faced one great obstacle: How could they get Chaos 21 into Russian airspace without being seen? The answer, as it turned out, had been sitting in their lap for some time.

The daily cargo flight from Yuzhno-Sakhalinsk Airport, on the southern tip of Sakhalin Island, had first appeared on the CIA's clandestine radar two years earlier. That was when the pilot who had been Kafelnikov's predecessor, an erratic island native, known only by his nom de guerre of Rex, had offered himself to the agency as an informant. As the owner-operator of a tiny air cargo company that carried illicit cargo on a government contract, Rex had proposed, for remuneration that bordered on extortion, to send photos of his nightly loads, including any paperwork that might suggest its provenance. Before any deal could be struck, Rex had ended up dead in a ditch, twin bullet holes stitched in his forehead—the consequence of double-crossing an island mob boss in an unrelated drug smuggling scheme. The entire disastrous affair lasted no more than a few weeks, and could easily have been forgotten, a fleeting glimmer of prospect in the vast constellation of Russia's corruption.

Thankfully, one team of agency analysts remained intrigued.

Sakhalin Island was a hub for natural gas production, and for decades Western energy companies had been deeply involved. When the war in Ukraine brought sanctions, curtailing the involvement of Shell and Exxon, production levels quickly collapsed. The Russian government's response was as predictable as it was crooked: a massive smuggling campaign was designed to scour the world for sanctioned hardware that would keep the nation's carbon-based lifeblood flowing. The CIA naturally countered with a crusade of its own, an effort to put as many fingers in the leaky parts-trafficking dike as possible. Eventually added to the list of possible vulnerabilities: one nightly transport flight between Yuzhno-Sakhalinsk and Khabarovsk, the logistics hub of Russia's Far East.

For over a year the agency had observed from afar. A new pilot had taken over the operation, and six nights a week he flew the same route, at the same speed, in the same airplane. It was the kind of predictability that spy agencies preyed upon. Yet while the nightly runs were easy to track, the question of how they could be put to good use had long gone unanswered.

Then, twenty-four hours ago, opportunity had struck like a bolt of lightning.

In the Khabarovsk area control center, Dmitri Popov watched his scope wearily. There were only two aircraft in his sector—one of the reasons he liked the night shift—a passenger flight en route to Vladivostok, and the nightly cargo run out of Yuzhno. He yawned, reached for the Styrofoam cup on his right, and tipped back the dregs of his coffee. The moment the cup came down, he noticed a half dozen new returns on his screen.

Popov blinked and did a double take. The new returns flickered in and out like short-circuiting Christmas lights. He had seen such false returns before and written them off as either flocks of birds or some random atmospheric phenomenon. They had also had issues with a software upgrade installed the previous summer. All in all, he wasn't concerned.

Then his screen went completely blank, losing the two dots he knew represented real aircraft.

"Hey, Mikael," he said, addressing his friend two workstations away at sector 6. "Is your screen working? Mine is acting strangely."

"Mine is fine," said Mikael. The older man pushed across the divide on his wheeled chair and looked at Popov's screen. "It will come back. I've seen this kind of thing before."

It was true—Mikael had seen this glitch precisely. What neither man knew was that neither birds nor a mischievous atmosphere was responsible. The culprit was instead a tightly controlled, and artfully crafted, Trojan horse inserted into the software by the NSA. The malware seized temporary control of the operating system, and for ten minutes, Popov's screen blinked and burped and occasionally went blank. He called each of the two aircraft he was controlling and got an immediate response from both. The radios were unaffected. Then, just as he was about to call for technical support, his screen burst back to life with complete normalcy.

As if by a miracle.

Popov settled back in his chair, and in no time, boredom set back in.

FIFTY-SEVEN

To the loadmaster, who was sitting on the cockpit jumpseat, the view out the front windscreen of Chaos 21 was unremarkable. To the two pilots in front of him, who were both wearing night vision goggles, the scene outside perfectly befit their call sign.

A mere thirty feet in front of them, an AN-2 Colt biplane burbled though the night sky on light turbulence, its silhouette startlingly clear in the latest wide-angle, white phosphor view. The proximity between the two aircraft was unnerving to say the least. The Osprey's massive twin rotors, each thirty-eight feet in diameter, scythed disconcertingly close to the Colt's tail, massive beaters in search of an egg.

Joining up with the Colt had been nothing short of a spectacle. The Osprey had a radar for mapping and following terrain, but it was useless for intercepting aircraft, and at any rate, it had been turned off in the name of electronic silence. To find the Colt, Gianakos had gotten vectors from an E-3 AWACS, flying safely in Japanese airspace, which were transmitted through the lone active datalink. As it turned out, the AWACS was the same airplane and crew, Darkstar 22, that had awaited the arrival of Primakov and Vektor days earlier.

"I'd feel better if you took her a little lower, boss," said Captain Bryan from the right seat, watching the propellers spin precipitously close to the Colt.

Gianakos, who was absolutely focused on flying formation with the little aircraft, took it as a welcome voice of reason. He descended ten feet and then tried to assimilate new references on the AN-2 to hold that position. All Air Force pilots get a dose of formation flying in pilot training, but holding a precise position behind a dissimilar aircraft using low-light goggles was a ballgame he'd never played. The nearest the major had come was during air-to-air refueling, connecting to a drogue behind a KC-10 tanker—a far more stable platform, and performed at a greater distance.

Compounding the equation were performance differences. The

CV-22 was no fast-mover, but the Colt was a relative snail, a biplane built for operating from short runways. This meant its cruising speed was not much above the stall speed for the Osprey in fixed-wing mode. It put Gianakos in an ungainly flight regime, the controls less responsive in his hands than usual—highly suboptimal for tight formation flying.

As he worked the controls furiously, spewing a constant stream of muttered expletives, Bryan took care of everything else. He cross-checked their navigation, monitored the Osprey's systems, and, most critically, checked the datalink regularly for warnings of trouble. Every other radio and transmitter on board had been turned off or disabled. Along the same lines, all the Osprey's external lights were extinguished, and the flight deck lighting was dimmed to the minimum necessary. The goal was simple—to make Chaos 21 all but invisible as it penetrated Russian airspace. The only person with a realistic chance of spotting her was fifty feet away in the Colt's cockpit. Thankfully, Boris Kafelnikov was unlikely to catch on. Other than checking his own wings for ice, he had little reason to turn and look over his shoulder. Even if he did glance back, the Colt's thick dual wings made checking his low six all but impossible, and with little moonlight, Chaos 21 was a barely discernable shadow.

All of this had been weighed in advance by JSOC planners as they wrestled with the mission's greatest shortcoming. Everyone agreed that the CV-22 was the only viable option for going deep into Russia and landing in the wilderness. The problem was that the Osprey, relative to stealthier military aircraft, had the radar cross section of the Hindenburg.

Thankfully, the cyberattack on Russia's air traffic control network seemed to have gone as planned. For ten minutes the Bumblehive—the NSA's Utah Data Center—had screwed with their radar systems, both civil and air defense, making one target invisible and adding a few spurious ones. In that window, Chaos 21 had jumped the boundary and tucked in beneath the unknowing Colt. There was no sign the Russians had sensed an intrusion, and so no digital gunfights had broken out.

Now, having blended with a known radar target, the burden fell upon Gianakos—he had to fly tight on the Colt's tail for another ninety minutes. At that point, in theory, the threat would lessen. Russian air defense networks, like those in all countries, were tailored to prevent intrusion, antennae positioned and angled accordingly. The vast interior of the country was more of an afterthought. As one major in the planning cell had phrased it, "Once we sneak through the front door, nobody will be watching the back."

As he thrashed on the controls and cussed a blue streak, feverishly trying to maintain position, Gianakos hoped to hell that theory held.

"Anything?" Kai asked.

"Not yet," Tru replied.

"Maybe they can't figure it out. I mean, the ice depth on a lake this remote?"

"Might have been a big ask."

She looked over her shoulder and saw Diaz shoveling snow off Vektor's right wing, the big tarps partially pulled away to provide access. "I guess it doesn't matter. I think I can make it without the extra gas."

He looked at her doubtfully, and as if on cue his satellite phone vibrated. It was the message they'd been waiting for. He saw one line of text and two lengthy attachments. The message was short and sweet, and sourced from a person he had never met: David Slaton, the recently installed director of the Special Activities Center.

YOUR REQUEST TO REQUISITION FUEL IS DENIED

Not surprised, Tru moved on to the two attachments. The first was the information he had requested regarding the current ice thickness of Zeya Reservoir, along with recommendations for driving on ice. The second was an instruction manual for operating a standard ZIL-131 transport, including a diagram of the ignition system, and how to measure available fuel in the tanker version.

Tru smiled. In a fleeting thought, he hoped he lived long enough to meet his new boss.

"Well?" Kai asked.

"Green light," he replied, pocketing the phone.

"No, it's not." She held him in a flinty stare. "But you're going to do it anyway."

"Look, you and our rescue bird could both use more gas to make it to Japan."

She seemed to weigh an argument, but then relented. "When will you leave?"

"It's dark now, but I'll wait another hour. Once I get back, we want just enough time to transfer the fuel, and then . . ." He made a zooming motion with a flattened hand.

"Any idea what—" Her words clipped off suddenly.

"What's wrong?" he asked, sensing her alarm.

Before she could answer, Tru heard it as well. The thumping of distant rotors. They went to the edge of the lake and saw them in the distance. First one, then a second.

"Hinds," he said.

"The two from town? Vega Group?"

"That'd be my guess. They're coming from that direction."

Primakov, having also heard the rotors, was already dousing the fire. He covered the embers with a section of tarp they'd cut away for that purpose. Diaz stood motionless on the wing.

They all watched the helicopters disappear over the northern hills.

"We've been watching and listening all day—that's the first sign of activity."

"Maybe. The town is far enough away that they could have flown off in a different direction without us hearing it."

"Do you think they're heading out to search for us?"

"Most likely."

"Good," she said. "They're not coming our way."

"Not yet. But they will." As the sound faded to nothing, he turned away. "I think my schedule just moved up. I should move while they're out flying."

"Makes sense."

As he began shouldering gear, she said, "Be careful out there."

"Aren't I always?" he said distractedly. Tru looked up, caught her gaze, and added a wry smile. Moments later, he was fading into the night once again.

Kai went over to Primakov and soon they were engaged in a deep conversation. It would be the most important flight briefing of her life.

FIFTY-EIGHT

"We're descending, boss," Bryan said from the right seat.

"No shit," Gianakos fussed, reducing power and nosing over to stay behind and beneath the Colt.

The show had been running for over an hour, Gianakos battling to stay in position behind the old transport. At one point, the Colt had jerked downward suddenly, forcing Gianakos to push over violently and turn to starboard. The reason, which neither American would ever know, was that Boris had sneezed, spilled his coffee, and bumped the controls hard enough to disengage the Colt's autopilot. The biplane righted quickly, and after a fusillade of invectives Gianakos worked his way back into place.

Now, however, with Khabarovsk airport, the Colt's destination, thirty miles ahead, decision points were nearing. The ingress plan had so far been relatively straightforward. And, as far as they knew, successful. There were no indications their intrusion into Russian airspace had been detected. Various ELINT and SIGINT assets were keeping constant watch, and no alarms had been raised in Russia's Far East air defense networks.

Descent, however, brought complications. The first involved simple aerodynamics. The two aircraft were vastly different in how they flew and handled, and transitioning to a descent could place the Osprey in an unsafe corner of its envelope. On top of that, after nearly two hours of hanging behind the Colt like a whipsawed kite, Gianakos was at the end of his tether. The muscles in his arms and hands ached, and his nerves were raw.

With Chaos 21 about to lose its ghost status, a massive question loomed: At what point should they break away?

Given the late hour, the control tower at Khabarovsk Airport was closed, and the regional air traffic center would be minimally staffed. NSA had no Trojans active in either of these facilities, so there was a chance the Osprey could be spotted when it broke away. Conversely, staying tight with the Colt to low altitude in a populated area meant that, even at night, they might be seen and reported by someone on the ground. There was no good answer, and the decision of when to separate had ultimately been left to the crew.

"How far out are we?" asked a stiff-necked Gianakos, his NVGs locked on the Colt.

"Twenty-eight miles from the airfield."

"Altitude?"

"Passing eight thousand. He's slowing, a hundred and twenty knots now. You won't be able to stay with him much longer."

"What's my course to the hills?"

"331 degrees. About thirty to your right."

The highlands to the west of the Amur basin were not particularly steep, but its craggy valleys were more than enough to mask a lone CV-22 on a dark night. Better yet, those highlands were all but uninhabited. If they could reach the foothills undetected, the route to Zeya would be clear.

Gianakos began making gentle S-turns. "He's getting too slow. I can't stay with him much longer."

"Twenty-five miles."

"Okay, here goes." The major made an aggressive turn to the right and began descending. No longer tied to the lumbering Colt, he accelerated the Osprey to near its red line.

Eight minutes later, Chaos 21 was three hundred feet above the ground and cloaked in a serpentine canyon. Bryan activated the radar for the first time to enable terrain following.

"Time to target?" Gianakos inquired, his attention riveted on the terrain outside.

"Show arrival at the LZ in sixty-two minutes. We're dead-on time."

For six hours Tarkhan followed the tracks on foot. He didn't miss the Lada, and he wasn't at all cold—moving was always the best way to stay warm in the forest. He wondered how long it had taken the American to reach this point. It had to have been many hours, yet still the length between his strides was like clockwork. There were no signs that he'd tired, no break in his rhythm.

He made a mental note to not underestimate this one.

He had just rounded a bend when the trail suddenly altered. He saw where the man had stopped and paused for a time. Then the twin tracks headed off into the woods on a perpendicular course.

The Cossack never hesitated. After readjusting his gear and getting his bearings, he too set out into the forest, keeping the same pace he had been holding all day.

Tru crossed the reservoir at a greater distance from town than the night before. He assumed his element of surprise was gone, and even though the helicopters were out flying, it was possible that watchful members of the Vega Group remained in town.

As he approached the clearing from the northeast, he adjusted his gear to preclude clatter. He was wearing the plate carrier he had stolen and carrying two weapons. Strapped to his back was an RPG-30 anti-tank grenade launcher, and on a sling in front he carried the guard's AK-12 assault rifle. He hoped neither was necessary, but there was un-deniable comfort in having options.

The glade came into view, and what he saw confused him at first. The heap of wreckage from last night's encounter was there, charred and rimmed with ice, the acrid scent of its fiery fate clinging to the air. The fuel trucks, however, were nowhere in sight. He wondered if last night's disaster had caused the unit to bug out. Had the Hinds flown away to some new staging area? Had the fuel trucks hit the road?

He edged carefully toward town, silent and watchful. He saw the bar, and in the distance the shuttered restaurant where he'd charged his phone. Finally, Tru spotted them—two hulking ZIL frames parked in tandem at the end of the main road. He wondered why they had been moved. For security? Was it possible they were empty?

The most important question then prevailed: Were the trucks being guarded? He observed the scene carefully for five minutes. Then he gave it five more. He watched a few bundled locals shuffle between buildings in town, saw the occasional light flick on or off in a window. He saw no one who was conceivably a member of Vega Group.

Nor did he see anyone near the trucks.

Tru plotted out the best approach path, skirting left behind a string of buildings and sheds. All at once, he was struck by the utter reckless-ness of his scheme. How could he possibly steal one of the trucks and not be noticed? Everyone in town would hear him crank the big diesel engine. The extra fuel could prove critical for both Kai and the exfil team, yet his plan for stealing it wasn't really a plan at all. With more time, he might come up with something stealthy and clever. As it was, he was stuck with loud and reckless.

He began moving, doing his best to stay out of sight. Reaching the first ZIL, he kept on the side away from town. Tru approached the cab carefully, his rifle poised. The front seat was empty. He tested the passenger-side door and found it unlocked. This wasn't a surprise—Vega Group had the run of Khvoyny and no one in their right mind was going to mess with one of their vehicles.

Not sure what that says about me, he thought idly.

Having reached the trucks, he now had to choose between them. From the research Slaton had delivered, he knew a full tanker carried roughly 11,000 pounds of gas—aviation fuel was always expressed in weight rather than volume, that being the relevant number for aircraft performance calculations. Some of that fuel, surely, had already been transferred to the Hinds, and the last thing Tru wanted to do was put his ass on the line to drive an empty gas truck across an ice field.

Thankfully, the new SAC director had included instructions on how to check the fuel level of a ZIL tanker in his message. All Tru had to do was power up the refueling panel on the side of the chassis and read a simple gauge. Thankfully, the panel was on the shielded side of both tankers, and in a matter of minutes he had his answer. The truck in front was nearly empty, less than a thousand pounds remaining. The other held roughly half a tank. Split between Vektor and the inbound Osprey, it would greatly improve the chances of both reaching safety.

Tru climbed into the cab through the passenger-side door. He unshouldered the RPG, set it securely on the floor, and then placed the AK on the seat beside him. Next, he rolled down the window, recalling a paragraph in the message about having an escape plan when driving on ice. When he'd first read it, Tru wrote off the tip as typical bureaucratic caution, but now he questioned Langley's confidence regarding the thickness of the ice.

No time for seconds thoughts.

Like most military vehicles, the ZIL had no key. Tru reached for the start button, then hesitated. Once he cranked the engine, there would be no turning back. The road ahead led to the shoreline, a gentle downhill grade, and he remembered the gravel boat ramp he'd seen last night. Noticing that the parking brake was set, he improvised. He put the shift lever in neutral and released the brake. The big ZIL shuddered once, then began rolling downhill, the only sound being that of gravel crunching under its tires. He turned toward the ramp, the steering wheel heavy but responsive, and made sure his foot was nowhere near the brake pedal—he didn't want the brake lights to flare. The truck gathered speed and he picked out the ramp easily.

The front wheels bounded onto the ice, and then the heavier back wheels stepped across. The transition to the new surface was audible, grinding rock giving way to mild crackling noises. Tru found himself holding his breath as Langley's calculations played out in real time. The ice seemed to hold.

Having reached a level surface, the speed began to drop off. Tru took a deep breath and sank the start button. The ZIL's diesel roared to life, shredding the night's silence. As he shifted into gear, he imagined lights snapping on behind him, curtains being flung open in windows. The ZIL accelerated, and he recalled another recommendation from the manual: driving slowly on ice gave the best margin for bearing weight, something about the dynamic pressure beneath the wheels increasing at higher speeds. He eased off the accelerator. Within seconds, adrenaline got the better of him. The dynamic pressure of the tires seemed far less relevant than the ballistic pressure he would face if Vega Group noticed his theft.

Tru stomped the accelerator to the floor and the ZIL lurched ahead, diesel smoke belching into a black night.

FIFTY-NINE

Tru's assessment that no one had been guarding the trucks was only half right.

Midway up one of Khvoyny's secondary streets, a man appeared in the window of a rundown house. He was naked and sleep-addled, having been awakened by the sound of a big diesel engine. Behind him a local woman lay beneath twisted layers of bedding, her eyes squinting into the darkness.

"What is it?" she asked.

Captain Volkov, the only member of Vega Group still in town, didn't answer. His eyes shot to the main road where the ZILs had been parked and he saw that only one remained. He'd been harboring vague suspicions since last night's disaster. But *this* he had never expected.

He rushed around the room searching for his clothes, but in the dark it was hopeless. He found his boxers on the floor, his pants on a bedpost. Two socks and one boot were near the wood stove. He wrestled it all on as fast as he could, grabbed his AK-12, and darted to the door.

He was halfway to the waterfront when the situation began to clarify. One of the ZILs was out on the lake, clouds of black soot steaming from its exhaust. He didn't know who had stolen it or for what reason. He only knew that if he didn't intervene, his life would become decidedly more difficult.

Volkov shouldered his AK, took aim, and began pouring rounds into the night.

Tru was trying to get his bearings, seeking a reference on the far shoreline, when he heard a sharp metallic ping. He didn't realize what it was at first—for all his training, he had never before come under direct fire from an enemy. The situation crystallized when the mirror outside the passenger door exploded. Tru leaned left, toward the open window, and ventured a quick glance toward shore. In the scant light he saw a half-naked man wearing one boot shooting at him with a rifle.

He drew back inside and told himself it was a manageable threat. There was plenty of metal between him and the shooter. *Not to mention a thousand gallons of flammable liquid.*

His right foot stayed hard on the accelerator. At the speed he was traveling, he would be out of range in roughly a minute. The more pressing problem: the half-dressed man would soon wield a more lethal weapon. A telephone or a radio.

And those the ZIL could never outrun.

Volkov emptied three magazines—all he was carrying in the pockets of his pants—to no avail. He was sure he had scored hits, but the ZIL wasn't going to be stopped by a handful of long-range 5.45mm rounds.

He lowered the rifle and cursed under his breath as the truck faded into the dark. He stood still in the frigid air, shirtless and wearing one boot, as the last of his doubts washed away; last night's debacle had been anything but an accident. He had stayed behind tonight because he'd sensed things accelerating. If the situation degraded, he'd reasoned, it would be easier to manage from town. That idea was about to be tested.

He set down the rifle and pulled out his phone.

The first call he placed was the one Tru had predicted. Volkov issued orders to be relayed though the regional command post—he could not talk directly to the Hinds, but his instructions would be forwarded via army radio links. After the sergeant on the other end read back his message, Volkov tapped out of the call and placed a second.

This one was answered after five rings, and the voice on the other end sounded sleepy.

"Things are going critical," Volkov said. "You need to get here right away."

SIXTY

Tru was half a mile from the encampment, all but standing on the accelerator, when the ice in front of the ZIL exploded. Bullets traced a line directly in his path, a wall of white erupting in the flood of the headlights. He instinctively heaved left on the wheel and the big truck flew into a swirling skid. Moments later a second line of bullets zippered to his right, peppering the windows with shards of ice and snow.

The ZIL spun out of control, tons of steel and gas going circular. On the second rotation Tru glimpsed a shadow flashing overhead. The ZIL came to rest; its engine had stalled, and the diesel roar was replaced by the thrum of a big helicopter. He craned his head to the right and saw what he expected: the familiar Hind repositioning for another strafing pass.

He could hardly imagine a worse scenario. He was completely exposed, the closest cover a mile away. He was in a truck loaded with fuel, and at least some of the inbound rounds had been incendiaries. He grabbed his weapons, tumbled out of the truck, and circled to the back. Peering over the rear bumper, he watched the Hind wheel out of a turn and settle its nose on the ZIL. At this range the gunsight might as well have been on his chest. He searched the sky all around but saw no trace of the second chopper. What did it matter? He was hiding behind a bomb.

He set down the AK and began prepping the RPG. He'd identified it as an RPG-30, similar to the RPG-27, which he had played with in training. This morning Tru had memorized the simple instructions printed on the side of the launch tube. He raised it to his shoulder, flipped up the front and rear sights. Once the rear sight was raised, the weapon was cocked and ready.

It was a lousy weapon for the situation. RPGs were unguided, and this one had a range of no more than two hundred meters. The Hind, thankfully, was hovering at a distance roughly half that. His biggest problem was that the RPG was a single-shot weapon. Tru would have only one chance. If he missed, he would be facing the scenario he'd avoided two days earlier: a gunfight with an assault helicopter. And this time, he knew the Hind was loaded with Spetznaz soldiers.

He stole another glance around the bumper. He would have to un-mask to get a decent shot. If the Hind's weapons officer opened up with the chin gun it would pulverize both him and the truck before he could get off a shot. Curiously, the Hind remained in a stable hover. *Why aren't they shooting?* The reason became clear when the chopper began to rotate. The side door came into view and Tru saw men preparing to exit. Vega Group didn't want to kill him—not yet. They wanted to capture him and ask questions first.

And that's their mistake.

He popped out from behind the truck and set his feet in a wide stance. The weapon was already on his shoulder. He lined up the sights as best he could and touched the trigger. His eyes were focused close-in, all attention on the two iron sights, yet he sensed frantic motion in the distance. The Hind began rotating again, the pilot seeing the danger. Trying to bring his guns to bear.

The trigger broke and the weapon launched as advertised. First came the precursor missile, a small projectile that streaked ahead as a decoy for reactive armor—a defensive measure found on tanks. A fraction of a second later, the main round belched from the tube.

The projectile took barely a second to reach its target. It seemed like an eternity.

The Hind was forty-five degrees off, a narrowing silhouette, when the 105mm tandem shaped charge struck near the open side door. Or possibly—Tru couldn't say for sure—it flew *through* the door. If the end-game trajectory was arguable, the result was not. The explosion was cataclysmic, a blinding orange fireball filling the night sky. The helicopter lurched to starboard as a rotor separated and flaming shards spun outward. Before Tru's eyes, what had moments ago been a functional aircraft cartwheeled toward the ice. The explosion when it struck was even greater than the primary.

A blast that could be seen and heard for miles.

And one that would register in outer space.

The smell of kerosene was a constant in the cabin of Chaos 21. The auxiliary tanks installed in the Osprey were notorious for leaking, and since they were hauling three for maximum range, there was no escaping the pungent odor. It was more a nuisance than a matter of safety, the main effect being psychological—the leaks were a constant reminder of the combustible nature of their mission.

"Twenty-eight minutes to go," Bryan said.

Both pilots were wearing their NVGs as Gianakos steered through a right turn. They were three hundred feet above the ground, plus or minus fifty due to the uneven terrain.

"Any updates from the LZ?" Gianakos asked.

"No news is good news. Must be quiet."

"Let's hope it stays that way."

"This guy is a nuclear fucking disaster!"

Anna Sorensen stared at the president. Elayne Cleveland was not typically disposed to profanity, but when the new images from Zeya Reservoir hit the screen in front of them—the flaming wreckage of yet another Russian helicopter—she simply lost it.

"He did what he had to do," Sorensen replied in what she hoped was a calm tone. They were alone together in the Oval Office, and she was thankful for that—the last thing she needed was a peanut gallery of national security experts slinging darts. The weight of the iconic trappings around them imbued all the gravitas necessary.

"You said he wasn't going to steal that fuel truck," said the president.

"I said he proposed stealing it, and that the SAC director ordered him not to."

"Are you telling me Rookie is no longer following Slaton's instructions?"

"He knows the situation on the ground better than we do. I suspect he made his own call."

"Well, his 'call' could push us into a damned war. I can understand a chance run-in with a guard, but now we've got multiple fatalities to answer for."

Sorensen couldn't argue otherwise. She wasn't surprised that Miller had gone after the truck, and she couldn't blame him for defending himself—the footage had shown the entire shootdown sequence. Still, she hadn't seen an altercation like this coming.

"Does the term 'mission creep' mean anything to you?" the president asked.

"Of course."

"This all started as a defection, a low-risk operation. All we had to do was put out a welcome mat, receive a fancy new jet, and tell one Russian pilot 'thank you very much.' Instead, I've got three Americans and our defector stranded deep inside Siberia, and that doesn't count the rescue mission." She looked at Sorensen somberly. "This was a mistake, Anna. But it's on me. I was too focused on the upside."

"We both knew there were risks going in. But the situation is still salvageable."

"What's the status of the rescue flight?"

Happy to change the subject, Sorensen checked her secure comm device. "They're half an hour out."

America's two top leaders looked at the screen uneasily. The president said what they were both thinking. "This could really blow up in our face."

"I know," Sorensen agreed. "But there's still a chance they can all get out before that happens."

Viktor Strelkov rushed across the tarmac at Skovorna at a virtual jog— the fastest his thick legs had moved in years.

Word had not yet reached him about the loss of the second Hind on Zeya Reservoir. He was aware, however, that a fuel truck had been heisted from under Volkov's nose. He wasn't sure what to make of that, nor did he know where Tarkhan had gone. Yet one thing was increasingly clear: he needed to get to Zeya before the situation became uncontrollable.

He climbed up into a churning Hip, the pilots regarding him warily—it was the same crew who had lifted Corporal Ivanov above the runway days earlier. Their instructions tonight were more conventional, and the Hip rose gently into a night sky that was about to become very crowded.

Two hundred miles east, Chaos 21 cut a weaving path through yet another shallow valley. Only a few turns remained before they reached their destination.

Unbeknownst to all of them, two other helicopters were converging on the same area, one from the north and another from the west.

As if that wasn't enough, on its improvised frozen taxiway, Russia's most advanced fighter was waking from a deep sleep.

SIXTY-ONE

Everyone at the camp had seen Tru's deadly encounter with the Hind, and they were waiting anxiously as the ZIL skidded to a stop on the ice near Vektor.

"Are you okay?" Kai asked the moment he climbed down from the cab.

"Yeah, I'm good," he said breathlessly. "We need to transfer this fuel fast."

"Faster than you think," she said, pointing to the back of the truck.

Tru looked and saw that the back half of the truck was riddled with holes. There were at least two in the tank itself, and fuel was dribbling onto the ice and forming a puddle.

"Like I said . . ." He checked his phone quickly, then shoved it back in his pocket. "No new updates, but the last one said the Osprey would arrive on time—that gives us a little over twenty minutes."

Diaz hurried toward the truck, his feet skidding on the ice. Tru had parked the ZIL roughly thirty meters from Vektor—according to Primakov, a standard refueling hose was thirty-five meters long. He didn't want to stress the frozen surface near the jet any more than necessary.

"Any idea how to read this gauge?" Diaz called out, studying the truck's refueling panel. "I don't speak Russian, and my metric conversions might not be great."

Tru said, "I think we've got about six thousand pounds. Just pump out half of whatever the gauge shows, and we'll save the rest for the Osprey."

"That I can do."

Everyone began working quickly, the sense of urgency heightened by the flaming wreckage in the distance.

Kai rushed around Vektor, performing a preflight inspection. The tarps were pulled away, and with the snow cleared from the wing, Tru saw the jet clearly for the first time. It looked sleek and ominous.

"You still sure about this?" he asked Kai. "You've never flown this jet."

"Just like riding a new bike . . . only a lot faster."

He smiled, although more at her attitude than her humor.

She said, "As soon as Diaz finishes fueling, I'll start flipping switches. The inertial platforms take about ten minutes to align. Once that's done, I'll crank the engines and I'm outta here. I guess I'll have to steer around that." She pointed to the smoldering crash.

Diaz, who was dragging a big fuel hose toward Vektor, said to Tru, "Two helicopters taken out on your first operational assignment—think that might be a record?"

"No idea, but if you add in Star Chaser . . . this lake is getting pretty full of airplane parts."

Kai said, "Let's not add any more."

She finished her inspection and approached the rope ladder. The evergreen scent of the forest was overcome by the stench of jet fuel leaking from the back of the ZIL.

"This feels weird," she said to Tru, pausing before climbing up. "I'm usually wearing a lot of gear to do this. Flight suit, G-suit, parachute harness. The colonel's stuff either doesn't fit or it's useless."

"What about a helmet?"

"That's the one thing I can use. It fits my head like a ten-gallon bucket, but the earphones and mic should at least give me radios."

Tru moved closer. "When you get to that O-club in Japan, order me a beer. I'll be there before it gets warm."

"I'll bet you're right." They exchanged an extended look, and she added, "Take care, Tru."

He watched her climb up the ladder and settle into the cockpit.

Moments later the jet began coming to life, the sound of its auxiliary power unit drowning out the silence. Tru diverted to where Primakov was sitting and began digging through the remaining survival gear from the ejection seat.

"That was a good shot," the Russian said.

Preoccupied, Tru didn't catch his meaning right away. "Oh . . . the RPG?"

"An unguided weapon, but still you scored a hit."

"The alternative wouldn't have been pretty."

"What are you looking for?"

"Handheld signal flares. Weren't there some in your kit?"

"Green nylon bag."

Tru found it.

"There are two," Primakov said, "one red and one green. What are you going to use them for?"

"I need to mark the LZ. The Osprey should be here in about fifteen minutes. They have GPS coordinates, but at night they might have trouble identifying the best spot for touchdown."

"The flares will burn for roughly five minutes. I would recommend the red at night. You should also consider the new distraction the crew will be facing."

"What's that?"

"The Hind that crashed. It's still burning, and I promise you that is the first thing the crew will see."

"Good point," Tru said, thankful to have a pilot's perspective.

"Go to the landing zone and take the compass. Calculate a bearing and approximate range from the crash, then pass it to the crew. That will give them a more complete picture."

Tru pocketed the flares. He was about to leave when Primakov said, "You operate very differently than we Russians do."

"How's that?"

"In the Russian military decisions are made at the highest levels, then dictated downward. Questioning them is never an option. You and the major do precisely the opposite. You make decisions here, in the field—even if they go against what headquarters is telling you."

"We'll answer for our choices later, so let's hope we're making the right calls."

"Generally, I think you have. And I would say it adds to your effectiveness."

"Great . . . you can put that in your five-star review."

Tru turned away, the Russian chuckling behind him.

The quickest way to reach the LZ was on a nearby game trail. Tru had spotted deer on it the first morning, and he'd been using it himself ever since. He sprinted over the snow-covered earth and reached the clearing in a matter of minutes. Hauling Primakov over the same route would be difficult, but Tru had already devised a workaround for that.

He stopped in the center of the clearing and took a compass shot to the wreckage, then estimated the distance. He removed his gloves, tapped it all into his phone, and waited. A response came ten seconds later.

COPY. CHAOS 21 TWENTY-ONE MINUTES OUT

Tru gauged where and when to pop the flares, double-checking that the ground was solid, and made a final check for obstructions on the perimeter. Finally, he scoured the area for loose debris, dragging a few old tree branches into the forest. Satisfied the LZ was as prepared as he could make it, he bolted back to camp.

Captain Longmire was in *Boxer*'s CIC watching the mission play out with his XO. The feed they were getting was a highly filtered version of what Langley was seeing, but enough to comprehend the big picture— essentially, one lonely blue dot traversing the expanses of eastern Russia. Chaos 21 was nearing the extraction point and the mission was going perfectly to script. Which only heightened his commander's sense of unease.

"So far, so good," Emerson said.

"If all goes well, we'll need the deck green for recovery in three hours. Maybe we should go roust Slaton—he'll want to watch this play out. I'm guessing he's in his cabin?"

"I haven't seen him since the launch."

"I'm sure he racked out. He's covered a lot of time zones in the last day. Go rattle his cage."

"Will do."

Longmire followed along on the monitor as Chaos 21 neared Zeya Reservoir. At the bottom of the screen was a JSOC message thread relating to the mission. Everything appeared quiet.

Five minutes later, Emerson returned to the CIC. His face had gone ashen. "Skipper, we have a problem . . ."

SIXTY-TWO

Tru's message reached Chaos 21 just in time.

"New incoming, skipper," Bryan announced. "It says a Hind has just gone down about a mile from our LZ."

"Gone down?" Gianakos repeated. "As in crashed?"

"Apparently. The snake-eater on the ground says it's still burning—he gave us a radial and distance from the LZ so that we can use it as a reference."

Bryan couldn't see the expression on the major's face because he was wearing NVGs. He had no trouble imagining it.

"Nice of him to think of us, but why the hell did a Hind crash right next to our LZ?"

"I was wondering the same thing."

"Fire back a reply. Find out what the hell's going on. If we're headed into some kind of damned hornet's nest, I wanna know about it."

Bryan input the query, his verbiage considerably more diplomatic, and hit send. As soon as he was done, he looked up, and said, "I think any answer is going to be too late."

"Why?"

"One o'clock, just below the horizon."

Gianakos looked right and saw a faint glow in the distance in his low-light view. The crash site. "Well, at least we know we're in the right spot. Give Jackson a five-minute call."

"Will do." Bryan tapped up the intercom and began talking to the loadmaster.

Tru and Diaz had brainstormed how to transfer Primakov to the LZ. The bound branches Tru had used as a sled were ungainly, and Diaz had come up with a solution. He'd lashed together fiberglass support poles and a section of material from the tarp to create a reasonable facsimile of a stretcher.

The question then became what route to take. Carrying the Russian on the stretcher through dense forest would be slow and awkward, while hauling him across the ice was a considerably farther distance. A better option, Tru decided, was sitting on the ice right in front of them. The ZIL had no flat outer surface on which they could place the stretcher, but the cab was spacious and the doors large. If they could slide Primakov in partially, leaving just enough room for Tru to drive, Diaz could ride the opposite runner with the door open and hold him in place.

Tru put the AK on the floor in the ZIL's cab—he hadn't been without it since his altercation with the Hind—and transformed from CIA paramilitary to hospital orderly. They moved Primakov as gently as they could—his leg hadn't been set properly, and they'd run out of pain meds.

Tru and Diaz lifted Primakov as carefully as possible. He was clearly in agony, but he never complained. Sliding their patient into the cab was the most difficult part, but eventually they managed it.

With Diaz on the runner, Tru rounded the ZIL to reach the driver's seat. He was almost there when two things seized his attention. The first was the distant sound of rotors. He initially took comfort in this until he noticed the second distraction: a new message on his phone.

SINGLE HIND INBOUND FROM NORTH. LZ NOT SECURE. ENGAGE
IF POSSIBLE.

Gianakos saw it just as Bryan was reading the urgent message. "Two o'clock, maybe five miles," he said. "Headed our way. The LZ is red!"

Gianakos banked into a hard right turn.

"Is this an abort?" the copilot asked.

"I put my ass on the line to get this far—no way I'm going home empty-handed. We'll lay low for a few minutes, see what happens."

Rolling out on the reverse course, Chaos 21 quickly disappeared behind a hill.

Tru dove into the cab for his AK, and shouted to Diaz, "Stay here!"

He ran full-bore onto the ice for fifty yards, then turned right to parallel the shore. Looking into the sky on his left he didn't see anything, but the sound was growing. He sprinted into the open with two objectives. The first was to stand out—if the Hind was headed this way, he wanted to draw the crew's eyes to him. Along the same lines, he wanted to put as much distance as possible between himself and the encampment.

Even if he succeeded, the distraction wouldn't last long. He heard Vektor's APU running, although Kai hadn't started its engines yet. The jet was uncovered and would stand out like a lighthouse. The idea of catching the attention of the Hind's crew was instinctive, but Tru had no idea what he would do at that point. He saw no sign of the Osprey, which was probably a good thing—as far as he knew, it wasn't an armed variant.

He was a hundred yards from the ZIL and Vektor when he caught a glint in the sky to his left. Soon a shadow emerged from the gloom, and between the dim moonlight and a bit of illumination from the aircraft's interior, the Hind materialized—almost surely the last remaining ship of the squadron he'd been decimating. Once more they had Tru in their sights, but this time they knew he could fight back.

Without breaking stride, he leveled his AK in the general direction of the big chopper. He squeezed off a single round. Then a few seconds later, another. At this range, roughly a thousand yards, he didn't have a prayer of getting a hit. Even if he did, the 5.45mm round wasn't going to penetrate the hardened windscreen of an assault helicopter. He was still just trying to become the focal point.

He squeezed off a third round, keenly aware that he didn't have ammo to burn. He scanned the shoreline to his right, searching for a particular feature. The Hind's closure lessened, and it appeared to stabilize. Sensing what was coming, Tru planted his foot to make a hard turn. He slipped and went sprawling across the ice.

In the next instant, the world around him erupted, rounds from the Hind's big gun walking past him a few yards away. He scrambled to his feet and sprinted toward shore, his arms windmilling for balance on the ice. Tru spotted what he was looking for in the gloom, a feature he'd noted yesterday—a massive boulder where the land met the ice.

The boulder was the size of a car, and he dove behind it moments before another string of rounds slammed in to his right. Bullets ripped into stone and shredded trees behind him. Tru scrambled ten feet to his right behind the boulder, popped up, and sighted on the Hind. It was two hundred yards away now, but stationary—the distant wreckage of their sister ship had made the pilots wary.

He fired three evenly spaced rounds, settling to take aim after each recoil. Then he ducked back down as the chin gun opened up again. He checked his pockets and felt two spare magazines. Thirty rounds each. He pulled out his phone and the most recent message glared at him. *Engage if possible.*

Yeah, easy for you to say, he thought.

He typed out a reply: INFORM INBOUND FLIGHT LZ IS UNDER FIRE FROM HIND. SITUATION CRITICAL. He hit send.

He returned fire again, then ejected an empty magazine and loaded a spare. It left one full mag in his pocket. The odds of hitting a vital part of the aircraft were virtually nil. But he was at least distracting them and doing it from solid cover.

But the stalemate wouldn't last long. Based on what he had learned from his reconnaissance, he figured there would be between six and ten Vega Group men inside the Hind. All of them would be hardened veterans, cut from the same cloth as the group who'd terrorized his sister. And on his team? One pilot with a broken leg, a skinny mechanic, and another pilot who was a confessed pacifist.

Tru didn't like the tactical landscape. Not one bit. If the chopper simply set down and let Vega Group go to work, he would quickly be outflanked. He had to do something to change the dynamic.

Nothing came to mind.

SIXTY-THREE

Despite the fact that she was seated at the controls of one of the world's most advanced machines of war, Kai had never felt so vulnerable. For all Vektor's potential lethality, it was at that moment little more than a duck on a frozen pond. And she was sitting on it.

She had seen Tru dart out onto the ice, rifle in hand, and so she knew trouble was brewing. He'd disappeared around a spit of shoreline, and soon after that she saw a Hind maneuvering in the distance. It came to a hover and began strafing in Tru's direction. She looked at Diaz and saw him frozen beside the ZIL. His job was to look after Primakov, so there was little he could do but watch and wait.

Kai considered her own response, but the options that came to mind were dismal.

It would take at least another five minutes to get Vektor airborne. She guessed the Hind's crew had spotted the jet parked near the shore, but they would view it as more a curiosity than a threat. The possibility that Vektor might actually start up and take off wouldn't register—not until the moment Kai cranked the first engine. At that point, the jet's infrared signature would be greater than the wreckage of the helicopter Tru had shot down.

Questions cascaded through her head.

Are there more Russians inbound? Almost certainly.

If I start the engines, is there any chance I could get airborne? Possibly, if Tru can distract them long enough.

For the next few minutes, in spite of the madness all around, Kai realized that her own situation remained unchanged. Getting Vektor airborne was her best chance to survive.

But what about the others? Tru was up against impossible odds, battling a helicopter gunship that was probably full of Spetznaz troops, and doing it with nothing more than one rifle. If he went down, it would leave Diaz and Primakov to fend for themselves. The inbound rescue flight would have no choice but to abort.

If Kai shut Vektor down, she might be able to join the fight. There was a second assault rifle somewhere. Yet small arms marksmanship wasn't her strength. If this were Hollywood, she could get airborne and shoot the Hind down. The real world, unfortunately, was far less dramatic. Vektor was in the experimental flight test stage of development. A year or two down the road, it would be certified to employ a broad array of missiles, bombs, and bullets. The jet she was sitting in, unfortunately, carried no weapons whatsoever—according to Primakov, the integral gun had actually been removed and replaced with ballast. This version of Vektor had but one superpower—it was invisible to radar. And that was useless for stopping the fusillade of bullets flying at Tru.

She smacked her palm hard on the Plexiglass canopy. Every bit of logic, every shred of common sense, shouted at her to crank the engines and get Vektor airborne. Instead, Kai unfastened her lap belt, stepped over the canopy rail, and clambered down the ladder.

There was a pause in the incoming rounds, and Tru ventured a look from behind the boulder. Seconds later, his fears were confirmed.

The Hind's pilot/weapons operator, who was seated at the forward station of the tandem cockpit, apparently wanted to end the standoff. With bullets not doing the job, he switched to rockets. From the pods on the side pylons, a salvo of fourteen S-8 80mm rockets lit up the night. The unguided rockets were a mix, some carrying high-explosive warheads, others incendiary. The resulting conflagration was spectacular.

Tru pressed deep into a notch at the base of the boulder as explosions slammed in all around. He was peppered with debris, earth and bark and stones raining in from every direction. His ears began ringing, but a quick self-assessment verified he hadn't taken any shrapnel. Or maybe he had and adrenaline was masking the pain.

More out of obstinance than anything else, he rose up and settled the AK's barrel on the Hind's nose section. He picked out the more forward of the high/low windscreens and took careful aim.

Tru let fly a single round.

To his utter amazement, the Hind jerked to one side, hesitated a hundred feet in the air, and then fell toward the ice like a buckshot vulture.

SIXTY-FOUR

Tru's shot had actually failed on every count.

To begin, he had taken aim at the wrong crew station—instead of the pilot flying in the rear seat, he had targeted the weapons operator in front. Even more deficiently, his bullet missed the Hind entirely, passing harmlessly a few feet left of the windscreen.

A second bullet, however, suffered neither error. This round, a fifty caliber, was far larger, carried a vastly higher velocity, and was designed to pierce armor. The bullet came at the helicopter from its ten o'clock position and struck with ruinous precision. It penetrated, in sequence, the pilot's side windscreen, his helmet, his brain, and then continued into an avionics panel. After inflicting massive damage there, the remains of the mangled round tumbled out the far side and into the night.

Seconds later, a second fifty caliber round slammed home, this one striking the main rotor gearbox. The round was designed to penetrate the engine blocks of large vehicles, such as the nearby ZIL, and so it had no trouble piercing the relatively lightweight housing of the Hind's main rotor transmission. Once inside, the damage it inflicted on the delicate meshwork of gears was nothing less than catastrophic. Metal flew and pinions failed as the powertrain chewed itself to shreds. At that point, the Hind was mortally wounded, its pilot dead and its power failing. Yet the passengers in back had one thing in their favor—the aircraft didn't have far to fall.

The helicopter smacked down on the ice hard, its left wing pod failing under the force of the collision. With its engines and rotors still churning by momentum, the aircraft thrashed through a half spin. Parts flew outward, one rotor blade separated, and flames spat from the port engine as it ingested debris. Yet ever so slowly, things began to settle. Unlike its downed sister ship, there was no great fireball, no thunderous explosion. Within seconds, the Hind simply disappeared, enveloped in a great cloud of smoke and icy mist.

Watching from behind the boulder, and having no idea what had just happened, Tru stood transfixed. He looked to his left, and through the broken line of trees he saw the ZIL, a spellbound Diaz standing next to it. Beyond that Vektor sat poised, the shrill sound of its APU taking over the night. Against all odds, they had come through unscathed.

Somehow.

He was contemplating sending a message, getting the rescue back on track, when the smoke began to clear. Tru saw the vague silhouette of the Hind, and then, as if emerging from a kicked anthill, smaller shapes began to appear and scatter in every direction. His spirits sank. Just when salvation seemed imminent, the situation turned worse than ever. The chopper was down, but Vega Group had survived.

He remained in cover long enough to determine how many men he was facing. And more importantly, how they were moving. He counted ten in all, two clusters of five that quickly organized into a pincer—one east and one west. Two of the men were limping, no doubt a result of the crash, but the rest looked perfectly capable. All of them carried weapons. He recalled from his time in Ukraine that members of that country's military referred to the Russian soldiers as orcs, an homage to the mindless humanoid brutes from Tolkien's *The Lord of the Rings*. He now understood.

Tru realized he had to move. He backed into the woods, then turned east, away from Vektor and the others. He ran as fast as the darkness allowed through the trees, and after fifty yards he turned back toward the shoreline. He paused behind a pine to scope out his adversaries. Still ten men, still evenly divided. He was a hundred yards from the eastern group, slightly more from the other.

Thankfully the AK he'd stolen was fitted with a low-light scope. He was sighting on his first target when something in their combined advance struck him as troubling. Both groups were reacting to his movement, and the western bunch were nearing the cover of the shoreline. If they reached it, his only advantage, having them in the open, would be lost. The Vega Group squad knew they had superior numbers, and they were armed with the same weapon and scope he was carrying. *Not to mention . . .*

Tru dropped to the ground just in time.

Kai found the spare AK near the tree where Primakov had been propped. She grabbed it and ran to the ZIL.

She knew that Diaz was something of a gun guy—he'd once told her he owned a half dozen weapons. For that reason—or so she told herself—she figured he would be a better shot. "You any good with one of these?"

"Never seen that model, but I can probably make it work."

She shoved it in his hands. "I'll stay with Primakov."

"What about Vektor?"

"I left everything powered up, but if we can't stop these guys there's not going to be any extraction."

He nodded, took up a kneeling position behind the ZIL's fender, and checked the weapon. He said, "I've only got three rounds here."

"Then I guess you better make 'em count."

The RPG flew over Tru's head and exploded behind him. Inbound rounds began pinging in. From behind the tree, he sighted on the western group and began firing. They were moving low and fast, approaching the trees. He dropped one with his third shot. Two rounds later another went down like he'd fallen through a trap door.

After that their movement became more erratic and he missed one shot after another. The eastern group stopped advancing and dropped to prone positions. They began firing at him at a high rate, trying to suppress his response until their comrades found cover. If they succeeded, the roles would switch.

And then I'm screwed.

Bullets came in a hail, and from different angles, forcing him to take cover behind a log. When he got his head up again, he saw a muzzle flash in the distant west. It had to be Diaz entering the fray with the spare AK from behind them. "Good man," Tru whispered. He then remembered that the second gun held only a few rounds. The crossfire wouldn't last long—but their adversaries didn't know that.

He saw one more man in the western group spin and go down, Diaz finding the mark with what might have been his last bullet. Tru shifted to concentrate on the eastern unit, and they exchanged fire until his magazine was empty. He switched out to his last mag, charged a round, and began firing again. As he did, he registered a notable silence from the west. He saw the last two Vega Group men advancing toward Vektor and the ZIL. They were no longer taking fire.

He took careful aim and dropped one man in the west. His last two rounds missed a fast-moving target, and the lone survivor of the group made it to cover, disappearing into the trees.

He shifted to the eastern section, who were moving now, and kept firing until the mag was empty. Only too late did he realize that he should have retained a few rounds for later—shots that had a higher probability of kill. It was a lesson he would have to take to another day.

If I get another day.

He rolled left, dropped into a swale, and began running back toward camp.

Only one satellite was in position to give Washington a view of the melee on Zeya Reservoir. That feed, for undetermined reasons, was of unusually poor quality. Technicians said something about interference from solar flares and were racing to fix the problem, but no one seemed to know how long that would take.

It left the decisionmakers, both at the White House and Langley, with an operational dilemma. The only information they could extract from the grainy feed was that a second Hind had gone down, after which a running gunfight had broken out between Vega Group and the handful of Americans on the ground. They also knew that Chaos 21, the rescue mission, was holding nearby in an attempt to stay clear of the fray—and burning precious fuel as it did so.

The White House made the only call that could be made. Chaos 21 was advised that the situation was fluid, and since they were nearest the action, with presumably the best situational awareness, they should make the call themselves: reach the Americans if it appeared safe, but under no circumstances remain on station so long that their fuel state would preclude a safe return.

On board Chaos 21, Major Gianakos had already established a "bingo fuel"—the fuel remaining at which they would bug out and head for home. After reaching it ten minutes earlier, he had revised it with a second number that carried razor-thin margins. With that number fast approaching on the fuel totalizer, he announced that if the situation on the ground didn't resolve in the next minute, he would abort the mission.

Captain Bryan seconded the plan, as did the loadmaster.

Then a fourth voice from the back intervened. And for the second time that night, Gianakos was ordered to fly closer.

SIXTY-FIVE

Silence took an icy grip on the cove.

Tru approached the camp warily, knowing that one man from the Vega Group unit was in the immediate area. He saw no sign of him, but what he did see was bad news—Kai was on a knee near the ZIL tending to Diaz who was splayed out on the ground. Tru rushed over with his head on a swivel.

Kai startled when she saw him emerge from the forest, but then relief washed over her when she realized who it was.

"What happened?" he asked, skidding down next to her.

Diaz actually answered. "Sorry . . . didn't move fast enough after I ran out of ammo."

"He took a round to his hip," Kai said as she worked on his wound. Using supplies from the combat medical kit, she had cut away the fabric of his pants and was applying a bandage with a clotting agent.

"You want me to take over?" Tru asked.

"I can manage. Probably better that you watch our back."

It was a valid point.

He stood and scanned the forest but saw no one. Not yet. But they were coming. And since Tru had already killed a good percentage of their unit, any encounter would not be a happy one. Then he made the mistake of considering what it would mean for the others, Kai in particular, and felt his rage rise.

He pushed the demons away, knowing that only rational thought was going to get them out of this bind. It occurred to him that carrying an empty weapon was probably a negative—it only made him a higher-priority target. He pulled off the sling and set down the AK. He felt naked without the weapon and realized that acquiring one was critical. The nearest rifle with bullets, presumably, was sixty yards away on the ice in front of him—next to the last man he'd dropped.

With a distinct feeling that eyes were on him, he turned to Kai, and said, "By my count, there are six guys still out there. Within the next few minutes, they'll either have shot us or taken us prisoner—maybe some combination of the two."

She looked up from her work and met his gaze, but didn't reply.

"Without a weapon we're done for. I'm going to run out and try for that one." He gestured to the downed man in the distance.

"You won't stand a chance out in the open."

"There's a chance—just not a good one. And staying here and doing nothing is as good as surrender."

"What can I do?"

"Maybe a little prayer?"

"Tru—"

Before she could say anything else, he gave her a grin that was completely at odds with the situation. Tru broke into a sprint, and ten yards later he was out in the open.

After twenty he was making good progress.

Then the bullets struck, and he went down hard.

All six surviving members of the Vega Group detachment emerged from the forest. Their weapons were poised, their eyes alert behind NVGs. Three were focused on the American who'd gone down and lay motionless on the ice. The others watched the contingent near the ZIL. They made a controlled, disciplined approach. The fact that they had broken cover spoke volumes for their confidence. It was clear the man they'd shot had been trying to reach a weapon. It was also apparent that he was the only true solider of the lot.

They closed the gap cautiously in a loose wedge formation. Captain Volkov, who'd been picked up from town, was in the lead. He kept his muzzle trained on the American, who hadn't moved since going down. Five steps away he paused, his barrel fixed on the man's head. Volkov could see his face—his eyes were open but vacant. The Russian flipped up his optic, wanting to meet the man's gaze if there was any life left in him. He wanted the American to know the price he was about to pay.

Then a distant sound broke his concentration—the thrum of rotors in the distance. He weighed who it might be, and two scenarios arose. Scenarios that would affect his next move greatly. Volkov fished his comm device out of his pocket and placed a call.

Tru had trouble focusing. He closed his eyes and then opened them a second time. His ribs on the right side felt like they'd been hit by a truck. He felt sharp pain on his inner right arm, and he looked down and saw blood. His plate carrier had taken hits, two or three at least judging by the shredded material. His arm had been nicked but might be functional. Worst of all was his head—he had slipped awkwardly and smacked it on the ice when he'd gone down. He recalled being told that most combat injuries weren't the result of direct fire. They were from collapsing walls, bad parachute landings, driving trucks into ditches . . . and tonight, apparently, bashing his head on a sheet of ice.

He tried to lift his head to comprehend the sideways world. What he saw was bleak. He was surrounded by the remains of the Vega Group, the nearest man a few yards away. He was wearing captain's rank, and the barrel of his AK was trained on Tru's face. He was fumbling one-handed with a phone, and when he realized Tru was conscious and looking at him, he said in English, "You are a hard one to kill. That is too bad—it would have been nicer for you if you had gone quickly."

Tru tried to move his injured arm and the barrel of the AK went rigid.

"No, no," the captain admonished.

Tru stopped moving, and the man went back to thumbing his phone.

Out here, Tru realized, the device had to be a satellite phone. Running a connection might take some time. He wondered how he could use that. He ignored the pain, pushed back the haze in his brain. He counted six men on the ice, the entire remaining group—at least, as far as he knew. Two were triangled off the captain, each five yards away. The other three were making their way toward the ZIL. They had their weapons level and were shouting commands he couldn't make out. He saw Kai standing in the distance, her arms raised in surrender. Diaz lay helpless on the ground.

The sound of rotors thrummed in the distance.

The image of Kai standing helpless pounded in his head.

Tru tried desperately to come up with a plan. Nothing came to mind.

Volkov's call took time to relay, but it was answered right away.

He said, "It's done, we have Primakov. There are three others, Americans, I think. I hear your helicopter. Do you want us to wait so you can finish this yourself?"

The voice on the other end began, "You hear my . . ." A lengthy pause, and then, "I am still fifty miles away."

Volkov was processing those words, turning in the direction of the thumping sound, when his head exploded. The remainder of his body collapsed to the ground.

The Vega group men all turned to look. They all saw their leader drop and were understandably stunned. Before any of them could react, one of the three nearing the ZIL was lifted off his feet in a cloud of red mist and thrown skidding across the ice.

SIXTY-SIX

For Tru it was the second miracle of the night, the first having been the inexplicable crash of the Hind. He didn't waste time analyzing precisely what has happening.

Because miracles were not to be wasted.

The captain fell only a few feet away, and Tru lunged headlong toward his body. Sliding over the ice on his belly like a greased seal, he seized the captain's AK and, leaving the sling around his inert form, twisted the barrel toward the man on his right—of the two who were near, he seemed to be moving quickest. Tru levered the trigger without referencing the sight and got the clatter of a two-round burst. The man sprawled backward and fell. Tru pried the barrel left toward the second man who was turning. He laced him with two rounds, then followed up with head shots for each—both were wearing body armor, and he didn't have time for wellness checks.

Still laying prone, he jerked the AK to the right, searching for the last two Vega Group men. It turned out to be unnecessary. Both were splayed motionless on the ice. Only now did all the sensations of the last frantic seconds catch up in his addled mind. His ears had registered at least three deep reports in the distance. He looked up the shoreline, and two hundred yards beyond the LZ he discerned the vague shadow of a CV-22 Osprey—the source of those sounds. The aircraft had settled along the shoreline in the next clearing to the north. Its wheels were on the ground and its rotors were idling. Facing away, its rear loading ramp was extended, exposing the darkened cargo bay to the night.

Finally, Tru realized what had happened. He relieved the dead captain of his AK, and with the rifle in hand, he quickly got to his feet. That turned out to be a grievous mistake. The world seemed to spin, and he stumbled to one side. His ribs screamed in pain. He checked carefully but saw no obvious hits aside from his upper arm.

Things began to stabilize, and he cradled the rifle under his good left arm. He looked again at the Osprey. With its rear ramp deployed, it was all but an invitation. He started weaving unevenly toward the fuel truck.

"You have a concussion," Kai said.

"There's no way you can know that," Tru argued.

"There's no way you can say you don't."

They were arguing over who would drive.

"The two of you sound like you are married," Primakov admonished. "We must go!"

Tru settled the dispute by sliding in behind the steering wheel.

Kai relented and took a spot on the opposite running board. With the passenger door open, she took a solid grip on Primakov's makeshift stretcher and nodded to say she was ready. Diaz was hunched on the floor on the passenger side, beside and below the colonel, grimacing in an awkward position. Everyone held on tight.

They reached the Osprey in a matter of minutes. A tall man that Tru took to be the loadmaster waved him closer until the ZIL was no more than ten feet from the ramp. Before Tru had even dismounted, the sergeant was dragging the ZIL's fuel hose inside the cargo bay to start the transfer.

A thickset Air Force major in a sanitized flight suit bounded down the ramp. After a flurry of introductions, he said, "We just got word two more helos are inbound."

"How long do we have?" Tru asked.

"Maybe twenty minutes."

Kai explained the condition of the two wounded men, and Tru was thankful she hadn't included him on her casualty list. Diaz explained the fueling system to the loadmaster, and as soon as gas was flowing the loadmaster and the pilot set to moving the two wounded men into the cargo bay.

Tru took up a position shoreside, his eyes moving and the AK ready—he couldn't be a hundred percent sure they had neutralized every threat. He was feeling more alert but still a bit woozy. He cast an occasional glance at the Osprey and saw a second silhouette on the flight deck, probably the copilot. He also caught glimpses of another figure deep at the forward limit of the cargo bay.

After a few minutes, Kai emerged and hurried toward him. "Everything is almost ready. I'm heading back to Vektor!"

When she turned toward the trail, Tru grabbed her arm to stop her. "After what just happened? You can't go back now!"

She jerked free of his grip. "Vektor is ready to go. You guys will be airborne in five minutes, and I'll be right behind you!"

"But what if—"

"No!" she said, holding out a forefinger to forestall any argument.

Tru considered throwing her over his shoulder and cave-manning her back to the Osprey. He quickly discounted the idea. For one thing, he wasn't sure he could pull it off in his addled state. He also understood exactly where she was coming from.

"All right," he said. "Then I'll see you at the O-club."

The stony look on her face softened. "Yeah . . . see you there." She set off toward the trail on a steady run.

SIXTY-SEVEN

As soon as the fueling was complete, Tru backed the ZIL clear and the Osprey's loading ramp was raised. The big twin rotors were already spinning when he ran back. The loadmaster stood waiting at the side entry door, poised to close it as soon as he was through.

Tru was nearly there when a distant sound sent him skidding to a stop. It was barely audible above the sound of the idling engines, but he had no doubt about what he'd heard . . . the scream of a woman.

He looked back toward the trail but saw nothing.

"Let's go!" the loadmaster shouted.

Tru never hesitated. "Kai needs help—head back without me! I got here on my own; I'll get out."

"Get back here, mister!" This was a voice Tru hadn't heard before. He never even bothered to look back.

As he disappeared into the woods, the loadmaster looked at the man behind him. After an extended, seething silence, he said, "All right, button her up. He's on his own."

The sergeant closed the door and gave an "all clear" to the flight deck. The Osprey powered up and lifted into the night.

Tru was fifty meters up the path when he realized his AK was in the Osprey—he'd given it to the loadmaster to stow while he'd moved the truck. It wasn't the first mistake he'd made on this op, but it might prove the costliest. There was a chance survivors from Vega Group remained. Even if not, it wasn't going to be long before the Russian Army descended on the surrounding hills.

His head was throbbing, his vision blurry as he lurched along the trail. He knew Kai was right—he had at least a minor concussion. The good news was that his symptoms didn't seem to be worsening.

A familiar curve in the trail told him he was nearing the end. The path straightened out, and when he saw what was ahead, he came to a hard stop. Twenty yards in front of him a hulking troglodyte of a man stood squarely in the middle of the trail. In his right hand was a pistol, possibly a Makarov. In his left was Kai. He had her upper arm vised in a vicious grip, but she was fighting him like a wildcat, fists swinging and elbows flying. The man seemed to not notice—he must have weighed twice what she did—and his eyes were padlocked on Tru.

Tru tried to decipher who this man was. He was tall, and heavier than Tru by a good margin. His dark features were as blank as the winter sky. Yet he wasn't part of the unit that had emerged from the crash—Tru would have remembered him, and he wasn't even dressed like a soldier. His clothing looked more like what a hunter would wear, a heavy overcoat and a fur hat. He had a fleeting thought that the man might be a local, drawn here by the commotion. *But if that was the case, why was he accosting Kai?*

She planted a solid kick to the man's leg, but he didn't react. Then she managed a half spin and planted a heel in his groin. This got the giant's attention. He bent forward slightly, then slowly straightened up. Once recovered, he launched a backhand swing with the grip of the Makarov that struck her squarely on the temple. Kai collapsed and he released her arm, leaving her motionless in the snow.

Through it all, the big man's eyes never left Tru. Then he did something completely unexpected. He pocketed the Makarov, and said in rough English, "Now I show you how Cossack fights."

Tru looked pointedly at Kai and replied in Russian, "You just showed me."

The man held his hands in front of him, palms up, and curled his fingers inward. A come-and-get-me taunt.

At The Farm, and later at Camp Peary, Tru had undergone extensive close-quarters training. He'd spent countless hours on mats since he was a teen. But engaging a giant like this, in Arctic conditions and with a rattled brain? Not a trainable event. As a longtime practitioner of various martial arts, he knew there were weight classes for a reason. The error of being without a weapon sank home. The best place to acquire one, he knew, was directly in front of him. The big man had a handgun in his right hip pocket. Any manner of bladed or blunt force weapon could be hidden in his great coat. If Tru possessed any of those, he would have put it to good use.

So what is this guy doing?

All his questions—who this Cossack was and why he was itching for a fight—faded away in the next moments. Perhaps he wasn't thinking clearly. The pounding in his head was relentless, the pain in his ribs constant. All logical thought was simply overtaken, subsumed by his reaction to one sight. A sight that had no tactical relevance whatsoever.

Kai collapsed motionless on the ground.

Tru rushed the giant, rage taking hold.

His world tunneled to the simplest of objectives. All his injuries evaporated as adrenaline spiked in. He ran hard and fast, a linebacker aiming for a tackling dummy. He was halfway to first contact, every muscle in his body straining, when one leg jerked to a violent stop—his right foot was seized by something sharp and vicious.

Tru slammed face-first into the ground, his momentum stopped instantly. Excruciating pain bolted through his right foot. He looked down and saw the jagged jaws of an animal trap clamped over his boot. Instinctively, he looked up at his adversary. The Cossack hadn't moved and seemed in no hurry. He bent down and picked up a wooden club—three feet of tapered hardwood that resembled a baseball bat, only twice the diameter. It was the perfect accessory to the trap on his foot—a tool used to put ensnared animals out of their misery.

He came at Tru slowly and paused ten feet away. He studied the ground for a moment, then used the club to poke a spot on the trail. A metallic snap cut the night air. Then he did it a second time, a few steps away, with the same result. Two more traps had been artfully concealed beneath forest debris. One was larger than the other two, its jaws seemingly sized for a bear.

Tru quickly bent down, got both hands on the trap on his foot. He struggled to lever it open. The spring was solid, but he managed to pry the metal jaws apart enough to extract his foot. The heavy rubber sole of his trail boot had taken much of the force, but his foot was gashed and bloody on both sides.

The Cossack closed in with his club, a hunter coming in for the kill. Tru tried to stand but immediately collapsed, unable to put weight on his right foot. The big man raised the club. Tru lifted himself with the aid of a tree trunk, then did the most counterintuitive thing he could think of—he attacked.

He pushed off with his good leg, and with every bit of strength aimed his left shoulder at the Cossack's knee. The club came down hard, but Tru was too close for the blow to be effective. He made contact with the man's weight-bearing knee and heard an audible pop as something gave way. The Cossack grunted and Tru kept driving, ignoring the pain in his foot. Both men tumbled into the leaf-cluttered forest, the club flying clear.

Tru tried to get to his feet but collapsed again. The Cossack howled with rage and rose unsteadily to his feet—Tru had done some damage. With blind fury the man swept his fist in a massive haymaker that cut down the only thing between them—a two-inch sapling that snapped like a matchstick. The Cossack came at him with surprising speed, this time staying low. He hit like a freight train, but Tru saw it coming and deflected much of the force. The two grappled and fell, and Tru twisted to avoid being pinned on his back. He almost got behind the man but an elbow to his head brought stars.

Tru immediately gave one right back.

The blow stunned the man, providing enough space for Tru to separate. Once more, he pulled himself up using a tree branch as a crutch. The Cossack did the same, and he somehow reacquired his club. He rushed in with a big arcing forehand, and Tru stumbled out of the way. Time and again the man swung for the fence, his face a mask of primal rage. Time and again Tru ducked and weaved, used tree trunks for cover. He could feel himself tiring and his right foot was barely responding.

Tru tripped and fell right back where they'd started. He crawled along the trail until his right hand felt something cold. He knew immediately what it was. With his back to the Cossack, but sensing him closing in, Tru worked with both hands. He had only seconds before the man would be on him. Tru rolled onto his back and lifted his hands over his head—something near a posture of surrender. But he never expected mercy.

The Russian dropped down and sank a massive knee onto his chest. Tru's body was immobilized, but his hands remained free. The man raised the club high, then hesitated for an instant to revel in his victory. Tru saw the glint of conquest in his eyes.

A moment of vanity that would cost him dearly.

Tru rotated both arms forward, lashing out with his improvised weapon. His strike was perfectly placed.

The Cossack screamed and his face went to a mask of crimson.

SIXTY-EIGHT

"Message from Chaos 21," said Sorensen, hanging up a call from JSOC. She was addressing the president and her advisors who'd gathered in the Oval Office to track the mission as it played out. "They're airborne with two evacuees."

Heads around the room shot back and forth, and the president said, "*Two?* Were they not supposed to bring out four?"

"That was the plan. I asked JSOC to expand and they said Primakov and Sergeant Diaz are on board. Both are injured but in stable condition."

"So where are Rookie and Major Benetton?"

Sorensen hesitated before saying, "We have no direct word on that. But reading between the lines, I noticed a couple of things in our satellite footage that might explain what's going on . . . at least, in part."

"Such as?"

"Vektor," General Carter replied. "I saw that as well. The tarps are gone, and someone cleared the snow off its wings."

Sorensen nodded. "And the fuel truck Rookie requisitioned stopped next to Vektor before heading to the LZ. I think I even caught a few frames where a hose was connected to the jet's refueling station."

"Are you saying what I think you're saying?" the president inquired acidly. "Major Benetton is going to attempt to *fly* Vektor out?"

"That would fit the evidence we have."

"And who authorized this?"

When no one ventured an answer, Sorensen felt obliged to say, "I suspect Major Benetton made the call."

Elayne Cleveland's expression went beyond wooden. It became a veritable lumberyard of doubt and wrath.

Carter said, "We should send a message to the Osprey, have them ask Sergeant Diaz what the hell is going on."

"Do it!" the president ordered. "And while you're at it, send a message to Slaton. Tell him if he can't manage his clandestine ops with more discipline that this, he is out of a job!"

Sorensen and Carter both nodded, then exchanged a private look—twenty minutes earlier they had taken a call from *Boxer*'s skipper, who'd urgently requested contact. The news from the Sea of Japan was even more unsettling, but until they confirmed their suspicions, they'd agreed there was no point in ruining a career. All the same, events halfway around the world seemed to be spiraling out of control.

There was a fine line between audaciousness and insubordination—and by all accounts, the entire team downrange seemed to be crossing it.

The Cossack's hands flew to his face, and Tru immediately fell back into a patch of frozen peat. He heaved on the metal chain for all he was worth. The jagged teeth of the bear trap tore deeper into the Cossack's flesh.

The giant spun like a man possessed, his arms swinging blindly. When he tried to stand, Tru leaned on the chain with all his weight. Its links were forged metal, designed to anchor a writhing half-ton bear. The bellow that resulted was animalistic, echoing through the valley. Tru lost his grip on the chain and rolled away.

The Cossack screamed and writhed, his arms lashing out blindly. The trap's lower jaw had sunk deep into his face, mauling one eye, his cheek, and the bridge of his nose. The opposing jaw was clamped over the back of his massive skull.

Tru hauled himself back to his feet. He looked at Kai and saw that she'd regained consciousness. She was on her knees, a trickle of blood streaming from her mouth. She got up slowly and moved toward Tru. They leaned on one another, neither able to stand on their own.

The Cossack began to recover. He paused his thrashings and used both hands to grip the trap. He pried it open in a Herculean pose, and nearly had it clear when his grip on one bloody metal edge slipped. The trap snapped back down on new flesh.

Stunningly, this time he uttered not a sound.

He made a second attempt and successfully levered the trap clear. He threw it aside and his hands went immediately to his shredded face. Head wounds are notoriously bloody, but the dozens of jagged gashes encircling his head left his entire upper body bathed in red. His right eye was little more than a socket of torn flesh, and the opposing mandible was exposed, white bone glinting in the dim light. Tru saw the club on the ground. He considered retrieving it, but the Russian put an end to the idea when he drew the Makarov from his pocket and began swinging it in a wide arc. Tru realized the man's vision was impaired, one eye grossly damaged and the other obscured by blood.

"Let's get out of here," Kai said in a hushed tone, tugging Tru up the trail.

Her voice must have registered. The Cossack spun a half turn, pointed the gun in their general direction, and snapped off a wild shot.

Tru and Kai bent low and stumbled away, gaining momentum as they went. Another shot rang out, then another, chasing the sound of their footsteps. Tru kept count, trying desperately to recall how many rounds were in a Makarov. He soon realized it was a pointless exercise—there were too many variables. He didn't know how many rounds had been in the gun to begin with or whether the man had another magazine. Didn't know precisely which variant he was carrying. After the ninth shot there was only silence.

Tru focused every fiber of his being on one task—he had to keep moving. Had to stay on his feet and get Kai to the jet safely. Soon they were out of range and moving more freely.

Vektor appeared before them.

SIXTY-NINE

"How long will it take you to get going?" Tru asked as they neared the boarding ladder.

"Three minutes, maybe four. All I have to do is start the engines and throw a few switches. The trickiest part will be getting the nose pointed in the right direction—I'm not sure if a hard ninety-degree turn is even possible on this ice. If I can get the nose aimed at the middle of the lake, the rest should be easy—light up the burners and she'll be airborne in no time."

She reached for the rope-and-wood ladder, but then paused before taking the first step. She stood staring at him.

"What?" he asked.

"Tru . . . you look like shit."

He looked down and performed a brief self-assessment. She had a point. His right foot was bloody, and he was standing crookedly. He probably had a concussion and bruised ribs, and he'd been intermittently dizzy. "I'm good to go."

"No, you're a mess. In an hour or two this place is going to be crawling with Russian troops. Even if you were a hundred percent, there's no way you could walk out like you walked in."

"I came in on skis, so that's how I'll leave."

"You're going to put a ski boot on that?" She pointed down to his foot.

"The Osprey is gone and it's not coming back—I made my choice."

"You came back for my sake."

"Don't worry, I'll figure something out."

She fell silent and looked up at the cockpit.

"Kai, you need to get going if—"

"Come with me," she said, interrupting him.

"*What?*"

"You climb in first. We'll lower the seat and I can sit in your lap."

He stared at her incredulously, then broke out laughing.

"It would *work*," she insisted. "I'm only five-five so we should be able to get the canopy down." She said this as if she was trying to convince herself, as if she was working out the details on the fly. "I'll still be able to reach the flight controls . . . except maybe the rudder pedals. But I won't need those—we're unarmed, so dogfights are out of the question."

He was laughing so hard his injured ribs hurt. "Yeah, who uses a rudder anymore? Do you know how crazy that sounds? I think you're the one with a concussion."

As if not hearing him, she said, "You need to understand that we won't be able to eject."

"And I was really looking forward to that."

She punched him hard on the shoulder. It actually hurt, and had what was probably the intended effect—he stopped laughing.

"Do you not comprehend your situation?" she shouted. "If you stay here, the Russians are going to capture you! You will be held as a spy, which is punishable by death. Then again, if the unit that captures you is tied to this one . . ." she pointed to all the bodies and smoldering wreckage on the ice, "they'll just shoot you outright."

His humor gave way to impatience. "You need to get out of here now!"

"Not without—" Her words were cut off by a primitive howl. They looked toward the trail and saw the Cossack lumbering out of the forest. Bloody and disfigured, he was limping straight toward them.

The mood at the White House was one of cautious optimism. Chaos 21 was well on its way to Japan, and so far, there were no indications that air defenses had been alerted. On the downside, two Americans remained on Zeya Reservoir. The president's query had been transmitted to Chaos 21, and Sergeant Diaz confirmed their suspicions: Major Benetton had taken the initiative to try and fly Vektor out, while Rookie had stayed behind for reasons that remained murky. It was a lot to digest. So far, the mission had avoided the disaster of Americans being captured. But the risk of that happening seemed higher than ever.

General Carter said what they were all thinking. "Why the hell aren't the Russians responding? They've lost two helicopters in a matter of hours and one of their Spetznaz units engaged in a running firefight. Still, we haven't picked up any radio or messaging traffic about reinforcements. By now there should be a battalion of helicopters inbound."

DNI Fuller said, "Our SIGINT coverage is pretty weak in that region. And even though we're pulling out all the stops, overhead surveillance has its limitations. We've been getting decent visuals over Zeya because the weather is good, but there's a lot of cloud cover in the surrounding areas. It's possible we don't have the full picture."

"Maybe the Russians don't either," Sorensen muttered almost to herself. Feeling everyone's eyes settle on her, she expanded. "There's been something screwy going on all along. Why were those three Hinds deployed to this area while the rest of the Russian Air Force has been beating circles in the sky hundreds of miles away? Why was Vega Group brought in for a routine search operation? That's all been bugging me . . . so I tasked a cell at CIA to do a little research."

"Research into what?" the president asked.

"Into *whom,* actually. We've all seen the executive summary on Colonel Maksim Primakov, but I did a deeper dive and found some concerning footnotes. The first involves his father-in-law, Viktor Strelkov."

"Strelkov?" the DNI repeated, clearly taken aback. "You're saying Primakov is married to the daughter of a GRU general?"

"Chief of the Third Directorate, responsible for intelligence across Asia. It's something we've known, but in the rush of Primakov's defection, it fell to the background. Our files on Strelkov are thick. By Russian standards, he's had a typical career progression. Twenty years ago, he was running protection rackets in St. Petersburg. In most countries that puts you under the scrutiny of law enforcement, but being a successful mob boss in Russia is grounds for promotion. The president deals out industries like playing cards, and he set Strelkov up in the oil and gas business. He did well, and in time, during one of the periodic house cleanings at GRU, he moved up another notch. Senior officers in military intelligence aren't selected based on experience or merit, but pure fealty. Within a few years, Strelkov ended up near the top of the GRU pyramid."

"What does this have to do with what's happening at Zeya?"

"The Hinds, Vega Group . . . those are exactly the kinds of assets Strelkov would have at his disposal. So I took things a step further. If his son-in-law were to defect with Vektor, Strelkov's career would go down in flames. But what if he learned about it and realized that it hadn't gone as planned . . ."

"He would do everything in his power to put a lid on it," the president said.

"That fits what we're seeing. I think Strelkov might have learned about the failed defection and committed every asset at his disposal to cover it up." She let the room chew on that for a few moments, then said, "This is all speculation, but I do see an upside. Depending on how things play out . . . there's a chance this entire mess will get swept under a Russian rug."

The president said, "We'll have a clearer picture in a few hours, but I think there's one imperative. If Chaos 21 and Vektor both reach safety, we have to keep it under wraps. In particular, keep Vektor and Primakov out of sight. If we can pull that off, then we sit back and watch closely, see what develops on the Russian end."

"What about Rookie?" the DNI asked.

"As usual, he's the wild card. I can't imagine why he would have stayed behind."

Sorensen added, "He's definitely screwed some things up. But he's also made some good calls, and he seems to have a knack for landing on his feet."

"Let's hope he can do it one more time," President Cleveland said. "Is there anything else about Strelkov we should know?"

"There was one thing, and it might or might not relate to what's happening. It has to do with Primakov's son . . ."

SEVENTY

"Go, go, go!" Tru shouted, shoving Kai toward the ladder.

Before she could protest, he turned and set off toward the Cossack.

Kai climbed up to the cockpit and sank into the seat. She began running through a checklist that Primakov had amended with notes and translations. Time and again, she shot glances to her left. Fifty feet away, the Russian stood like a creature from a horror movie, his face a crimson mass of tissue. He repeatedly swiped away blood from his good eye and was limping severely, one leg dragging behind him like deadweight.

Tru was hardly better off. He was moving cautiously, favoring his good foot and blading his body to protect his injured ribs. They ended up a few steps apart, both wary and calculating. It was nothing less than a contest of wills.

Kai wanted desperately to help Tru, but she stayed put for two reasons. First was that if the Russian could get past him, he might find a way to stop her from getting Vektor airborne. Until the jet began moving, it could be disabled—a few rocks or chunks of ice in an engine intake was all it would take. She also knew that without a weapon there was little she could do to stop the giant.

And would I use a weapon if I had one? she asked herself.

With all systems up and running, she tried to start the starboard engine. It didn't begin spooling right away, and her spirits lurched. Diaz had checked things out earlier, but the jet had been sitting in subzero cold for days. What if the starter valve had frozen? What if snow had collected in the inlet when they'd cleaned the wings? The engine coughed, and then mercifully began to spin. By the time it reached idle the shrill backdrop of the turbojet overrode every other sound.

She started spinning the port engine, and as it accelerated she ventured another look at Tru. He looked poised and ready. Then the Cossack pulled the Makarov from his pocket and pointed it at Tru's head.

"So that's how a Cossack fights," Tru shouted above the din of the engines. It was hard to read the expression on the man's shredded face, but a hesitation made him think he'd hit a nerve. Which was a good thing—staring down a gun barrel from five feet away had a way of altering one's perspective of time.

"A Cossack wins," he growled through his mangled jaw. "That is all that matters."

Tru caught a flash of motion from Vektor's cockpit—he and the Russian had spun a wary half circle, leaving the Cossack with his back to the jet. Kai was holding one finger in the air, the universal signal for "wait a sec." *Wait?* he thought. *Wait for what?*

Tru had no idea what she was up to, but he figured anything he could do to buy a few more moments on earth was a plus.

"You're not Vega Group," he said.

The Cossack spat out a wad of blood. Possibly as an answer, but more likely because he was having trouble breathing. He looked across the ice at the devasted Spetznaz force. "You are worthy, I give you that. But those men did not fight well enough. Now you have met your match."

"If you're not Spetznaz, then who are you? Who do you work for?"

The gun wavered, then settled on his head. No answer came.

"Before you pull the trigger," Tru said in the most reasonable tone he could muster, "I should at least tell you who I am . . ."

Kai saw Tru talking to the man. She prayed he could keep it up for a few more seconds.

With both engines running, she reached for the controls and hoped to hell he would read her intentions. She released the parking brake and stepped hard on the left wheel brake. She added power to the starboard engine. Vektor responded with a shudder as wheels that had been frozen for days began to turn. The jet pivoted on the locked left wheel and its nose spun toward the lake.

The Russian must have sensed Vektor's noise and movement, but he couldn't take his eyes off Tru. Soon Kai was craning her neck back to five o'clock to keep the men in sight, much as she would in a defensive dogfight with a bandit on her tail. She could see Tru shouting over the noise, but his eyes were on her, on Vektor. She played the right throttle and brake until she had the exact geometry she wanted.

Then she held her right arm out straight and made a giant palm-down motion.

Then she did it again and again.

Frantically.

Tru saw the signal clearly, but he had no idea what Kai was doing. The jet had performed a neat pirouette. It was still turning, but more slowly, pointed almost directly away. Then its nose suddenly bucked lower, like a car braking for a red light.

Her arm was flapping like a fledgling raptor trying to leave its nest.

The engine noise increased.

And just like that, he understood.

Tru fell to the ice and covered his head with his arms.

The engines accelerated, Vektor's twin exhaust nozzles narrowing a mere forty feet away. The Cossack ignored the maelstrom behind him, more concerned by Tru's sudden movement. He lowered the barrel of his weapon, then took the time to wipe blood from his good eye. In those added seconds, Kai made her move.

With the brakes set, she shoved Vektor's throttles around one detent and all the way to the forward stops. The jet's afterburners lit, massive amounts of raw fuel funneling into the exhaust. In a tight cone directed by the vectoring nozzles, twin sixty-foot bolts of blue flame leapt from the engines. In barely more than a heartbeat, the temperature behind Vektor went from zero to three thousand degrees.

Tru stayed low on the ice, rolling to one side. The engines were mounted eight feet above the ground, and the exhaust plume rocketed past just above him. It felt like the sun itself was coursing over his head.

His vision obscured, the Cossack didn't sense the danger until it was too late. His instinctive reaction to the rising wave of exhaust was to stand strong and lean into it—a mountain man bracing against the elements. Then the hurricane morphed instantaneously into a horizontal torrent of flame. In a fraction of a second his body was lifted into the conflagration. Flesh and bone and cloth were incinerated, the ashes swept away by 75,000 pounds of thrust. All that remained in the end: one superheated Makarov spinning into a distant snowbank.

Tru kept moving, clawing clear to avoid cremation. He had good separation, but even twenty feet from the exhaust plume the heat was extreme. The flames and noise dissipated as quickly as they'd begun.

He looked over his shoulder to see Vektor skidding across the ice with all the grace of a three-legged gazelle. The jet came to a stop after spinning a full circle, Newtonian principles playing out with a vengeance.

When the jet finally fell still, Kai looked back at him.

Tru struggled to his feet and gave her a thumbs-up. Then he noticed an oddly chemical smell and felt warmth on his back. He pulled off his plate carrier—it was singed and smoking, two of its plastic buckles melted. He dropped it on the ice and hobbled toward Vektor.

Kai beckoned him closer, and then used hand motions to indicate he should take a wide arc around the nose—Vektor's engines were still idling. The rope and wood ladder remained in place, and he climbed up to the canopy rail.

All he could think to say was, "Thanks."

"You're welcome . . . sort of."

"You're kind of a failure at being a pacifist."

"Only because you're a failure as an assassin."

"Yeah, well . . . maybe I could work on my—" He stopped midsentence, noticing her green eyes. They were locked on something behind him. He turned, followed her line of sight, and spotted it in the distance—a helicopter was approaching. He couldn't tell the exact type, but it wasn't a Hind. It was smaller, without the deadly protuberances, and its navigation lights were illuminated. None of that made it less threatening.

"Time to go," she said.

They looked at one another, riding the same thought. The same question.

Tru made his choice. "Okay . . . move over."

SEVENTY-ONE

With the canopy lowered, they fit in the cockpit like two turtles sharing a shell. Space was so tight, Kai had been forced to throw Primakov's helmet out onto the ice. Tru was pressed deep into the seat, and she was sitting on his lap. Even after lowering the seat to the limit, the crown of her head was brushing the Plexiglass above. The arrangement had all the clumsiness of two kids sharing a bike, but it was the only way they could make it work.

"Can you shift a little right?" he fussed.

"Shut up!" she snapped as Vektor began to move. "We have to turn right, so I need you to step on the right rudder pedal."

"You said we weren't going to need the rudder thing."

"We won't once we're in the air, but that's the only way to steer on the ground."

He pushed on the pedal and Vektor's nose slewed right. Tru canted his head left and right, but he couldn't see any of the forward quadrant. Her short ponytail flogged him repeatedly.

"Okay, stop there!" Kai said.

He took his foot off the rudder pedal. Tru leaned as far right as he could and saw the helicopter approaching. It was still half a mile away but headed straight for them. He was about to mention it to Kai when she shoved the throttles to the firewall.

Tru had felt acceleration before. He'd driven fast cars and motorcycles. This was from another galaxy. The afterburners lit and the massive machine leapt ahead, snapping his head back against the headrest. Speed built quickly, the frozen lake turning to a blur in the dim light.

If the helicopter's pilots hadn't seen them before, they surely did now; twin cylinders of flame shot behind Vektor like industrial furnaces. He could feel Kai's hands on the flight controls, her shoulder muscles flexing as she blended with the jet. The ride became rougher as speed built, the surface of the reservoir pocked with patches of snow and ice.

Then everything suddenly smoothed out as the jet lifted into its element. Kai raised the landing gear and flaps. The speed kept building. Tru again leaned far to his right. He saw the helicopter directly in front of them.

With Vektor still accelerating, he felt like he was riding a horizontal rocket.

The helicopter seemed to fill the windscreen.

"Kai! What the hell—"

His words were cut off when Vektor's nose wrenched violently skyward. Tru was slammed downward by G-forces, and Kai's weight in his lap increased sixfold. He couldn't move his head—it was pinned sideways between the seat and the side canopy, his neck muscles overcome. Finally, the forces eased, and when his eyes refocused, he saw the night sky and horizon clearly.

Vektor was pointed straight up. Still accelerating and headed for the heavens.

Strelkov was ashen as he stepped from the Hip onto solid ground. He was still hyperventilating, the near miss having shaken him to the core.

He'd been up front, looking out the forward windscreen, when the pilots had pointed out a jet taking off on the frozen reservoir. It could only have been Vektor. And it could only have been his son-in-law flying it. The jet bolted straight at them and collision seemed imminent. Then the Hip's pilot jerked the controls left at the last instant. Strelkov vaguely remembered hearing a scream. Vektor pitched skyward, missing them by a mere few meters, and its aerodynamic wake nearly threw them out of control. The pilot battled the controls and was able to right the Hip.

That had been five minutes ago. Safely settled now on a clearing near the shoreline, everyone bailed out as soon as the rotors went still. The rattled pilots tended to the Hip, while Strelkov's four security men who'd been in back and hadn't seen the near miss, fanned out around him. They were wary and watchful.

And with good reason.

At the water's edge Strelkov paused to take in the scene. It was nothing short of apocalyptic. He saw two downed Hinds. The one in the distance was little more than a charred hulk, part of which had dropped through the ice. The nearer bird was a total loss, crumpled and beaten, but had not caught fire.

And then there were the men—more than a dozen bodies lay strewn on an icy battlefield. The general had no doubt who they were—his personal Vega Group detachment had been decimated. *But how? And by whom?* By Tarkhan's logic, they were searching for two men—Primakov and a CIA paramilitary. The two of them, surely, could not be responsible for this.

Strelkov breathed deeply, and his heart rate began to lower. It was only a temporary reprieve. Vektor was once more on its way to America, Maksim at the controls. Had it been here since the night it had gone lost? If so, for what reason? And where was Tarkhan?

Strelkov had so many questions; yet one overrode all the others: *What to do now?*

Vektor had to be headed to Japan or South Korea. Who could help him stop it? Was it even *possible* to stop it without making admissions that would author his own death warrant? A fleeting thought came to mind that perhaps he should join Maksim—commandeer the Hip, fly east, and defect himself in order to save his skin. Surely the Americans would welcome a man with his insider's knowledge.

His desperate musings were clipped when he spotted something in the distance—a lone pair of red and green lights skimming over the moonlit reservoir. Who the hell was this? he wondered. An army bird responding to something Volkov had reported? Tarkhan in the Hip he had been allocated? *Or perhaps Maksim has come back for a strafing pass to put me out of my misery.*

The form resolved into yet another helicopter—the default method of reaching this place in winter. Yet it wasn't a military bird. Instead, he recognized a sleek executive model, the ride favored by the elites of Moscow. Which, for Strelkov, carried infinitely more menace than rocket pods or chain guns.

He watched the bird settle near his own, saw the entry door open. A set of stairs extended, and he immediately recognized the silhouette that stepped down. It was the last person on earth he expected to see.

Strelkov breathed a huge sigh of relief.

SEVENTY-TWO

Tru felt like he was riding in the world's fastest clown car. He did his best to stay out of Kai's way, but with arms and legs akimbo in the tight confines of the cockpit, he had already inadvertently activated two switches. Neither turned out to be anything critical, but Kai admonished him to keep his fat hands and knees to himself. A number of smartass replies came to mind, but seeing how busy she was he held back.

"What's our ETA?" he asked.

"About an hour—assuming we don't have to maneuver to avoid complications."

"Complications?"

"Enemy fighters, surface-to-air missiles."

"Sorry I asked. What can I do to help?" Tru couldn't see her face, but at this point he knew her well enough to imagine her thoughtful expression.

"See that gauge?" she said, pointing to an old fashioned "steam gauge" with a needle and colored arcs.

"Sure."

"It shows the pressurization inside the cockpit. It's in the green band, but Primakov mentioned that the system is a little quirky. We're not wearing oxygen masks, so if it gets near the yellow, I need to know right away—we'd have to descend to a lower altitude."

"Okay. What's the red line mean?"

"I think that's Armstrong's Limit, which is roughly 63,000 feet."

"Is that significant?"

"At that altitude, the outside pressure is so low that blood boils at body temperature."

"And how high are we?"

"Right now . . . somewhere in the high fifties."

"You're a fountain of cheer."

"It's not all bad. Loading that extra gas was a huge plus—it lets us fly high and fast. Primakov said Vektor is capable of supercruise—that's going supersonic without using afterburners—and he was right. We're doing Mach 1.7 and the fuel flow is reasonable."

"Good. The faster we get out of Russian airspace, the better."

"Let's hope whoever was in that helicopter doesn't figure out where we're headed and alert the air defenses. If that happens, our smooth sailing could come to an end. So far, I'm not seeing any sign of it. The radar warning receiver is clear."

Tru should have felt relief. The worst, surely, was behind them. Three wrecked helicopters. More than a dozen dead soldiers. One atomized Cossack. And in front of them? Nothing but clear skies and good prospects all the way to Kamchatka.

"There's something else you can do," she said.

"What's that?"

"I can't turn on the radar to search for bogeys without highlighting us, so our best chance of spotting threats is with the old Mark-1 eyeball. Help me keep an eye outside."

"Will do." Tru scanned every bit of night sky in his field of view, taking in stars, a few ground lights, and the silver of a crescent moon. He saw nothing troubling. "My leg's going numb. Mind if I readjust?"

She raised her weight off him as best she could. "Knock yourself out."

Tru shifted to the right. "That's better."

She sat back down, and he gave a loud grunt.

"Oh, give me a break. I weigh one-twenty."

"It's not that . . . it's just that I've got a few sore spots."

"Suck it up, soldier." She checked the nav display. "Fifty-eight minutes, and we're home free."

Strelkov looked on in disbelief as his daughter approached. "What the hell are you doing here?"

"And hello to you too, Father."

There was no embrace, no alternating cheek kisses. Oksana simply stopped next to him and gazed indifferently across the reservoir.

He looked back and forth between her and the sleek helicopter. "Two questions," he said.

She waited.

"Who authorized you to use that helicopter?"

His daughter could not suppress a smile. "You have been busy lately, Father. Too busy to notice that I have merited another promotion."

"A promotion? To what division?"

"I am now a colonel in the Political Section."

His train of thought derailed. The Political Section was unique in the GRU. It didn't keep watch on Russia's enemies, but on the agency itself. It was the organizational snitch, a bastard child of the *zampolit* of the Soviet era—the internal black hats who oversaw security and allegiance to the regime. The Political Section was headed by Pavel Zhurov, one of the few men who wielded more clout than Strelkov himself.

"You have transferred to Zhurov's section?"

"It was not something I sought, but he seems to have taken a personal interest in my career. He approached me a few months ago and explained that he has been monitoring my advancement closely. He said he needed someone to help with certain delicate internal projects."

"Do you not see his ploy?" he spat derisively. "A man like Zhurov does not recruit the daughter of a rival based on merit."

"Is that what the two of you are? Rivals? He never mentioned it."

Strelkov felt as though the earth was shifting beneath him.

"And your second question, Father?"

After a lengthy pause, he asked, "How did you know I was here?"

Instead of speaking, Oksana walked out onto the ice. He followed her as she led him to the nearest collection of bodies.

She passed the first uniformed corpse without comment, then stopped at the second and looked down. "Poor Volkov," she said. "I imagine he did his best."

Once more, Strelkov stood dumbstruck. "How do you know . . ." The cues came slowly. Then they gathered like a storm. "You have been tracking Volkov? You learned that he worked for me?"

"Poor Father, you *have* lost a step. Do you still not see? Captain Volkov works . . . or should I say, worked, for me."

His daughter locked him in a frigid gaze and her hands went deep into the pockets of her jacket.

"How much does Zhukov know?" he said weakly.

"Enough to be suspicious. But not everything. He knows you have a deep interest in this crash, and also that your relationship with Maksim has long been in tatters." She surveyed the mess on the ice. "So where have they all gone? Primakov, the Americans, Vektor? Everything Volkov told me about is now missing."

"Vektor flew out as I was arriving—it had to have been Maksim. If there were Americans here, I never saw them."

She shook her head. "When my pilot landed, he pointed out impressions in the earth. He said another aircraft had been there very recently. Combine that with what we see before us . . ." She gestured to the frozen killing field around them. "Could the situation be any worse for you, Father? I see only two possible excuses—incompetence or complicity. I doubt President Petrov would look favorably upon either."

Finally, Strelkov saw a thread of hope. "Yes, those are my choices . . . but they apply to you as well. As my daughter, as Maksim's wife, you also will be held accountable."

"I knew nothing about any of this. I am only here to pursue General Zhukov's suspicions."

Strelkov glanced at his security men—they were still back by the shore. He lowered his voice. "Our only chance is to go to the West, follow Maksim's lead. We could—"

Oksana's left hand came out of her pocket. It was holding a phone and she showed him the screen. The record button was running, capturing his words. She tapped the screen to stop it.

His rage peaked. "Zhukov has turned you against me. *Me! Your own flesh and blood!*"

"No," she countered, "you only have yourself to blame. Zhukov merely brought your disloyalty to my attention."

"What are you saying?"

"He told me what happened to Nik."

The words sank like a dagger. "Lies! Whatever he told you, it was lies!"

Her head shook with unwavering certainty. "He showed me the letter you wrote to General Olenev. Olenev ordered Nik assigned to his division when he was called up for the special military operation in Ukraine. He had arranged a very safe job for him in the rear echelon, no doubt as a favor to you that would one day be called for repayment. When you learned of it, you wrote back insisting that he be sent to the front."

"No, I never—"

"I verified these facts with Olenev himself!" she barked, cutting him off. "His recollection of the story was identical. Apart from that, I know it is precisely the kind of thing you *would* do. You saw a personal advantage to be had. If Nik survived, you would have a hero to celebrate. If he died defending the Motherland, then you would earn sympathy. Either way, by sending him into the grinder you stood to gain."

"No . . . I . . ." He couldn't manage a coherent thought.

"You sent your only grandson to the front lines, where he . . ." for the first time, Oksana's voice cracked, ". . . where he lasted less than a week. My son, the love of my life, was blown to pieces."

He opened his mouth to say something, but she cut him off in the most inarticulate way imaginable—she pulled a handgun from her pocket and pointed it at his chest. "Don't disgrace yourself by trying to deny it!" she hissed.

Strelkov cast a desperate glance at his security men. They stood like statues on the shoreline, perfectly aware of what was happening. He locked eyes with Dmitri, the lead, who gave a simple shake of his head. Zhukov had thought of everything. Or if not Zhukov, someone every bit as ruthless.

He looked pleadingly at his daughter. "That recording means nothing. If you kill me, Petrov will see through it."

"I think not. He will see me as a mother who has given her only child to Russia. And a daughter who, in the name of state security, was willing to take her father's life."

His jaw dropped, but no words emerged. Not before the bullet flew straight and true into his heart.

SEVENTY-THREE

Oksana walked away from her father's body. Some distance away, she drew to a stop on the naked ice. She stared out at the faceless winter feeling strangely hollow. No guilt, no relief, no sense of satisfaction. There was simply . . . emptiness. A soft snow had started to fall, fluttering through the blackness. Lost in thought, she didn't move for a very long time. Not until she sensed a presence behind her.

She glanced back and saw Dmitri approaching. He would be expecting new orders. It occurred to her that the gun was still in her hand. She slid it back into her jacket pocket.

The confrontation with her father had gone to script. She'd done what she had come here to do. Her next moves, however, required careful thought. The next hour would be critical. Indeed, her very survival depended on it. Her father had not been completely off the mark. Maksim's defection, which was not yet sealed, would be a reputational disaster to Russia and its president. Her father had paid the ultimate price, and the question of how it would affect her was yet to be answered.

Her father had also been right in another respect: her usefulness to General Zhukov was at an end. Yet given the scope of this debacle, and the embarrassment it entailed, there was an excellent chance it would be covered up. And what she had just done, in full view of the security team . . . Oksana thought it might prove convincing. It was possible she would be spared.

President Petrov himself would make that call.

Dmitri came to a stop behind her.

She glanced at her watch. *One hour . . . if I can buy Maksim that, it might save both of us.*

"I will go straight back to Moscow," she said, turning. "I want you and your men to stay here until help arrives to clean up this mess."

"I understand," the security man said.

"I will make the call for assistance once I am airborne." She looked directly at the thick-jawed man to emphasize her next words. "This is a *very* delicate situation. I am giving you and your men strictest orders to contact no one—you will leave all communications to me. Answer calls from no one but me. Is that clear?"

"Yes, Colonel." He pointed into the distance. The pilots of Strelkov's Hip stood waiting by their aircraft. "What about those two?"

Oksana considered it. Eliminating them would not fit the greater script. "The same. Keep them here and ensure they contact no one."

Dmitri acknowledged the order, and she set out toward her own helicopter. Minutes later she was airborne and streaking west. It would be an interminable ride to Moscow.

For fifty minutes, Oksana waited. Then she gave it ten more for old time's sake. Finally, she picked up the helicopter's secure handset and placed a call to report the situation on Zeya Reservoir. As the connection ran, her lips mimicked voicelessly, *"Godspeed, Maksim."*

The 24th Air Defense Division, Eastern Military District, received its orders and immediately sprang into action. Alerts were issued across the network and radars began scouring the sky frantically, their operators looking for any trace of an unidentified outbound target.

Three separate fighter aviation regiments sent interceptors from alert facilities shrieking into the sky. Their air-to-air radars swept in overlapping arcs, covering every inch of the assigned area: the eastern coast of Russia between Vladivostok and Sakhalin Island. Because night still held its grip, winter's dawn being hours away, there was no hope of getting a visual on the suspected bogey.

Nearly everyone came up empty.

Yet there was one hint of a contact.

Midway across the Tatar Strait, the stretch of sea between the Russian mainland and Sakhalin Island, the lead aircraft of a pair of Su-35 Flankers notched a lock-on with its infrared search and track system, or IRSTS. It registered a dim, mid-aspect target headed for the Sea of Japan. The pilot did his best to intercept the shadow, which was traveling at an excessive rate of speed.

He took the best possible intercept angle, yet just as he was closing in from abeam, with almost enough moonlight to make a visual ID, the target disappeared into a dense cloud bank. The moisture caused the infrared system to immediately break lock. The frustrated pilot banked away, curious as to why neither his nor his wingman's powerful radars, which were not affected by moisture, showed no sign of a contact.

The lead aircraft radioed a report to their controller, but soon after was forced to break away to avoid violating Japanese airspace.

"That was close," Kai said. "Glad you've got a sharp eye."

"Maybe I should've been a pilot," Tru replied.

"Are you kidding? Wastewater plants, railways, helicopter squadrons . . . you're a destroyer of worlds."

"That cloud layer was convenient."

"Right on the border." She then made the announcement Tru had been waiting for. "That's it—we are now officially in Japanese airspace."

They broke out of the weather, and Tru squirmed to one side and saw lights ahead. "Hope the Japanese don't shoot us down."

"They're expecting us. That's the island of Hokkaido. Our destination is Chitose Air Base, on the southwest side."

Fifteen minutes later they were skimming in at low altitude. Kai had talked to no one on the radio, but she seemed confident the runway was clear and that Vektor would be welcomed.

"It's going to be your job to stop us," she said. "A few seconds after we touch down, I'll tell you to get on the brakes—you push the toes of the rudder pedals. The pedals will also steer left and right, so try to keep us on the runway."

"Rudder stuff again. Okay, I'll do my best."

The lights of the city seemed to grow, and it struck Tru that for the first time in days he wasn't surrounded by frozen wilderness. Five miles out he picked up the runway lights, and the final approach seemed smooth. On short final he saw a sight that validated Kai's confidence: next to the runway were a handful of vehicles, including a fire truck and a tug. Vektor swept past them at speed, but as it did Tru caught a momentary glimpse of an unsettling sight: one of the firemen was waving a flashlight frantically out the side window, as if he was trying to wave them off.

"Hey, did you see that guy in the fire truck?"

"Not now!" Kai fussed. The control stick was working furiously as she settled the jet to a landing. The main wheels touched down gently, and she kept the nose in the air to take advantage of aerodynamic braking. Tru had his feet poised over the rudder pedals, waiting for her cue. Kai gently lowered the nosewheel to the runway.

And that was when everything went wrong.

The fireman with the flashlight had been trying to draw their attention to the problem. If Kai hadn't been forced to ditch Primakov's helmet, she would have heard the tower controller's warning on the radio. The issue was Vektor's nosewheel. Instead of extending in line with the jet's path, a malfunction—later determined to be a steering cylinder damaged by the cold on Zeya—had left the wheel cocked thirty degrees to the left. The instant Vektor's nose touched the runway, the jet swerved sharply in that direction.

Kai instantly knew something was wrong, and she manipulated the flight controls as best she could to maintain directional control. It had almost no effect. The airfield was well lit, so she had a good view of what was ahead. Vektor was in a full-blown skid and there was nothing in the forward windscreen but grass.

She shouted, "Right brake! Right brake!"

Tru's right foot searched in vain for the pedal, but the lateral forces of the skid had thrown him sideways in the seat. His right foot, still mangled from an encounter with a wolf trap and encased by a damaged trail shoe, was trapped outside the rudder well.

Realizing they were about to depart the runway, Kai shut down both engines. Vektor was skidding sideways when it hit the grass, and clods of dirt loosened by the recent rains flew into the air. A main wheel struck a drainage culvert and the jet bounded upward, sending Kai and Tru airborne in the cramped confines of the cockpit. Vektor spun a second turn, mud still flying, before it churned to a stop in the infield.

A sudden, uneasy silence enveloped the cockpit. Kai and Tru remained still, assessing both themselves and Vektor. They had been tossed around with considerable force, and neither was strapped in. She ended up folded against the port side canopy rail. Tru had been bucked to starboard and was sitting on a radio panel. No longer stacked in the seat, as they'd been for over an hour, they were now jammed sideways and facing one another.

After days of close calls, so many near misses, the idea that they had nearly burst into flames at the last instant seemed nothing short of absurd. Yet here they were, still intact, their limbs tangled and their faces inches apart. They stared at one another with wide-eyed disbelief.

Out of nowhere, a smile broke onto Tru's face.

Kai echoed it.

Soon they were laughing uncontrollably beneath the Plexiglass dome. It carried on for a long time, and when it finally faded neither seemed able to disengage from the other's eyes.

They sat that way for nearly a minute. Both silent, neither making any attempt to move.

A rattle to one side finally broke their trance.

A fireman in full gear appeared at the side of the canopy. He removed his hood and stared incredulously at two people shoehorned into a single-seat cockpit.

The look on his face was priceless.

SEVENTY-FOUR

The weather forecast held, and Chaos 21 touched down on *Boxer* under considerably improved conditions. The eastern sky was just beginning to glow with the arrival of a new day. As Major Gianakos shut down the engines, he noted eighteen minutes of fuel remaining. It was a slim margin, and one that had been boosted by the fuel they'd uploaded downrange. As they were guided to a parking spot, he and Bryan couldn't resist a fist bump.

With considerable relief, Captain Longmire and his exec, Emerson, waited in the lee of the island. As soon as the Osprey's back ramp motored down, the ship's medical staff rushed on board. Within minutes they were transferring Diaz and Primakov below. Only after they were clear did the last passenger emerge.

Slaton stepped onto the deck hauling a fifty-inch soft case. He walked toward the two officers, and with an easy smile, said, "See? I told you it would all work out."

The Navy men exchanged an uneasy glance. The skipper responded, "Well, like I said when you got here . . . it's your rodeo. I just didn't figure you to be a rider. I'm just glad everybody got back safe."

"So am I."

The two exchanged a handshake.

Slaton said, "Is there a cup of coffee anywhere on this ship?"

Longmire grinned. "I think we can scare one up."

Tru spent his first hour at the base hospital. His foot required two sets of stitches, and various parts of his body were scanned. After the results came back negative, he was provided new clothes and released to his minder, a U.S. Army major who ushered him to a small room in the biggest building on base.

The initial debriefing lasted three hours. He was isolated from Kai, but this came as no surprise—it was standard procedure to obtain individual accounts of operations. He did his best to power through, fighting growing fatigue. He had gotten little rest in recent days, and the Siberian cold only magnified his exhaustion. When the interviews ended, he was reunited with Kai. They were given a hot meal and issued adjacent rooms in the visiting officer quarters. Both took extended hot showers and then slept for twelve hours.

The next evening, they made good on the agreement they'd made the previous night. The bar was not an official O-club, few of which existed anymore, but it was as close as they could get on a Japanese air base. One row of ten stools lined the lounge of the on-base restaurant. The place was quiet, the beer was cold, and for the first time in days they didn't have to tend to the fire—faux gas logs burned warmly at the hearth on the far side of the room.

"They've got me on a flight out later tonight," he said. "You?"

"I'm supposed to hang here for a few days. The justification is that Primakov knows me. They performed surgery on his leg, so he'll be laid up for a while. I'm also going to help go over Vektor."

He nodded. "Diaz?"

"They tell me he's doing well. There'll be some rehab on his leg, but no long-term problems."

"Great to hear. I'll check in on him before I go. So, who did your interviews?"

"One guy was definitely DOD. I think the other might have been CIA. They mostly wanted details of what happened at Zeya. We'll have plenty of time to study Vektor, but right now everyone is spun up about the potential for a diplomatic disaster."

"I got the same impression. From what I've heard, things are quiet so far. Vektor is locked down tight in a hangar and there's nothing in the media about the engagement on the reservoir."

"President Petrov must know by now," she said. "Do you think he'll play it down?"

"It's hard to ignore a punch in the face, but a little easier when nobody sees it. From a Russian point of view, this was an embarrassment across the board. Petrov might decide he doesn't want to draw attention to it. I'd say if it goes another day, maybe two, without a stink being raised . . . we probably got away with it."

Kai took an extended pull on her beer.

"Did we break the jet?" he asked.

"We *delivered* that jet, Tru. The nosewheel needs some work, but other than that just a few dings. She'll fly again. At least, if that's how DOD decides to play things."

"Have you gotten any pushback about your decision to fly Vektor out?"

"Not yet, but it's coming. I'm guessing it'll be one of those times when you get a loud reprimand and a quiet commendation."

"Think you'll ever get a chance to take her up again?"

"No telling, but I'd like to."

"If you do, I hope your next flight is less eventful."

They both studied their bottles for a time.

"What you did for me last night, Kai, when that Russian had a gun in my face . . . I know that wasn't easy for you. Thanks."

"I wouldn't have had the chance if you hadn't come back for me."

They tapped the necks of their bottles.

"And for what it's worth," he added, "I think you'll make a damned good Buddhist."

She looked at him oddly, then laughed. "I don't have plans for a tombstone, but if I did, that could be my epitaph: A damned good Buddhist."

Tru grinned. "Glad to help."

She gave him an appraising look.

"What?" he asked.

"You shaved."

"Might have missed a few spots—I did it before I crashed."

"You shouldn't use that word with a pilot—say slept."

"Even if I survived one with her?"

"Especially then."

He checked his watch, then drained the last of his beer. "I gotta get ready to go."

He fished into his pocket but came up dry. "Anybody give you money?"

"A little. Don't worry, I've got you covered."

"Thanks," he said. "Next time it's on me."

She nodded. "Next time."

As Tru got up to leave, they exchanged an awkward look.

When he started to turn, she said, "Tru, about what happened . . . right after we landed."

"No, Kai. No need to explain." He knew exactly what was on her mind. "We survived some big scares, but that last one came out of nowhere. Our emotions were running high."

"Yeah, that's it. Just the adrenaline hitting us."

They looked at one another for a long beat.

And then Tru turned away and was gone.

SEVENTY-FIVE

The patio was the largest Slaton had ever built, more than a thousand square feet of tumbled travertine and matching stone structures. Aside from the main sitting area, there was a fire pit, two planters, and a walking path around the southern side of the house. He had been working on the project for the best part of a month. Not that there was any deadline. Slaton never added constraints without reason.

The tile saw shrieked as he made cuts to fashion a curve in the pathway. When he finished and removed his hearing protection, he immediately registered the sound of a vehicle. Slaton couldn't see the driveway from where he stood, but the engine noise told him all he needed to know. Not his wife's minivan, but a big-block SUV. Christine had taken the kids to a doctor's appointment, and after that they were headed for a playdate. They wouldn't be home for hours.

He had timed the arrival for precisely that reason.

Hearing footsteps approaching on the walkway, he removed his gloves and used a rag to wipe down his arms and face—he'd been working all morning and was covered in dust. The engine in the driveway fell quiet. As per his instructions, the man and woman he'd sent to fetch his visitor would wait by the SUV.

Truman Miller came into view. When he saw Slaton, he drew to a stop. This was the first time they had met face to face. Miller had been back in the D.C. area for two days, but Slaton had decided to allow him an interval of rest and recuperation. And he was busy himself managing fallout from the recent mission.

They regarded one another from a distance, until Slaton diverted to a roughed-in section of travertine at the back. He rearranged two Adirondack chairs and took a seat in one.

Recognizing this as something near an invitation, the paramilitary everyone called Tru walked closer. Instead of sitting, however, he remained on his feet. It might have been because he was stiff after a forty-minute car ride. More likely because he was obstinate. There was no need for a handshake or introductions. Each knew the other's name, and they were not, at this point in time, friends. Yet there was a curious undercurrent, a distinct bond between them.

Slaton had expected it.

Tru had not.

Standing with his hands in his pockets, looking across the wintering lawn at a stand of leafless trees, Tru took the lead. "I guess I should thank you."

"For what?"

"It was you . . . on the Osprey that night. You took down the Hind, then a good number of the Vega Group men."

The SAC director didn't reply.

"Rumor is that you were a sniper, IDF or Mossad."

"What I am is the head of your section. That's all you need to know."

A measured nod. "Has there been pushback from Moscow yet?"

"Surprisingly, no. They've cleaned things up on the reservoir and haven't mentioned it. I'm sure there will be payback of some kind, but you didn't start a war."

"Great. So why am I here?"

"Because I've got a decision to make. I'm getting pressure from above, from the very top, to let a certain operator go. He went into a mission that demanded stealth and nuance, and blew it up—literally and repeatedly." He paused to let that sink in, then added, "This operator also achieved every mission objective, and went above and beyond to acquire a valuable piece of enemy technology."

Slaton got up and diverted to a nearby table in the grass. He picked up a half-full water bottle, took a long draw, and said, "So that's my dilemma."

"You're asking me whether you should fire me? I turned in a detailed mission report that tells you everything you need to know."

"Does it?"

Tru didn't respond.

"Do you *want* to keep your job?" The way Slaton said it, his pitch and inflection, made it sound like a sincere question. He really didn't know.

"I've been wondering that myself. The agency spent two and a half years teaching me tradecraft, teaching me to kill people. Next thing I know, I'm standing knee-deep in sewage."

"And then you were sent to Russia on a high-stakes op. The needs of the agency always take precedence."

"I was sent into Russia because I was the only operator within a thousand miles."

"Correct. But that's where you've been wanting to go all along, right?"

"I speak the language, know a good deal about the country. Isn't that how it works at the agency? You send people where they have the most expertise?"

Slaton paused, knowing where he had to go next.

"We need to talk about your sister."

"Do *not* bring her into this!"

"I didn't—you did! You take her with you everywhere you go, all the way from Ukraine to Camp Peary to Siberia. If you are going to work for this agency, you can only do it with a clear head. Without that, you are putting lives at risk—judging by what I've seen, you don't care about your own, but I can't let you endanger everyone you work with."

"If I'm going to work for the CIA, I'll do it on my terms. Period."

Slaton's gray eyes drilled across the divide.

Tru glared right back.

Slaton dialed down, his voice going quiet. "Let me tell you something nobody at this agency knows. I was a little younger than you when I was recruited by Mossad, and I had a tragedy in my own background that was similar to yours. I was desperate to extract payback on a particular Arab faction. Mossad not only knew that—they made every effort to use it. Looking back, I see that turning me into a killer was easy. All they had to do was channel my rage into something productive. Or from their viewpoint, something kinetic."

He studied Tru for a long moment, as if making a choice. He finally said, "Come with me. There's something I want to show you."

Slaton led the way to the back door, then through a kitchen and a hallway. He turned into an office that was a work in progress. Empty shelves stood waiting for books that were stuffed in boxes all around. The big desk in the center of the room was empty except for one file folder on the blotter. The folder was hatched in red and stenciled with the highest level of classification.

Slaton said, "My job is to put people in harm's way. I won't do that without knowing them, understanding what makes them tick. It's true, I sent you into Russia because you were the only option. But the minute I did, I began researching you. In the course of it, I talked to Bob Stansell."

"He told you about my sister."

"He told me what you told him. But I didn't stop there. I followed up, had a couple of analysts do an in-depth search." He pointed to the folder. "They came up with information I don't think you're aware of."

Tru looked at it warily. "What kind of information?"

Slaton moved between Tru and the desk. "I know you're still battling this, dealing with what happened to Kate. You've got potential as an operator, and I could use you in SAC. But it will never work the way things stand."

"So that's it? You're giving me the boot?"

"I'm giving you the one thing Mossad never gave me at the beginning . . . the truth." He edged toward the door. "I'll give you one hour. Nothing in that folder leaves this room."

Tru nodded, and Slaton disappeared. He heard the tile saw spin back up, saw dust flying high in the window. He stared at the folder like it was radioactive.

Tru knew he had crossed a threshold in Russia. His private war had morphed into something sanctioned—or as close as it could ever be. Yet in the course of fulfilling his mission objectives, Tru had gone beyond his mandate. Far, far beyond. He couldn't fault Slaton if he did decide to take him off the board.

His eyes locked on the file.

Had his recent actions done anything to purge the demons inside? He had killed a number of Russians—he would never know the exact count—yet in doing so an unforeseen question had arisen. Was he merely transferring his pain? Propagating his suffering to a new generation of wives and children and parents? Or had he actually performed a service to the world by removing some bad players?

The saw blade began to howl.

The file on the desk drew him in with what seemed like a gravitational pull. He felt like his life was poised on a perfectly balanced scale, and the few pieces of paper before him would tip things one way or the other.

Tru reached for the file, opened it, and began to read.

ACKNOWLEDGMENTS

First and foremost, I want to thank you. Without readers there would be no stories, and I appreciate the trust you put in me. Time is valuable to all of us, and I hope this book has met the entertainment standard you expect and deserve.

I have a terrific team at Tor/Forge Books. Linda Quinton, Libby Collins, Angus Johnston, Troix Jackson, and Eileen Lawrence—your help and understanding has long been instrumental, and for that you have my deepest thanks.

Much appreciation to Adrian Speckert and Cory Todd Hughes for helping guide David Slaton toward the big screen. We are not to the finish line, but surely it's near. And as always, or so it seems, thanks to P. J. Ochlan for so brilliantly bringing *Dark Vector* to life on audio.

To my editor, Robert Davis, your expertise and patience are enduring. And Bob and Susan Gleason, thank you for bringing me into such wonderful company.

James Abt and his legion of reviewers at Best Thriller Books (Best ThrillerBooks.com) are the best in the business. The same can be said of David Temple (*The Thriller Zone* podcast) and Mike and Chris (*No Limits: The Mitch Rapp Podcast*).

And finally, thanks to my family. The shelf is getting full, but your patience and support never waver.

ABOUT THE AUTHOR

Jack Larsen

WARD LARSEN is a *USA Today* bestselling author and multiple-time winner of the Florida Book Award. His work has been nominated for both the Edgar and Macavity Awards. A former U.S. Air Force fighter pilot, Larsen flew more than twenty missions in Operation Desert Storm. He also served as a federal law enforcement officer and is a trained aircraft accident investigator. His first thriller, *The Perfect Assassin,* is being adapted into a major motion picture.